His A...
M...

MARGARET MAYO
TRISH WYLIE
TINA DUNCAN

MILLS & BOON

All rights reserved including the right of reproduction in whole or in part in any form. This edition is published by arrangement with Harlequin Books S.A.

This is a work of fiction. Names, characters, places, locations and incidents are purely fictional and bear no relationship to any real life individuals, living or dead, or to any actual places, business establishments, locations, events or incidents. Any resemblance is entirely coincidental.

This book is sold subject to the condition that it shall not, by way of trade or otherwise, be lent, resold, hired out or otherwise circulated without the prior consent of the publisher in any form of binding or cover other than that in which it is published and without a similar condition including this condition being imposed on the subsequent purchaser.

® and ™ are trademarks owned and used by the trademark owner and/or its licensee. Trademarks marked with ® are registered with the United Kingdom Patent Office and/or the Office for Harmonisation in the Internal Market and in other countries.

Published in Great Britain 2015
by Mills & Boon, an imprint of Harlequin (UK) Limited,
Eton House, 18-24 Paradise Road, Richmond, Surrey, TW9 1SR

HIS AFTER-HOURS MISTRESS © 2015 Harlequin Books S. A.

The Rich Man's Reluctant Mistress, *The Inconvenient Laws of Attraction* and *Playing His Dangerous Game* were first published in Great Britain by Harlequin (UK) Limited.

The Rich Man's Reluctant Mistress © 2007 Margaret Mayo
The Inconvenient Laws of Attraction © 2011 Trish Wylie
Playing His Dangerous Game © 2011 Tina Duncan

ISBN: 978-0-263-25232-3

05-1015

Harlequin (UK) Limited's policy is to use papers that are natural, renewable and recyclable products and made from wood grown in sustainable forests. The logging and manufacturing processes conform to the legal environmental regulations of the country of origin.

Printed and bound in Spain
by CPI, Barcelona

THE RICH MAN'S RELUCTANT MISTRESS

BY
MARGARET MAYO

Margaret Mayo was reading Mills & Boon® romances long before she began to write them. In fact she never had any plans to become a writer. After an idea for a short story popped into her head she was thrilled when it turned into a full-scale novel. Now, over twenty-five years later, she is still happily writing, and says she has no intention of stopping. She lives with her husband Ken in a rural part of Staffordshire. She has two children—Adrian, who now lives in America, and Tina. Margaret's hobbies are reading, photography and, more recently, watercolour painting, which she says has honed her observational skills and is a definite advantage when it comes to writing.

CHAPTER ONE

SMOKY blue eyes looked with shocked disbelief into delicate green ones. Seconds ticked away. Zane was the first to speak.

'You!' he exclaimed, his voice deep and gruff and entirely disbelieving, almost accusatory.

Lucinda nodded, slowly and deliberately. 'Yes, it's me, and I'm as surprised as you are.'

Except that surprised was far too mild a word. Even shocked wasn't good enough. Stunned perhaps. And had she known who to expect she would never have come here today. Zane Alexander was not on her list of favourite people. Her experience working for him a few years ago had shown he was insensitive, uncaring and a whole host of other adjectives she could have put her mind to had she wanted. Except—that business was business.

'What are you doing here?' came the next curt question.

'You sent for me.' Her eyes were full of innocence. 'I have an appointment.'

'But—you're a *nanny*!'

Lucinda allowed her lips to curve into a smile. Not that it held any pleasure. Her only pleasure was in seeing this man at a loss. 'I *was* a nanny,' she corrected. 'And, by the way, how's Tim?'

'Very well,' he responded.

'And I only did it to fund myself while I was preparing to go into business,' she explained.

Zane Alexander frowned. 'But it couldn't have been more than two years ago. Three at the most! How can you possibly be—'

'Experienced?' she suggested sweetly. 'Believe me, Mr Alexander, I'm very experienced.'

Blue eyes narrowed and one brow crooked upwards. Although Lucinda knew what he was thinking she didn't let it show. She kept a cool smile on her lips and a question in her eyes.

Zane Alexander's brow dropped again until his eyes levelled on hers. 'Show me your credentials.'

Lucinda reached out her portfolio and sat there quietly while he studied it. In turn she chose to study him. He was really quite a handsome man—it was a pity he didn't have a handsome character to match. In the few weeks she had worked for him she had seen enough to recognise that he thought more of going out with one of his numerous lady friends than he did caring for his son.

He had medium blond hair that waved in gorgeous disarray. It was cut reasonably short in an effort to tame it but without much success. She bet it was the only thing in his life he couldn't take control of.

His eyes were beautifully shaped and a dusky sort of blue, like smoke out of a chimney, with fair lashes and light eyebrows that matched his hair both in colour and disobedience. His mouth was full and wide and at this moment compressed. It was a very mobile mouth, though. She had seen it smiling and even laughing, as well as expressing the grimness he showed at this moment. It was a nice mouth, she admitted reluctantly.

'I have to confess,' he said now, waving the folder, 'that this is very impressive. And you did come highly recommended.'

'Is that a compliment?' she asked, eyes wide and questioning.

'Not at all!' came the swift reply. 'I'm not in the habit of handing out compliments to people I hardly know. But I can see that you'll be capable of doing the job I want.'

'And that would be?' she asked. When his PA had phoned to make the appointment with her secretary, apart from saying that it was a prestigious interior design job for Mr Alexander of Revelation Holdings, no further details had been given. The name Alexander had meant nothing to her. She certainly hadn't equated it with the Mr Alexander she had done the nannying job for and she was deeply curious as to why he had sent for her.

Nothing around here needed refurbishing. His office block was modern, immaculate and totally awe-inspiring. All the best quality materials had been used, the colours were muted and restful and the right accents added. And, from memory, his house was the same! Large and impressive and flawless.

Perhaps he was moving? Perhaps he'd bought a second home? Perhaps his business was expanding? There was no end of possibilities. She waited patiently for him to tell her.

It was rare for Zane Alexander to be taken by surprise, but today he had been literally swept off his feet when

Lucinda Oliver had walked into his office. When he'd last seen her she had simply introduced herself as Lucy, and although she was a lovely looking girl he hadn't thought about her since.

Today she looked far more grown-up, with her flaming Titian hair brushed back in some sort of fancy loop, revealing the fine bone structure of her face and her long elegant neck. Carefully made-up green eyes shone from a matt complexion, her nose was beautifully straight and her mouth held only the merest hint of lip-gloss.

He suddenly realised that she was waiting to hear about the job and he was forced to give his head a mental shake before he could take his eyes from her. He pressed a button on the console on his desk to draw the window blinds, then another to slide down a huge screen that took up most of one wall.

'Are you ready?' he asked.

A tiny nod of her head was all the response he got.

The first image appeared on the screen. 'This is a property I've recently acquired,' he announced. 'I've had one or two alterations made to it but now I need someone to add the finishing touches. I've been told you're the best.'

Lucinda lifted well-shaped brows. 'I thank whoever said that, although personally I don't think I have yet achieved such stardom, but I do pride myself on my work and I've already won an award, if that's good enough for you. Where is this property?' It was a sprawling one-storey building, set amongst palm trees and tropical blue skies. 'Not in England, that's for sure,' she added.

'You're right. I wasn't going to tell you until you'd

seen the rest of the photographs, but since you've asked—it's in St Lucia.'

'The Caribbean?' Her green eyes widened ever so slightly and he realised how beautiful they were—wide-spaced and long-lashed—and he wondered why he had never noticed them before. They were expressive eyes and at this moment they revealed an inner tension. She was clearly feeling apprehensive. Perhaps it was because of who he was? Perhaps she had never taken on a job out of England? Perhaps he was asking too much of her?

'That's right,' he answered, watching her closely.

'And you expect me to go all the way out there?' An even deeper incredulity darkened her eyes.

'All expenses paid, of course,' he answered smoothly, smiling now at her expression. 'I take it that you're not accustomed to jetting around the world for the sake of your job?'

'No, I'm not.'

'Would you object to it?' He hoped not. He was enjoying her company and would like to see more of her. Lucy the nanny had done nothing for him. But Lucinda the interior designer was surely every man's dream.

It was a hot day and she was dressed in ivory silk wide-legged trousers and a jacket that skimmed her waist. Around her neck hung a bronze three-tiered pendant which almost disappeared into her delectable cleavage. It was matched by bronze earrings and even her nails wore bronze polish.

She was elegance personified and nothing like the girl who had turned up at his house in blue jeans and a T-shirt. It alarmed him to realise that he would enjoy the pleasure of peeling the suit off her slow inch by slow inch and feasting his eyes on the sylphlike body beneath.

'It all depends,' she said with a faint grimace.

Zane berated himself. It was ridiculous to let his thoughts run in such a foolish direction. 'On what?' he asked briskly. 'On how much I'd pay you?'

'Amongst other things,' she acknowledged, her eyes steady on his now, no sign of the tension he had seen earlier. 'For instance, where would I be staying? Is the house habitable?'

'Absolutely,' he concurred, pleased to hear that she was considering his proposition. Perhaps she'd suddenly realised that she was on to a good thing.

'And how long would I be away?' she asked. 'I'm not used to—'

'Do you have family commitments?' he interrupted sharply, glancing curiously at her left hand. He felt strangely relieved when he saw no ring, then asked himself why. So long as she could do the job, her personal affairs were inconsequential.

'None at all,' she answered. 'You needn't fear that there's anything to get in the way of my work.'

'No boyfriend who'd object to you being away for a few weeks?' He watched her face closely. He was intrigued. In almost three years she had changed from a girl, a well-adjusted girl admittedly, to a sophisticated, confident woman whose rise up the ladder of success was truly remarkable.

Lucinda's smile was wry. 'No boyfriend.'

Was that regret he heard in her voice? Had there been someone recently? He wanted to know but it was too soon for such personal questions. And he had to ask himself why he was taking such an inordinate interest in her private life. Purely to safeguard his interests, of course! He didn't want someone who couldn't give one hundred per cent of her attention.

'Then I think we should look at the rest of the photographs,' he said quietly. 'And tonight I'll take you out to dinner so that we can discuss the project properly.' He pushed back a cuff and glanced at his watch.

'And what is wrong with discussing it now?' asked Lucinda, hearing the crossness in her voice but ignoring it.

Brows rose disapprovingly. 'Although you come highly recommended, I prefer to make my own judgement.'

Lucinda tossed her head, her eyes flashing crossly. 'I thought you'd convinced yourself that I was good enough?'

'And of course,' he added, ignoring her question, 'I need to make sure that you and I get on.'

His eyes connected with hers as he spoke and his meaning was very clear. Lucinda felt the hairs on the back of her neck bristle. Anger flared hot and fluid through her veins and her green eyes sparked fire. But when she spoke there was no hint in her voice that she knew what he had in mind.

'You think that taking me out to dinner is the best way of doing it? I think not, Mr Alexander. Whatever needs to be discussed can be done right here and now. If that doesn't suit you then perhaps I shouldn't be here at all.'

She got up and headed for the door but Zane was there before her, moving remarkably quickly for such a tall man. She guessed he was about six-four—wide-shouldered and hard-muscled, as though he worked out several times a week.

His face was grim, brows pulled tightly together. 'Hardly a professional attitude.'

'I beg your pardon?' Lucinda glared and stood that little bit taller. Not that she was intimidated by him! She was five feet eight herself and equalled most men. 'My attitude has nothing to do with it. It's yours that's in question,' she parried accusingly. 'Admit it, you were doubtful once you saw who I was.' But it didn't alter the fact that he had designs on her! She could tell that by the way he looked at her. Would he be accompanying her to St Lucia? Would they be sharing his house? Lucinda suddenly realised what a dangerous situation she could be getting herself into.

Broad shoulders shrugged. 'Can you blame me?' It was more a statement than a question.

'So recommendations weren't enough?' Lord, she wanted to take a swipe at him, knock that superior expression off his face.

'I like to make up my own mind.'

In more ways than one, she thought edgily. She'd had enough of this conversation and reached for the door handle.

'Not so quickly,' breathed Zane. 'You're here for a purpose. Please, allow me to finish the show.' And, with complete disregard for her feelings, he steered her back into the room and pushed her unceremoniously on to the chair.

Lucinda's blood boiled and she took several deep steadying breaths. Never in her life had she found a man more irritating than Zane Alexander. She didn't trust him, so how could she work for him? She would be on tenterhooks the whole time. On the other hand, his business would be highly profitable. For that reason alone she would be foolish to turn him down.

She had no idea how lovely she looked with her face flaming almost as red as her hair and her eyes a more brilliant green than they'd ever been before. All she knew was that she was spitting mad and that this man was the cause.

'We're inside the house now and this is the living area.'

Zane's voice interrupted her thoughts and she fixed her attention on the screen. The room was huge.

'I've had two rooms knocked into one. I like to have plenty of space. And here we have the main bedroom.'

Oh, Lord, if she took this job she would be expected to dress this room. To suit him! Immediately she had a vision of steel and silver and ice-blue. Cold and hard and totally devoid of feeling! 'Would you be accompanying me to St Lucia?' she asked in a breathless voice.

'Obviously.'

A shiver ran down her spine. 'And we'd both be staying at the house?'

'Of course,' he answered and, without giving her time to object, he carried on with the show. 'This is bedroom number two and, as you can see, they are both fully furnished. And here are numbers three and four, the main bathroom, the kitchen.' He had realised she wasn't listening and consequently rushed through the rest of the images. 'What do you think?'

What did she think? That she didn't want to be living there with him. 'I think I'd prefer to stay in a hotel.'

Smoky blue eyes locked on to hers. 'No deal!' he announced shortly. 'The house is remote; there's no hotel for miles. It would be inconvenient for you to—'

'Damn the convenience!' she cried. 'How about the propriety?'

A faint smile curved his mouth. 'Who's to know?'

Lucinda did not find it funny. 'It's unethical.'

'You think I might take advantage of the situation?'

The hot colour in Lucinda's cheeks gave her away. 'Actually, yes.'

But she knew she had to trust him—although those wicked blue eyes didn't invite trust. His lips quirked. 'Perhaps it's yourself you're afraid of. Don't think I haven't noticed that you're very much aware of me.'

Lucinda's eyes flashed and she ignored the hot streak through her veins. 'Of all the conceited, overbearing men, you take the biscuit. You know exactly how I feel about you.'

'The point is, do *you* know how you feel?' he asked with quiet innuendo.

Lucinda closed her eyes. The argument was lost; she might as well give in gracefully. It would be foolish to turn down this dream job because of what might happen. If Zane decided to make advances on her, surely she was woman enough to deal with him?

Zane saw her weakening and took advantage. His smile was wide and confident. 'So,' he said, 'is it dinner with me tonight or not?'

CHAPTER TWO

LUCINDA studied her wardrobe, wondering what to wear for her evening out with Zane Alexander. The red slinky number, or perhaps something more decorous? She didn't want him getting the wrong impression. How about the amber suit? Or even the lime-green dress, which everyone else hated but she loved? It was certainly demure.

She had thought long and hard about accepting Zane's dinner invitation but ultimately decided to put her personal issues about him to one side. This project was too good an opportunity to miss. Now, though, as she stepped into an elegant black dress, she wondered whether she was doing the right thing.

A job in St Lucia! It sounded too good to be true. Except that she would be out there with Zane, a man she didn't particularly like. But whom she found devastatingly attractive! It was an admission she hated making—but it happened to be true. There really was something about him that could not be ignored.

Would he stay while she developed thoughts and ideas? Would he want to talk them over with her as she went along? Or would he simply show her around and then wait to hear what suggestions she came up with?

He was a very busy man, of that she was well aware. When she had looked after his two-year-old son, Zane had spent very little time at home. In fact Tim had rarely seen him. Zane was not a good father. On the other hand, perhaps because of Tim, he would not stay on the island the whole time she was there—unless, of course, he had business interests in St Lucia? It could well be the case.

They certainly had a lot to discuss.

And time was running out. Zane was picking her up at seven-thirty; he would expect her to be ready. She finished her make-up and ran a final brush through her hair. It was long and silky, almost to her waist, and her pride and joy. At the last minute, though, she decided to sweep it up. She didn't want Zane Alexander thinking she looked anything less than professional.

She watched for him to arrive and was out of the door almost before he had stopped his car. Lucinda lived with her mother and stepfather in a large house where she had her own suite of offices. It didn't really suit her and her bank balance was such these days that she was almost ready to buy a place of her own. In fact she'd been looking at property only the other day.

'A lady who's prompt,' commented Zane with a dry smile, jumping out to open the door for her. 'I like that. And may I say how elegant you look.'

Lucinda inclined her head in thanks. Zane looked pretty good himself in an oatmeal linen jacket and crisp dark trousers, and as he slid into the sleek silver Mercedes beside her the faint smell of his cologne wafted beneath her nostrils. It was masculine and woody and reminded her of nights spent on an exotic island paradise.

She suddenly realised where her mind was going

and checked it. How would she know what it felt like? Was she thinking about the job that lay ahead? Was it wishful thinking? Never! Not with Zane Alexander. Not in a million years.

Besides, wasn't he married? Not that there'd been a wife around. Maybe they were divorced. Maybe there wasn't a Mrs Alexander any longer. Maybe she'd dumped the child on him on that occasion and, Zane being Zane, he hadn't wanted to give up his precious time.

'You must be doing rather well for yourself, judging by where you live,' commented Zane as he pulled away from the house.

'It's not mine,' she answered quickly. 'It belongs to my stepfather. I'm moving out shortly.'

'You're not happy there?' he asked intuitively.

Perhaps her tone had given too much away. But she didn't get on well with David Goldberg. He had once told her that she hadn't the imagination of a sparrow and would never enter the world of business. How she had loved proving him wrong. Her own father had died when she was fifteen and her mother had remarried far too quickly in Lucinda's opinion. They'd gone from being very poor to very rich in a short space of time; not that she had accepted any help from her stepfather when setting up her design company.

'I feel it's time I have a place of my own,' she answered quietly.

'Of course.'

She had expected him to probe, to make some disparaging remark about her still living at home, but he didn't.

'How old are you?' he asked instead.

'Twenty-eight,' she answered.

'And running your own successful business. Congratulations.'

His compliment pleased her.

'What is your ambition?' He kept his eyes on the road in front where it looked like a young mother was ready to roll a pushchair out in front of them. 'To have a team of workers under you so that you can sit back and count your pennies? Or to always be a hands-on person?'

Lucinda thought she heard sarcasm and tossed her head. 'Ultimately I want to get married and have children. I love children; I used to earn money looking after them when I was a student.'

'The nanny job?'

Lucinda nodded. 'I could have made it a career but it would have been a waste of the design course I was taking. I'd always set my heart on interior design. Each job is different. It's a new challenge. I love it.'

'Then I shall very much look forward to showing you over my place in St Lucia.'

'You're assuming I'll take the job?' she questioned, glancing at him, seeing nothing but the hard contours of his profile. Until he turned briefly to look at her and she caught a twinkle in his smoky eyes.

'I thought you already had,' he said. 'Otherwise why would you be here?' And he looked back at the road.

There was nothing more for Lucinda to say. There was trepidation in her heart but a sense of excitement too.

The restaurant was small and intimate and not the sort of place where business deals were done. It had a more romantic atmosphere, where couples looked into each other's eyes and drank champagne and wished for the moon. Lucinda felt uncomfortable, her heart beating far louder than it should.

'Have you been here before?' Zane asked.

Lucinda shook her head.

'Then you should have,' he admonished. 'The food is superb and the head chef incidentally is a very good friend of mine.'

They sipped their drinks as they studied the menu and, while they were waiting to be seated, Zane made no attempt to talk business. Instead he asked her questions about herself, almost as though they were on a date. Which made her feel even more uncomfortable.

'I don't see that it has anything to do with the job,' she protested when he wanted to know whether she had any brothers or sisters.

'I'm curious about you, that's all,' he answered with a disarming smile, a smile that probably made many women go weak at the knees. And she was in grave danger of following suit!

'All you need to know are my qualifications,' she told him, her voice a little more cool than she had intended, 'and you've already seen those. When are we going to get down to business?'

Zane smiled, his teeth amazingly white in his subtly tanned face. 'There's not really much to discuss, is there, not until we arrive on site, so to speak? I've already decided I want you to do the job; this is merely an opportunity to get to know you.'

Lucinda swallowed hard. 'A complete waste of time.'

Zane frowned. 'I don't understand?'

'Is this the way you usually conduct your business

affairs?' she questioned coolly. Perhaps it was. Especially with members of the opposite sex! And how did he expect the evening to end? Lucinda realised she was being fanciful. There was nothing in his attitude at this moment to suggest that he wanted anything more from her. It was all in her mind. But then didn't she have reason to be fearful?

Simon, her ex-fiancé, whom she'd met at university, had left her wary of men. He had wooed and won her, they'd had a long and happy engagement, they'd even been planning their wedding, and then he'd dumped her without any real explanation except to say that their relationship wasn't working. She'd heard afterwards that he'd met someone else—and it hadn't done much for her ego. From that day on she had sworn she would be careful not to lose her heart so easily to another man. Especially one like Zane Alexander!

'If you mean do I enjoy taking beautiful young ladies out to dinner, then the answer is yes.'

Lucinda frowned. 'And your wife, what does she have to say about it?' Thinking about Simon had made her feel angry and her voice was waspish.

Well-marked brows rose; his surprise very evident. 'I don't have a wife.'

'You mean you're divorced?' she asked sharply.

'I've never been married,' he answered, more puzzlement in his tone. 'I've never met anyone I've wanted to settle down with.'

'So where does Tim fit into the equation?' she asked, feeling hopelessly lost now.

'Ah!' Enlightenment dawned on Zane's handsome face. 'You think Tim is my son?'

'Well, isn't he?' she questioned crossly.

'Actually, no, he's my brother's child. I was merely looking after him.'

Lucinda leaned back in her seat and stared. '*You* were looking after him?' She couldn't believe what she was hearing. It was an even worse scenario than she had thought. 'That is disgraceful—paying someone to look after a child who'd been put into your care.' Her eyes were a vivid angry green and she sat forward on the edge of her seat, wanting to take a swipe at him. 'How could you do such a thing?'

'Perhaps I should enlighten you,' Zane said tersely. A waiter showing them to their table had interrupted their conversation, but once their first course had been placed in front of them he could hold his tongue no longer. Who the hell did Lucinda Oliver think she was? How dared she condemn him?

'Nothing you can say will excuse the fact that you let your nephew down,' Lucinda snapped. 'How could you offload Tim on to a stranger?'

'Just listen,' he rasped, annoyed now by her determination to cast him as the bad guy. 'To start with, my brother and his wife died in a road accident when Tim was eighteen months old.'

Lucinda's lovely eyes widened. 'That's awful; I didn't know.'

'Of course you didn't,' he snarled. 'His maternal grandmother took him in. When one day she was rushed into hospital there was no one to look after him except me. Unfortunately I had a series of extremely important business meetings—hence employing you.' Damn, why was he explaining this to her? She didn't deserve an explanation. Except that she was beginning to get under his skin like no other woman ever had!

'Not that I expect you to understand,' he declared shortly. 'I think maybe this evening was a mistake. Let's go.' And he pushed back his chair.

'I'm sorry,' said Lucinda quietly.

'And that's supposed to make it better, is it?' he growled. Two miserable little words of apology after she'd made aspersions on his character. It wasn't good enough. He'd had his fill of this woman and her patronising behaviour.

'I love kids, that's all,' she added, as if reading his thoughts. 'I don't think they should be given a hard time. But I can see now that you did the best you could, and I'm sorry I thought ill of you. Have I blotted my copybook as far as the job's concerned?'

Her eyes were wide and apologetic—and incredibly beautiful. Zane felt himself weakening and hated himself for it. 'I really haven't time to start looking for someone all over again.'

'So you still want me?' she asked, her voice husky now.

Want her? Of course he wanted her! Far too badly! She was exceptionally fine-looking—too gorgeous to ignore. He loved the little black dress with its rhinestone straps and a *décolletage* that stopped just short of revealing the delightful fullness of her breasts. Her skin was velvety smooth and her perfume sweet and tantalising. She looked stylish, yet there was an innocent freshness about her as well.

He drew in a long breath and let it go slowly before pulling his chair back up to the table. 'Let's talk about it.'

* * *

By the end of the evening Lucinda began to look forward to working in St Lucia. Zane was going to fly her out in a few days, giving them both time to sort their diaries. It would be the most exciting job of her career.

As they sipped their coffee, Lucinda telling Zane that she already had some ideas, the head chef came out to say hello.

'Zane, it is good to see you again.' The two men shook hands. He was French and short and rotund, and he looked curiously at Lucinda.

'This is Lucinda Oliver,' introduced Zane, 'an interior designer who's going to do some work for me.'

'She is beautiful, is she not, you lucky old dog,' said the chef. And then, in his native language, 'Is she your girlfriend as well, or is that what you would like her to be?'

Zane answered in French also. 'She is not my girlfriend.'

'But you are working on her? And who can blame you? She is—extraordinarily attractive. If I were not married I would pursue her myself.'

'You would not stand a chance, my friend,' said Zane with a dazzling smile.

Of all the conceited men, Zane Alexander took the biscuit! Lucinda flashed her green eyes and, speaking in perfect French, said, 'Excuse me, gentlemen, but I do not like being talked about like this.'

The chef's mouth fell open and, in English, he said, *'Mademoiselle*, I am so sorry. Do accept my apologies. But you are indeed beautiful.'

Lucinda smiled and waited for Zane's apology also—but it didn't materialise. And when his friend had gone back to the kitchen she turned on him. 'Do you normally talk like that about someone who's going to do a job for you?'

'Only when they're particularly lovely,' he acknowledged with a tiny tug at the corners of his mouth. He looked not in the least concerned that he had been found out. Instead he said, 'I congratulate you on your fluent French.'

Lucinda huffed but said nothing more, finishing her coffee instead and then pronouncing herself ready to leave. Of one thing she was very sure—she was not going to be Zane's girlfriend, no matter how hard he tried. Or how much she was attracted to him!

After her experience with her ex-fiancé, she had no intention of taking any man at face value; trust would have to be earned over a long period. Far longer than the few weeks this project would take. In any case, she felt sure that Zane Alexander had no real interest in her long-term. It would simply amuse him to try and seduce her while on the island.

She imagined him to be somewhere in his late thirties and if he wasn't married there had to be a good reason for it. In all probability it was because he enjoyed playing the field. Not that she had any proof; it was all pure conjecture on her part, but why else would he still be a bachelor?

When Lucinda told her mother about her plans she was thrilled for her. 'What a wonderful opportunity,' she said. 'I almost wish I was coming with you.' Not that Ruth was ever short of exotic holidays. If David was too busy to go with her she went with one of her many friends.

'It will be pure work,' reminded Lucinda. 'There won't be much pleasure in it.'

'Nonsense!' chided Ruth. 'All work and no play? I don't believe it for a second. What's this Zane Alexander like? Is he married? Perhaps you need to work your charm on him. It's time you found yourself another boyfriend. He sounds interesting.'

Because he had money, thought Lucinda bitterly. It was all her mother ever thought of.

'What's this about Zane Alexander?' Lucinda's stepfather walked into the room and looked enquiringly at the two women. He was a tall striking man, not particularly good-looking, but there was something about him that most women found attractive. Not so Lucinda. She had never felt happy about her mother marrying him and in turn David did not show much love for his stepdaughter.

'Lucinda's going with him to St Lucia,' answered Ruth excitedly.

David Goldberg frowned harshly and was about to say something when Lucinda interrupted.

'It's purely business. I'm doing a job for him.'

Goldberg snorted in a derogatory manner. 'He's out of your league.'

Lucinda lifted her chin. 'We'll see about that.' Ever since she had started her business, her stepfather had taken great pleasure in putting her down, and it grieved him to think that she was succeeding under her own steam. He would have liked it better had she gone crawling to him for money. But never in her life would she give him that satisfaction. Where money was concerned she was as different from her mother as chalk from cheese.

'Are you sure that doing a job is all he wants from you?' asked David. 'Zane Alexander is a playboy. Surely you must know that?'

'Actually I'd never heard of him until he approached me,' confessed Lucinda, not wishing to admit that she had formed the same opinion. Or that she had met him previously.

'Then, unless you want to spend the entire time in his bed, I'd get out of it fast,' he advised.

Lucinda shook her head. 'I can't do that. This will be my most valuable job yet. I can handle him.'

'Of course you can, darling,' said her mother. 'In any case, you're only young once. Enjoy yourself…'

David's dark brows rose. 'You mark my words; it will be all play and no reward. He's got you where he wants you, girl.'

Lucinda refused to listen, though there were times in the days that followed when she couldn't help wondering whether David was right. Zane's words to his chef had suggested that he might be after something more than a business relationship.

CHAPTER THREE

ZANE sent a car to pick Lucinda up and drive her to the airport. Not the Mercedes he had driven himself, but a sleek black limousine with a liveried driver. The man was young but polite and courteous and, although he looked at Lucinda curiously, he asked no questions.

She was not entirely surprised when she was met and escorted to a private jet, having already gained the impression that Zane enjoyed all the trappings his extreme wealth could give him. When she climbed on board he was already there. She saw white teeth and glittering eyes and for a fraction of a second Lucinda considered turning round and making a quick exit.

She felt as if she was bearding a lion in his den, or a wolf ready to snarl and snap and swallow her down whole. David's warning still rang in her ears. But somehow she managed to fix a smile to her lips.

'You made it, then,' growled Zane. 'I did wonder whether you would change your mind.'

'I'd given my word,' announced Lucinda stiffly.

'Then relax, I don't bite,' he told her tersely. 'Take off your jacket. Sit down. We have a long flight in front of us.'

The plane had a luxurious black leather interior with

one part partitioned for use as an office, another area for dining and amazing deep sofas for relaxing. Lucinda looked about her curiously, smiled at the two pretty flight attendants and shrugged off her coat, which was immediately whisked away.

'You certainly believe in doing things in style,' she commented.

'Why not?' he asked with a smile.

Why not indeed! With his money he could do anything he liked—including whisking her away to a tropical island! Again Lucinda couldn't help wondering whether she'd made a terrible mistake.

'You look apprehensive,' he said, motioning her to sit down. 'Is something wrong? Are you having second thoughts?'

'Not at all.' Lucinda took hold of herself and smiled. Not for anything was she going to let this man know that he disturbed her.

'That's good because I've given up a lot of my time to make this trip with you.'

'You didn't have to,' she protested. Zane wore a black open-necked shirt and black close-fitting trousers which should have made him almost invisible against the upholstery. But it didn't. He was long and lithe and incredibly sexy. Out of formal clothing he was relaxed and somehow different, more threatening to her sanity.

'How else would you have known what I wanted?' he asked, an eyebrow lifted quizzically.

'It seems to me you're going to a lot of trouble for a holiday home.'

And now he frowned. 'Who said it was a holiday home?'

'So what is it?' she asked, staring right into those smoky blue eyes. They made her insides shiver but she resolutely ignored it and continued to look at him.

'It is a home, yes, but not solely for holidays; I rarely take those. My business interests take me all over the world. It gets tiresome staying in hotels.'

'I see,' she said, but she didn't, and if her stepfather was right in his declaration that Zane Alexander was a playboy then this was just going to be another place set up for that purpose. All of a sudden the job didn't seem like such a good idea.

'What's wrong?' His eyes narrowed on hers, trying to see into her mind, to guess at the thoughts that had suddenly disturbed her.

'Nothing,' she said, trying her hardest to keep her unease at bay.

'In that case, let me offer you a drink.' He gave a nod to one of his attendants and immediately crystal flutes of champagne were produced. Zane held his up towards her. 'Here's to a successful business relationship.' Those were his words but not what his eyes told her. They were intent, boring into her soul, reading her, almost telling her what sort of a relationship he hoped to have with her.

Almost but not quite!

Nevertheless something stirred in Lucinda's stomach. She clamped it down firmly, lifting her chin instead, returning his gaze with a firm one of her own. 'To business.'

The champagne slid coolly down her throat, fizzing quietly in her stomach, joining the apprehension. Maybe she ought to have realised that this job would be like no other. Maybe she ought to have considered the danger instead of jumping at the opportunity of adding to her portfolio.

Too late now! They were well and truly on their way.

If she had expected that Zane would spend the whole journey chatting to her she was wrong. 'Please excuse me, I have work to do,' he announced after he had finished his drink. 'Just relax and enjoy the flight.'

In truth Zane knew that he had to keep away from Lucinda. He found her truly exciting and it was going to take all of his not inconsiderable willpower to resist her. She had given every indication that she wanted a strictly business relationship and if he didn't want to frighten her away before she had even started the job he must respect that and keep his feelings well hidden.

Nevertheless it would be interesting to find out what made her tick. To see whether there were any cracks in her armour. He might even stay on the island longer than he had originally planned!

He smiled at the thought and then concentrated on his paperwork. At least he tried to concentrate, but in reality his mind was with the stunning Titian-haired woman sitting just the other side of the partition. She was as nervous as hell and he could hardly blame her. She was flying thousands of miles with a stranger. She had put her faith and trust in him.

Again he tried to concentrate but within a few minutes he gave up and joined her. She'd had her glass refilled and was scanning the skies and when he sat down she turned with a smile. 'I love cloudscapes, don't you?'

He'd never really thought about it. And even now he didn't want to look out the window, he wanted to feast his eyes on his beautiful companion. 'I must confess I rarely study the sky.'

'You're always too busy.'

It was almost an accusation. However, he inclined his head and said nothing.

'Have you finished what you were doing?'

'I didn't think it fair to leave you here alone.'

Green eyes looked scathingly into his. 'And I'm supposed to believe that? A man who can offload an upset little nephew on to a complete stranger won't think twice about leaving someone who's simply doing a job for him alone. Go to your work; I don't need you with me.'

Strong words. He admired her for it but it didn't please him.

For the rest of the flight Zane left Lucinda strictly alone. She had seen his displeasure at her outburst, his face turning thunderous when she reminded him of his behaviour, but she wasn't sorry and felt immense relief when he returned to his little office area.

Now they were nearing their destination. Below them the sea was a glorious turquoise and when the Windward Islands came into view Lucinda gasped with pleasure. As they lost height she could see long white beaches and lush green hinterland and when they finally landed on St Lucia she had forgotten her resentment and turned to Zane with a smile wide enough to split her face in two. 'It looks fantastic. I can't believe I've come here to work. It's like a dream.'

Zane's face lost some of its hardness. 'It is indeed very beautiful and it will be my pleasure to show you around.' But his voice was businesslike and Lucinda didn't know whether to be happy or sad.

They were met by a car and driver and whisked away to a spacious single-storey home that sat on a promontory miles away from any other dwelling. Mindful that they were here on business, Zane gave her a whistle-stop tour of the house and Lucinda felt like a child in paradise. The furnishings were shabby, the paintwork peeling, but it had tremendous potential and Lucinda could see why Zane had bought it.

The rooms were large and airy; it really needed not much more than a lick of paint and some new furniture. She could hardly believe that he was paying her to organise so little. Not that she was complaining. This was an opportunity too good to miss.

The only fly in the ointment, as far as she could see, was that they would be living here together. It troubled her deeply and she knew that she would need to be on her guard at all times.

Outside she discovered a swimming pool and a Jacuzzi and they ended their tour on the sun deck, where they were able to watch the antics of a brilliantly coloured parrot in one of the many trees growing in the steeply sloping garden. 'So,' said Zane, turning to her, 'what do you think now that you've seen it all?'

Lucinda smiled broadly; she couldn't help it. 'I think it's wonderful. How did you find such a place?' Far below was a bay dotted with boats and, even though the day was hot, at this height there was a most welcome mountain breeze.

'It used to belong to a colleague of mine,' answered Zane. 'He nursed his wife through a long illness and I'm afraid everything got neglected. When she died he had no interest in it.'

'I'm sorry,' said Lucinda. 'Have you stayed here yet?'

Zane shook his head and a wicked twinkle sparked in his eyes. 'You have the honour of sharing my pleasure.'

Sharing! Lucinda wasn't sure that she liked his choice of word. And, even though he'd had the foresight to have two bedrooms made habitable, she had noticed that there were no locks on the doors.

'What are you thinking?' he asked, noticing her frown.

Lucinda shook her head, not wishing to reveal her fears.

'If it will make you feel any better, you have my word that I won't enter your space.'

Which was one way of putting it, she thought. But what happened if she entered his? They would be living in such close proximity that she could hardly avoid him. She knew that she had to trust Zane, but somehow those wicked blue eyes didn't invite trust.

'Perhaps you're afraid of being tempted to stray into my room?' he suggested casually.

Lucinda's eyes flashed and she ignored the hot streak through her veins. 'You are unbelievable, Zane Alexander. I've made it clear how I feel about you.'

'But are you sure you know how you feel?' he asked.

Lucinda moved away, not wishing to take part in such a conversation. And then she felt a hand on her arm and a ripple of pleasurable heat where his fingers touched. Intense heat! Burning heat!

She found herself looking into smouldering blue depths, close enough to see the attractive dark line around his irises, the clear whites, the amazing length of his lashes. They were quite magnificent eyes for a man and she was mesmerised by them. She felt them drawing her in, feeding a need inside her that she had not known was there.

After Simon she had felt nothing for any man and had been determined to keep it that way. Why then was this particular man affecting her to such an extent that she wanted to turn tail and run? She gritted her teeth and said the first thing that came into her head. 'Which bedroom is mine?'

A mere flicker suggested that he knew the fight she'd had, but there was nothing in his voice to confirm it. 'Let's go and look, shall we?'

Both of the bedrooms had fabulous views over the bay, each with its own *en suite* bathroom. 'The choice is yours,' said Zane.

The house was kept cool by an ancient air-conditioning system that creaked and groaned and definitely needed replacing. But the warmth on the back of her neck had nothing to do with it not running properly. It was Zane standing far too close for comfort.

She stepped further into the room. 'I'll take this one,' she announced. It was the second one along the hallway. Zane would have no need to walk past it. Small comfort, but better than nothing.

There were four bedrooms altogether, each with beautiful high ceilings and floor to ceiling windows, which allowed them to fill with light. Zane could host a whole harem of girls here, thought Lucinda, and then despised herself for such unworthy thoughts.

'In that case I'll get your suitcase brought in,' said Zane.

He did more than that. A maid appeared as if from nowhere and unpacked their cases and in no time a buffet meal and chilled drinks had been placed on a table outside in the shade.

Lucinda helped herself to aubergine and peppers in a sweet and sour sauce and smoked mahi mahi served with crispy potato and onion. She slowly sipped pineapple juice before finally admitting she could eat no more.

Zane's appetite was healthy too and there wasn't much food left by the time they had finished. He leaned back in his chair. 'I suggest we rest now before taking a dip in the pool.'

Lucinda shook her head, the thought of swimming with Zane, seeing him half naked, filling her with dread. She could imagine a hard body, smooth golden skin, firm stomach, long legs and everything else that went with it. 'I'm here to work,' she reminded him firmly. 'You rest if you want to but I need to wander around again and familiarise myself with each of the rooms in turn before I can even begin to think about design.'

Zane put a hand over hers where it rested on the table. 'There's plenty of time for that. Today you can relax. Today I would appreciate your company.' And he meant it. The touch of his hand was firm, his smoky eyes narrowed and warning.

A heat that had nothing to do with the climate swept through her and Lucinda wanted to pull her hand free. But of course she couldn't do that; she couldn't give away the fact that his touch sent shivers of apprehension rushing through her limbs. So she looked him squarely in the eye and said, 'It's not what I'm getting paid for.'

'What are you, a workaholic?' he asked harshly,

letting his hand drop back to his side. 'Don't you believe in a little pleasure?'

'I thought you wanted the job done as quickly as possible,' asserted Lucinda. Pleasure was the last thing she wanted. Pleasure in her surroundings, yes, in the warmth of the sun, in the glorious blue skies, but not in Zane Alexander's company. He was too discomfiting by far. 'And I can't believe that you're willing to waste time like this. If anyone's a workaholic it's you.'

'I agree,' he said with a shrug, 'but there's a time and place for everything. I declare today an official holiday. Lucinda Oliver, you are not allowed to work.'

She couldn't help smiling. This was a side to Zane that she hadn't seen before. Relaxed, cheerful, teasing. And she couldn't deny that she liked it. 'In that case I think I'd like to change into something more relaxing,' she announced and headed indoors.

She chose a gypsy skirt and a cool camisole top and as she had popped in a bikini at the last minute—just in case—she donned that as well and rejoined Zane on the sun deck.

He had moved to a reclining chair and still wore the black shirt and trousers. Lucinda had half expected him to change too, and she had listened carefully while in her room but heard no movement next door. For the moment he appeared to be a different man but she did not altogether trust him and knew that she still needed to be on her guard.

Zane patted the reclining chair he had placed near to his and reluctantly Lucinda slid on to it. It felt intimate, far too cosy for comfort. She lay back and closed her eyes but he was impossible to ignore. She could hear his breathing, she could smell the faint tang of his cologne, and knew that he was looking at her.

When the silence ran into minutes Lucinda could stand it no longer. She shot open her eyes, ready to lambaste him, or at the very least to jump to her feet and return indoors. To her amazement his lids were closed and when she looked closer she could see by his deepened breathing that he was asleep.

He had undone the buttons on his shirt and as expected his skin was firm and bronzed and she had the irrational urge to touch. Her eyes skimmed over the rest of him, over the hard flatness of his stomach and the long length of his legs. He was an extremely sexy man, even fully clothed, and it was going to be hard denying the fact.

'Like what you see?'

Lucinda hadn't noticed Zane open his eyes and swift heat shot through her, though she did her best to appear undisturbed. 'You have a good physique. Do you work out?'

He nodded. 'I have a gym in my London home.'

'And was a swimming pool a requisite here?'

'Of course.'

'Do you have other homes?' There was a lot about Zane that she didn't know. Not that it was any business of hers, but sitting here in his relaxed company it didn't feel like an intrusion of privacy.

He nodded. 'LA, Australia, the south of France.'

Lucinda shook her head. 'How can you warrant them?'

Zane's lips tugged wryly up at the corners. 'What else do I have to spend my money on?'

Your women friends, she felt tempted to say, but

wisely kept her own counsel. 'Why have you never married?' she asked instead. 'Or is that a stupid question? I guess you're too busy making money.'

'Not the right answer,' he informed her tersely, his eyes flashing almost silver. 'I've simply never met anyone I want to spend the rest of my life with.'

'Let me guess,' she dared to say. 'Most girls are only ever interested in the state of your bank balance?'

'Something like that,' he agreed.

'Are you resigned to staying a bachelor?'

'It doesn't worry me, though it does worry my mother,' he admitted. 'My parents live in Australia and my mother is for ever nagging me to get married. She wants more grandchildren.' He smiled ruefully. 'Here am I almost telling you my life story and I know nothing about you. Except that you don't have a boyfriend. Which I find extremely odd because you're a very attractive lady.'

As he spoke he looked at her appreciatively, just as she had looked at him earlier. Only he did it blatantly, not caring that she watched. Every part of her responded! Nerves tingled; hormones leapt into life; nipples tautened and strained against her soft cotton top—and he missed nothing.

'So—tell me about yourself,' he said, his eyes finally moving up to her face, narrowing sharply when he observed the tip of her tongue moistening her lips.

Lucinda hoped that he didn't take it as a sign of encouragement. Her mouth had gone nervously dry and the butterflies in her stomach intensified. Heaven knew how much she wanted to dislike this man, so why didn't she? What was it about him that caused every one of her senses to go into overdrive?

'There's not much to tell,' she answered, alarmed to hear how husky her voice sounded. Damn the man! Why was he confusing her like this? Or, more importantly, why was she allowing it? Why was she letting him affect her?

Because he was one hell of a sexy man, that was the answer. She couldn't help herself. She didn't want to like him but was constantly pulled towards him in a cycle that would be difficult to break.

Zane probably took it for granted that most women, if not all, would fall at his feet. He could bed any woman he liked. *But she didn't have to be one of them!* Without any shadow of doubt she would need to be on her guard at all times.

'Your mother's remarried. What happened to your father?'

'He died,' she answered bluntly, trying to hide the pain that still shot through her whenever she spoke about him.

'I'm sorry. How did that happen?'

'He'd been ill a long time. It was inevitable,' she told him, while knowing that he didn't really care.

'I'm genuinely interested,' he assured her, reading her expression. 'I'm interested in people. I like to find out what motivates them. I already know that you don't like your stepfather.' Lucinda frowned and sat up just a little bit straighter. 'I didn't tell you that.'

'No, but you gave the impression.'

'Actually, it's true.' Her shoulders relaxed a little. 'I hate him, and the feeling's mutual—except that he doesn't let my mother know it. And I hate my mother for marrying him simply for his money,' she added bitterly.

'She did that?'

'It's what many women do,' she retorted, her eyes shooting sparks of angry fire. 'Not that I have any intention of falling into that same trap! I'll make my own money, thank you.'

Zane pursed his lips and nodded his head. 'Wise woman! We're two of a kind, you and I.'

Lucinda frowned. She knew what he meant but she didn't like being lumped into the same category. She would never spend her money on lavish houses all over the world, not if she had a thousand million in the bank. Such extravagances didn't appeal. The fact that people did it, and needed the likes of her to improve their interiors, was a different matter altogether.

'So—tell me about your father,' he said encouragingly. 'How old were you when he died?'

Lucinda pursed her lips and her eyes grew sad. 'Fifteen. I was heartbroken. He'd spent most of his life in and out of hospitals; we didn't have any money, but he more than made up for it. There was always love and laughter in our house. I was so happy. What I didn't know was that my mother gradually resented the fact that we were poor.

'After my father died she met Goldberg, a very wealthy property developer. She shamelessly threw herself at him and within a few months they were married. We moved from our tiny rented property into his palatial mansion. He paid for my higher education; I appreciate that, but he will never replace my father. He was the most wonderful man.'

Tears misted her eyes and instantly Zane leaned forward and gathered her into his arms, dabbing her eyes with his handkerchief, murmuring words of reassurance. At first Lucinda didn't resist; she actually felt comforted by his action, but then the reality of the situation hit her.

This man had employed her to do a job, and he was in the same league as David Goldberg; there was no way in this world that she was going to have an affair with him. He may have been only consoling her, but that wasn't the point. She had seen the hungry look in his eyes; she knew his reputation. If she weren't careful she would end up in his bed.

'I'm sorry,' she said, straining to pull away. 'It always gets to me when I talk about my father. If he knew what my mother had done he'd turn in his grave. He loved her so much. Love was all he had to give. And he gave it in bucketfuls.' Tears welled again.

Zane pushed her head into his shoulder and held her there until she began to feel better. He stroked her hair, which had become free from its restraining tie. It amazed Lucinda that a man as important as Zane Alexander should have this caring side to him. It was totally unexpected.

Unless, of course, it wasn't because he cared! Maybe he was using her distress as a way of getting through to her? Maybe he thought it would lead to other things? Even as the thought occurred to her Lucinda pushed her hands hard against his chest. 'I'm all right now.'

'Are you sure?' He blocked her escape by cupping her face between warm firm hands. There was something almost primeval in his eyes as they locked with hers, a desire as old as man himself, and Lucinda felt unwanted warmth steal into her. It started in her toes and gradually worked its way through each limb until her whole body raged with fire. This was a situation she had told herself she would avoid at all costs. This was Zane the playboy in action. And already her needs were being fuelled by his closeness.

CHAPTER FOUR

ZANE knew that Lucinda was torn between letting him kiss her and doing the right thing and pushing him away. He was sorry about her father, of course he was, and when he persuaded her into his arms it hadn't been his intention to take the situation any further. But holding her against him, feeling the warmth of her body and smelling its sweetness, had aroused all of his base instincts. He wanted her! And he wanted her now.

It took all of Lucinda's will-power to move out of Zane's embrace. It felt as though she was wrenching herself free of an iron clamp instead of the light touch of his hands. It really had been a big mistake coming here. She had put greed for his business before what was best for her.

'I wish you hadn't done that,' she told him tightly, the words crackling out of a throat gone tremendously dry.

'Done what?'

Did he really need her to spell it out? 'You know what I'm talking about,' she retorted. 'I appreciate the use of your handkerchief but I don't need comforting in other ways.'

'And what way would that be?'

A steely glint appeared in his eyes and Lucinda began to wonder whether she had misjudged him. Whether it was her fertile imagination that had seen something that wasn't there. Whatever, he looked far from pleased.

She shook her head and got up from her chair. 'It doesn't matter.'

'And I say it does matter,' he rejoined fiercely. 'I do not like being criticised.'

'It doesn't count that you're already cast as a playboy?'

'You've heard the rumour?' A faint smile curved his lips. 'Who told you that, I wonder?'

Lucinda jutted her chin and stared hostilely. 'Actually I'd had my suspicions, but my stepfather confirmed it.'

'Ah!' Enlightenment filled his eyes. 'And you took his word as truth? A man you incidentally hate the sight of? It didn't occur to you that he could be saying it because he didn't want you working for me?'

It was true; David Goldberg definitely didn't like to think that her career was taking off. He liked to think that she hadn't the intelligence to do well for herself. Why, she had no idea. Maybe because she had always resented him! At the age of fifteen her hormones had been all over the place; she'd just lost her beloved father, her mother had all too quickly remarried and Lucinda's resentment of the new man in their life had caused ill feelings between them, which had never gone away.

'I don't care whether it's true or not,' she told him now. 'And I have no wish to continue this conversation.' She sprang up from her seat and ran round to the other side of the house, where she stripped off her skirt and top and dived cleanly into the pool. She desperately needed to cool off.

She was feverishly hot and the water mercifully cold, and after a few energetic lengths her ragged nerves were calmed. She had half expected Zane to follow and was both relieved and pleased when there was no sign of him. She kept telling herself that it wasn't going to work, staying here with him, feeling his presence, knowing that at any minute she could give in to temptation. And he was a big temptation. She could hardly believe that she was attracted to him. It was totally inconceivable.

Finally she hauled herself out of the pool, rinsed herself down beneath the huge outdoor shower and headed back towards the house. Zane appeared in front of her as if from nowhere.

'You swim like a mermaid,' he complimented. 'Graceful, swift and beautiful.' A pair of dark glasses shielded his eyes but she felt his eyes studying her body in its neat white bikini. The heat returned.

'You were watching me?' Accusation made her voice shrill.

Zane inclined his head. 'And very pleasant it was too. I wanted to join you but I wasn't sure that you'd appreciate it.'

'No, I wouldn't have done,' snapped Lucinda, her green eyes flashing magnificently. 'In fact I don't appreciate your presence here at all.'

'That's a pity,' he said with a disarming smile, 'because I was actually enjoying myself. And I think I'd enjoy myself more if you'd allow me to…'

His words ceased as his hands caught her hips and

urged her against him and, before she could even draw breath to ask what the hell he thought he was doing, his mouth found hers.

It was a heart-stopping kiss that filled her body with intense pleasure. How a man she didn't particularly like and certainly didn't trust could do this to her she did not know. Thankfully he let her go just as abruptly. 'I'm sorry, I just had to do that,' he declared immediately. 'You have no idea how tempting you looked.'

Lucinda struggled for breath. She didn't believe his apology for one second. He'd planned this. He'd known from the moment he invited her out here that he would make a play for her. It was what he did. And she had been a fool to think otherwise.

'Not only do you swim like a mermaid but you also looked like one as you stood there with your hair hanging loose.' His eyes lowered and Lucinda became aware of her nipples pushing against the silky fabric of her top. It was plain white and far too revealing. In fact, she realised with instant horror, it had gone almost transparent!

Her cheeks flamed. It was a new bikini, not tried out in the water, bought more for sunbathing than anything else. She had thought it would look good against a tan. Inwardly, though, she stiffened her spine. Not for anything would she let Zane see her embarrassment. With her chin high she met his gaze. 'Maybe I was one in a previous life.'

'I'm surprised you don't have a boyfriend.'

The statement was sudden and unexpected and Lucinda's eyes widened. 'Why do you want to know?'

'Because it's unusual for a woman as beautiful as you.'

Lucinda shook her head, wishing he wouldn't keep complimenting her. She knew he was doing it so that she'd feel flattered and fall into his arms. Hadn't he realised yet that he'd picked the wrong person?

'I was engaged once,' she finally admitted.

Blue eyes expressed interest. 'And?' he prompted when she didn't continue.

'I went out with him for nearly four years.'

Zane's eyebrows rose and his interest increased. 'That's a long time.'

'Too long, I guess,' she acknowledged with a hint of irony in her voice.

'So what happened?'

'He dropped me for someone else. We'd actually planned the wedding. I was devastated.' Lord, why on earth was she opening up to him? It was so out of character. And in any case Zane was the last person she wanted to tell her life story to. She couldn't believe the effect he was having on her. First she'd let him kiss her, now she was revealing confidences. What next?

Zane saw the pain in her eyes, mistook it for unhappiness over her past and immediately pulled her into his arms.

'I'm sorry,' he said.

The hell he was! How could he be when he didn't know her or Simon? It was another excuse to get close. She should never have told him. She'd actually given him some ammunition. 'I don't need your pity,' she declared, struggling to free herself. 'I'm over it now.'

Zane released her but he didn't move away. 'No, you're not,' he declared. 'You've erected a barrier.'

He was right; Simon *was* her defence. She had only

to think about the way he'd treated her to put her off any man who tried to get close. And that included the gorgeous, extremely sexy Zane Alexander.

It didn't count that his brief kiss of a few seconds ago had aroused feelings that she had thought long since dead. And, if she were honest with herself, they were sensations that went incredibly deeper than any she had ever felt with Simon. Simon had been her one and only lover so she'd had no one to compare him with. Until now!

At this point Lucinda angrily dashed her thoughts away. They were unwanted. It didn't matter whether Zane was the most fantastic lover of all time; she had no intention of finding out.

'I don't want to discuss this any more,' she declared tightly. 'I'm going to rest in my room for a while.' She might even stay there until morning. She'd had enough of Zane's company for one day.

Zane's smile told her that he knew exactly what she was thinking. 'Have you ever sat outside on a tropical night and watched the stars?' he asked quietly. 'Have you ever listened to the chirruping of cicadas? Have you smelled the heady perfume of the flowers? Don't miss out on it all because of a misguided sense of trust.'

Misguided? Lucinda didn't think so. Zane was forgetting that she knew exactly the sort of uncaring person he was. He might try to romance her, to seduce her even, but once they returned to England and her job was finished she would be just as quickly forgotten. Maybe other girls were into affairs, especially with rich, handsome men, but not this one.

To her relief Zane didn't insist on an answer. She fled to her room, showered and then flung herself down on the bed. To take her mind off Zane and his kiss, she began planning how she would decorate the room. She had brought several fabric swatches with her as well as paint samples and pages out of furniture catalogues, but it soon became clear that she would be far better going into Castries and seeing what they had to offer there. It needed something with a local flavour. The capital was sure to have a good selection of shops. She would suggest it to Zane tomorrow and hopefully he would put a car and driver at her disposal.

But all thoughts of decorating left her when a tap came on her door. Instantly she thought it was Zane and was prepared to tell him to go away, when the door was pushed tentatively open and the maid popped her head inside. 'Excuse me, Miss Oliver. Mr Alexander has asked for you to join him,' she announced with a wide smile.

It was easy to see that she thought the sun shone out of Zane's eyes.

'Tell him I'm tired and that I'm staying here,' said Lucinda.

'He said not to take no for an answer,' the pretty dark-skinned girl answered, looking worried. 'He is ready to eat.'

Lucinda groaned inwardly. 'Very well,' she agreed, not wishing to get the maid into trouble. 'Tell him I'll be along shortly.'

Her shortly amounted to half an hour and when she opened her bedroom door she was taken aback to see a thunderous Zane about to make an entrance. 'I was just coming to fetch you,' he growled. 'What the hell have you been doing?'

'Reluctantly getting myself ready,' she answered,

chin high. 'I rather fancied an early night. You're forgetting the time difference.' Her tone was sharp, her eyes growing as angry as his. 'I would have been in bed were I at home. You're being unreasonable, Zane.' But then wasn't that Zane Alexander all over?

'And you're not?' he grunted, his eyes roving over the coral silk blouse she had donned with a pair of matching trousers. It was loose enough to be cool and also not to show the way her nipples stood to attention under his scrutiny.

It was a long, hard look he gave her before he swung on his heel and she had no choice but to follow him through to the dining room. Someone had done their best to make it look cheerful with tastefully arranged urns of flowers but Lucinda's professional eye was soon making changes. Like all the other rooms, it was spacious and light and it had the most wonderful views, but it was badly in need of a makeover. The furniture was old and jaded and the curtains at the windows had certainly seen better days.

Their table was placed so that they both sat looking out through the open window with its glorious view. By this time the sun had gone down and the sky was filled with stunning colours—gold and scarlet, the inkiest of blacks and the richest purples, all reflected with even more intensity in the calm waters of the Caribbean Sea. Her mood mellowed as she sat looking at it.

And when dishes of food were placed in front of them she discovered a hunger that she hadn't suspected. Fish broth, Creole baked chicken, fresh fruit. She tasted them all. She enjoyed them all. They hardly spoke; such was the enchantment of the evening. Or was it because

Zane was still angry with her that he didn't say much? Lucinda couldn't be sure.

Afterwards, as they sat outside on the terrace sipping wine, listening to the sounds of the night and gazing at the stars that were surely more brilliant than they ever were in England, she felt amazingly content. This was an experience that would stay with her for a long time.

Until suddenly she became aware that Zane was watching her and not the darkening sky, and although the night air was cool her skin grew moist with sudden heat. This was truly a place made for lovers—and he was looking at her as though that was his intention.

'You're very beautiful, Lucinda,' he said roughly. 'Far more beautiful than I remember.'

'That's because when I was babysitting Tim you were never there,' she reminded him, unable to keep a note of censure from her voice. 'You hardly had time to notice me.'

'I guess I did have other things on my mind,' he agreed. 'But not so now. This is one of those rare occasions when I can relax. And I have you to keep me company. What more could a man ask for? A beautiful lady in a most beautiful part of the world.'

'I'm here to work,' she reminded him. She didn't like the way he was talking—as though their time here was for his pleasure alone.

'You know what they say about all work and no play,' he reminded her, his eyes a dark blue in the light that spilled out from the dining room. It gilded his features with bronze. His face was beautifully sculpted with an almost Roman nose and chiselled cheek bones and a mouth that was fluent and kissable and… She stopped her thoughts right there.

What he looked like was of no interest to her whatsoever, and she'd do well to remember it. Except that he'd set light to a fire inside her and she couldn't help but wonder what it would be like to be kissed by him again out here in the moonlight.

That earlier brief kiss, no matter how much she had resented it, had opened up her defences. She was susceptible to him now. And, judging by the look in his eyes, he knew it! They were narrowed and intent on hers, reading her dilemma, knowing exactly how she felt. It was time she left. But when she pushed back her chair and stood up a hand shot out and caught her wrist.

'Don't leave yet,' said Zane. 'The evening is still young and I have no wish to spend it alone.' And all the time he was speaking he was pulling her inexorably towards him.

The air between them crackled with tension, warning her that if she didn't escape now it would be too late. But did she want to escape? Wasn't this devastatingly attractive man setting alight fires inside her that had never been lit before? Wasn't he arousing passions that no one else but he could quench?

Yes, but…

But what? asked an inner voice.

But nothing! There was no but about it. She was being foolish. If she didn't put a stop to things now she would hate herself later. 'I want to go to my room,' she told him firmly, trying to no avail to tug her hand free. 'I really am very tired.'

'And I'd like you here with me. Please stay.'

Their eyes met and held, his fingers relaxed and

suddenly her hand was free, but instead of turning and running Lucinda amazed herself by slipping quietly back on to her chair. It was the way he'd said 'Please stay' that had done it. It had been an unexpected 'please'. Not what she was used to from this man. Perhaps he was lonely? After all they were both in a strange place with no one else to turn to for company.

'Very well,' she agreed quietly, 'but not for long. I should go to bed.'

Gradually she relaxed. Zane seemed to be in a mood for not saying very much and she too was content to sit quietly. Nevertheless his nearness could not be ignored. The heady scent of him invaded her nostrils and if she closed her eyes and listened intently she could even hear him breathing. There were so many other night sounds around them and yet Zane's breathing and the constant thud of her heart were the only ones that she heard.

'What are you thinking?'

His voice broke the silence and made her jump. 'How beautiful it is out here,' she lied.

'But not as beautiful as you.'

Her eyes shot wide and her heart rate increased. 'You shouldn't be saying that, Zane. We're here on business. Or at least I am.' But never had a job taken her to such a faraway magical place. Everything here was beautiful.

He inched his chair nearer to hers. 'I'm glad you said that *you're* here on business and not me, because I don't normally like to mix business with pleasure. As things stand, I have no such dilemma.' Again he edged his chair closer, so close this time that there was but a hair's breadth between them.

Lucinda drew in a swift breath, trying to ignore the

alarming sensations that were pulsing in every single one of her cells. He was going to kiss her; she was very much aware of it, and if she had any sense she would flee. But sense and sensibility didn't show their heads; instead she felt an aching need that only he could assuage and when he tipped her chin with a firm finger she willingly parted her lips.

Zane had wanted to do this ever since Lucinda had walked into his office just over a week ago. She had transformed herself into a stunningly beautiful businesswoman. Not only beautiful but hellishly sexy as well.

But *he* was aware, very much so, and she was driving him crazy. He had begun to think that he would never get anywhere with her—and he had taken a huge gamble when he'd kissed her earlier. Brief though that kiss had been, he had become immediately aware that she wasn't immune to him. It had given him the encouragement he needed.

He had heard it said that St Lucia was born beautiful. That was true of Lucinda as well. Just as the beauty of nature enhanced the island, an inner beauty made Lucinda one of the most striking women he had ever met. She was completely unaware of it but to him it was like a beckoning beacon. He wanted her so badly that it hurt.

And when she showed no sign of resisting him, when she seemed to melt into his arms, he groaned deep within his throat and, pulling her on to his lap, he deepened his kiss.

He traced her lips with his tongue, he tasted the nectarlike sweetness of her, he explored the intricacies of her mouth, and all the time he could feel the throb of her heart getting stronger and stronger. And the soft warmth of her body growing hotter and hotter.

His own desire surged and when Lucinda wriggled against him he knew that she was aware of his arousal. The beauty of it was that it didn't frighten her away. On the contrary, she sucked in his kisses like a drowning woman, letting her tongue play with his, her hands shaping his head, fingers twisting in his hair, her passion growing with each second that passed.

What he wanted to do, what he really wanted to do, was pick her up and take her to bed. But he knew that it was far too soon. So he continued to kiss her and slowly he let his hand glide over one of her breasts. When he discovered that she was not wearing a bra beneath the coral silk it nearly drove him wild.

He rubbed the pad of his thumb over her nipple until it tightened into a hard nub. And then he did the same to her other breast. And all the time she said nothing. Not that he wasn't aware of her heightened excitement. Her breathing came in much shorter gasps and her fingers tightened in his hair until he felt that if she wasn't careful she would pull it out by the roots.

Very slowly he released his mouth from hers and with even more painfully slow progress he nibbled his way down to her beckoning breasts, at the same time flipping open her blouse buttons so that they were revealed in all their naked glory to his greedy eyes.

Then he sucked each burning nipple in turn into his mouth, exulting when he heard her moans of pleasure, when she held him against her as though she never wanted him to stop. She tasted as sweet as she smelled and he knew he ought to call a halt before he came to the point when he couldn't.

It was a tiny noise that did it. The sound of something shattering inside the house! A dropped plate perhaps, or a glass! Followed by a smothered cry. And it broke the spell.

He lifted his face to look at her. He saw sweetness and softness and wonderment. Lips that were moist and slightly swollen. Eyes that were glowing orbs of pleasure but with a question in them too. She was asking herself how this could have happened.

And he wanted to ask the same.

Was it the sweet night air that had seduced their senses? Was it their exotic surroundings? Was it the magic of the island? Or was it simply that when push came to shove she couldn't resist him? He'd really given her little choice. She had wanted to retire to her room. Instead he had insisted she join him. What had happened next was inevitable. Except that for some reason his conscience bothered him. It didn't normally. Most women he knew enjoyed his kisses. But Lucinda was different.

'I shouldn't have done that,' he growled, but he said it so quietly that it was possible she hadn't heard.

'No, you shouldn't,' she agreed, also very quietly. 'It went beyond the bounds of our contract. However, I'm prepared to forget it, provided it never happens again.' And with that she pulled her blouse together and walked away with her head held high.

Lucinda could not believe that she had let Zane kiss her again. And not only on the lips! She'd let him undress her and taste her breasts, and touch them, and arouse them, and make her lose her mind. Oh, God, the pleasure he had given her! Even thinking about it re-created the sensations.

Indoors in her room she touched where he had touched. She looked at herself in the mirror. Saw the dreamy arousal in her eyes, the soft glow to her skin, and when she grazed her thumb lightly over her nipples the full sweet sensations winged once again through the very heart of her.

What was she to do? Amazingly he had apologised so perhaps he wouldn't touch her again. But Lord help her—she wanted him to. He had given her a taste of what it could be like between them and she wanted to feed from it like a starving animal.

It was this island that did it, she felt sure. It was an exotic paradise just made for lovers. Had Zane known that when he brought her here? Or had St Lucia woven its spell over him too? He struck her as a man well able to control his emotions—so what had happened?

He needed a woman, that was what had happened. And she had been the only one available!

Looking at it like that made Lucinda tighten her lips. The magic was over, the spell broken. It didn't have to be her; it could have been anyone. Zane Alexander had an insatiable sexual appetite. She must never forget that. He was used to a whole coterie of women sitting at his feet, waiting for his favours. He'd probably never been turned down.

What a shock he had in store!

CHAPTER FIVE

NOT surprisingly Lucinda's body refused to settle down and she slept little that night. She could still feel Zane's touch, still smell the male scent of him, still experience rushes of pleasure whenever she remembered what he had done to her.

And the thought that he was in the next room played a big part as well. She had lain awake listening for him to come to bed and an hour or more had passed before she heard his soft footsteps and his door opening and closing. Even then she strained to hear the sounds of him moving about the room—and it was well into the early hours before all was still and quiet.

She slept intermittently but as soon as the first lazy fingers of dawn stretched across the sky Lucinda sprang out of bed. She pulled on a pair of shorts and a T-shirt, tied her hair back in a ponytail and set off to explore. The temperature outside was perfect, but she knew that all too soon the heat of the day would take over and she would wish herself back in the air-conditioned house.

The gardens were lush and green with a plethora of ferns and palms and exotic flowers that she did not know the names of. She discovered a path and followed it down the hillside. It became steeper and steeper with a handrail to the side and eventually Lucinda found herself on the shore, with the bay to her right with its dozens of moored yachts and cruisers, and to her left a long stretch of almost white sand.

By now the sun had painted the sky in a fleeting burst of red and apricot, until it rose majestically above the horizon and the colours muted and disappeared altogether. There was not another soul about and Lucinda kicked off her sandals and walked along the shore. The sea was tempting and although she had nothing to change into she ran into the lapping waves, laughing and splashing, until she was in deep enough to swim.

The water felt like silk against her skin and she raised her arms in long lazy strokes, enjoying the feeling of being at one with nature. She floated on her back, watched the birds wheeling and crying above, and was thinking of returning to the house when she became conscious of someone swimming beside her.

'Zane!' How had he got here? In no time flutters of anxiety filled her nerves. She had been enjoying her time alone. Now all she could remember was last night and him kissing her.

Zane grinned at her shocked face. 'Is that all you have to say? Zane?'

'I didn't expect you. I didn't even see you,' she retorted, annoyed to feel her heart racing all over again.

'Why are you up so early? Couldn't you sleep? Wasn't the bed comfortable?'

As if by mutual consent, they both turned and headed for the shore. 'The bed was very comfortable, thank you,' she replied, looking him straight in the eye. 'It was my thoughts that kept me awake.'

'Now let me think,' he said, a faint smile tugging at the corners of his mouth. 'Would they be thoughts about the project in hand? Were you busy imagining how you are going to transform my place? Or would your thoughts have been about—' he paused deliberately, his eyes twinkling with humour '—what happened between us last night? I know I said I shouldn't have done it, but I'm not sorry I did. Your boyfriend was a fool to let you go.'

By now they had reached shallow waters and they waded out and stood for a moment on the shore facing each other. Lord, he was sexy, thought Lucinda. He wore a pair of brief black swim-shorts and his body was tanned and firm and her fingers simply itched to touch him.

Heat flooded her. They were insane thoughts. She must learn to curb them. 'Don't flatter yourself,' she said with a hint of anger in her voice. 'It was the project I was thinking about. I'd actually like to go into Castries and see what's on offer. Do you have a car I can use?'

'Better still, I'll come with you,' he said without hesitation.

'No!' Lucinda's voice came out in something like a panic-ridden shriek and she immediately amended it. 'I mean, no, I'll be better off alone. I'll probably spend hours looking around. You'd be totally bored.'

His eyes told her that he could never be bored in her company, but what he said was, 'Do you not think I should have a say in what you're going to do?'

'Naturally,' said Lucinda. 'But not until I've developed a few ideas. I need time to myself. Both in your house and when I'm sourcing furniture and materials.'

'Mmm!' Zane touched a finger to his lips. 'That might be difficult.'

Lucinda frowned.

'You see I'm not very good at spending time by myself. I need company.' Blue eyes challenged hers, sending shivers of sensation down her spine.

Lucinda shook off the feeling as well as she could. Not easy when the sexiest man in the universe was standing less than a metre away. 'You more or less told me that this would be a base,' she declared resentfully. 'Can't you go and do some work somewhere?'

'I could,' he agreed. 'But you know what they say about all work and no play making Jack a dull boy. I should hate to appear dull.'

That would be impossible, thought Lucinda. Zane? Dull? Never!

His mouth twitched as he waited for her response.

'Since I am here to work,' she told him, 'I see no reason why you shouldn't work also. You can't possibly sit around for days on end.'

'I don't intend to do that,' he told her. 'This transformation of my house, or whatever you like to call it, is going to be a joint effort. It's so rare I take time off work that I'm actually looking forward to it.'

Lucinda groaned inwardly. She hadn't really thought about what Zane would do while she was working; but she most certainly hadn't imagined he would want to spend much of his time with her—certainly not all of it! It would make her job impossible.

Maybe if he hadn't kissed her, maybe if she weren't so very much aware of the way her body reacted to his, then it would work. But already, after only a few hours on the island, she could see the physical impossibility of anything like that happening.

'How can I think with you around?' she asked him bluntly.

And how could he act normally when a woman as exceptionally beautiful and desirable as Lucinda was living with him but was taboo? Zane knew he was behaving like a complete moron. It wasn't usual for him to lust over a member of the opposite sex. It was usually they who came to him.

Women hung around him in droves. And he knew why. Money! Power! It was an aphrodisiac to some of the female population. Lucinda was different. She'd had a bad experience, and a bad role model in her mother apparently, and was well and truly off men.

Although—and it pleased him somewhat to realise this—she hadn't been entirely averse to his kiss last night. It had eventually sent her running, yes, but she had nevertheless enjoyed it. Indeed her reaction had been far more intense and exciting than he had expected.

'As a professional woman I'm quite sure you'll be able to get on with your job,' he assured her, 'despite my presence. Now, let's go up and have some breakfast. I don't know about you, but that swim's made me hungry.'

He touched a hand to her elbow and led her to a door in the cliff face. A glass door! He smiled at her surprised expression. 'The previous owner had a lift installed for his invalid wife. We may as well make use of it; it's a stiff climb otherwise.'

Zane could see the doubt in Lucinda's eyes—and quite incredible green eyes they were too. Sometimes they were as dark as the deepest ocean and at others, like now, they were the lightest aquamarine. They enchanted him. But he could see that she wasn't happy about sharing the lift. Maybe she was thinking about last night's kiss. That incredible kiss! She had run like a scared rabbit afterwards but he had a feeling that she had enjoyed it as much as he had.

It was so unusual for him to be happy about taking time off from his business affairs that he knew this attractive woman had something to do with it. A lot to do with it, in fact! Everything to do with it! She was totally gorgeous. Although he wasn't ready for a serious relationship, Lucinda had a lot more going for her than most of the women he dated.

As Lucinda stepped into the lift and the door swished closed behind her she felt a shiver of apprehension. The confined space worried her. She knew what Zane could do to her senses—without even touching her. And here, now, he was so close that she could almost feel the electricity crackling between them.

She tried to concentrate on the view instead. It was totally magical being whisked silently upwards with the whole panorama opening out in front of them. The yachts grew smaller, the ocean wider, the sky immense. And inside their little space the walls were padded with ocean coloured leather. It was out of this world.

Except that it was a tiny world holding just her and Zane. She could feel the heat of his body, inhale the fresh scent of him, and her fingers curled into fists at her sides.

'Is something wrong?'

She hadn't realised that Zane had observed her tension.

'Are you scared of heights?' The shore was a long way below them now.

Lucinda grabbed the excuse. 'Yes,' she lied faintly. But it was entirely the wrong thing to have said. The next second Zane's arms were wrapped protectively around her, her head held firmly against his chest, her eyes shaded from the view outside.

'A few more moments,' he told her.

More like a lifetime, she thought, fighting to control the sensations that were whizzing through her veins. And when he, oh so gently, stroked damp strands of hair from her face such was her surge of feelings that she wanted to press herself even closer to him.

Fortunately, before she had time to give herself away, the lift came to a halt and the doors opened. Zane immediately released her and Lucinda stepped out. They were at the side of the pump house, near the pool. It was no wonder that she hadn't seen the lift before.

'I'll go and get showered,' she said at once.

Zane nodded. 'We'll meet at breakfast and afterwards we'll make that trip into Castries.'

Lucinda did not want him to accompany her, but she knew without a shadow of doubt that he wouldn't take no for an answer so she smiled bravely.

Their *en suite* bathrooms were back to back and when Lucinda finished her shower she could hear Zane's water still running and above it she could hear him humming. It depressed her. He was clearly happy with the situation even though she wasn't. But if it was in his mind to start an affair then he would need to think again. There was no way she was going to take part in anything like that. No way!

This job was unlike any other she had worked on. She had thought, initially, that it would be a good experience. And it would be, if it weren't for Zane. Had she known they would be spending so much time together, she would most certainly not have taken the job. How did he expect her to do what he was paying her for if he insisted on commandeering her attention? He had told her that he had business interests here in St Lucia, so why wasn't he out there working?

Lucinda took her time dressing and Zane was already sitting at the breakfast table when she walked out to the sun deck. The air was warmer now but the mountain breeze ruffled her hair and was very welcome, although not all of the heat in her body was due to the weather.

On the table was a huge dish of fresh fruit, already peeled and sliced; there were bread rolls and butter and cheeses and ham, a selection of juices and cereals. 'I wasn't sure whether you'd like a cooked breakfast?' he asked.

Lucinda shook her head. She didn't feel that she could eat a thing.

'Likewise. I always eat continental when I'm in a hot country. At least we have something in common.'

Not quite sure how to answer that, Lucinda let it go and poured herself a glass of mango juice.

'Tell me more about this guy who let you down,' said Zane conversationally when she had selected a bread roll and buttered it carefully. So carefully in fact that it took her ages and she hadn't noticed that Zane was watching her. 'He's really affected you, hasn't he?'

Lucinda frowned. 'What do you mean?'

'Isn't it obvious?' he asked. 'You seem extremely wary of men—unless it's just me?'

'It's not you,' she lied, 'although it was definitely a mistake letting you kiss me. Rest assured it won't happen again. This is a business trip, neither of us must forget that.' She felt sudden heat flood her cheeks as she reminded him of the kiss and hoped he would put it down to the warmth of the day.

'So in future you're Miss Prim, is that it?' His smoky blue eyes teased her. 'Or would it be Miss Untouchable?'

'I happen to take my work seriously,' she reminded him fiercely. 'I wouldn't have got where I am quite so quickly if I didn't.'

'Tell me about your ex-fiancé. I'm interested in him.'

Lucinda sighed and leaned back in her chair. 'There's not much to tell.'

'Four years was a long relationship. Time enough surely for you to both know your own minds?'

Lucinda nodded. 'I was so sure he was the one.'

'Most people get married or at least move in together in far less time than that,' he observed. 'Which perhaps suggests that he was never the right person for you. Did you ever have reservations?'

'None at all,' she answered, feeling the pain of their parting all over again. 'Simon and I met at university. It wasn't love at first sight or anything like that. But we gradually began to see more of each other and I suppose we slipped into the relationship. Nevertheless I did love him; I could see a future for us together. But obviously he didn't. I don't know who he left me for and I don't really care.' But she had cared when it happened and she had tried to find out who the other woman was. Not that it would have done her any good. Simon had gone, deserted her. All the love he had sworn for her had sailed into thin air.

Zane reached across the table and put his hand over hers. 'You're well rid of him. You deserve better.'

And when she looked into the smoky depths of his eyes Lucinda saw compassion and wondered if he was suggesting himself. He didn't stand a cat in hell's chance. She definitely felt attracted to him, but that was pure sex, nothing more. When, or if, she ever did fall in love again he would have to be someone special, someone whom she could trust and love unconditionally, and who felt the same way. Zane Alexander most definitely didn't fit that bill.

She pulled her hand away, trying to do it so that he didn't realise how much he had the power to disturb her. And she broke off a piece of bread and popped it into her mouth.

'Anyway, we're not here to talk about ourselves,' she said firmly.

'So what else is there to talk about?'

Anything but themselves!

'Would you like to tell me what you're thinking of doing to my bedroom, for instance?' he asked with a hint of a smile.

Swift heat flooded her. Bedrooms were as much a taboo subject as Simon and her manless state. She still thought of silver and grey and ice-blue, although maybe the ice part wasn't right any more. He was a man of passion. Maybe hot red or fiery purple would make more sense.

Careful not to let him see that the thought of discussing his bedroom disturbed her, she looked at him with cool green eyes. 'You've not yet given me time to come up with any ideas.'

'There's a reason behind that,' he announced calmly.

Lucinda frowned.

'Before you can design for me you need to get to know me. Properly know me, I mean. Isn't that the way you usually work?'

'I like to get a general idea of what clients like and dislike, a little about their personalities perhaps, but—'

'That's exactly what I mean,' Zane declared in triumph. 'My personality! Can you honestly say that you know me yet?'

She knew enough, thought Lucinda. Enough to want to steer clear of him, to avoid him like the plague, in fact. Even now, sitting here, talking to him, she couldn't ignore his sexuality. Even his hair was sexy. It was dry now and back to its golden colour, totally untamed, and she wanted to run her fingers through it and stroke it into place. Crazy, she knew, but she couldn't help herself.

'No, you can't, can you?' he said when she didn't answer. 'We need a few days together before you start the thinking process. We'll go into Castries together, and you can look all you like at whatever it is you need to look at, but primarily it should be pleasure, not work. We'll dine there—I know a perfect restaurant—and then—'

'Stop!' It was Lucinda's turn to hold up her hand. 'Don't run away with yourself. My time's money, don't forget. The longer I'm here, the more it's going to cost you.'

'I don't mind,' he declared indifferently, just as she had known he would. 'I haven't had a proper holiday in years.'

'This isn't a holiday,' she reminded him.

His voice went an octave lower. 'Wouldn't you like it to be?'

Yes, she would, very much so. But it was far too dangerous. Zane was dangerous. The most dangerous man she had ever met. He was sex on two legs. He did dangerous things to her without even trying.

Even now, sitting here in this most beautiful of places, she was indifferent to her surroundings. Zane was the whole focus of her attention. He had made it that way. And, try as she might, she could not rid herself of him. He filled her thoughts to the extent of all else. How she was going to complete the job she was being paid for she did not know.

'You haven't answered my question.' The low rumble of his voice as he leaned slightly forward reverberated through her nerve-endings as though he was touching each one of them singly, as though he was tuning her body for—for whatever he wanted to do to her. Lucinda felt her breathing quicken and she was afraid to look at him.

'Business and pleasure don't mix,' she declared firmly. Was it she who'd said that before, or Zane? She couldn't remember. Nothing in her mind was clear any more.

'It seems to me that you need taking in hand, Lucinda Oliver,' he said sternly. 'You're far too serious. Come, eat some more breakfast and we'll go out and have fun.'

Castries was a mixture of ancient and modern—glass, concrete and steel vied with wooden buildings with graceful balconies and latticework. 'It's because they've had a series of fires over the centuries,' Zane told her when Lucinda commented on the diversity of the architecture.

The market-place was busy and colourful and full of the aroma of spices and tropical fruit. Everyone was friendly and talkative and Lucinda began to relax and enjoy herself. Zane too was being friendly and nothing more. He made no demands of her and for this she was grateful.

They left the main shopping area until last and when Lucinda lost herself in swathes of materials and grew ecstatic over oceans of beautiful furniture Zane left her to her own devices. He was either bored, she decided, or being tactful. Whichever, she appreciated it and when she finally decided that she'd had enough she was weighed down with brochures and samples and ideas.

They had arranged to meet at a restaurant he had pointed out to her earlier. The best one in Castries, so Zane had said. An attentive waiter took away her packages and showed her to the bar where Zane was waiting for her. At first she did not see him; then she discovered him sitting in a deep armchair—and opposite him, laughing at something he had said, was a very beautiful young woman, dusky-skinned and black-haired and very, very sensuous.

For a few seconds Lucinda stood watching them. She saw an intimacy that made her feel uneasy. Zane was at his flirtatious best and his companion was hanging on to his every word, and on to every look from those gorgeous bluey-grey eyes and every breath that he took.

Lucinda suddenly felt as if she was an unwanted

third party. Her happiness evaporated as quickly as smoke from a chimney and she turned swiftly on her heel. At the same time Zane looked up and saw her.

CHAPTER SIX

'LUCINDA!'

Lucinda ignored Zane. She didn't want to listen to any fancy excuses. He had just compounded her belief that members of the female sex were his playthings. And, Lord help her, she had almost fallen into the trap herself.

It was maybe a good thing that she had caught him working his charm. Judging by what she had seen, his companion was well and truly besotted. Was it someone he had picked up while waiting for her? Or someone he already knew? Whatever the case, Lucinda felt well and truly let down. In fact she felt an idiot. She had been in grave danger of making a very big fool of herself.

'Lucinda!' Zane's hand fell heavily on her shoulder. 'Where are you going?'

'I didn't want to intrude on what looked like a very cosy twosome,' she told him coolly, shrugging his hand away and continuing her swift exit.

'Nonsense, you wouldn't be intruding,' said Zane firmly. 'Serafine is a friend of mine; I'd like you to meet her.'

'Why?' she demanded. 'You were clearly bored following me around—I did tell you that I'd prefer to do the job my myself—and she is a welcome diversion. I have no wish to come between you.' She hated to acknowledge the fact, even to herself, that she felt deadly jealous of Zane's beautiful friend and she most certainly wasn't going to let Zane know. 'I'll make my own way back.'

'Oh, no, you won't,' growled Zane. 'You'll join us for dinner.' And he took her by the elbow and forcibly led her across the room.

Serafine smiled as they approached. 'Lucinda, it's good to meet you,' she exclaimed. 'Zane has told me how clever you are.'

Lucinda wanted to ignore Serafine's outstretched hand, but one glance at Zane's stern face and she decided against it. 'It is good to meet a friend of Zane's too,' she said quietly, hoping she sounded more sincere than she felt.

'I would not know where to start if I were transforming his house. It is all right when you are doing it for yourself, but for someone else—how do you do that? Unless you know that person intimately?'

Lucinda had no wish to discuss her job with this woman, with her huge expressive brown eyes and a wide smile which revealed beautifully even white teeth. She was stunning, and would have been even if she weren't dressed in a haute couture suit and expensive jewellery.

Serafine fingered a diamond and emerald ring as she looked at Zane and Lucinda couldn't help wondering whether he had bought it for her. The way Serafine kept touching it, and the way she looked at Zane as she did so, was highly suspicious. Maybe Serafine had been throwing out a big hint when she'd mentioned intimate relationships. Not that it worried her. Why should it? She already knew that Zane was into relationships. Nothing permanent, just fun while they lasted!

And she had very nearly become a statistic! Just as Serafine would be one! Did the girl know it? Was she as used as Zane to playing the field?

'You do need to get to know your client,' she answered. 'Their preferences, their dislikes, et cetera. It would be pointless filling a place with furniture that they absolutely hated.'

'Hence you and Zane staying in the house together?' suggested Serafine, her brown eyes steady on Lucinda's. 'Zane is a man of mystery as far as I am concerned. He never tells me much about himself. Maybe now that he has bought a house here it will change? Perhaps I will see more of him.' Her eyes switched to Zane, brilliant and flirtatious, suggesting that she would like something far more permanent from their relationship.

Zane's smile was enigmatic; Lucinda was not sure what to read into it. Serafine, on the other hand, touched her hand to his and he took it, his smile changing, becoming gradually more intimate. 'Maybe,' he agreed, his voice a low seductive growl.

Lucinda wanted to get up and walk out; she felt sickened by this open display of—of what? Not simple affection, that was for sure. Lust, perhaps. Physical need. As she had once experienced with Zane!

It had been powerful and she regretted it now. And, looking at Serafine, she knew that this woman had also experienced the magic of Zane's kisses. They'd probably even made love! Lucinda's throat closed painfully and she wanted to get up and walk away, but of course that was impossible. She had no intention of letting Zane know how much his attitude towards Serafine affected her.

She was annoyed with herself actually for feeling this way—especially so soon after the Simon affair.

'What would you like to drink, Lucinda?' Zane's attention was once again on her.

'Whatever you're having,' she answered with a shrug. She didn't care. What she really wanted was to go home. Home? It was odd to be calling Zane's house home, but she supposed that that was what it was for the time being, and she ought to be there working, not sitting around with Zane and one of his female friends.

With her drink placed in front of her Lucinda continued to seethe over the situation into which she had been forced, and when the three of them went through to the restaurant she felt like screaming. Nevertheless she did her best to be pleasant and talkative and when the time came for them to leave she smiled warmly at Serafine. 'It's been nice meeting you.'

'You too,' agreed the other woman. 'You must ask Zane to bring you to my restaurant again.'

'That was Serafine's restaurant?' asked Lucinda with a frown once she had collected her parcels and they were outside. 'She owns it?'

Zane smiled and nodded, taking the packets off Lucinda and tucking them beneath his arm. 'She's some girl. It's not the only place she owns.'

'But she never said.' Lucinda felt that she had been left in ignorance deliberately.

'That's because she's extremely modest,' said Zane, more than a hint of admiration in his voice.

'Have you known her long?'

'We met at a conference in England a few years ago,' he answered and Lucinda thought she saw a faraway look in his eyes. 'And I've seen her on and off ever since. I'm very fond of her.'

And Serafine was more than fond of Zane!

'Why all the questions?' His blue eyes levelled on hers curiously. 'Forgive me for saying it, but you sound jealous.'

'Me? Jealous?' Lucinda was alarmed to hear a faint squeak in her voice. 'Why would I be jealous of a friend of someone I'm simply doing a job for?'

'You did kiss me.'

He looked highly indignant and Lucinda was about to make some scathing remark when she realised that he was teasing her and she smiled faintly. 'Nevertheless,' she said firmly, 'I have no intention of being one of your numerous conquests.'

'Numerous?' he repeated, his eyes narrowing.

'I bet there's a girl in every corner of the world willing to go to bed with you.'

'You think Serafine and I are lovers?'

'Well, aren't you?'

Zane gave a mysterious smile. 'My private life is just that, Lucinda. Private.'

They reached the car, where the driver sat patiently waiting, and as she climbed into it Lucinda was left thinking the worst. It shouldn't have worried her; Zane was employing her to do a job for him—nothing more, nothing less. The fact that he had kissed her was of no consequence. It meant nothing to him; it should have meant nothing to her. The trouble was she couldn't forget the kiss. It played over and over in her mind and she hated to admit it but she wanted more.

The next day Lucinda kept well out of Zane's way, studying the rooms, consulting her samples, doing the work she was being paid to do. She had brought her laptop with her and spent time building up composites of each of the rooms in turn. In fact she kept herself so busy that until she stopped work she wasn't aware that Zane had left the house.

'Mr Alexander went out before lunch,' the maid informed her, and it wasn't difficult to guess where he had gone. Zane craved female company and since she wasn't making herself available...

Images of the beautiful Serafine kept popping into her head and when Zane didn't come home until late that evening Lucinda knew that her assumption was correct.

'Where are you going?' he asked as he walked into the house and saw her heading towards her bedroom.

'Bed, of course,' she answered. 'It's late.'

'You've shut me out the whole day,' he said. 'I think I deserve a little of your time now.'

'*I've* shut *you* out?' she questioned sharply. 'I've merely been doing the job you're paying me for.'

'And I have been out on business too. So a little leisure time together will do us both good.' He sounded cross, as though he was paying her to spend time with him and she was failing in her duty.

'If you insist,' she conceded irritably. 'I am rather tired, though; I've had a busy day.'

'And a productive one, I hope?' he asked, an eyebrow raised questioningly. 'When am I going to see these ideas of yours?'

'Whenever you like,' answered Lucinda. 'I'm about ready to discuss them with you. I realise that there will probably be things you don't like, but—'

'Hold on!' Zane held up his hand. 'I have no intention of talking business tonight. I simply want your company.'

And what else? she couldn't help wondering. But it didn't stop her agreeing to stay with him. In actual fact she wanted his company too, needed it even. One taste of him and she had become infatuated. One taste and she wanted more, even though she had sworn to herself that she would never let him kiss her again. Surely they could sit together and talk like two sensible adults and not take their relationship any further?

They sat outside beneath the moon and the stars, sipping wine and not saying very much at all. The sky was midnight-blue. The sea shimmered with silver highlights. There were a few sounds of the night—faint strains of music from one of the boats moored far below them, an animal moving through the undergrowth, cicadas chirruping—and their own breathing!

Zane's was deep and regular, as though he had fallen asleep. Lucinda glanced across and was startled to see that he was watching her.

'Have you any idea how beautiful you look in the moonlight?' he asked.

Lucinda shook her head. 'I don't want your compliments.'

'Then that's a pity because I believe that all beautiful woman should receive their fair share. And you're lovelier than most, Lucinda. I'm very fortunate to have obtained your services.'

'You have no idea yet how I'll perform,' she retorted.

'Oh, I think I do.'

Maybe his expression wasn't clear but the meaning in his voice certainly was and Lucinda huffed. 'I'm talking about my work.' And her body went hot all over.

'Naturally,' he agreed, and she could hear a smile in his voice.

Lucinda shook her head vigorously and her hair, which she had brushed earlier and left loose about her shoulders, flew over her face. She flicked it away with an impatient hand.

'You should have let me do that,' growled Zane, inching closer. 'You have gorgeous hair, Lucinda. Has anyone ever told you that? I wish you would wear it down more often.' And then he surprised her with a complete change of subject. 'Are you afraid of men?' he asked, his voice low and considered.

'I'm not afraid of you,' retorted Lucinda.

Zane raised his brows. 'No? Most women I know wouldn't settle for sitting quietly by my side. They'd want something more.'

'I'm not most women.'

'And, as I said, it's because of Simon.'

Their eyes met and held and Lucinda felt the disturbing power of him. 'If all you want to talk to me about is my ex-fiancé then I'm going to bed,' she declared crossly, jumping to her feet.

Lucinda stuck her nose in the air, spun on her heel and walked away. To her relief, Zane let her go. But later, as she lay in bed, she couldn't help wondering why he had asked all those questions. And it made her think about Simon, to wonder how much she had really enjoyed his lovemaking.

Would it be better with Zane? He certainly made her feel different. Even that one kiss had stirred emotions she had never felt before. What sort of a lover would Zane be? The answer was simple. Exciting! Innovative! Passionate! Considerate! All of these things and more.

And why was she even thinking about it when she had no intention of ever letting him touch her again? Because, answered an inner voice, you want to know what it feels like to be made love to by an expert in the art of seduction. His kiss has given you a taste of what a powerful lover he can be and you want more. Admit it!

She couldn't get to sleep and even when Zane went to bed over an hour later she still lay there thinking about him. When finally she did drop off to sleep she was woken what seemed like mere seconds later by a loud noise. She shot up in bed and listened. There it was again. It sounded like someone trying to break into the house. Goosebumps rose on her skin. Had Zane heard? She couldn't hear him moving.

Thoroughly scared but knowing that she needed to do something, Lucinda left her room and pushed open Zane's door. Instantly he was awake. 'Lucinda, what's wrong?'

'I heard a noise, like someone breaking in,' she said in a loud whisper.

Zane sprang out of bed—and, to Lucinda's horror, he was naked. Quickly she averted her eyes, even though the room was lit only by moonlight. And he didn't even bother to put anything on before he raced out of the room.

Lucinda stayed where she was, fearful of the feelings he had aroused in her—feelings which were much more intense than those of fear she had felt earlier. It was wrong, all wrong, and she didn't know what to do about it. If Zane should continue to demand her company, if he should attempt to kiss her again, would she be weak and foolish? Or would she find an inner strength?

When he returned she was still standing in the dark in his bedroom. 'Panic over!' he said quietly. 'It was a mongoose. Nothing to worry about.'

Zane touched his hand to Lucinda's arm and when he felt her trembling he pulled her hard against him. She felt soft and warm and vulnerable and a whole host of sensations rushed through his body. This woman was so different from any other he had known. She might own her own business—was indeed very successful, according to all that he'd heard—but beneath her veneer was a hurt woman. And he wanted to do something about it; he wanted to help her through her pain, to protect her, help her to see that there were men in the world who would treat her as she deserved to be treated.

Why he should feel angry that her fiancé had let her down he didn't know, but he did. Very much so. And if he ever met him... His thoughts ended there. He wasn't sure what he would do, but it wouldn't be gentlemanly, that was certain. And why he was associating her fear now with Simon, he wasn't sure about either. But somehow he felt the two were intermingled.

'It's all right,' he said softly in her ear. 'There's nothing more to worry about. I'll take care of you.' And when she didn't struggle, when she didn't attempt to move away from him, his arms tightened about her.

'It's because I'm in a strange place,' Lucinda excused herself. 'I'm not normally scared of the slightest sound.' And she lifted her face to his.

There was nothing he could do about it. His lips came down on hers almost of their own volition. He tasted sweetness and hunger as well as faint fear. And when she didn't resist he guided her over to the bed.

They lay down together, mouths still clinging, and when Lucinda's arms wrapped around him he drew in a deep shuddering breath. He wanted to make love to her but knew that he daren't. Not yet. There was much ground to cover first; it was too soon—she was only just starting to put her trust in him.

Was she really doing that? Trusting him not to take advantage? Simply to kiss her and comfort her and make her feel better? It couldn't be. She wanted him to make love to her, otherwise why would she have remained in his room? Why would she have let him kiss her? Why would she have put up no resistance when he led her to the bed?

Once he had followed those thoughts through, Zane no longer stemmed the tide of passion that filled him.

Lucinda knew that what she was doing was crazy but there was something inside her that refused to let go. She wanted his kisses; she wanted him to make love to her. She wanted everything he had to give. Something exciting had happened to her out here on this tropical island and all she wanted now was Zane.

Her job was forgotten; it was as though she was here

with this man for a very different purpose—the cleansing of Simon from her system! Zane was the only person who could do it, who could make her forget. She would let him bury himself in her, let him transport her to a world where only senses mattered—and what happened after that—well, she would take care of that when the time came. For now she would lose herself in an affair that she would remember for the rest of her life. It was totally unlike her, went against every principle she held, but strangely it felt right.

Thumb and forefinger played with her nipple through the thin cotton of her nightdress, sending spirals of pleasure through every inch of her body. 'Take my nightie off,' she urged him, lying back with her arms above her head.

Zane needed no second bidding and this time it was his mouth that pleasured her, closing over her nipples, playing one against the other, making her squirm and wriggle and cry out in deepest pleasure. She threaded her fingers through the thick springiness of his hair and held him against her, not wanting him to ever stop.

'This is all right for you?' He paused and lifted his head slightly to look at her, his eyes dark and seductive in the moonlight. In fact the whole of him felt seductive, his body shining as though cast in pewter—except that it didn't feel like hard metal at all; it felt warm and firm and infinitely touchable.

She traced her fingers over his back, feeling muscle and sinew and warm, intoxicating man, and she felt as if she wanted to keep him close to her for ever more. Of course she knew that wasn't possible, but she could dream, couldn't she? She could take a few moments in the time span of life to let her hair down and enjoy herself. Since the death of her father she had taken life very seriously—it was time for a change.

'Yes,' she whispered, unaware of how brightly her eyes were shining, how beautiful they looked in the light from the moon. It was a night made for love and she intended to take the challenge.

In response he took her mouth again, kissing deeply and excitingly, setting alight fires, and then slowly and seductively his mouth moved down her body, nibbling the soft column of her neck, touching his tongue to the strongly beating pulse at the base of her throat, seeking yet again her all too sensitive nipples, making her squirm and cry out and hold him against her.

The excitement was almost too much. She had never experienced such intense feelings. They filled her body, making her feel that she would explode at any minute—and he had hardly started!

She had been right in thinking that he would know exactly what to do to send a woman wild, to spin her out of this world and into the next. She felt faintly cheated when he moved away from her breasts to leave a trail of kisses over her stomach—and she wondered where he was going next!

Without even realising what she was doing Lucinda wriggled invitingly. But it wasn't his tongue that found the hot core of her. He touched her with gentle fingers.

Lucinda couldn't speak; her throat was far too tight. All she wanted was to feel him inside her. She had never in the whole of her life reached such a pinnacle of desire—and she knew there was more to come.

Briefly he pulled away and Lucinda felt a faint

moment's disappointment. Until suddenly she felt him entering her, slowly, carefully, excitingly! Zane knew exactly what to do to keep her in a state of heightened arousal. She wasn't living in this earthly world any more; he had taken her into another dimension where only senses mattered.

She lifted heavy lids and looked up at him and saw the same pleasure on his face, the glazing of his eyes, and she heard the sounds of intense passion that were being drawn from his throat.

And she realised that she was moaning too. Strange sounds that she had never uttered before! Pleasure, pain, need, greed!

She closed her eyes again and then felt his fingers on her cheek. And when she looked at him he was asking if it was good for her. Not with words—he was beyond speaking—but simply by the expression in his eyes.

Lucinda nodded and clung to him, urging him more deeply inside her. This was a world of wonderland, of feelings and excitement, like minor explosions taking place inside her body. Every one of her nerve-endings sizzled, her hormones danced, and finally she threw back her head and let it all happen.

She had no idea that she screamed out; no idea that her body bucked and rolled. And when she felt that she could stand no more she experienced such an explosion of feeling that the world spun away into space. And only seconds afterwards she heard Zane cry out and sink himself even further into her as he reached his own shattering climax.

Not until their bodies had stopped heaving did he withdraw and he looked at her with such tenderness in his eyes that Lucinda wanted to weep. 'No regrets?' he asked softly.

Lucinda shook her head. 'None. None at all!'

CHAPTER SEVEN

IN THE days that followed Lucinda and Zane spent every second of their time together. He didn't seem to care that she was getting no work done. If they weren't making love then they were out on his yacht or dining at some fabulous restaurant.

She was living, thought Lucinda, in a world of the very rich, far removed from her own particular lifestyle.

Her stepfather was admittedly wealthy but she had never wanted any part of it, nor was ever likely to. She was happy in her own little world, building up her business and planning for the future.

A no-strings affair with Zane suited her perfectly. She knew very well that she and Zane moved in different circles and there could never be anything serious between them. But why turn her back on the experience of a lifetime? He was so gorgeously sexy that no one in her right mind would resist him.

He had the most amazing eyes she had ever seen. Eyes that constantly twinkled, as though he was planning what his next move would be! How to make life even more exciting! He was a very innovative lover and she was under no illusion that life after Zane would be anything but very empty and mundane.

All the more reason to make the most of what she had now, Lucinda kept telling herself whenever any faint doubts crept into her mind.

When Zane had first taken her out on his yacht she had been extremely impressed. He had proudly told her that at sixty-four feet long and weighing twenty-eight tonnes it was the top of its range. The decks were teak and extremely spacious, the cockpit vast, and below, besides four double berths, was a saloon with sumptuous white leather seating. And the galley was to die for. 'Not that I do any cooking myself,' he had explained when she had gone into raptures. 'I have two crew members who do everything. It's used mainly for corporate entertaining, but I thought it might be fun to bring it out here and make use of it.'

And they had certainly done that!

And today they were out on it again.

'I thought,' said Zane, as they sunbathed on one of the decks, 'that we might stay out for the night. Have you ever been on the water at night with no land in sight? Where a canopy of stars is your whole world? It's a truly remarkable experience. Will you share it with me?'

What could she say except yes? Lucinda nodded happily. 'It sounds perfect. I didn't realise that you were so poetic.'

'There's a lot about me you don't know.' His voice was soft and low, almost a rumble. It was incredibly sexy and sent a tremor through her veins. Everything about this man was sexy. Even when they weren't making love he kept her in a state of suspended readiness. One look in his eyes and she could see what he was thinking and her body would surge into life. She even felt disappointed when nothing happened. But when it did—then the whole world rocked on its axis.

Tonight, she knew, was going to be very special. A night to be locked away in the memories of her mind for ever.

'Do you mind that I'm not getting any work done?' she asked him idly while he was smoothing sun oil on to her back.

'Would I have brought you out here today if I did?' he countered. 'Would I have taken up so much of your time?' he asked softly, his fingers kneading her back in a way that he knew melted her senses.

'I guess not,' she said, wriggling uncontrollably. 'You're paying whether I work or not. But you do realise that your bill will go up for all the time I spend away?'

She had said it half jokingly but when Zane said, 'So long as I get what I want you'll get what you want,' it reminded her very clearly that this was but a game to him. Once home, her job done, she would be completely forgotten.

It made her feel very sad. It also made her feel that she was giving her body to him for his selfish pleasure. But then Zane nuzzled her neck and cupped one of her breasts possessively and all was forgotten except the heady excitement of being with him.

Before lunch they went swimming, diving into the clear waters of the Caribbean and playing like porpoises. And after their light meal, consisting mainly of fruit and fish prepared by one of his very expert crew, they lay down in their cabin for a siesta. At least that was the plan. The heat outside was unbearable, but here in the air-conditioned interior sleep didn't seem so important.

'I would never have believed,' said Lucinda dreamily as she lay at Zane's side in the superbly fitted master bedroom, 'that you could take so much time off work. I always thought that you were a real workaholic.'

'Maybe it's because I've never met a woman as beautiful as you,' he answered. She lay in his arms, still in the camisole and Indian skirt that she had donned for their lunch. And his fingers stroked wherever the fancy took him. 'A woman who takes my mind off all other things! You're a siren in disguise, Lucinda. Do you know that?'

A siren! No one had ever called her that before. Didn't it mean a dangerously fascinating and sexy woman? Was that what she was to him? The thought pleased her. 'Am I the most captivating woman you've ever met?' It was a leading question and one that she wasn't sure she ought to have asked. She waited for his answer with bated breath.

He smiled slowly. 'Captivating? You're certainly that. And, what's more, Lucinda, I'm thoroughly enjoying our time here. Are you?'

She swallowed hard and nodded. 'It's something I'll remember for the rest of my life.' One part of her hoped that he would say the same, even that she was beginning to mean something to him. Instead he pulled her closer, lifting her skirt and seeking that private place that he had made his own.

All too soon her misgivings faded and she was lost in their lovemaking. And afterwards, while the yacht sailed on when they were both fully sated, they drifted into sleep.

* * *

Zane woke with the knowledge that something was wrong. He hadn't felt well all morning, but had thought it was nothing more than an over-indulgence of food and drink. But his headache had got worse and he felt as though he were burning up.

Lucinda still lay at his side and when he touched her forehead her skin felt quite cool. So it wasn't the air-conditioning that had failed. He really was ill.

Feeling him move, Lucinda opened her eyes and then did a double-take. 'Are you all right, Zane? You look very flushed.'

'It's nothing,' he said, unwilling to tell her how he felt. How manly was it to become ill when he had promised her a romantic trip? When he wanted to give her the best time of her life? This sort of thing never happened to him. He was always in control, always in command of every situation. And he had been of this one—until now!

He had been enjoying his education of Lucinda. Although she had never said anything, he was aware that he had taught her lots of new and wonderful things. And she had responded in a way far beyond his wildest dreams. She was a woman to surpass all women where making love was concerned and he would be sorry when it ended. As of course it must. Lucinda Oliver was not for him. No woman was. Not long-term. Of that he was very sure.

'It looks more than nothing to me. How do you feel?'

He swallowed with difficulty. 'I have a raging headache and I'm burning up. Probably sunstroke. But it won't last. I feel all right.'

'But you've always been careful!' exclaimed

Lucinda. 'We both have. If it's sunstroke, though, it could be serious. I'll ask Fabian to head back to shore. You need to see a doctor.'

'I don't want to spoil your day,' he said, struggling to his feet, feeling extremely mortified when dizziness forced him back down on the bed. 'Maybe you're right,' he agreed reluctantly. 'But let's get a doctor out here. I don't want you to miss out on your star-spangled night.' Except that he wouldn't be able to share it with her in quite the way he had imagined!

'And I don't want you to be a martyr,' she retorted crossly. 'What is it with men that they won't admit defeat?'

He managed a smile. 'It's not good for our image.' Especially in front of a woman he was trying to impress. No sooner had the thought entered his head than he asked himself whether it was true. Was he trying to impress Lucinda with his sexual prowess, with his private yacht and his Caribbean villa? And, if so, why?

In point of fact she gave the impression that she thought they were unnecessary appendages. Money simply didn't interest her. So long as she had enough for her daily needs she was happy. And he admired her for that. In fact there was a lot about Lucinda that he admired.

He closed his eyes and tried to shut out both his thoughts and the heat in his body. Perhaps Lucinda was right. He ought to go back. He certainly wasn't any good to her here. But they had been sailing for hours and unhappily he didn't feel that he could go that long without medical attention.

'Ask Fabian to phone for a doctor,' he croaked.

Lucinda shot up on deck and explained Zane's predicament and immediately arrangements were made. Money spoke, thought Lucinda as she went back to Zane. There was nothing that couldn't be acquired. It didn't make her feel happy. Her mother might be a slave to money, but she definitely was not.

'The doctor will be here as soon as he can,' she told Zane, alarmed to see that his fever had increased. She wet some towels and pressed them to his face and his skin, all the time murmuring words of comfort. He seemed to drift in and out of consciousness. Or was it her imagination? Was he just closing his eyes?

And as she sat there watching him, doing all she could to make him feel comfortable, Lucinda made an alarming discovery. She was falling in love with Zane. Properly in love! Not just a sex thing. She wanted to spend the rest of her life—or at least a large part of it— with him. How stupid was that? Zane had made it clear that he didn't intend to settle down with anyone. He enjoyed playing the field. He would probably do it until he was too old or too tired!

And, besides, she didn't enjoy the trappings of wealth. She could see no point in them. So why would she want to bind herself to Zane? She was out of her head. Probably going down with the same illness. She touched a hand to her brow. Perfectly normal! She wasn't ill, no, just plain crazy.

Perhaps Zane's illness had come in the nick of time. Before she made a complete fool of herself and told him how she felt. As she continued to mop his brow, to try to cool his fever with wet towels, she knew that she had gone far beyond the point of no return. She loved him to distraction, and probably always would, even though she knew without a shadow of doubt that once they returned to England and her job was finished she would never see him again.

In less than an hour a doctor arrived by helicopter and was lowered on to the deck. He confirmed that Zane was indeed suffering from a mild case of sunstroke.

'You must get him into a cool bath straight away,' he told Lucinda. 'And you must gently massage his skin and keep taking his temperature. Can you do that?'

Lucinda glanced at Zane, who looked anything but happy about the situation, and then back at the doctor. After all their lovemaking, when there wasn't a part of his body that she hadn't explored, it should be an easy task. She nodded.

'After that you must put him in a cool room, still checking his temperature—because if it should continue to drop then you must keep him warm. Have you got that?'

'Yes,' agreed Lucinda.

'Massaging must continue, to encourage circulation. He may need to stay in bed for several days.'

Lucinda couldn't see Zane agreeing to this, but she nodded anyway. 'I'll see to it, doctor.'

'If you don't follow my instructions there is a danger that he will get worse and have to be hospitalised. But hopefully he will recover quite quickly. How did he get in this state?'

'I don't know,' answered Lucinda. 'We're always careful in the sun.'

'Obviously not careful enough!' he admonished. 'And it's not always the sun itself. Any prolonged exposure to high temperatures can cause it. You might feel you're safe sitting on the deck in the shade but, believe me, it can be just as dangerous. Or playing energetic games. They all add up. I fear your friend has overdone it. You'll need to keep your eye on him.'

Zane had hardly spoken, except to thank the doctor for coming, and once he'd gone he glared at Lucinda. 'The man's exaggerating. I'm not that ill.'

'Oh, yes, you are,' answered Lucinda firmly, 'and you know it. Thank goodness there's a bathtub on board. Excuse me.' She went through to the *en suite* bathroom and filled the tub with cool water.

Zane looked very sorry for himself as he lay in the bath and allowed Lucinda to massage him. But eventually he gave a wry smile. 'I'm not so ill that I'm unaware of what you're doing. In fact I rather like it.' And he thrust out a hand and brought her face close to his. 'I've half a mind to pull you in here with me.'

'Don't you dare!' laughed Lucinda. 'It's freezing.'

As she continued to massage him after he'd left the bath and lay on the bed, Zane in turn continued to turn the whole exercise into a sensual experience. She knew that he still wasn't feeling well, but it didn't alter the fact that he didn't want to spoil her time out here and he made a tremendous effort to keep her happy—and excited—and aroused!

Oh, how she loved this man, Lucinda thought. It would break her heart when the day came for them to part company.

By the end of the day Zane was feeling much better—well enough, he said, to lie out on the deck with her and watch the stars. The air had cooled by then and, although she didn't agree with him being outside, he insisted.

The yacht had dropped anchor and the crew had discreetly disappeared. On a table beside them was a bottle of vintage champagne and some nuts and fruit. 'The cashew nuts are grown here on the island,' Zane informed her when he saw her nibbling them. 'And did you know that they've made many films on St Lucia?'

Lucinda didn't but she could see why. It was such a magical island. So lush! Such gorgeous white beaches! It was really beautiful.

Zane had taken her to the Botanical Gardens one day, where she'd seen incredible plants growing and a Japanese water garden. And they'd been to a lovely warm waterfall where they sat in the pool beneath the falls and drank bubbly. In fact she'd never drank so much champagne in her life, thought Lucinda now as Zane refilled her glass.

He wasn't touching the stuff himself. All he had beside him was a glass of iced water and Lucinda was fearful that he wasn't really up to this.

When she'd had enough to eat and drink Lucinda edged herself on to Zane's lounger and, locked in each other's arms, they lay back and looked at the stars. It was as though there were only the two of them in the whole universe.

'I did want to make love to you out here,' he confessed. 'It was my initial plan. But I'm not sure now that I have the strength.'

'And you'd be going against doctor's orders,' Lucinda warned him. 'He says you're to rest.'

'And that's exactly what I'm doing,' he said. 'But

there's nothing stopping me touching you.' His voice had dropped to a low sensual growl.

Lucinda wore a thin cotton shift dress with nothing beneath and when he touched her breasts they reacted immediately. She was unsure how wise it would be to reveal the sensations he was arousing. She was so afraid he would push himself too far. He looked a hundred times better than he had earlier, but even so...

'You're a naughty girl dressing like this when you know I haven't the energy to do anything,' he admonished.

'I thought it would give you pleasure.'

He groaned loudly. 'You've no idea how much. I've never met a woman quite like you before. You're ready to try anything at any time, aren't you?'

She nodded, suddenly shy.

'I curse this illness that means I can't take control.'

'Maybe I ought to take advantage of you,' she suggested with a cheeky smile.

He groaned loudly. 'You have a cruel streak, Lucinda Oliver. No woman's going to seduce me if I can't do anything about it.'

'Then we'll just hold each other,' she said. And they lay there and he pointed out some of the stars. It was a truly magical night. The sky was so big, the stars so bright—they filled it like glittering diamonds.

How long they lay there she wasn't sure. At one stage Zane fell asleep, and then she did too. And when she awoke he was gently stroking her breasts. It made a change to be held by him and not make mad passionate love. This was a different kind of lovemaking and if it was all he could manage then she was content.

It was past midnight before he suggested they go to

bed and as she helped him down into their cabin Lucinda felt her love flowing fiercely. 'Thank you for a magical few hours,' she said.

'The pleasure was all mine,' answered Zane, his smile weak. 'And never fear, I'll make this up to you.'

He had nothing to make up, thought Lucinda. She would remember this night for the rest of her life.

Early the next morning they headed back to shore, but it was still a few days before Zane was his old self. They spent their time sitting quietly, talking, lighting fires within each other but doing nothing about it, which Lucinda found an incredible experience. She would never have dreamt that they could make love without touching each other—but in some strange way that was what they managed to do.

And then came a phone call which changed everything.

'Tim's grandmother's been taken into hospital,' Zane told her. 'I have to go home.'

'What do you want me to do?' asked Lucinda. 'My work here's not finished.' Spending all her time with Zane, she'd done precious little during the last few days.

'You should come back with me. There's no point in you staying,' he said. 'I'm sure you have done everything you need to for the time being. In fact I don't think you'll even need my approval because you know me better than anyone else does. And I certainly trust you.'

Lucinda's eyes widened. 'That's quite a compliment.'

During the flight back Zane asked himself whether he was falling for Lucinda. He had never felt quite like this about any woman before—but, dammit, he didn't want to fall in love. Love had no part to play in his life. The best thing he could do when they got home was to not see her again.

It might even be best to forget the interior design project. He'd get someone else to do it—someone in St Lucia! Serafine would help him find someone.

It was going to be hard walking away from Lucinda. But he daren't give way to the feelings burning inside him. It was far too dangerous. He didn't want to believe that Lucinda was like other women, but how could he tell?

His lifelong friend had had a bad experience—his marriage had broken down and his wife had all but ruined him with her demands. And yet she'd seemed like a lovely woman. No one would have expected it of her.

Prenuptial agreements were the way to go these days, but that was being cold and calculating and, although he could be both of these things in his business affairs, it didn't seem right to bring it into the realms of love. Best not to love than be hurt.

He enjoyed his playboy image, though he didn't date half as many women as had been suggested by the press. And Lucinda was the first one to really get through to him. He had to ask himself why. How was she different?

Maybe because she'd shown no interest in him initially. It was something that had never happened to him before. Once she had let herself go, though, the world had rocked. Lucinda was incredible.

Perhaps she wouldn't expect to continue the relationship once they were back in England? Her ex had put the fear of hell into her where commitment was concerned. Perhaps she'd decided on a good time, knowing that she could leave it behind when her job was finished.

The thought should have pleased him but, for some reason, it didn't and when they eventually landed his mood was black.

CHAPTER EIGHT

LUCINDA couldn't work out why Zane's mood had changed so dramatically. Unless he was telling her that their affair was over. That it had been good while it lasted but now it was goodbye. He'd hardly spoken during the flight, shutting himself in his on-board office for most of the time.

It should have been a relief, so why wasn't it? It was clearly back to business for him and it should be the same for her. But women weren't programmed the same as men. It wasn't so easy to shut out what had happened between them during the last couple of weeks. But by the time they touched down in England she'd accepted that this was what she'd have to do.

She felt utterly miserable and when he put her into a separate car at the airport and didn't even say whether he would see her again, Lucinda felt like breaking down in tears. Of course she didn't; she lifted her chin and pretended that she wasn't hurt.

It could be that he was worried about his little nephew's grandmother, but somehow she didn't think so. It was something *she* had said or done. Perhaps he'd been afraid that she was the clinging type, that she wouldn't want to let go? Which was ridiculous, because she'd known from the beginning that there was no future in their relationship. Even if that really was the case, he needn't have cut her out of his life quite so abruptly.

During the next few days Lucinda threw herself into her work. There was a lot to catch up on and she pushed Zane Alexander to the back of her mind. Or at least she tried to. It was practically impossible, especially when she lay alone in her bed at night. They'd had so many nights of passion that it killed her. She wanted Zane with her for ever more.

Then her secretary put a call through. 'It's Mr Alexander,' she declared in a hushed voice.

Lucinda was aware that Amanda had been curious about her visit to the Caribbean, but she'd kept deliberately quiet, saying only that the project hadn't materialised, not wanting to tell anyone what had happened. She hadn't even told her mother, even though Ruth had questioned her time and time again.

Now her heart raced erratically. 'Lucinda Oliver,' she announced, keeping her tone brisk and businesslike. 'How may I help you?'

'Lucinda.'

It was his voice that did it. That incredible growl that made her toes curl and her stomach turn over. She closed her eyes and attempted to hold on to her dignity.

'I need to see you.'

Heavens! Was he talking about what she hoped he was talking about? Had he, like her, spent sleepless nights wishing they were together again? Had he realised that he couldn't live without her? That what they had was something special, far removed from a brief affair? Her heartbeats were loud and heavy in her breast and she put a hand to her throat.

'I need you to help me look after Timothy.'

Lucinda's spirits fell like a sledgehammer, slamming into her senses, making her realise how stupid she had been. Of course he wouldn't want her for any other reason; he had made that perfectly clear. She had been stupid to even think it. 'Why?' she asked, hoping he couldn't hear the sudden dryness in her throat. 'Why me?'

'Because he knows you, he likes you.'

'I'm not a nanny any longer,' she reminded him curtly, swallowing her disappointment. Lord knew what she had thought he would say but it certainly hadn't been anything like that. 'Besides, how can he remember me when it was so long ago?'

A brief silence, then, 'You're someone I know and can trust.'

Lucinda shook her head. He sounded brisk and businesslike, not a man whose bed she had shared night after night. 'I'm very busy, Zane. I have a lot to catch up on.'

'Tim's grandmother's very poorly. The poor boy has no one but me to look after him.'

'And you're naturally too busy.' Lucinda couldn't keep the sarcasm out of her voice. 'And you also have a nerve thinking I'll drop everything to do your work for you.'

'I'm missing you, Lucinda.' It was said quietly, almost regretfully, and she was aware how much it must have cost him to say that. She couldn't curb a tiny smile. So he wasn't entirely immune to her? Their brief affair had meant something! Quite what she couldn't be sure, but it meant that he was possibly suffering the same as she was. Except that she loved him and his feelings were nothing more than lust.

Nevertheless, the thought of seeing him again was extremely tempting.

'I could set you up an office here so that you won't get behind with your work.' And when she didn't answer he added, 'Whatever you need will be yours.'

I need you, she thought desperately. I need your love. Not an office. Not looking after your nephew. *You!* Would this be second best? If she moved into his house, would their affair rekindle itself? Would Zane realise what he was missing? Would he learn to love her the same as she loved him?

Lucinda found it hard to believe that she had fallen in love with Zane after vowing to herself never to trust another man. It just went to show that when the right man came along…

Was Zane the right man? She wouldn't know unless she took up his challenge. It was the only chance she'd have of seeing him again.

'Lucinda? Give me your answer.'

She threw her shoulders back, drew in a deep breath and said, 'I don't see why I should, but, yes, I suppose I will. Until you sort yourself out at least.' Whether she'd regret it later she didn't know, but for the moment she was being given a second chance and she knew that it was something she had to do.

She heard the soft whistle of his breath, knew that he'd been holding it while he waited for her answer. 'Thank you, Lucinda. I'll make sure you never regret it. I'll send a car for you now.'

'Oh, no, you won't!' declared Lucinda vehemently.

'I have a day's work to finish. Then I need to go home and pack. I'll start in the morning.'

'But—'

'But nothing, Zane! I'll come in the morning or not at all.' And she put down the phone, guessing that he had never had anyone do that to him before. But she didn't care. He couldn't walk all over her; she wouldn't let him. And even now, only seconds after agreeing to help him out, she was having doubts. Would she be making a fool of herself? Was it really only for Tim's sake that he needed her? Nothing to do with his own feelings! Or was she walking into a trap? He wanted her to mind Tim, yes, but that could be an excuse because he also wanted her body.

For the rest of the day Lucinda found it difficult to concentrate and when she went home that evening and told her mother what she was doing Ruth was delighted. 'Forget the nanny stuff,' she declared. 'He's missing you. This is fantastic, Lucinda. He's quite a catch.'

'I'm not interested in his money, Mother, you know that.'

Ruth shrugged. 'Whatever. I know he has a reputation, but I think he's finally been hooked. I knew when you came back from St Lucia that something had happened between you; I could see it in your eyes. I'm happy for you, darling.'

Lucinda didn't feel happy. She felt worried. And excited! It was an odd mixture of feelings—apprehension laced with anticipation.

When the car came to pick her up she was still feeling unsure. She'd had an almost sleepless night worrying whether she was doing the right thing. It was her heart leading her, not her head, and she feared that she might be on course for disaster. Nevertheless she had to go through with it. Some demon inside drove her on.

The last time she'd been here, recalled Lucinda as the car proceeded along a winding drive lined with plane trees, was when Tim was two. Zane had said that his nephew remembered her but Lucinda wasn't so sure. Three years was a long time for a child. She had a feeling that Zane had used that as an excuse.

But when they got to the house—a huge red brick building with formal lawns at the front and a swimming pool at the back—she remembered the pool because she had always been fearful that Tim might wander out there and drown—the door opened and Timothy himself stood shyly on the step. She caught sight of an older woman in the background.

How he had grown! She hurried towards him and gave him a big hug. 'I've missed you,' she said with a warm smile. 'What a big boy you are now.'

He smiled at her then. 'I remember you,' he said slowly. 'I think. You looked after me.'

'I certainly did and I'm going to look after you again. Where's your uncle?'

'At work,' he announced importantly. 'He's a very busy man, that's why he needs someone else to look after me while Nanna is in hospital. She's very poorly.'

Lucinda nodded. 'So I hear. Shall we go inside?'

Tim nodded and put his hand trustingly into hers.

Lucinda's heart went out to him.

Her bags were carried up to the room she had used the last time she was here. It was next to Tim's and the fact that she had been given this room told her in no uncertain manner that this was going to be her place, that Zane had no intention of asking her to share his bed. She ought to have known. And, for just a few seconds, she wished that she had never come. And then she looked at Tim and knew that she had done the right thing.

Zane had a housekeeper, Mrs Burton, and a maid and sometimes a butler if he was entertaining, but none of them were qualified to look after Tim. Had he left his nephew in their care these last few days? she wondered. Or had he taken time off himself? Somehow she doubted it; he'd been away from his affairs too long, the same as she had.

His staff had probably coped but he'd felt that he needed someone more professional. Though why he had asked her when he could have rung any agency he liked she didn't know. If her sleeping arrangements had been any different she would have suspected that he wanted to carry on their affair—but his instructions told her very clearly that this was not the case.

It was late evening before Zane came home, which was very much what Lucinda had expected. There was not much about him that surprised her. She was curled up on a sofa in the sitting room watching TV. She had been tempted to go to her room, to make a point of telling him that she knew where her place was, but had decided against it at the last minute.

And she hadn't really been watching TV. Her ears had been alerted to his return and she'd scarcely heard what the characters in the film were saying.

'So you really came.'

Lucinda's heart thumped so hard that she thought he must surely see it throbbing against her ribcage. Zane hadn't changed at all. He was still magnificently handsome, still had the same gorgeous smoky blue eyes and still had the power to turn her world upside down.

Not surprising considering it was only a few days since she had last seen him. Yet it felt like a lifetime. And now she was here Lucinda wondered whether she had made a big mistake. There was nothing in Zane's eyes to tell her that he was as delighted as she. They were matter of fact and considering, watching her gravely for a few seconds before he stepped further into the room.

'How's Tim?'

Not *How are you*? But *How's Tim*? Not, *I've missed you*. Nothing like that! It felt like a slap in the face. 'He's fast asleep.'

'Was he pleased to see you?'

Lucinda nodded. 'I was surprised he remembered me.'

'He couldn't stop talking about the lady who was here before. He remembered you all right. As do I,' he added *sotto voce*.

She almost didn't catch those last words; perhaps she wasn't intended to. But it made her look at him questioningly. Of course he remembered her. Was there some hidden meaning behind them? Perhaps he meant he was remembering their nights of passion?

They had been unforgettable nights. But they may as well never have happened if they meant so little to him. 'How's your health these days?' she asked instead.

'Back to normal,' he acknowledged. 'If you'll excuse me I'll take a shower and then I'll join you.'

'Fraternising with the hired help?' The words slipped out without her intending them to. But he was making her feel like that. After all they'd gone through together, it would have been perfectly normal for him to stride across the room and take her into his arms. Instead he stood there in the doorway making no attempt to come any closer. He couldn't have made it any clearer that that particular part of their life was over.

Zane's lips tightened. 'I'll try to ignore that remark.'

'It's what you make me feel like.'

'Nonsense!'

'Is it?' she asked pointedly. 'You used me, Zane Alexander. And for that I will never forgive you.'

'And yet you came here today?' Sandy brows rose, blue eyes looked coolly into hers. 'Doesn't that tell you something? It certainly does me.'

Lucinda frowned. What did it tell him? That she was still his for the taking? Lord help her, it would be so easy. But she could see Zane clearly now for what he was and she stiffened her resolve. While she was living in Zane's house she would never let him touch her, never let him kiss her.

She ought to walk out. It would be best all round. But young Tim had taken to her so willingly and completely that she couldn't bear to let him down. It was bad enough that his beloved grandmother was so poorly. He didn't need any more instability in his life. No, she would stay until the woman recovered. She would do what she had come here for, but that was all. Zane Alexander could go and take a running jump. She would never let him near her again.

Zane's feelings were running high as he showered off his tiredness. He had been looking forward to coming home and finding Lucinda here. What he hadn't expected was her animosity towards him. He'd given her a good time in St Lucia. He'd done nothing to hurt her. So what was it all about?

He had half wondered, when she'd agreed to look after Tim, if she would want to carry on their affair. He had been pleased and relieved that she'd accepted—of course he had—but nevertheless he couldn't help speculating whether it might be because she wanted something more from him.

Clearly, though, nothing was further from her mind. He was shocked by how cool and distant she was towards him. Their brief affair might never have happened. But if that was the way she wanted to play it—then that was all right by him.

When he rejoined her Lucinda was deeply engrossed in the film showing on television and wasn't aware of his presence, so he stood in the doorway watching her. She was even more stunning than he remembered. Her auburn hair was tied back in a ponytail but he knew how enticingly sexy it was when she left it loose around her shoulders. He had threaded his fingers through it so many times; he had used it to pull her face close to his; he had covered her naked breasts with it, enjoyed the intriguing little glimpses of her exciting nipples.

So many things they had done together and they all came rushing back in a brief moment of madness. Inhaling the sweet fragrance that was essentially Lucinda made him want to leap on her and make love until they were both senseless.

She was so gorgeously sexy. It had definitely been a

big mistake to invite her into his house. When Tim had cried in his sleep and refused to be consoled he had been at his wits' end. He'd taken time off work but even so he wasn't used to young children and there had been times over the past few days when he had been at a complete loss.

That was when he had thought of Lucinda. He hadn't dared hope she might agree to his request; indeed he had been shocked when she had. Shocked but pleased. Very pleased, because it meant that he would see her again.

It hadn't occurred to him how much he had missed her until he'd heard her voice on the phone. Because he had thrown himself into his work, because he had Tim to look after as well, because he had fallen into bed each night dog-tired, Lucinda had not been on his mind. Now she was very much to the forefront and his male hormones began to take over.

Lucinda had shocked him when she'd stated that he had used her. How could that be when she had been a willing partner? And that comment about fraternising with the hired help. Where had that come from? Didn't what they'd gone through together mean anything to her?

Zane felt both confused and not a little bit angry. She needn't have come if this was the attitude she was going to take. He cleared his throat and she looked up and, for just a second, he thought he saw desire in her lovely green eyes. Gone in an instant; he might even have imagined it, because they were hard now, almost questioning his presence.

'I didn't see you there,' she lied. In actual fact she had been aware of his presence the whole time; it would be impossible not to be. This house was full of him. Wherever she went Zane was there, whether in the flesh or not. But in the flesh, as now, she had sensed him, felt him, had never been more aware of him. And it made her realise what a big mistake she had made in coming here.

No doubt she would weather the storm, but it would be hard denying her feelings, pretending an immunity she did not feel. All she could hope was that he wouldn't attempt to carry on their affair. It would be a bittersweet relationship, knowing it could end again once Tim's grandmother was well enough to take him back. She couldn't go through with it.

He came into the room. 'A drink?' he asked, walking over to a mini-bar in the far corner. The room was high-ceilinged and tall-windowed, with beautiful gold silk curtains against a wall of palest blue. The carpet had a blue and gold pattern and all of the furniture was antique. Money well spent, she thought. Not that it was to her taste; she preferred something more modern, but it suited Zane. The whole house suited him.

Even now, dressed down in black jeans and T-shirt, he didn't look out of place. While she was all keyed up inside, he looked relaxed and perfectly at ease. And, while she didn't really want a drink, Lucinda nodded, feeling it might help settle her uneasy stomach.

He poured her a gin and tonic without even asking what she would like and, with a tumbler of whisky for himself, he sat down on the settee opposite her.

The film finished and Lucinda hoped he wouldn't ask her what it was about because she hadn't the slightest idea.

'So tell me,' he said, 'what's been happening in your life since we got home?'

Lucinda shrugged. 'I've been working hard, that's all. I had a lot to catch up on.'

'And how's my project doing?'

She frowned. 'You still want me to carry on with it?' This was the last thing she had expected.

'Why wouldn't I? I didn't go to all the trouble of flying you out there for nothing. Is that what you thought? That I took you out to have my evil way with you? Is that why you looked at me earlier as though I were the devil incarnate? Believe me, Lucinda, what happened was as much your choice as mine.'

Lucinda wasn't sure she would agree with that. He was the one who had started the affair. If he hadn't she would have got all her work done and she wouldn't be feeling as though he had robbed her of a very precious part of her being.

'You look as though you don't agree.'

There was hardness in his eyes, turning them steel-blue instead of smoky blue and Lucinda felt everything inside her go tense. 'You were the one who started it.' Oh, Lord, how childish was that?

'One of us had to,' he declared pragmatically. 'We couldn't have got through our time there feeling as we did if we didn't give in to our feelings. Don't you agree?'

Lucinda shrugged. 'It's never happened to me before.'

'And do you regret it?' He paused, his glass poised before his lips.

'Yes, actually,' answered Lucinda. Honesty was the best policy here or she could see him attacking her defences yet again. And she would unfortunately let him. He was a man who could not be ignored.

Zane took a long swallow of his drink, put his glass

down carefully on a side table and looked at her intently. 'Are you saying to me that if I took you into my arms right now and kissed you, you wouldn't respond? That your body wouldn't melt and your arms wouldn't go around my neck and you'd beg me for more? Are you saying that, Lucinda?'

She eyed him coolly. 'Yes!' And her voice crackled into the air like breaking ice.

Well-marked brows rose. 'And I'm supposed to believe it?'

'You can believe what you like,' she threw at him even more crisply. 'It happens to be the truth. You used me out there and you're not going to do it again. Actually, I think the location seduced me more than you did.'

His eyes flickered but he said nothing.

'And now that I'm back on home ground my head is level and I have no wish to carry on an affair with you.' In fact he was the one who had put an end to it by his behaviour on the plane. But she didn't tell him that; she didn't tell him how much he had hurt her. She was glad now that it was finished because it would have hurt even more the longer it had gone on.

She was under no delusion that he would ever have turned their relationship into something more serious. That was way out of his agenda. All Zane was interested in was a good time.

And that was what they'd had. She couldn't deny it. The only fly in the ointment had been Serafine. Lucinda had been excruciatingly jealous of her.

'Who's saying I want to?'

His callous statement took Lucinda's breath away.

'I asked you here to look after Tim. If you've put any other connotations on it then it's your fault.'

Lucinda felt her skin burning. He really knew how to turn the knife. 'At least we know where we stand,' she declared fiercely. 'I don't think I want this drink. I'm going to bed.'

'Lucinda!'

She turned halfway across the room and glared at him. She had never felt so humiliated in her whole life.

'Don't run away.'

'I'm not running,' she snapped. 'I'm tired.'

'Then relax here with me.'

'It's impossible.'

'Is it?' An eyebrow rose. 'Or is it that you don't like the way the conversation is going? We could change it. We could talk about the project. We could talk about Tim. We could talk about anything you like.'

Lucinda drew in a deep breath and struggled with her conscience. This whole uncomfortable issue was her fault and she didn't want to be anywhere near Zane for the time being. She needed space; she needed to get her head round things. She needed to ask herself what the real reason was that she had come here today.

CHAPTER NINE

'DID you find your office?'

Lucinda looked at Zane across the breakfast table and frowned.

'Yesterday, when you came,' he enlarged. 'Did you see it? Is there everything you need?'

'I didn't know that you'd already set up a room for me,' she answered. 'I was busy with Tim.' And she didn't really see how she could work at her job with a five-year-old to look after. Actually, she hadn't thought it through very well at all. And the main reason being? She had wanted to see Zane! It was stupid; it was irrational and totally unlike her. And, after last night's fiasco, she wished that she had never come.

She had lain awake most of the night berating herself for letting Zane get through to her, for even mentioning their affair. It had been stupid of her, irrational, and she felt all kinds of a fool.

Tim had come into her room early and snuggled down in bed with her and then she had washed and dressed him and given him his breakfast. At the moment he was helping in the kitchen. And later she had promised to take him to the hospital to see his beloved

Nanna. How she had thought she could do her job as well as look after Zane's nephew she had no idea. It was another case of her heart ruling her head.

'Then I'll show you afterwards,' declared Zane. 'Did you sleep well?'

She hadn't stayed and talked when he'd asked her to; she had run away like a scared rabbit. 'As well as could be expected in a strange house,' she answered.

'I'm afraid I'll be away tonight but I'll give you my mobile number in case there's an emergency.'

Lucinda nodded but didn't answer. The only thought that ran through her mind was—whose bed would he be sharing?

'Lucinda, do you regret what happened between us?'

The question was unexpected and she looked at him with shocked eyes. 'Didn't I make myself clear yesterday? Of course I regret it. I'm only here because of Tim, so don't dare go getting any other ideas. Have your flings with whomever you like, but don't count me on your list of conquests.'

She missed the shadow that darkened his brow, heard only the harshness in his voice. 'Well, I'm off, then.' He threw a card down in front of her. 'Here's my number. Have a good day.' At the door he turned. 'If there's anything else you need for your office ring my PA. He will see to it.'

He? Lucinda stared after Zane's retreating back. He had a male assistant? Unbelievable! Men like him usually surrounded themselves with pretty women.

After breakfast, curious to find out what he had provided in the way of an office, Lucinda pushed open doors until she found the room. It had a desk in front of the window with very fine views over sweeping lawns, a tennis court and a corner of the swimming pool.

The massive desk held a computer, with a little note attached to it saying that Zane had had it networked with her system at the office. Thoughtful of him, she felt, but he had taken a liberty, one that she wasn't sure she approved of.

On another table was a printer and scanner and copier. There was a stock of stationery and a couple of easy chairs as well as a very fine black leather executive chair. She tried it out for size, twisting around with her feet in the air. Perfect!

Zane had thought of everything.

At that moment Tim came running into the room and all thoughts of Zane were forgotten.

She let him swing on the chair while she phoned her secretary and then got someone to bring in a desk and chair for Tim out of his bedroom. He played there happily while she made a few phone calls and checked the correspondence that Amanda had scanned on to the computer for her.

She even managed to do some work on a new project before it was time to take Tim to the hospital. Perhaps the arrangement was going to work after all, she thought. Tim was a good child and, although she had no intention of keeping him cooped up in her office the whole time, he had proved that for short periods he was more than happy to sit with her.

Tim's grandmother, Helen, didn't look at all well. She was more than pleased to see Lucinda and her darling grandson—and he was delighted to see her, hugging her and hugging her as though he never wanted to let her go—but she was clearly exhausted after only a few minutes. 'It's my heart,' she explained. 'It's giving up, I'm afraid.'

She was much older than Lucinda had expected, probably in her mid-seventies, and far too old to be looking after a child as young as Timothy. Lucinda couldn't believe that Zane had let her do it. Surely the duty should have fallen on his shoulders?

But of course business always came first with Zane. That was why she had been totally surprised when he'd taken so much time off in St Lucia. And how disastrous the outcome of that had been! Lucinda returned to his house with her heart both heavy and angry.

After she had put Tim to bed that evening Lucinda went to her newly acquired office and worked until almost midnight. She needed the mental challenge to take her mind off Zane. It wasn't easy. She kept seeing twinkling blue eyes and a sexy smile and her body remembered the way he had taken her to the top of the universe and back.

She really oughtn't to think of him like this any more. It had been but a brief interlude and was not likely to be repeated. Not if she had anything to do with it. She wouldn't put it past Zane to try while she was here, but forewarned was forearmed, wasn't that what they said? And she certainly knew all there was to know about Zane Alexander.

The next day Tim wanted to go swimming. It was an almost Olympic-sized pool and Lucinda was nervous, but he told her that his uncle Zane took him swimming there. She had noticed yesterday that Zane had had a fence erected around the whole pool area, which had pleased her enormously, and now as they let themselves in she was startled when Tim ran over to the shallow end and jumped in.

She needn't have feared. Even at five years old he could swim like a fish. 'I used to swim with my daddy,' he said matter-of-factly when Lucinda congratulated him on his prowess. 'I miss my daddy.'

'Of course you do,' she said sympathetically, marvelling that he could remember so well.

'And my mummy! Will they ever come back?'

Lucinda winced inside. 'I'm afraid not, sweetie. But they're up there watching you and thinking about you all the time. That's why you must be good.'

'I am good,' he said importantly.

Lucinda hugged him. 'You're the best boy I know. And the best swimmer I know. Let's have a race.'

After all his swimming Tim was tired out and once lunch was over Lucinda put him in bed. 'I'm going to do some work in my office, sweetheart. If you wake up, come and find me.'

Tim nodded and yawned and in seconds he was asleep.

Lucinda had showered and changed into jeans and a knitted top and was so busy on her new computer that she didn't hear Zane enter the room. She didn't even know that he had come home. 'You're early,' she said, looking round in surprise when he spoke her name.

'I thought I owed you some of my time. Where's Tim?'

'In bed,' announced Lucinda.

'He's not ill?'

She smiled. 'We've been swimming. What a fantastic little swimmer he is. He wore himself out.'

'So you've coped all right?'

Lucinda nodded. 'We went to the hospital yesterday to see his grandmother.'

'Ah.' He dropped into one of the easy chairs. 'I was going to take him there this afternoon. How was she?'

'Not well at all,' answered Lucinda crisply. 'I can't believe that you've let her take care of Tim all this time. She's far too old. He's such a handful; it's not fair on her. No wonder her heart's giving up.'

'Is that what she told you?'

'Not the Tim bit, but she did mention her heart. She can hardly get her breath.' Lucinda was really fired up about the whole thing and her voice rose. 'You should be the one looking after Tim, not his grandmother. Goodness, what were you thinking?'

'I'm thinking I have a full-time job,' he answered fiercely.

'Nevertheless you could still have him living here with you,' she slammed. 'He starts back to school in September. Lots of one-parent families cope. Even working parents. They get help. You could have done that instead of putting all the pressure on Helen.'

'Helen wanted to look after him,' informed Zane, his brow thunderous now.

'And you let her.' Lucinda was really fired up now. 'You didn't stop to think that it might be too much for her. Oh, no, having Tim here would spoil your nights of passion with whichever woman is your current favourite. I despise you, Zane Alexander.'

Once the words were out Lucinda wished that she hadn't uttered them. He'd gone to a lot of trouble to set things up for her here, and this was how she repaid him. Goodness, she wouldn't blame him if he told her to go. Right now!

'And how about *our* nights of passion?' he asked with amazing calmness.

Actually he was too calm. It worried Lucinda.

'How do you rate those? Were they sordid?'

Lucinda winced. They definitely hadn't seemed it at the time. They had been beautiful and sensual and her heart had sung with sheer happiness. Even now, despite her reservations, she still looked on them with pleasure.

'Of course they weren't,' he answered for her. 'You're letting your emotions run away with you, Lucinda. You know nothing about my private life.'

'I know what I read in the glossies.'

'And you believe it?'

'And I know that you've done wrong by your brother.'

Zane closed his eyes and laced his fingers tightly together. 'I sometimes think I could strangle you, Lucinda Oliver. And at other times—' he opened his eyes and looked straight at her '—I want to take you to bed. In fact, I think that's what I might do right now. A form of punishment, shall we say, for daring to turn on me.' And, with that, he scooped her up into his arms.

Lucinda's struggles were to no avail and, to be honest, she didn't struggle too hard. Zane had made up his mind and that was that. He kicked open the door to his bedroom and she had a quick impression of masculine browns and beiges and a dark green carpet before he laid her down on the bed.

In a matter of seconds he had ripped off his clothes and then he did the same to her. She was utterly at his mercy, her eyes wide and shocked and appealing, but it made no difference. Zane wanted and Zane was going to take. And she, Lord help her, was powerless to do anything about it.

She could have left. While he was undressing she could have got off his bed and made for the door. So why hadn't she? Because she wanted it as much as he did! She had lain there and watched as each inch of his flesh was exposed. It was so familiar to her, so incredibly powerful, that she hadn't been able to move.

And this time when he made love to her there were no preliminaries. No long drawn out foreplay, no teasing, no enticing and encouraging. He held himself over her for just a second before he entered her, a second when his eyes were asking whether she wanted to run.

But by then Lucinda's heart was racing and her hormones dancing and the very thought of him taking her like this held a very different kind of excitement. It wasn't until he had entered her that she realised he was not using protection. On all other occasions he had, but this time he'd been in too much of a hurry.

It was too late now to worry about it and with a bit of luck it was the wrong time of her monthly cycle. There were much deeper issues to think about. Like the fact that she was still in love with him—despite everything! And the fact that his lovemaking was coming to a grand finale far too quickly!

She could feel her climax rising within her and she knew that Zane was nearing his own. She cried out as he collapsed on top of her, his breathing ragged, hers the same as sensation after exquisite sensation made her writhe beneath him, as her whole body throbbed and her throat went tight.

And then they were still.

For a long time they were still.

Until Zane slowly rolled away from her! Their eyes met and his no longer twinkled. They were filled with soul-destroying sadness instead.

Lucinda turned away; she couldn't bear to look at him. She didn't know why he was sad. Anger she could have understood—it was what had started this off, but sadness? Perhaps he wanted their affair to carry on but knew that it couldn't? No, that wouldn't make him sad. Zane was the sort of man who hopped from one girl to another without giving them a second thought.

She must have been mistaken because he sat up now and looked at her again and there was nothing to suggest sadness. 'I had to do that, Lucinda.'

She nodded.

'You could have stopped me.'

She nodded again.

'Am I to take it then that you didn't mind?'

How could she answer that? She did and she didn't. She was crazy where this man was concerned. It didn't matter what rational thoughts entered her head, they took off in all the wrong directions whenever he chose to take control.

He was very good at taking control. It was almost as though he hypnotised her into doing things against her will. He had the power to make her think that she wanted what he wanted. How could that be?

'Lucinda?'

He touched a finger to her chin and forced her to look at him. 'I asked whether you minded?'

Slowly she shook her head. 'But I would like to go to

my room.' She got up off the bed and, hugging her clothes to her, headed for the door. He let her go. And, completely naked, she walked along the corridor to her own room. Where she threw herself down on the bed and cried.

Zane was shocked by how easily Lucinda had capitulated, and ashamed for forcing himself on her. He would have let her go if she had fought him off, but she hadn't, and now he felt guilty. He didn't feel the pleasure he normally associated with making love to Lucinda, and this was alien to him.

Out in St Lucia, each time they had made love it had been an experience to surpass all other experiences. They had both risen to great heights and no regrets had ever been felt. Now he felt a heel. He ought not to have done it. On the other hand, Lucinda could have stopped him. It was her fault as much as his.

He made himself think that as he showered and dressed and when he went downstairs Tim had woken and was demanding his attention. 'Where's Lucy?' his nephew asked.

'She's resting,' answered Zane. 'I think you wore her out swimming.'

'She says I'm good,' said Tim proudly.

'You are.'

'Can I swim again, then?'

Zane shook his head. 'Not today! I'm going to take you to see Nanna. Lucinda has work to do.' He wasn't sure about that but he did know that she would not welcome spending time with him. Which was a shame because that was the reason he had come home early.

And what had he done? Hurt her beyond measure.

How could he even look her in the face again? His only consolation was that she hadn't stopped him. It must mean that she still felt something. When they were on the island she had often instigated their lovemaking, making him believe that she was as happy with the situation as he was.

Why then, now that they were back here in London, had she completely changed? Was it the location that had turned her into a sultry seductress? Was she not normally like that? He didn't know what to think any more. All he knew was that he couldn't get her out of his head. Unlike other girls he'd slept with, Lucinda had left a lasting impression.

At the hospital Helen looked so very much worse than the last time he had seen her and he could understand why Lucinda had railed against him. If Helen didn't improve then it looked very much as though he would have to take Tim on full-time. Who, though, would he get to look after him?

A full-time nanny—*or a wife*? This was something he had never contemplated before. Didn't want to contemplate. On the other hand, he couldn't let Tim down. He was such an engaging little boy. If he ever had children, heaven forbid, he would like them to be just like Tim.

Lucinda spent the rest of the afternoon at her desk. She had heard Zane and Tim go out and couldn't begin to describe the relief she felt. How could she have let Zane make love to her again? Her brain must have fried out there in the Caribbean. She was no more over him than she had been during those magical days.

Love came in many guises and hers had crept up on

her unawares and unhappily refused to go away. She was so afraid that Zane would see how she felt and that he would take advantage. Today had proven how weak she was and if he had any idea her life wouldn't be her own any more.

And the cruellest part of all would be when he dumped her at the end, when he'd tired of her, as he most probably would. Zane's type never committed. It really had been the biggest mistake of her life coming here. Zane had her in his clutches—again; maybe that was even what he'd had in mind. Maybe it wasn't for Tim's sake.

Lucinda's anger grew and when they returned she made a fuss of Tim but totally ignored Zane. She pretended not to notice his frown, the way he kept looking at her and asking silent questions.

She played with Tim, she gave him his tea, she bathed him and put him to bed and all the time she said not one single word to Zane.

But she might have known that she couldn't go through the rest of the night like that. As soon as he had her to himself Zane demanded to know what was wrong.

'Nothing,' she answered coolly, averting her eyes because she knew that if she looked into his she would weaken. They mesmerised her. They were like pools of silky smooth water that she could dive into—and then drown in a sea of passion.

'Don't be ridiculous,' he snarled. 'You've ignored me completely for the last few hours. I'm not a fool, Lucinda.'

'And nor am I,' she tossed back furiously. 'So don't take me for one.'

Zane frowned. 'I don't understand.'

'Don't ever,' she spat, *'ever* take advantage of me again.'

'So that's it, is it?' he asked, enlightenment in his eyes. 'Forgive me if I'm wrong, but you didn't complain at the time.'

'Maybe,' she snapped, 'but I've changed my mind. 'It was a foolish mistake, one that I'm not likely to make again.'

'Even though your body still craves mine?'

'Who's saying it does?' Lucinda's eyes flashed a furious green.

Zane smiled, slowly and confidently. It crinkled the corners of his eyes and made him look boyish and charming and Lucinda felt an unwanted quickening of her pulses, which added to her annoyance.

'I'm saying it does,' announced Zane. 'Words are easy, Lucinda. It's body language that counts. And, believe me, I can read your body language any day.'

Lucinda felt like slapping him. 'You're talking nonsense,' she responded haughtily, 'and I have no wish to continue such a conversation.'

'Very well,' he agreed, much to her surprise. 'The next item on the agenda is dinner. I thought I'd take you out.'

'Then you thought wrong,' she snapped. 'Besides, aren't I supposed to be looking after Tim?'

'Mrs Burton can do that tonight,' he said carelessly. 'Besides, he very rarely wakes.'

'The answer's still no,' she retorted, fighting a whole host of inflammatory sensations. It had to be no. For ever no! For her own peace of mind!

Zane drew in a deep breath, his chest rising and his height increasing. She had angered him but she didn't care. Why should he think that he had only to click his fingers and she'd do as he asked? She was her own woman; hadn't he found that out yet?

'Maybe you'll condescend to dine with me here, then?' he growled.

Lucinda wanted to say no but she didn't think that she could face any more of Zane's wrath. So she inclined her head. 'That would be nice.'

'And before then? Can I expect the honour of your company?'

His voice was dry and sarcastic and Lucinda shook her head. 'I still have work to do.'

Zane frowned and glanced at his watch 'It's nearly seven.'

'And I spent much of the day playing with Tim,' she reminded him. 'I can't afford to let my business go.'

Her remark hit home and his eyes shot daggers. 'Then I'll see you at eight.' And with that he whirled on his heel and left the room.

They were halfway through their meal when the phone was brought in to Zane. 'The hospital,' said his housekeeper gravely.

Zane listened for a moment or two and then shot up from his chair. 'I have to go,' he said apologetically. 'Helen's taken a turn for the worse.'

CHAPTER TEN

LUCINDA waited on tenterhooks to hear about Helen. Her main thoughts were with Tim. He'd lost both his parents and now it looked as though he might lose his grandmother too. How shocking would that be for him, poor little soul? How upsetting?

It was almost midnight when Zane returned home. Lucinda had waited up for him and she met him in the hallway. He shook his head, his lips clamped tightly together, his eyes sad.

'She's gone?'

'I'm afraid so,' he answered quietly.

'How are you going to tell Tim? He idolised her.'

Zane heaved a sigh and nodded. 'It won't be easy.'

Nor was it.

The following morning when Tim awoke Zane took him to one side. Lucinda watched from a distance, saw the disbelief on the boy's face, saw it crumple, and then he ran from the room.

'I'll see to him,' said Lucinda.

She found Tim in his bedroom, curled up in bed, sucking a corner of the cover. He turned away when she went in. Lucinda sat beside him quietly for a few moments, not saying anything, and gradually his hand found hers. 'Why has Nanna left me?' he whimpered.

'Because she was very poorly, sweetheart! Because she was in a lot of pain and couldn't stand it any longer! She's gone to your mummy and daddy in the sky.'

'I want her, though.'

'I know, my darling.'

'Who'll look after me?'

'Uncle Zane, of course.' Lucinda mentally crossed her fingers as she said this. It couldn't be counted on, that was for sure.

'And you?' He looked trustingly into her face.

Lucinda felt tears prick the backs of her eyelids too. 'I don't know about that, Tim. But I will come and see you often, I promise.'

He turned his face away from her and buried it in the pillow and at that moment Zane entered the room.

They stood there hand in hand and looked down at the little boy. It was a moment of togetherness that was totally different from anything else she had shared with Zane. There weren't the two of them this time—there were three. And her heart went out to both of them.

'You will help Tim through this?' asked Zane that evening after his nephew had been put to bed. It had been a long sad day and, although Timothy had perked up as the day had worn on, they both knew how much damage it could do to him.

He needed constant love now; he needed to know that he still had a home and someone to care for him. At one point, after his parents had died, the authorities had mooted foster parents, but Tim's Nanna would have none of it and Zane had declared that he felt the same.

'He is my responsibility now,' he said firmly. 'I know I won't be the best of fathers, but I'll do what I can. I'll employ a full-time nanny—unless you—' He looked questioningly at Lucinda, but she shook her head. It would be wrong to let herself get sucked into a situation that in the end would cause nothing but heartache.

'I thought not,' he said, 'but you will come and see Tim sometimes? He's really taken to you.'

'Of course I will,' she said. Though she wasn't sure whether even that was a good idea.

The funeral came and went and even then Zane did nothing about finding another nanny. Helen's wishes had been that he became Tim's legal guardian and he had agreed to do this, and somehow Lucinda was managing to run her business and look after Tim at the same time. She hated herself for being weak, for letting Zane take advantage of her, and in defiance she refused to share his bed again.

'I've had an idea,' he said one evening over dinner. 'It's not ideal for you, running two offices. Why not set up shop here? Bring Amanda and all the rest of your stuff. You can have another room; you can have as many rooms as you like.'

'So long as I continue to look after Tim for you?' asked Lucinda, appalled by his nerve, but congratulating him at the same time. 'What happened about finding another nanny?'

'I would have done,' he apologised, 'but Tim's had enough upsets for the time being. And I thought this would be a good compromise.'

Lucinda's eyes flashed. 'It's nothing to do with *you* wanting me here? It's just Tim you're thinking of?'

'Of course,' he answered, but Lucinda knew he was lying. She knew that he still wanted her in his bed; she had seen it in his eyes when he thought she wasn't looking. And if he had her here permanently...

The trouble was the longer Lucinda lived here the deeper her feelings grew and the less disposed she was to move back to her stepfather's house. She cursed the day she had ever set eyes on Zane Alexander. There was no other man for her now.

And yet all he wanted was a good time! She was sadly aware of that fact. Marriage was definitely not on Zane's agenda. Never had been, never would be.

'I might regret it,' she said slowly now, 'but yes, it sounds like a good idea for the time being. I am planning to buy a place of my own, you do realise that? This won't be a permanent arrangement.'

Zane nodded. 'Of course.'

And so she moved in. Her stepfather didn't have a good word to say about it. 'You're making a big mistake, you know. Zane Alexander's using you. He wants you as a built in babysitter as well as a stable mate; you won't have a chance to do any work. Not that I ever expected you to succeed.'

But her mother was all for it. 'Darling, that's wonderful news. I did wonder what was going on between you two. I didn't believe all that stuff about looking after his nephew. Will I be hearing wedding bells soon? He's such a catch.'

'*Mother!*' exclaimed Lucinda. 'It's nothing like that. It's a business proposition.'

'Of course,' said her mother, but Lucinda could see that she didn't believe her.

Once settled in her new suite of offices, with Amanda on hand to deal with all the day-to-day problems, Lucinda found little time to worry about her mother or stepfather. Her hands were full juggling her job and minding Tim.

With the remarkable resilience of children he had come bouncing back, and although he talked frequently about his beloved Nanna as well as his parents, he got on with the job of enjoying life as only young children could.

Lucinda's days were full and often when Amanda went home and Tim was in bed she would shut herself in her office and catch up on her work.

On one such evening the door opened and Zane came in, carrying a tray with a bottle of wine and two glasses. 'You work too hard,' he said. 'It's time to relax. And, as you won't come to me, then you leave me no choice.'

Frequently he had invited her to join him but always she had used the excuse of work. Living here with him, seeing him every day, drinking in the heady essence of him, feeling her emotions throb, had been almost more than she could stand. Her nerves were raw; even Amanda had noticed how jittery she was and asked what was wrong.

Now Zane took her hand and led her from her desk to one of the easy chairs, then he filled their glasses and joined her. 'I didn't expect you to work every night. You'll kill yourself.'

'Someone has to do it,' she told him, her chin high and her eyes defiant. 'And as my days are filled with looking after Tim, then I'm left with little option.'

'You could employ someone to help you.'

'Leaving me to become a full-time nanny?' she asked

scathingly. 'I don't think so. It's not what I had in mind when I took my design course. And, since you've brought the subject up, I don't think it's working, looking after Tim and running my business as well. I'm going to give you notice, Zane.'

It wasn't something she had thought about; in fact it had only just occurred to her. But the situation really was intolerable. She couldn't go on like it. She hadn't failed to notice that Zane was doing his part, coming home reasonably early each day and going out only rarely, but even so the onus on her was far bigger than she had anticipated. And, compounded with her love for him, it really was a far from ideal state of affairs.

'You can't do that!' Zane's reaction to her suggestion was immediate and hostile. 'You can't leave me.'

If she hadn't been so wound up Lucinda would have laughed. He sounded like Tim when they'd been playing games and she'd wanted to go indoors. *You can't leave me now, Lucy. Who's going to play with me?*

And that was exactly what Zane was saying. Who was going to play with him? Not that there had been any love games since the funeral. She had deliberately kept a distance between them, and Zane, to give him his due, had respected her wishes. Now it looked as though his patience was running out. He wanted her! It was there in his eyes. It was there in the bottle of wine that sat between them suggesting temptation.

She sipped slowly and carefully and let her eyes meet his. A big mistake! Once they had locked together she couldn't escape. There was something in their depths that tightened her stomach muscles and sent curls of sensation through the very heart of her.

Knowing that if she tugged her eyes away he would know why, Lucinda maintained eye contact but she knew what he was thinking. He wanted her, and he wanted her badly. And, Lord help her, she wanted him too. She should have known that it would only be a matter of time before their feelings got the better of them. If she had thought they could maintain a purely business relationship then she was a fool. An even bigger one than she'd already been.

'What choice do I have?' she asked now, taking another slow sip from the beautiful crystal glass. 'My business is the most important thing in my life.'

'You don't need to be earning when you have me,' he suggested softly. 'I'll take care of all your financial needs. I want you here with me. I don't want to let you go.'

Exactly how much was he offering her? thought Lucinda. A roof over her head! A place in his bed! But what else? Not marriage, that was for sure. Could she settle for second best? And how long would it last? That was the crucial question. She could give her all and then be kicked out within a few months.

On the other hand, wasn't it better to have loved and lost than never to have loved at all? There would never be anyone else in her life; she knew that for certain. It was the real thing she felt for Zane. Why not take what he was offering? A few crumbs were better than none at all.

'I can't give up my business,' she said quietly.

'But? I hear a but coming.' Zane's smoky eyes held a hopeful smile and he leaned that little bit closer towards her.

He smelled so gorgeous that Lucinda wanted to leap at him and let him hold her against his strongly beating heart. She had missed their lovemaking. Her body craved his so intensely at times that it hurt. Especially in bed at night! The hours were long and lonely and many a time she had thought she'd heard him outside her door and her hormones had driven her crazy. But always there had been silence and she knew that it was her overactive imagination.

'I might change my mind and stay,' she said softly, closing her eyes briefly now, breaking the contact, hoping she wasn't going to live to regret her decision.

Zane's smile was wide and consuming. 'You'll let me employ someone to help you, someone who really knows the business and can take charge when you're otherwise engaged?'

'I'm not going to be a full-time nanny,' she declared vehemently. 'I still want to be in charge of the running of it.'

'Of course,' he answered smoothly. 'It will still be yours, you'll still be in control; it's just that life will be a little easier for you. And for me,' he added wryly. 'I won't have to sit night after night on my own knowing you're beavering away in here and that it's all my fault.'

He pushed himself up and stood in front of her. Then he reached out his hands and Lucinda took them. When he had pulled her to her feet their eyes locked and their mouths came together.

It was like drinking sweet nectar, thought Lucinda. How much she had missed his kisses, the feel of him against her and the excitement of his lovemaking. How very, very much!

She heard Zane groan deep in his throat, felt his arms tighten and the burgeoning fullness of him against her. And suddenly it didn't matter whether he was prepared to commit to her or not. She wanted him and he wanted her. It was as simple as that.

Zane's life had felt empty since Helen died and Lucinda had shut him out. He had begun to think that he would never feel her in his arms again, never experience her in bed beside him and never recreate the magic of their lovemaking. In fact he'd felt that he had made a big mistake in inviting her to live with him. He ought to have hired someone else to look after Tim and forgotten Lucinda.

But how could he? Hadn't she got beneath his skin like no one else ever had? He was even, Lord help him, contemplating asking her to marry him. Of course that was in the future; he had to be totally sure first. But he needed her so much. The pain of lying in bed at night knowing she was just a few rooms away was killing him.

More than once he had been tempted to go to her; he had even ventured as far as her door, but common sense had always sent him back to his room.

But now things were looking up. Lucinda had agreed to stay and he was going to get help for her, which meant she would have more time to spend with him! He wanted to shout it from the rooftops, he felt so ridiculously happy. He felt like a teenager again instead of a respectable businessman of thirty-five.

Now he experienced again the sweetness of her mouth, the feel of her soft slender body against him. She was actually trembling. And he wanted her so very much. But only once had he let his emotions run away with him; he couldn't do that to her again. It had horrified him to think that he might have made her pregnant.

There was no sign of it, though. No morning sickness, no accusations, and he'd begun to relax again. He held her gently, trying to ignore his own raging need, and suggested they take their drinks into his sitting room where it was more comfortable.

But no sooner had they settled, no sooner had Lucinda snuggled up against Zane in anticipation of what was to come, than Tim came running into the room.

'I had a nasty dream,' he told them, his face screwing up in tears. 'I'm frightened. I want you with me, Lucy.'

Lucinda looked at Zane and gave a wry shrug.

'You'd best go,' Zane whispered. 'I'll see you later.'

But later never came. Lucinda curled up in bed with Tim and, without even being aware of it, she fell asleep. When she awoke it was morning and Zane had already left for the office.

But mid-morning he phoned her. 'So what happened to you last night?'

'I must have fallen asleep,' she answered apologetically.

'And very beautiful you were. I came to find you, Lucinda. You looked like an angel. I wanted to carry you off to my lair but I was afraid I'd wake Tim.' His voice went down another octave. 'You're not going to get away with it again though. Come what may, tonight belongs to me.'

He sounded so determined that Lucinda's body went into overdrive. Already she was envisaging what they would do or, more to the point, what he would do to her. He was the most exciting man she had ever met and she couldn't wait.

When Zane came home she already had Timothy in bed and she had bathed and put on a kingfisher-blue dress that he had never seen before. It was a semi-fitted shift with a low neck and tiny cap sleeves and it shimmered as she walked. Her high-heeled sandals were a similar iridescent blue.

'Wow, you look sensational,' applauded Zane. 'Far too amazing to stay in! I'll save your *ravishment* for later. I want to show you off to the world. I'll ask Mrs Burton to keep an ear open for Tim. Let me just go and get changed; I won't be long.'

Lucinda loved his compliments. They made her feel even more sexy and she wasn't sure that she wanted to go out. Perhaps they ought to make love first? It had been so long that her body couldn't wait.

She almost ran upstairs and pushed open Zane's bedroom door. He was nowhere in sight but she could hear the shower running. With her heart beating at twice its normal rate, she kicked off her shoes and slipped out of her dress and, with a boldness that was completely alien to her character, she slid open the shower door and stepped in beside him.

Zane's reaction was explosive. First he gasped, next he grinned in admiration, and then he lifted her high and with excruciating slowness he let her body slide down the length of his. It created some of the most exciting sensations Lucinda had ever felt. She let her head fall back, her hair, which she had so carefully brushed earlier, soaking wet now, hanging like a silken curtain, and she arched her body into him. Zane caught her by the hips and held her close, made her achingly aware of his need. 'You little minx,

Lucinda! This wasn't in my plan of things at all. I was going to take—'

Lucinda put a finger to his lips. 'Shh, Zane, this is my game.' And then she traced her finger all the way down his body until she reached what she was searching for and held him in her hand, where she continued to torture him.

Zane drew in an excruciating breath but she wasn't finished. She stooped down and took him into her mouth instead, the hot water jets on her back and shoulders drumming in the same hungry rhythm.

Her excitement was so intense that she felt ready to explode. Zane's hands were on her head, holding her, encouraging, urging. And at the same time his body shuddered and his groans were like those of a man in pain.

'Enough! Enough!' His hoarse voice penetrated Lucinda's concentration. 'Now it is my turn.'

He hauled her up straight and captured her mouth with his, kissing her, perhaps even tasting himself, she thought briefly. Whatever he was doing to her, she had lost her senses. She felt like a floppy rag doll and was his to do with as he liked. He pressed her up against the wall and with his hands on her bottom he entered her.

'Lucinda, my Lucinda, I hadn't meant to do this so soon. It's your fault, you shouldn't have—'

'It's all right,' she said, silencing him. 'I want it too. I want you; I want you so much, Zane.' And again her head dropped back, her hips grinding against his, their two bodies made one by this act of pure animal hunger.

Not until their limbs went limp did they part. And even then Lucinda draped herself over him, her head on his shoulder, and it seemed like an age before he finally turned off the shower and suggested they towel themselves dry.

Actually he towelled her dry and Lucinda did the same to him. And there was not a part of each that didn't receive their full attention. When they had finished Zane picked Lucinda up and carried her to his bed, where he began making love to her all over again.

This time, though, he took it more slowly. In fact their lovemaking lasted all evening and they never made it to dinner. He had strawberries and champagne sent up instead and fed them to her one by one. Eventually they fell asleep, waking long past midnight, both of them starving.

They crept down to the kitchen like two naughty children and ate sandwiches and cake and drank milk, and then they went back to bed and they once more made love. It was as though neither of them could get enough of each other.

Eventually, when first light stretched across the sky, they went to sleep. But not for long because they were woken by Tim bouncing on the bed. 'Wake up, Uncle Zane; wake up, Lucy. You promised we could swim.'

Lucy groaned. She wanted to turn over and go back to sleep. Then she realised that she was in Zane's bed and Tim was jumping on them. What must he be thinking?

But Tim saw nothing wrong in them being together and he began to drag the covers off. 'Come on, get up.'

Knowing they were both naked, Lucinda held on to the duvet for all her life.

Zane grinned at her embarrassment. 'That's right, Tim, and we will—later. You run down to Mrs Burton now and tell her you're ready for breakfast. We'll meet you down there.'

Not until he had gone did Lucinda relax. 'That was a close shave.'

'There's nothing wrong with nude bodies,' said Zane, one hand touching her breast, teasing a nipple into exquisite life.

'Please,' she begged. 'Not again.'

'Perhaps not now—' Zane smiled '—but later, Lucinda. Later.'

For the next few days their lives followed a similar pattern and Lucinda began to feel that perhaps they might have a future together after all.

Zane was as good as his word and found Lucinda a suitable assistant, thus relieving her of an enormous amount of responsibility. Maria was good and had exactly the same mindset as Lucinda herself, and she felt that she could safely leave a lot of the designing in her hands.

Everything worked wonderfully until Lucinda began to have her suspicions that Zane might be seeing another woman.

CHAPTER ELEVEN

IT WASN'T that Zane was any different towards Lucinda. They still made the most wonderful and exciting love, but he was later and later getting home. Since Helen's death he had made a point of getting away from the office early to spend his evenings with her and Tim, but gradually his times changed until sometimes it was almost midnight.

'Where's Uncle Zane?' asked Tim constantly and Lucinda was compelled to tell him that he was a very busy man and was still at work. And this was what she would have liked to believe, except that occasionally, just occasionally, she thought she could smell another woman's perfume on him.

So much for her theory that they might have a future together! What wishful thinking that had been! Zane would never change; she ought to have known that. He simply wasn't the settling down type. He'd even admitted it to her, so why had she begun to dream?

Her mood had swung from one of intense happiness to one of deep despair and she decided to return to her own bed, asking herself how she could sleep with a man who was two-timing her. No, that was wrong. He wasn't two-timing her because they didn't have a serious relationship. He had never declared his love for her, had never mentioned anything long-term. They had simply fallen into the habit of sharing his bed. That was all it was. Nothing serious, nothing long-term! No commitment on his part. So she really had nothing to grumble about.

Until Zane came home and charged into her room! 'What's going on?' he demanded crossly, standing over her.

It was not a question, more a condemnation. Yet why, when he was the one who had strayed, Lucinda had no idea. She sat up abruptly. 'What do you mean, what's going on? I could ask you the same question.' Even though she knew that she had no right. He had promised her nothing, so how could she expect anything?

Except that he had seemed to be changing. Except that he had seemed happy to spend most of his time with her. She ought to have known differently.

'Why have you moved back in here?' Blue eyes looked almost black in the artificial light. He had snapped on the switch when he entered, making her blink at the suddenness of the light.

She swung her legs over the edge of the bed now and stood up, feeling at a complete disadvantage with Zane towering over her. 'It is my room.'

'And one you haven't slept in for weeks,' he accused.

Lucinda gave a dismissive shrug. 'I saw no point in lying in your bed waiting for you when you hardly ever come home before I'm asleep. I thought I'd make myself comfortable here.'

'I do have a business to run, Lucinda,' he said shortly. 'One I've been neglecting lately.'

He looked tired, she thought, and wondered whether she had misjudged him. But she couldn't get that faint smell of perfume out of her head. You didn't get the scent of a woman's perfume on your collar if you weren't intimate.

Zane liked women. It was as simple as that. She had been a challenge, someone different, someone who hadn't fallen immediately into his arms, but now that she had, now that she freely gave herself to him, he was tired of her and needed someone else to turn his fatal charms on.

'And Tim? How do you think he's taking it?' she demanded. 'He thinks you don't love him any more.' Quite why she was using Tim as her defence she wasn't sure. But it was certainly true.

'He's said that?' Zane frowned.

'Not in so many words,' answered Lucinda, folding her arms defensively across her chest, because even in the heat of their argument she couldn't escape the fact that Zane still had the power to turn her on. 'But he constantly asks where you are.'

'And you tell him what?' Zane folded his arms too and stood looking down his nose at her.

Lucinda had never felt quite so inadequate in his presence. She wished that she were dressed. She wished that she had some protective armour against this man who had stolen her heart. 'That you're working, of course.'

'You make it sound as though you're not sure. What is it you think I'm doing, Lucinda? Seeing another woman?'

Lifting her shoulders, Lucinda avoided looking him in the eye.

'So you do think that?' His hands gripped her shoulders so brutally that he hurt, and she was compelled to look up into his eyes. She saw fierce denial, but of course he would deny it, wouldn't he? He still needed her, if only to look after Tim, so he wouldn't tell her that he had tired of her body and was finding his pleasure elsewhere.

'What am I supposed to think?' she asked quietly. 'You never offer any excuses. All you do is come home late and then use me.'

Her words hurt. She saw it in his eyes and immediately wished she could retract them.

'And that's all you think I'm doing, is it?' he demanded. 'Taking advantage when you offer yourself so beautifully to me?' His fingers tightened and he shook her ever so lightly. 'Do you know, Lucinda, that you can be maddening? But your jealousy pleases me.'

'Who says I'm jealous?' Lucinda lifted her green eyes to his, trying to show innocence, but knowing that she dismally failed.

'And instead,' he said, ignoring her question, 'I'll join you in *your* bed for a change. Allow me one moment to shower.' And, so saying, he stripped off his clothes and disappeared into her bathroom.

Lucinda could only stand with her mouth open. What she ought to have done was leap into electric life and order him out. Instead she had more or less agreed to let him make love to her. It was a dreadful state to be in. She was his prisoner as surely as if she were behind bars.

And when he came out of the shower she was still standing there. Numb with shock. Appalled at the way things were going. But completely unable to do anything about it.

He came to her, as naked as the day he was born, no inhibitions whatsoever, his eyes meeting her eyes, locking into them so that there was no looking away. Silently he slid her nightdress from her shoulders and when it fell in a pool at her feet he pulled her to him, holding her there for several long seconds, not speaking, not doing anything, simply pressing her close.

And then slowly he began stroking. First her hair—he loved her hair, he had told her that many times. He loved entwining his fingers in it and making her his prisoner. But not tonight; he simply let it slide through his fingers in a gentle caress. Afterwards he massaged her shoulders and back—long sensual strokes that aroused and disturbed and made her want to urge herself against him.

She didn't, of course. She made herself stand very still. His hands reached down to her buttocks and there they stayed as he urged her against him. She could feel his powerful erection pressing into her but he made no further move. It was almost as though he was now waiting for her!

And when she didn't respond, when she stood there like a frozen statue, when she thought he would give up and condemn her to hell, he left one hand where it was but with his other he lifted her chin and stared deeply into her eyes.

'Do you want me, Lucinda?' he asked in a voice gruff with emotion.

Did she want him? Desperately so! Why did he even need to ask the question? And finally her reserve broke. 'Like never before,' she whispered hoarsely, ashamed to admit that her body was weaker than her mind. He wasn't playing the game fair and yet here she was, hungering for everything he had to offer.

It was all the encouragement he needed.

With a groan his mouth came down on hers, hungry, demanding, taking. Lucinda's whole body burst into glorious life, all the negative feelings of the last few days disappearing into thin air. She had told herself that she would enjoy this affair while it lasted and, even though she knew it was nearing its end, she wanted to savour every last minute of it, every hour, every day, for however long it took before Zane finally cut the ties.

It might be some time, of course, because of Tim, but, fool that she was, she was prepared to accept that. Never in her whole life had her mind been so weak. She knew it was wrong, she knew it would end in heartbreak, and yet something still drove her on. Love had turned her mind, made her blinkered to everything except her feelings.

She held his head between her palms and returned his kisses with a hunger so deep that it felt as though she was giving her soul and she urged her hips against him, gyrating until it drove him crazy too.

He swung her up into his arms and carried her to the bed. He took her urgently and hungrily, and somewhere in the back of her mind she remembered thinking that it was as though he hadn't had sex for a long time. It couldn't be, of course; it was only last night—and with whomever he had been out with this evening! He was a man with an insatiable sexual appetite and he had turned her into a sex-hungry woman as well.

She couldn't deny the fact that she loved his body, loved what he did to her, how he knew exactly which were her most erogenous zones, how he made her feel as though she was being transported to a different planet. She wasn't in this world, that was for sure. She was floating somewhere in the heavens—and she didn't want to come down.

But, like all good things, it couldn't last for ever. With fierce abandonment they both reached the pinnacle of their desire, their bodies out of control, coming down to earth only slowly. Lucinda didn't want to lose the feeling; she wanted it to stay with her all night long. She was at such a fever pitch that tears rolled down her cheeks.

Instantly Zane asked what was wrong. 'Have I hurt you, my darling?'

My darling! He had never called her that before. Was it a slip of the tongue? Was he thinking of someone else? Or had he really begun to think of her in those terms? How would she know? How would she ever know? She wouldn't, because one day she would no longer be a part of his life! That was a fact.

She shook her head and when their bodies finally recovered Lucinda half expected Zane to go back to his room. But instead he stayed with her; he kept her close in his arms the whole night long. And when morning began to break he woke her with a kiss, with a gentle touch, and she was instantly aroused. She turned to him and touched him too, but when she showed signs of wanting a replay of last night, he smiled and said softly, 'There's no hurry this morning.' And he tortured her with deliberate light touches and kisses; there was no part of her that he missed, and yet he wouldn't let her turn her hunger into anything else.

He made her writhe on the bed until she felt that she was going out of her mind and when she clawed at him he gently removed her hands. 'Lie still, Lucinda,' he admonished softly. 'I haven't finished with you yet.'

Not finished! When he was driving her delirious. How impossible was that? 'Zane! Zane!' she groaned.

But he smothered her mouth with kisses. 'Don't talk!'

Oh, Lord, he was asking the impossible. Her body bucked and, unable to stop herself, she was overcome by the biggest orgasm she'd ever had. Never in her life had this happened to her in this way. She couldn't believe that it had happened, and she lay there panting and lifting her hips as wave after wave of exquisite sensation ravaged her body.

'I'm sorry, Zane,' she said quietly at last.

'Sorry? Don't be sorry, my darling. You've just made me one hell of a happy man.'

Lucinda frowned. 'I don't understand.'

'You've given me something very precious.'

'I have?'

He groaned and kissed her and, before Lucinda knew it, he was entering her and it was his turn to scale the heights. It was the ultimate lovemaking session, one that would remain with her for ever. Long after Zane had gone out of her life.

To her surprise and pleasure Zane came home early that evening; nevertheless she still couldn't stop a niggle of suspicion that there was someone else in his life. Perhaps she ought to make a concerted effort to fill his life with so much sex that he wouldn't have the energy for anyone else?

It was an amusing thought but Lucinda knew very well that she wouldn't do it. It would be like waging war on an invisible army. How would she ever know that she had won?

But, as she had expected, the early evenings didn't

last and Lucinda's disappointment grew to such an extent that she really felt she couldn't carry on any longer. She went to see Zane in his study one evening. He had come home early but had shut himself away after dinner, declaring that he still had work to do. Normally Lucinda wouldn't dream of interrupting him, but she was so wound up that she pushed open the door without even knocking.

'Zane, I'm leaving,' she said without preamble. 'I cannot—' and then came to a sudden halt when she heard him on the phone.

'Serafine, I have to go, I'll see you later.'

It was her worst nightmare come true, all her suspicions confirmed. The woman Zane was seeing was Serafine! The St Lucian girl was the one keeping him out at night. Lucinda found it hard to believe, but she had heard him say her name. There was no disputing the fact.

'Serafine?' she asked in a choked little voice. 'Serafine is here?'

Zane nodded. 'She's working over here for the time being.' And he didn't look in the least guilty.

'So she's the one who's been keeping you out late at night?' Lucinda accused, unaware of how shrill her voice had gone.

'I've taken her to dinner occasionally,' he admitted, looking not in the least concerned. 'She's alone in a strange country. It would be rude of me to ignore her.'

And what else had he provided besides dinner? wondered Lucinda bitterly. A hotel room? Entertainment in the way he knew best? Her heart turned to stone. Her heartbeats seemed to stop.

'So what is so important that you came charging in

here as though all the hounds in hell were after you?' he asked pleasantly.

The hounds had pounced! They had caught their prey. And she was about to be chewed into little pieces and spat out. This really was the end of their relationship. Not a moment too soon had she decided to return to her stepfather's house. In fact, she wouldn't even go there. She would rent an office and some rooms and look around for a house of her own. She could afford to spend a little time looking around.

'I came to tell you I'm leaving,' she announced, her chin high, her eyes defensive.

Zane frowned. 'I beg your pardon?' His smoky blue eyes narrowed and he pushed himself up from the chair.

'I think you heard,' she declared unflinchingly.

'But why?' And he closed the gap between them.

Lucinda stepped backwards. She daren't let him touch her or it would be her undoing. 'Because it's not working. I cannot concentrate on two jobs. You'll be much better off finding someone else to look after Tim.'

'I thought we'd solved that problem when Maria joined your team.'

'I like to be at the helm,' she announced coldly. 'Surely you above all people can understand that.'

'I also know that sometimes it's necessary to delegate.'

'Not when other things take up your time,' she tossed. 'If I didn't have Tim to look after, I could double my output. I happen to enjoy my work, Zane. I appreciate all you've done for me, but the time has definitely come to go my own way.'

'Just like that?' he asked, his voice deadly quiet now. 'You're going to walk out on me just like that?'

Lucinda nodded and took another step backwards.

'And if I say I won't let you go?'

She heard thinly controlled anger deep in his voice. 'You have no choice. I don't belong to you. I made no commitment.'

Zane put his fingertips to his brow and rubbed it worriedly. 'How do you think Tim's going to react to all this?'

Lucinda closed her eyes momentarily. 'Not good,' she whispered.

'You're damn right,' he roared, bouncing over to stand a few inches in front of her. 'Have you considered what that poor boy's gone through recently? How can you do this to him?'

'He'll get over it,' said Lucinda softly. But inside she was crying because she knew that Tim was the one who would get hurt most.

'Of course, children always do, isn't that what you once told me? But who knows what sort of repercussions it might have in later life? Think about it, Lucinda. Think carefully before you make any rash decisions.'

'It's not rash,' she protested. 'I've thought about it a lot.'

'And do you know what you'll be giving up?'

Her life, she thought miserably. Zane! Zane was her life. She'd be giving up the only man she'd ever truly loved. It would be an enormous wrench, but she had always known that their relationship could never be permanent. Not that he was talking about himself. He could walk away and leave her without a moment's compunction. She meant nothing to him. Women were there to be used. Serafine hadn't learned that lesson yet. She had come over here after him but all too soon she would find herself thrown on to the used pile like every other girl he had bedded.

'I'll be giving you up,' she answered. 'Not that it will be any great loss. It's been good while it lasted, Zane, but as you know I have no intention of committing myself to any man, ever. Simon taught me the hard way that men are not to be trusted.'

A deep flush rose from Zane's throat and filled his whole face and his eyes grew as hard as bullets. 'And you're saying you don't trust me. If that's how you feel, Lucinda, then don't let me stand in your way. In fact I'll help you move out.'

'There's no need,' she answered. 'I can manage perfectly well on my own.' And with that parting shot she turned and walked away.

CHAPTER TWELVE

ZANE felt as though he'd been poleaxed. He found it hard to believe that Lucinda had been using him. He'd used women in the past but never to the extent that they'd lost their hearts to him. He had known exactly when to call a halt to proceedings.

With Lucinda it had been different. From the beginning she had tugged at a corner of his heart. And it had been in his plan of things to change her mind about men. He thought he had succeeded. He had even considered changing his mind about marriage; he had even thought about proposing to her. She had got through to him where no one else had succeeded.

And now this!

He couldn't let her go! *He couldn't!*

'Lucinda!' He called her name but already she was out of earshot. He could hear her running up the stairs. His initial thought was to go after her—but would that solve anything? She had been so adamant. So cruel even! He didn't want to believe that she had been using him, but why would she lie?

This wasn't the first time that she'd threatened to leave, but this time she had been absolutely determined.

He sat down and dropped his head in his hands. He really had thought they had a future together. He'd been making plans; he'd been so very sure she'd be pleased. Now it seemed as though it was all pointless.

Lucinda felt tears streaming down her face as she fled to her room. She had to go through with her plan even though it was utterly painful. She couldn't share Zane, not with anyone. If he wanted Serafine, then he could have her.

In the morning she would make a few phone calls, she would find herself somewhere to live, somewhere to run her business, and then she would be out of here. She ought to have known from the beginning that it would be a dreadful mistake. In fact she had, but she had foolishly ignored it. To her downfall!

She half expected Zane to follow her, to plead with her to stay. Not that pleading was one of Zane's virtues. Come to think of it, did he have any? Zane thought only of himself. She would be well rid of him.

The next morning she didn't go down to breakfast until she was sure that he was out of the house. She took Tim to school, then spent her time on the phone arranging her future. It wasn't as easy as she'd thought to get an immediate let and she was left with the choice of going back to her stepfather's house temporarily or holding on until everything was organised.

She opted to stay, though whether she would regret it she didn't know. At least it would give her time to prepare Tim for her departure. He had known it would come; she had told him so after the funeral when she hadn't been sure what her future would hold.

The trouble was they had built quite a strong bond

and it would upset her as well to leave him. But not as much as it would hurt to leave Zane! She had been a fool letting herself fall in love with him. And more of a fool for letting their relationship blossom to such a degree that her heart was now breaking.

How she would miss him! How she would miss their nights of passion! It hurt to think that he would have the lovely Serafine sharing his bed now.

Tim was highly excited when she fetched him from school that afternoon. 'I'm in the school concert,' he announced importantly.

'Darling, that's wonderful,' exclaimed Lucinda, knowing that she couldn't burst his bubble at this moment by telling him that she was leaving.

'You will come and see me, won't you?' he asked, his hand tucked into hers, his upturned face shiny and happy. 'And Uncle Zane?'

'Of course we will, sweetheart,' she said, squeezing his hand and kissing his forehead. 'When is it?'

Tim frowned. 'It's Hallo—Hallo—something.'

'Halloween?' suggested Lucinda.

'That's it, Halloween,' he confirmed. 'I'm going to be a ghost.'

Lucinda groaned inwardly. Halloween was nearly six weeks away. She couldn't carry on that long; she simply couldn't. It was heartbreaking enough knowing that Zane was seeing someone else without having to live through it for several more weeks. But how did she tell Tim that?

She would, of course, attend the concert; she wouldn't let him down in that respect, but she most certainly couldn't live with Zane until then, breathing in the very essence of him, feeling the pain of her love, while suspecting that he was bedding another woman. The mere thought of it sliced through her heart, hurting every thought, filling her with so much agony that all she wanted to do was run.

She wanted to get as far away from him as possible. The other side of the world sounded good. Except that she had a business to run and a healthy order book. Since Maria had joined her everything had gone up and up. And she had thought her love life was on the up as well.

She had thought that she could trust Zane. It had taken her a long time to accept this, but she really had begun to believe that he would never let her down. Not that Zane had ever declared his love. Perhaps she'd been a fool for even thinking along the lines of something permanent.

They reached Zane's house and as they walked up the long winding drive Lucinda realised how much she was going to miss this place. The house was a mixture of old and new, but done so sympathetically that it all blended together. It was huge, and in moments of madness she had envisaged getting married there, with the reception in the ballroom, or outside if the weather permitted. And lots of children to fill it.

She was horrified now by these thoughts. How could she have entertained them? Zane had never given her the slightest hint that he wanted to marry. He'd enjoyed bedding her; it was all they ever seemed to do, but as for anything else—it was a figment of her imagination.

She was such a fool.

'Why are you crying?'

Lucinda suddenly realised that Tim was staring up

at her and she had tears rolling down her cheeks. 'I'm not crying, sweetheart, it's the wind.' She fished a handkerchief out of her pocket and dabbed her eyes. She really would need to be more careful. She mustn't let her thoughts run away with her—unless she was in the privacy of her own room, of course, where she could cry to her heart's content.

Actually, why was she crying? Men like Zane weren't worth losing sleep over. She would be well rid of him. A lesson learned, yes, but sorrow, no! She squared her shoulders and lifted her chin and by the time they were indoors Lucinda had control of herself.

To her amazement Zane was at home and came to meet them in the hall. He had changed from his business suit into a pair of off-white chinos and a white T-shirt that faithfully followed every line of his body. He looked lean and sexy and she turned away quickly as Tim went running to tell him about the concert.

Upstairs she put out Tim's clothes ready for him to change into and then went to her office. With Zane at home her duties were done. Or so she thought. Zane had different ideas.

Her phone rang and it was Zane. He had never called her on her office line before. He'd had no need. She frowned and ignored the sudden racing of her heart.

'Yes?' she asked impatiently.

'You rushed off.' It was almost an accusation.

'I thought with you at home to look after Tim I could get on with some work.' She kept her voice cool and professional. Not that she felt cool. Her skin was at melting point and her pulses were dancing all over the place. It was what he did to her. Even the sound of his voice was enough to send a charge of electricity through her body.

'I wish to speak with you.'

'We have nothing to talk about.'

'You're still intent on leaving?'

'Yes.'

'We need to discuss it.'

'Nothing will change my mind.'

'We still need to talk. I'll give you five minutes. I'll be in my study.' And the line went dead.

Lucinda was furious. She had said all she wanted to say. If he wanted her he could come to her; she certainly wasn't going to run at his bidding.

But five minutes later Lucinda found herself outside Zane's office. She had thought about it and didn't want a heated discussion in front of her staff. She pushed open the door, ignored her thudding heart and stood just inside the room. 'There's nothing you can say that will make me change my mind,' she announced firmly.

Zane sat at his desk, the normal twinkle gone from his eyes. They were as cold as an icy sea and just as stormy. 'Have you told Tim yet that you're leaving?'

Lucinda shook her head.

'So when are you going to deliver that little gem?'

She shrugged. 'I was going to do it today but he was so full of his part in the school play that I couldn't. I know it won't be easy for him. But I have my own life to consider. Tim is your responsibility, not mine. I'll go to see him in his play, of course I will, but I'm not staying on for his benefit alone.'

'So how soon exactly are you planning on leaving?' he asked, his voice as icy as his eyes.

Lucinda shivered. 'I have to find somewhere to live first, and an office. It's not going to be as easy as I thought.'

'So you're not going back home?'

She shook her head. 'My stepfather would crow. I couldn't bear that.'

'You don't have to go at all.' There was a subtle change in his voice. He wasn't pleading—oh, no, Zane didn't plead—but it was a suggestion that she might like to change her mind.

'I do,' she said. 'I'm sorry, but—'

'You're not damn sorry at all,' he grated, jumping to his feet and crossing the room towards her. 'I cannot work you out, Lucinda. I thought you were happy here.'

'I am—was,' she corrected. 'But you must have known it couldn't last for ever.'

Zane's brows dragged together into a formidable frown. 'What couldn't last? You working here? Or our relationship?'

'Both,' she snapped. 'And I see no point in going over this conversation again. I thought it was all sorted last night. The only thing that's different is that I will be staying a little longer than I expected. Unless of course you would rather I go now?'

Lord knew what she expected him to say, but it certainly wasn't the answer he gave her.

'I think it might be best,' he announced, his voice deadly calm now. And there was nothing in his eyes to suggest that he would feel any heartbreak over it. Instead he strode to the window and looked out.

Lucinda stood for a moment or two, wondering,

waiting, and then spun on her heel and fled to her room. She refused to let tears come. He was an out-and-out swine and she hated him.

It wasn't going to be that easy moving immediately. For one thing she'd have to go back home, much as she hated the idea. And for another she didn't like the thought of having to tell Amanda and Maria that they were moving office. They would be sure to ask questions. They both loved the environment they worked in and only the other day Amanda had asked her how serious her relationship with Zane was. As far as they were concerned, the sun shone out of his eyes.

And there was Tim to consider too. She had to tell Tim. She didn't want to run away and leave Zane to do it for her. She wanted to make sure he was all right with the situation.

Later she bathed Tim and put him to bed, but he was still so full of his part in the school play that she couldn't bring herself to tell him.

It wasn't until she took him to school the following morning that she found the courage and, as gently as she could, she said, 'I won't be picking you up this afternoon, Tim. I'm going back to my own home to live. Uncle Zane will find you a new nanny. Someone you like, of course.'

She saw tears well in his eyes. 'I like *you*, Lucy. I love you.'

'I love you too, sweetheart,' she said softly, 'but my job looking after you has ended. I'll still come to your school play. I want to see you in that so much.'

Tim's head bowed and Lucinda knew that he was trying to be brave. But how brave could a five-year-old be when he was going to lose someone else he'd learned to love? It must seem to him as though everyone he'd ever loved in his whole life was leaving him.

He turned to her then and wrapped his arms around her legs. Lucinda picked him up and hugged him tightly and planted a big kiss on his cheek. 'You'll still see me sometimes, I promise,' she whispered, then set him down again and he scampered away.

She stood there for a moment and watched as he entered the school building and then she turned and headed back, her footsteps slow, her heart heavy. Today was the end of her hopes and dreams.

When she got back to the house she told her employees that they could take the rest of the day off. 'I'm moving back to my stepfather's house,' she declared. 'I'll see you there in the morning.'

'But—' began Amanda.

'I don't want any questions asked. Please do as I say.'

When they had gone, curiosity killing them, Lucinda busied herself packing. She could have got them to help, of course, but she wanted time on her own. She didn't want the third degree either. The situation was already too upsetting by far.

She hadn't been working long when there was a phone call from Tim's teacher. 'I was wondering, Miss Oliver, why Tim isn't in school today. Is he ill?'

Lucinda's heart seemed to stop for a moment. She clapped a hand over her mouth. 'Not in school?' And she felt anxiety rush through her like a red-hot knife. 'But I dropped him off there myself. I saw him go inside.'

There was a pause on the other end and then, 'Are you sure about that?'

'Of course I'm sure.' Lucinda was almost screeching by now. 'If he's not there, then where is he? Have you looked everywhere? He's had some—bad news—he might be hiding.'

'We'll set up a search,' said the woman. 'In the meantime, I think you ought to come.'

'Of course, yes,' said Lucinda, shaking her dazed head. Oh, goodness, what had happened to him? Where was he? If he wasn't in school, where had he gone? He was only five, for goodness' sake. He could have wandered anywhere.

The first thing she did was phone Zane.

'Alexander,' he barked in her ear, not sounding in the best of moods.

'Zane, it's me, Lucinda. The school's phoned; Tim's missing.' Her words fell over themselves.

A moment's pause, and then, 'What do you mean, Tim's missing?'

Lucinda had to hold the phone away from her ear to avoid Zane's ear-splitting roar.

'I mean he's not in school.' Oh, Lord, this was the worst thing that had ever happened to her.

'Did you take him there?'

'Of course I did. I saw him safely inside.'

'And did you tell him you were leaving us?'

Lucinda winced. 'Yes, I did.' And she heard Zane's exasperated sigh.

'How did he take it?'

'He was upset.'

'Then this whole thing is your fault,' he yelled. 'Where are you now?'

'I'm just leaving for the school.'

'I'll see you there. And if anything has happened to him, then…' His voice tailed off.

When Lucinda arrived the whole school had been searched and there was no sign of Tim. 'We've alerted the police,' said the headmistress. 'I'm sure nothing's happened to him. I'm sure he just wandered away and he'll be found safe and sound.'

Lucinda prayed that this was so. She knew the school gates were locked once everyone was inside so he must have run away the moment she'd gone. Her heart wept for him. He'd suffered so much in his short life and now she had added to it.

Zane turned up, striding into the school like an enraged lion. He blamed Lucinda. He blamed the teachers. He blamed anyone who got in his way. 'You'll not hear the last of this,' he warned. 'Come, Lucinda, we'll go looking for him.'

Lucinda hadn't the slightest idea where to look. They drove around the local streets but there was no sign of him and their search took them further and further afield until Lucinda had an idea.

'Do you think,' she asked Zane hesitantly, because by this time he was hardly speaking to her, 'that he could have found his way to his Nanna's house? He loved it there.'

'I suppose it is a possibility,' he admitted, his voice deep and gruff with anxiety. 'Anything's worth a try. It is a couple of miles away, though. Could he walk that far? Would he know where to go?'

Lucinda lifted her shoulders and winced. 'He might. And there's only one major road to—' Oh, God, it didn't bear thinking about. If anything had happened to Tim, she would never forgive herself. Never!

When they arrived at the house Lucinda was taken aback. She saw scaffolding and workmen and the whole place looked like a building site. She'd had no idea that the house had already been sold.

'Tim can't be here,' she said. 'Even if he came this way he wouldn't want to stay. It looks nothing like his old home.'

'I'll make some enquiries,' rasped Zane, leaping out of the car.

Lucinda moved at a much slower pace, her eyes searching, her heart thumping and the tears she had bravely tried to hold back raced unchecked down her cheeks.

She stopped a workman and asked but he shook his head.

She stopped another but got the same response.

And then suddenly she heard Zane's voice rise in a roar of exultation. 'Timothy!'

She ran inside and there was Tim, cradled in Zane's arms. Her tears turned to sobs and she hid her face so that they wouldn't see. But Timothy put his arms out to her and called her name. 'Lucy! Lucy! Don't leave me.'

The three of them stood in a circle, arms entwined, faces streaming with tears of both relief and distress. Zane finally smiled but Lucinda knew that she hadn't heard the end of it. And Tim smiled too. 'You stay now?'

Slowly she nodded. What else could she do?

CHAPTER THIRTEEN

'DID you mean it?'

Lucinda looked at Zane and frowned. 'Did I mean what?'

'About staying? Or were you humouring Tim?'

They were home and Tim was in bed and asleep, worn out after his marathon walk. Zane was still in the devil of a mood.

'Yes, I meant it,' she said quietly.

'For how long?'

'As long as he needs me.' She might regret it, but she would never forget Tim's face when he'd seen her at his Nanna's house. His smile had stretched from ear to ear. She would have had to be inhuman to resist him.

'And if I need you?' The growl was low in Zane's throat and his eyes were hooded as he looked at her, telling her nothing.

Lucinda swallowed a sudden constricting lump. 'I don't know what you mean.' Her voice was equally low, tension trembling in the air between them like an unseen tightrope.

'God dammit, Lucinda,' he roared, 'have you no idea how I feel?'

'None at all,' she told him truthfully. He enjoyed her body, but what else? He had an insatiable sexual appetite, but she wasn't the only one with whom he sought pleasure.

Zane shook his head as if he couldn't believe what he was hearing. 'You sometimes amaze me, Lucinda. Do you really think that I would have taken you into my bed if I hadn't felt something for you?'

'I know you have a huge sexual appetite,' she told him, keeping her tone quiet and her face impassive. She was afraid to believe what she was hearing. There had to be some misunderstanding.

He almost smiled then. 'Hark at the pot calling the kettle black!'

Lucinda shrugged, trying to pretend that she didn't know what he was talking about. But deep down inside she felt secretly pleased.

'It was not only sex, Lucinda, good though it was. It was much, much more. Come here.' And he beckoned her towards him.

Lucinda crossed the room slowly, cautiously, not sure what he expected or even wanted. She knew her spirits had lifted a fraction. She knew that the future didn't look entirely bleak. But beyond that she was afraid to think.

When she reached Zane he pulled her down on to his lap. And he put his mouth close to her ear. 'I think I'm in love with you, Lucinda.'

The shock was complete, but then the heavens were suddenly filled with beautiful light and she bowed her head and whispered too. 'You only think?' She felt suddenly daring and dangerous and she wanted to jump up and dance around the room. She wanted to declare her love too, but knew that she must wait, that she must be perfectly sure. She didn't want to make a fool of herself.

'I know I am,' he said firmly this time. 'I've fought it, Lucinda. Really hard. I've always been of the opinion that love never lasts. I've seen proof of it. The same as you have. But suddenly I can't let that hold me back any more. I love you. I want to love you for the rest of your life. If you'll have me.'

He sounded humble, which was so unlike Zane that yet again she felt close to tears.

'I love you too, Zane. I think you already know that.'

'I thought so at one time,' he agreed. 'But when you threatened to walk away I was devastated. I thought I'd misread the signals. I thought all you'd wanted from me was sex.'

'Which is what I thought you wanted from me,' she said with a laugh.

'You have to agree it was good.'

Lucinda jigged up and down on his lap. 'More than good. Fantastic. Out of this world. Unique. Wonderful.'

'I think I get the picture,' he said, his mouth crooked up at the corners. 'And if you carry on doing that I think I might have to carry out some of these fantastic, wonderful, out of this world experiences. Could you manage that?'

'Whenever and wherever,' she answered with a wicked smile.

In response Zane swept her into his arms and carried her upstairs and they lost themselves in the exquisite pleasure of each other's bodies.

It was the sound of Timothy waking that made them scramble off the bed and into their clothes. 'We still have a lot more talking to do,' warned Zane, 'but I think we should wait until Tim's safely tucked up again tonight. In the meantime the poor little fellow needs more reassurance that you're not going to leave us. Actually—I need reassurance too. Would you really have left me?'

Lucinda inclined her head.

'Would it have broken your heart?'

'Absolutely,' she agreed, her lips wry, 'but I thought I had just cause.'

Zane frowned. 'And what's that supposed to mean?'

'Serafine!' Lucinda smiled weakly and self-consciously as she said the other woman's name. 'I thought you were having an affair with her. Are you?'

A look of complete astonishment crossed Zane's face. 'Would I have declared my love for you if I were? Whatever gave you that idea?'

'You've been staying out late. What was I to think? She's very beautiful. I was even jealous of her when we were in St Lucia.'

'She's not as beautiful as you, my darling Lucinda. But I'm glad that you were jealous,' he added with a grin, ' because it tells me how much you love me.'

'With the whole of my heart,' she declared, her eyes locked into his, her arms around his waist, pulling him close. 'I will love you for ever, Zane.'

'And I you,' he returned, kissing her lightly.

For the rest of the day they played with Tim. He was highly delighted to be given a day off school, but as expected he needed lots of reassurance from Lucinda that she was not going to leave them.

It was not until evening, over dinner in Zane's fantastic dining room with its views over the valley, that he said to her, 'Aren't you a teeny bit curious as to what's going on at Helen's house?'

Lucinda shook her head, her lovely Titian hair swinging across her shoulders. Zane liked her to wear it loose and most of the time she did. He reached out now and touched it and stroked the back of his hand across her cheek and there was a mountain of love in his eyes. Lucinda felt that it was more than she deserved. 'I'm assuming it's been sold. Poor Tim; I bet he hated finding it like that.'

'Actually,' said Zane with a mysterious smile, 'Helen left it to me. All her money, and she had a fair amount, has been put into trust for Tim, but she wanted me to have the house.'

'Why?' asked Lucinda simply. It wasn't as if Zane needed it. He was so rich that he could have bought the whole neighbourhood.

'I don't know,' he answered, his expression as quizzical as hers. 'I've always liked the house; it has a lot of potential. Helen used to say, after her husband died, that she'd like to turn it into a restaurant. But she never did anything about it.'

'So is that what you're doing?' asked Lucinda.

Zane nodded. 'It was to be a surprise.'

Lucinda had no idea what he was talking about. 'For whom?'

'You, my darling.'

'Me?' She was completely confused now.

'I was—still am,' he amended quickly, 'going to ask you to marry me. And the restaurant was to be your wedding present. I'm going to call it Lucinda's.'

'Oh, Zane!' Lucinda jumped up from her seat and hugged him. 'What a good man you are. I'm sorry I ever doubted you; I don't deserve your love.'

'Don't ever say that!' he warned, lifting a finger. 'I didn't exactly show my love, did I? I guess I was afraid. But not any more, my precious one. Not any more. It won't be only my body you'll get, but my devoted attention for the rest of your days.'

His housekeeper bringing in their dessert interrupted their kiss. Lucinda jumped away hurriedly, but Zane smiled. 'Mrs Burton, you can be the first to congratulate us. Lucinda's just agreed to be my wife.'

'I have?' asked Lucinda, her eyes wide with surprise. 'I don't recall you asking.'

He grinned. 'I thought it was a foregone conclusion. Let me make amends.' He got up from his chair and knelt down on one knee and, taking her hand, he looked up into her face with smiling blue eyes. 'Lucinda Oliver, will you please do me the honour of becoming my wife?'

'I will,' she said unsteadily, trying to stop herself from laughing. Not because it was funny, but because she was out-of-this-world happy.

Mrs Burton clapped. 'You make a fine couple, if I may say so.'

'You may,' said Zane seriously as he stood up. And, before his housekeeper had even left the room, he pulled Lucinda into his arms and kissed her again.

Later that evening, much later, when Lucinda's euphoria had died down a little, but not much, because today was the happiest day of her life, and she was able to sit without jumping up and down with excitement, she asked Zane about Serafine. 'What exactly does she mean to you?'

'You have nothing to fear where she is concerned,' Zane assured her.

'But why is she here, in England?'

'Because I asked her to come.'

Lucinda frowned, a sudden uneasy feeling in the pit of her stomach. He might say she had nothing to fear, but...

'Serafine's an expert in the restaurant business, as you know,' he told her. 'I sought her help in converting Helen's house. I could have asked you, of course, but that would have spoilt my surprise. In fact it's already spoiled so I might have to think up something else for a wedding present.'

'Zane!' Lucinda was appalled. 'You can't do that. I don't want anything else. I'm even overwhelmed that you should name a restaurant after me.'

'Not only name it, my darling, I'm giving it you.'

'OK,' she agreed, 'but all the profits will go into Tim's trust fund,' she announced firmly.

The next morning, when they told Tim that they were going to get married, he was so happy and excited that he couldn't sit still and he was impatient to go to school to tell everyone.

When Lucinda came back from taking him she was surprised to find Zane still at the house. He usually went out before her—long before her—and although he'd joined them for breakfast she hadn't expected to see him again until evening.

'Why aren't you at work?' she asked after he had kissed her soundly and very satisfyingly.

'Because I've been thinking,' he said. 'I have something to discuss with you.'

Lucinda lifted her brows and waited.

'As you know, one of Helen's requests was that I become Tim's legal guardian, but, my precious darling, what do you think about adoption? Once we're married, of course. Then he'll be our real son.'

'You mean as well as the one I'm carrying?' asked Lucinda shyly. It had been her big secret. She'd had no morning sickness, nothing at all to warn her that she was pregnant, but she knew.

Zane stood stock-still. 'You can't be serious?'

She nodded.

And sudden anger crossed his face. 'You were going to run away and not tell me? You were going to deny me my own child?'

Lucinda hadn't expected this reaction. She had thought he would be as pleased and excited as she was. She could understand him, in one way. She hadn't been too happy herself when she'd first discovered that she was carrying Zane's baby. Not that she'd been surprised, because they'd been a bit remiss about protection on occasions, but she had wondered how she would cope.

'Lucinda, tell me!' He took her by the shoulders and shook her. 'Were you going to do that?'

She nodded slowly, unhappiness in her eyes now. 'I didn't want you to feel responsible. I knew you weren't the settling down type. I couldn't shackle you with a child.'

'My playboy image?' he asked, cold anger still in his eyes.

Again Lucinda nodded.

'Let me tell you something, Lucinda. I am no playboy.

I make no secret of the fact that I like women. I like their company. I like to entertain them. But all those lurid stories in the tabloids are completely untrue. They see me with someone and make up the rest. You are the first and the only woman I've ever loved and I've tried to treat you with respect and dignity. I'm not saying I've never made love to anyone else in the past; I have, but it's been pure sex. It's not that way with you and I thought you felt the same. Was it a game with you, Lucinda?'

'No!' she cried. 'No! Of course not! At first, admittedly, I enjoyed the sex. It's what I thought you wanted and it was good, the best I've ever known. It was entirely out of character for me to behave like that, but I lost control of my body.'

When he said nothing she went on. 'Very quickly, though, I realised that I was falling in love with you. And I was afraid. When I discovered that I was pregnant I was even more afraid. I'm sorry, Zane.'

Gradually his grip on her shoulders relaxed and he pulled her against him, holding her quietly, saying nothing.

'I really am sorry,' she said again, her voice whisper-quiet. 'I hope you understand my reasoning.' If he should change his mind about marrying her it would break her heart. And he could well do that. What would happen to their child then? Would he want custody? It didn't bear thinking about.

'I love you, Lucinda,' he said at length. 'It's sad that you felt the need to run away, but I understand. You're a strong woman and I admire you for that.' And for a long time he held her, neither speaking, simply feeling their love flow from one to the other.

* * *

'Lucinda, will you take Zane to be your husband? Will you love him, comfort him, honour and protect him and, forsaking all others, be faithful to him for as long as you both shall live?'

'I will,' said Lucinda with so much love and feeling in her voice that she heard a collective sigh go through the small group of people who were attending their wedding in St Lucia.

It had been Zane's idea to get married at his Caribbean home. 'It's where we first made love,' he said, 'where we both discovered, although we didn't know it at the time, that we couldn't live without each other. It's the perfect place.'

Lucinda had agreed wholeheartedly and when they'd told Tim, when they'd said he could be their pageboy and best man all rolled into one, he had been very excited. He wasn't old enough to understand the importance and significance of what was happening but he was so proud and happy.

And on this very special day he held a cushion with their rings nestling on it, and there in the sunshine, overlooking the ocean with its deep blues and greens and translucent turquoise, they exchanged their vows.

Lucinda's mother had flown over for the occasion, as had Zane's parents from Australia. Her stepfather had declined, arguing that pressure of work forbade it, and she wasn't sorry because he would have made her feel uncomfortable.

The rest of the colourful congregation was made up of locals whom Zane had got to know during the time he spent there. Some were simply friends, others were business contacts, but they were all open friendly people who delighted in seeing the good-looking Englishman who had made a home on their island marry his beautiful bride.

And, of course, there was Serafine.

Lucinda wasn't entirely sure that nothing had ever gone on between this woman and Zane and, although Serafine had been very pleasant towards her, Lucinda had seen the way she looked at Zane and intuitively knew that she was in love with him. Maybe Zane wasn't in love with Serafine, but something had gone on between them, and Serafine looked as though she wasn't happy that it had ended.

For the moment, though, Lucinda pushed these thoughts to the back of her mind. She wanted nothing to spoil this magical day. There was music and dancing and enough food to feed an army, and when they finally went to bed that night Lucinda felt happier than she ever had in her life.

'I love you, Mr Alexander,' she told him.

'And I love you, Mrs Alexander, with all of my heart,' he declared firmly. 'You are the most beautiful bride ever.'

Their lovemaking took on a new dimension and when morning broke, when they began their first day as man and wife, Lucinda felt as though she was walking on air. She didn't want this feeling to ever go.

Zane's parents and her mother were staying in a hotel. It was their decision—they'd said that it would be wrong to share with the newlyweds—and although Lucinda hadn't truly liked the idea, especially Zane's mother and father whom he hadn't seen for so long, she was secretly pleased that she and Zane were alone.

Their parents had even insisted on having Tim with them for the first night.

A few days later their parents left for their respective homes on opposite sides of the world and Lucinda and Tim took a walk on the beach. Zane had apologised and said he had a little business to take care of. He had kissed her gently as he said it. 'I won't be long, I promise.'

Lucinda knew that she would have to get used to Zane's obsession with his business affairs and she didn't really mind because they were having such a spectacular time. It would be a shame to go home and come back to earth.

What made her look up towards the house she didn't know, but a figure stood there and waved and then slowly began making her way down the cliff path to the shore. It was not until she got closer that Lucinda realised it was Serafine.

Lucinda clutched Tim's hand tightly, though why she had no idea. She had nothing to fear from this woman. Perhaps not, reasoned an inner voice, but she might want to tell you things that you'd rather not know. A woman scorned and all that. It could be a difficult confrontation.

Serafine smiled. 'I thought it was you. Where's Zane? Not gone off and left you already?' She was barefooted but carried a pair of high heels and she wore a georgette dress in the same colours as the sea. She looked beautiful.

'He's working,' answered Lucinda reluctantly.

'Shame on him!' scolded Serafine.

'I'll tell him you called,' said Lucinda pleasantly. Not that she was feeling pleasant. The woman had a gall, coming here when they'd only been married a few days.

'You don't like me, do you, Lucinda?' asked Serafine, her wide dark eyes troubled.

Lucinda shrugged. 'I don't really know you.'

'You see me as a threat, I can tell. Perhaps I should explain what sort of relationship Zane and I have.'

'I don't want to know.' Lucinda turned and began walking away, dragging Tim with her.

'Wait!' Serafine's voice was so urgent that Lucinda had no choice but to stop. But she didn't turn; she waited for the St Lucian girl to catch her up.

'Zane and I have known each other for a long time,' said Serafine. 'We've done business together. I admire him—but I also love him,' she added faintly.

Lucinda's heart stammered and then stopped and finally fell into the bottom of her stomach.

'But,' went on the dark-skinned girl, 'Zane doesn't love me. He never has. We've never made love; he's not even kissed me, except as a friend. I've always hoped, and I was heartbroken when he met you. But why I've come here today is to wish you every happiness. I'm glad Zane's out because it's given me the chance to tell you exactly how I feel.'

Lucinda was speechless. She certainly hadn't expected this.

'I know that you've always thought Zane and I were having an affair,' went on Serafine. 'I wish we were,' she added sadly, 'but the truth is you have nothing to be jealous about. I'll get over him. And what I want to say is that I wish you both a long and happy marriage.' And with those words she turned and ran back the way she had come.

But not before Lucinda had seen the glint of tears in

her eyes and she knew how much it must have cost Serafine to come here today. She silently thanked the woman a million times over for setting the matter straight, because now she could get on with the rest of her life without having to fear that Zane might be tempted by the beautiful St Lucian girl.

'Wait!' Lucinda called, belatedly wanting to thank Serafine for her help in turning Helen's house into a restaurant, but already Serafine was out of earshot. Or if she wasn't she didn't want to hear whatever else Lucinda might have to say.

When Zane came home Lucinda told him about Serafine's visit. But she didn't tell him the real reason for it, only that she'd come to wish them all the best in their married life. And as far as Lucinda could see there was now not one single thing on the horizon to spoil it for them.

Life would be totally perfect.

EPILOGUE

JEREMY ELLIS ALEXANDER was born the following spring. Tim was delighted to have a baby brother and Lucinda had never been happier. Zane was the perfect husband and father. Tim was now their legal son and she had given up her business to become a full-time wife and mother.

'Happy?' asked Zane one evening when both their children were in bed and they were able to settle down to some quality time together.

'I've never been happier,' answered Lucinda.

'No regrets?'

'Not one.'

'I have one tiny one,' he admitted.

Lucinda looked at him with a frown.

Zane tried his hardest to hide a smile. 'I wanted a daughter.'

Lucinda knew he was joking because they'd talked about this before. But she went along with him. 'Then, my darling husband, I think we should go upstairs and try for another baby right now. And I think we should go on trying until we get what we want.'

Zane didn't have to say another word.

THE INCONVENIENT
LAWS OF ATTRACTION

**BY
TRISH WYLIE**

Trish Wylie worked on a long career of careers to get to the one she wanted from her late teens. She flicked her blonde hair over her shoulder while playing the promotions game, patted her manicured hands on the backs of musicians in the music business, smiled sweetly at awkward customers during the retail nightmare known as the run-up to Christmas, and has got completely lost in her car in every single town in Ireland while working as a sales rep. And it took all that character-building and a healthy sense of humour to get her dream job, she feels—where she spends her days in reindeer slippers, with her hair in whatever band she can find to keep it out of the way, make-up as vague and distant a memory as manicured nails, while she gets to create the kind of dream man she'd still like to believe is out there somewhere. If it turns out he is, she promises she'll let you know...after she's been out for a new wardrobe, a manicure and a make-over...

For everyone who kept me from hitting the ground
until I remembered how to fly again.

CHAPTER ONE

'OLIVIA BRANNIGAN. Blake Clayton?'

Continuing to rehearse below her breath, she tugged firmly on her jacket as she walked up the path. 'I represent Wagner, Liebstrahm, Barker and DeLuise, and…'

It was what came after the 'and' she was struggling with most. Informing him of a legacy was one thing, breaking the news that came with it was another, even if the news was several weeks old. But the man would have to live in a cave to have avoided hearing about it and they couldn't have been *that* close—not when it had taken so long to find him.

The Stars And Stripes hanging from the porch fluttered gently in a welcome hint of air movement as she took a deep breath and pressed the buzzer.

'I regret to have to inform you…'

She hated that line. Last time she'd made a death notification it had been more than difficult: It had been the final act in a series of events that altered the course of her life.

When the door swung open, a heavy-set man holding a half-eaten hamburger looked her over from head to toe.

'Mr Clayton?'

'Yo, Blake!' he yelled.

'What?' a voice yelled in answer.

'Anyone suing you?'

'Not this week.'

'Guess you can come in then.' The man grinned, issuing an invitation with a jerk of his head.

Following him down the hallway, Olivia's heels clicked in an even, businesslike rhythm while she focused on their destination and the man she would discover when she got there. In a matter of seconds he would be a living, breathing person instead of someone she'd spent entirely too much time trying to picture in her mind while she was searching for him. She wouldn't have to imagine what he looked like or wonder how he was going to react.

The mystery would be solved.

Anticipation built with each step as she prepared for the disappointment of reality when compared to the uncharacteristic flights of fantasy she'd been engaged in of late. There was just something about this case that got to her, and with her track record when it came to emotional involvement in the workplace, that wasn't good.

The sooner she wrapped it up, the better.

The room she walked into was in a chaotic state of construction. There were four men in it: two chewing hamburgers, one hunkered down sanding a door-frame and another by large windows covered in opaque plastic. Since the man by the windows was looking at her, she approached him and held out a hand. 'Mr Clayton, I'm Olivia Brannigan from—'

'Over here, sweetheart.' A deep, rough-edged voice drew her gaze to the man sanding the door-frame.

'You're Blake Clayton?' She turned around. Considering how long it had taken to find him, she had to be sure. 'Blake *Anders* Clayton.'

There was a snort of laughter behind her.

'Thanks for that.' He shook his head, dropping his chin

and lifting a hand to remove the dust mask from his face as he stood up. 'So what'd I do this time?'

Opening her mouth to set his mind at ease, anything resembling coherent thought scrambled when he set the mask aside and looked directly at her. The room contracted; it was suddenly smaller and tighter and felt as if all the oxygen had been sucked out of it. Everything in her peripheral vision blurred as her gaze locked on him and doggedly refused to let go. But who could blame a girl for staring?

A little heads-up on how he looked might have helped.

Six foot two, possibly three, lean at the waist, broad at the shoulders, with short spikes of unruly chocolate-brown hair and dark eyes that sparkled with more than a hint of the guy a girl's mother would warn her about; Blake Clayton was the living, breathing definition of *seriously smokin' hot*.

When her gaze dropped briefly to the jut of a full lower lip that begged for immediate, audience-be-damned attention, Olivia ran her tongue over her teeth. Would he taste as good as he looked? She'd just bet he did.

The woman inside her purred appreciatively. The professional forced a businesslike tone to her voice. 'I represent the legal firm of Wagner, Liebstrahm, Barker and DeLuise, and—'

'Bet that's a bitch to put on a business card.' A corner of his mouth hitched with amusement.

The woman sighed contentedly while the professional frowned at how difficult it was to focus. Her flights of fantasy had fallen woefully short of reality.

'Is there somewhere we could talk?'

'We're talking now.'

'Mr Clayton, I'm afraid I have bad news,' she announced more bluntly than she'd intended.

'I heard,' he said tightly, the change in him immediate.

Her voice softened 'I'm sorry for your loss.'

'Don't be.' Stepping past her to lift a mug from a worktop, he sat down beside one of the men eating lunch, spreading long, jeans-clad legs while tipping the rim of the mug to his mouth. 'We done?'

Glancing at their audience, she found them watching her like some kind of floor show. Surely he didn't want to—

'You can say whatever you have to say in front of them,' he added as if he'd read her mind.

Considering her thoughts since she'd laid eyes on him, Olivia sincerely hoped he hadn't.

'No secrets among friends,' the man who'd answered the door added. 'Offer us the right money, we could tell you enough to get him arrested in a half-dozen states.'

'And Canada,' added a chorus of voices.

'You got something you need me to sign, hand it over,' Blake said over the sound of laughter. 'You can mail whatever memento I've got coming my way.'

'I'm afraid I can't do that,' Olivia replied patiently. 'You're the sole beneficiary. He left everything to you.'

'Everything?'

'Yes.'

'All of it?'

'Yes.' She nodded. He obviously hadn't known. Not that the flat tone to his deep voice gave any indication he was happy with the news. The majority of people would have been turning cartwheels.

'There's no one else?'

Confused by the question after her use of the term 'sole beneficiary', she shook her head. 'No.' Thanks to Charles Warren's will, his son was one of the richest, most powerful men in America. 'I know it must seem daunting to take on the responsibility of—'

'Such a great legacy?' A dark brow lifted. 'Wrong tactic, Miss—what did you say your name was again?'

'Brannigan.' She tried not to be piqued by the fact he hadn't remembered. 'Olivia Brannigan.'

'Well, *Liv*—' he leaned forward '—someone should probably have warned you: I don't give a rat's ass how great a legacy it is. I don't want it.'

Was he *insane*?

'I understand you need time to process everything, b—'

'There's nothing to process.' Setting his mug down, he pushed to his feet. 'What I *need* is to get this job done.'

As she faltered, he walked past her and picked up his tools. She'd never been in such a surreal situation. What did he expect her to do? Go back to the office, walk up to her boss and say, *Sorry, no go, we have to find someone else we can give billions of dollars' worth of property and assets to?* They could hold a raffle.

When she didn't move, he glanced at her from the corner of his eye. 'Am I supposed to tip you?'

Seriously?

The professional stepped forward and smiled smoothly. 'I don't think you understand, Mr Clayton. Allow me to make it clear: you're it. Whether you want it or not, you're the sole beneficiary of Charles Warren's will.'

'*The* Charles Warren?' an incredulous voice asked behind her.

'Your father made his wishes very clear.'

'*Father?*' said the same incredulous voice. 'You're kidding me, right?'

So much for no secrets between friends…

He took a step forward and lowered his voice. 'Look, lady, I get that you're trying to do your job but, in case you didn't get it, allow *me* to make it clear: *I'm not your man*. So unless you're planning on setting down that briefcase and picking up a power tool, I suggest you hightail it back to Manhattan and tell Wagner, Liebstrahm, Barker and DeLuise—or whoever it is you answer to further down the food chain—they best find a distant Warren relative they can lay this on. I have a life. I'm not living someone else's.'

'This isn't going anywhere,' she insisted with a deceptive calmness that masked the effect his proximity was having on her body.

'Maybe not,' he allowed. 'But *I* can.'

What about the life he'd said he had? Olivia found herself wondering if there was a woman in it; one who would miss him when he was gone. Somehow she doubted he was the type to stick around long enough to let anyone get that close. Judging by the number of addresses she'd discovered in various different states—some of which he'd only resided in for a matter of weeks—any relationships he had were short-lived. Not that looking the way he did would leave him short of company for long.

Squaring her shoulders, she reached into the front of the briefcase he'd mentioned and held out her hand. 'I'll leave my card. When you've had time to think things over—'

'Not gonna happen.'

Olivia stood her ground.

'I take it you can find the door on your own?'

Okay. If he wanted to play hardball, she'd play. Lowering her gaze to his broad chest, she relaxed her shoulders and took a step forward, standing within inches of his large body and slowly lifting her lashes until she was looking deep into dark eyes. She ran her tongue over her lips and smoothed them together, watching his gaze lower and smiling when he frowned. She spoke in a low voice just loud enough for their audience to hear.

'Tomorrow morning...all over the state...thousands of

Warren Enterprises employees are going to turn up for work. I'd like to be able to tell them they'll have a job a month from now, especially in this economy.' She angled her head. 'Wouldn't you?'

Reaching out, she set her business card on a plank of wood beside him before turning on her heel and walking back down the hall. Her hand was on the door when she heard a voice ask, 'Charles Warren is your old man?'

Silence.

'You know my cousin Mike works for Warren Tech? He's got a wife and three kids…'

Olivia smiled as she opened the door. There was no question in her mind she'd be seeing him again.

She was looking forward to it already.

Blake had always liked cities better than small towns. Cities were anonymous, no one wanted to poke their nose in anyone else's business; it was easy to disappear into the crowd in the city. At least it used to be…

'Isn't that your lawyer lady from the other day?'

'Yup.' He'd known she was there from the minute she appeared with her mismatched set of friends. His gaze found her in the crowded bar with the same accuracy as a heat-seeking missile.

'Sure fills out a pair of jeans,' Marty observed.

'I'm sure Chrissy will be glad to hear you noticed.'

'I'm married, not blind.'

Without her power suit she was different, there was no denying that. Dressed in hip-hugging jeans and a scoop-necked blouse that highlighted her narrow waist, pale skin and the swell of her breasts, it had been hard to ignore her presence since she arrived. If there'd been the remotest chance they might cross paths again, he would never have accepted Marty's usual end-of-the-working-week invitation for a beer and a game of pool in the nearest bar to the restoration project they'd been working on in the West Village. But it was too late now. It was only a matter of time before she crossed the room.

Bending over to line up his shot, Blake's gaze was drawn upward by the appearance of distinctly feminine, jeans-clad thighs at the other side of the table.

'Gentlemen...'

And there she was.

Sinking a ball into the pocket in front of her before standing upright, he set the end of his cue on the floor, folding his fingers around it as he looked her over.

American pool halls had once been the exclusive realm of men who smoked cigars and drank beer while they growled and spit tobacco. Young truants cleaned tables and floors, racking balls for new games while they learnt pool hustling and miscreant behaviour. It had been a poor man's men's club, devoid of female company.

Blake couldn't help thinking it would have been better for Olivia Brannigan if it had stayed that way.

Because the second his gaze swept over her, he had the exact same reaction he'd had the first time. The tips of his fingers itched to be thrust into her sleek blond mane and mess it up until it framed her face the way it would after a session of the kind of hot, sweaty, mutually gratifying sex he doubted she'd ever experienced. He wanted to set the pad of his thumb on her full lips and smear away any hint of lipstick before he set his mouth on hers, to place a palm to the small of her back, melding her body to his as—

He took a measured breath. 'Want to play, do you?'

'So it would seem.'

There was a brief spark of light in the cool blue of her eyes that suggested a challenge did it for her. The fact she'd answered in a low voice which could easily have been described as sultry didn't escape him either.

'Reckon you can take me on?'

'I guess we'll find out, won't we?'

Indeed they would.

'Rack 'em up, Marty.'

While Marty handed over his cue and started gathering balls from the pockets, Blake stepped around the table to issue a low warning. 'If you're over here to discuss my luck in the legacy department, you can forget it.'

'Well, I don't know about you,' she replied brightly, 'but *I'm* off the clock.'

Looking down at her from the corner of his eye, he saw her check the face of a neat wristwatch. A wave of softly curled hair hid her profile from him until she lifted her chin and added, 'As of an hour and ten minutes ago.'

'You're the kind of gal who's never off the clock.'

'Maybe you don't know me as well as you like to think you do.'

'Meaning I should get to know you better?'

'We're set,' Marty said.

Blake held out an arm. 'Ladies first.'

'Don't hold back on my account.'

He leaned towards her as he walked by. 'Never do.'

'She know what she's doing?' Marty asked as he joined him at the bar.

Time would tell. Since every town had a pool table, they'd been one of the few constants in Blake's life growing up. He knew a lot of pool was simple physics. Watching men who'd been playing for most of their lives, he knew it was all about the angles, the action and reaction, knowing when to exert a little force and when to use a finer touch. He'd learnt a lot of valuable life lessons from the game of pool. Watching Olivia Brannigan in action turned it into something altogether different: less physics, a whole lot more to do with chemistry.

Didn't matter which side of the table she took her shot from, either way it provided the kind of view any red-blooded male could appreciate. When she was on the far side of the table, bending over the cue, it allowed a clean line of sight down her blouse to a hint of coloured ribbon that became the equivalent of an apple in Eden. A side view let his gaze skim over the sweep of her spine, the sweet curve of her ass, down legs that would never have ended if it hadn't been for the floor.

As a card-carrying one hundred per cent red-blooded male, his body's reaction to her was understandable. *Unwelcome*, considering what she represented, but understandable. Not to mention a timely reminder he'd obviously been all work and no play for too long. Something he would have to rectify, soon.

Standing upright, her gaze collided with his as she walked around the table with a hint of a smile on her face. Turning, she bent over to line up her next shot, gently swaying her hips from side to side: *right in front of him*.

'She's good,' Marty said appreciatively as a ball ricocheted off a cushion directly into a corner pocket.

Blake's silent agreement had nothing to do with her pool skills. Setting his bottle down, he stepped towards her. 'Hustling me, Liv?'

'It's Olivia,' she informed him, twisting on her heel and backing away with a sweet smile. 'And if I wanted to hustle you, wouldn't it make more sense to play badly before making a wager?'

'You just popped over here to play a friendly little game of pool with the boys?'

Standing still long enough to efficiently chalk the tip of

her cue with short, sharp movements, she continued walking around the table. 'Is that illegal?'

'You're the lawyer. You tell me.'

'I know it's not in the state of New York.' She bent down. 'But I'd have to check the rules for Canada.'

When another ball disappeared off the table, she smiled a small, satisfied smile as she stood up.

'I'm not talking to you about the will.'

'I didn't ask you to.'

'You're going to.'

'You can see into the future?' A flicker of amusement sparkled in her eyes. 'Wouldn't happen to know next week's lottery numbers, would you?' She shrugged a shoulder as she walked around the table.

'Not that you need them.'

'You know I can take out a restraining order against everyone at your firm if I have to…'

'Be a pretty long list of names.'

'I'd know who to put at the top.'

When he set his palm on the wooden edge of the table as she bent over her cue again, a brief upward flicker of her lashes revealed what might almost have been taken for hesitation. Did she realise she was playing in the big leagues? *Good.* Considering her options? *More likely.* Looking back down the cue, she swayed her hips again, a move that could have been misconstrued as preparation for her next shot to the untrained eye. Blake recognised it for what it was.

What bugged him was how well it was working.

'I didn't know you'd be here, if that's what you're suggesting,' she said in a matter-of-fact tone.

That he was more likely to believe. How could she when he hadn't known himself until a little under an hour ago? He never did from one Friday to the next. It was the nature of the job, the story of his life.

There was a sharp click and another ball disappeared off the table. 'But, since we are here, maybe if you told me what the problem is, we could talk about it.'

'We could—' he rocked forward as she stood up '—if I hadn't already said I *wasn't* talking about it.'

'You brought it up.'

'Pity you're off the clock then, isn't it?'

She sighed. 'It's a lot of money to ignore.'

If money meant as much to him as she seemed to think it should, she might have a point. Rocking back on his heels, Blake stilled, his gaze scanning the crowd. He wondered what she'd think if she knew, given the option, he'd prefer every cent to disappear. He didn't want to be responsible for thousands of people's lives. A rolling stone could end up looking like the Rockies if it gathered that much moss.

'I know it's an intimidating prospect, running a company that large—' her voice softened to a hum that washed across his senses with the same burn as the first sip of a smooth Scotch '—but there are people who have been with the company for decades…'

She was playing the guilt card again? When he looked down at her from the corner of his eye, she tacked on a soft smile and added, 'They could run it for you.'

'That's exactly what I—'

Blake set an arm across Marty's chest when he stepped forward to add his two cents.

'You think I'm avoiding this because the leap from carpenter to CEO is beyond me?'

'I didn't say that.'

Not in so many words. But she was smarter than that.

Tucking the cue into the crook of his arm, he folded his arms across his chest. 'So you're gonna do what? Talk me through a pie chart? Help me pick out a suit for the office? Hold my hand while I go play with the big boys?' He narrowed his eyes and smiled tightly. 'Don't think I don't know what you're doing, sweetheart.'

'It's called trying to help.'

'That's going well.' He nodded. 'For future reference—insulting my intelligence? Not a good place to start.'

Stepping around her to get to the bar, he lifted his bottle and tilted it to his mouth. His gaze followed her in the mirror as she followed him.

'I wasn't trying to insult you,' she said in the sultry tone that travelled directly from ear to groin.

Blake gritted his teeth. Sure she wasn't.

'Would hardly be the best way to start a working relationship, would it?'

What working relationship?

'It's really none of my business why you want to turn your back on billions of dollars. But, like I said, the responsibility isn't going anywhere. The board's hands are tied. You have controlling interest in the company—they can't do anything without your say-so. It's how your father wanted it.'

The woman didn't know when to quit.

Her voice lowered. 'I know you're still grieving. The last thing you want right now is—'

'Grieving?' A burst of sarcastic laughter split the air as he set his bottle down with a slam and turned on her, frustration mixing with anger. 'Lady, you don't know anything about—'

'Blake…' Marty used a hand on his upper arm to hold him still and allow him time to take a breath; his voice was filled with the same rock-steady calmness he'd used in the old days when Blake had been prone to standing up to guys twice his size. It had been the curse of the new kid and since Blake had always been the new kid…

With a nod from Blake to indicate he was good, Marty

stepped away. Blake looked at Olivia and saw she was staring at him with a mixture of suspicion and curiosity. Not fear, he noted. Part of him respected the hell out of her for that when guys much bigger than her had been known to baulk. It was enough to make him step towards her again; the fact she stood her ground increased his perception of her as a woman who could hold her own.

He shook his head when his libido buzzed with the numerous possibilities that came with the thought. Strong women who could take him on both in and out of the bedroom—preferably without needing emotional entanglement—did it for him. Always had, always would.

He took a short breath. 'As much of a pain in the ass as you're proving to be, you didn't deserve that.'

She arched a brow. 'Is that an apology?'

'It's as close as I ever get to giving one.' A corner of his mouth tugged wryly. 'I'd run with it if I were you.'

Considering him with a tilt of her head, she came back with, 'Know what you could do to make it up to me?'

Wasn't going to like this, was he?

'You know what the Warren Foundation is?'

And now he was an idiot again.

'They're hosting a benefit a couple of weeks from now. If you showed up—even for an hour or two—you might encourage people to reach deeper into their pockets to impress the new owner of the company.' She shrugged as if she didn't care one way or another if he showed. 'As well as helping a worthy cause, you can meet some of the people who work for you in a social environment.'

'You're one of those women who calls in the middle of the night to tell a guy his phone is ringing, aren't you?'

When she continued calmly holding his gaze, Blake wondered if she ever cut loose. What would it take to get the real Olivia Brannigan to come on down and—the question immediately jumped to the front of his mind—just how far was she willing to go to get what she wanted?

He was tempted to find out.

'It's at the Empire hotel,' she added with a nod as if he'd already agreed, her gaze lowering to travel over his body from the middle of his chest to the toes of his boots.

Digging in the pocket of his jeans as he turned away, Blake frowned at the immediate response the invisible touch had on him. 'I'll think about it.'

'It's formal. You'll need a tux.'

'I said I'll think about it.' Tossing several bills on the bar, he turned to face her again. 'While I do, I suggest you think about what you're getting yourself into.'

'Meaning?'

He stepped closer, forcing her to lift her chin. Searching her eyes, he noted the spark it took a blink of long lashes to conceal and smiled a slow smile. As aware of him as he was of her, wasn't she? Unless he was mistaken—which he doubted—she'd known exactly what she was doing around the pool table. She thought she was in control of the situation and could use her sexuality to her advantage. He was fine with her attempting the latter, but if she wanted to take him on at more than a simple game of pool there were a few things she needed to understand.

'Meaning you gamble, you best be prepared to ante-up, so think long and hard about what you're bringing to the table, sweetheart.' He closed the gap and moved his face closer to hers, his gaze lowering to her mouth, then shifting sharply to tangle with hers. 'Because I'll collect, and I think you know exactly what I mean by that.'

The almost imperceptible narrowing of her eyes told him she'd got the message. Blake smiled lazily when the next thing he saw was a spark of light that said it was 'game on' as far as she was concerned.

It was enough, for now.

Walking across the crowded room without looking back, he swung open the door and stepped out into oppressively humid air, pacing up and down on the sidewalk while he waited for Marty. Maybe he should just get the hell on with it. The sooner he did something about offloading property, dumping stocks and signing things over to people who might want them, the sooner he could leave it behind and get on with his life. It was more constructive than waiting around for a hint of grief to make an appearance. Especially when the lack of it was starting to make him feel like a heartless son-of-a—

Shouldn't he feel *something*? When he looked inside at the dark corner where he'd tucked away his memories of the past, there was nothing: a big, black vacuum of nothing. That should have made him feel guilty; but nope, still nothing. Not a thing. As if part of him was missing.

When the door swung open again, he made a snap decision. 'Think you can keep an eye on the crew?'

'Sure.' Marty's shrug wouldn't have inspired confidence if Blake hadn't known him better. 'Do what you gotta do, *Anders*.'

That was that, then. Another thought occurred to him and he began to smile as they walked towards the subway station. No reason he couldn't have some fun along the way. Never let it be said he couldn't multitask.

Olivia Brannigan's life was about to get interesting.

CHAPTER TWO

'Now, remember, you can't kill a client.'

Be prepared to ante-up? He would *collect*? Who did he think he was? Inside her head, Olivia was laughing the derogatory laugh of a woman in serious self-denial. But who was she kidding? She hadn't been able to resist a battle of wills since the second grade.

'Potential client,' she corrected, tucking her cellphone between her shoulder and her ear so she could reach into her briefcase. 'And right now I'm not even sure I can work with this guy. He's—'

'Sexy as sin?' Jo asked in a tone that suggested she was batting her eyelashes.

'Not helping.'

Grimacing at the pain from a rapidly growing blister, Olivia checked the address on the folded piece of paper and lifted her gaze to the numbers above the doors in a neat row of brownstones. Being forced across the Brooklyn Bridge in searing midday temperatures to play messenger girl in the most inappropriate heels known to messenger-kind helped—as did the fact he'd demanded the files *immediately*.

Difficult clients she could handle. Raging sexual attraction to a man she might have to work with on a daily basis, *not so much*—and since a simple game of pool had felt a tad too much like foreplay...

Catching sight of a dumpster outside one of the houses, she checked for traffic and crossed the street.

'You know what *would* help?' Jo asked.

'I'm not having sex with him,' she answered firmly, wondering just who it was she was trying to convince. 'He's a *client*.'

'*Potential* client and you can't tell me you haven't thought about it.'

Not under oath she couldn't. Her imagination had been having a field day, particularly in the restless hours she spent tossing and turning in bed before her alarm went off.

The number above the door matched the one on the piece of paper. Olivia's voice lowered to mutter, 'Here we go.'

'I'm just saying...' cajoled the voice in her ear.

'I know. I meant I've got to go. I'm here.'

'Ooh, call me back with the blow-by-blow. I want details. What he's wearing. How he looks. What he says. Don't leave *anything* out!'

Olivia smiled. 'I'm hanging up now.'

With her cellphone tucked safely away in a pocket at the front of her briefcase, she put her jacket on over her sleeveless blouse and buttoned it up as she walked up the steps to the open door, pausing to remove her sunglasses and check her appearance in a nearby window. Loud music echoed from the floor above while she sidestepped debris in the hall and sighed heavily. No air conditioning. *Great*.

'Hello?'

The downstairs rooms were deserted but on the first floor landing the loud squeal of a power tool drew her to a room where she waved a hand to have her presence acknowledged. 'Do you know where I can find Blake Clayton?'

The man pointed upward before continuing his work. On the second floor, she met a semi-naked man in shorts.

'Blake Clayton?'

'Top floor.'

Of course he was. She brushed her shoulder on a wall while trying to avoid a stepladder, and then twisted her neck to search for signs of damage to her jacket as she moved to the next set of stairs. It was getting hotter by the floor. Wasn't hell supposed to be *downstairs*?

'Whoa!' Two large hands grasped her elbows when she caught her heel on a loose floorboard and stumbled forward. 'Careful, lady.'

Scowling briefly at the dusty fingerprints semi-naked man number two had left on her linen sleeves, she forced a smile as she lifted her chin. 'Olivia Brannigan from Wagner, Liebstrahm, Barker and DeLuise. I wonder if—'

'You should get that printed on a T-shirt,' a rough-edged voice said above her head, sending a shiver of awareness down her spine. 'Save time on the introductions.'

Her gaze lifted to where he was leaning casually on the banister, her breath catching. Did he look sexier than he had the last time? How was that possible? Before she could open her mouth, he turned and disappeared, leaving her to make her way up the stairs and peek through several doors until she found him again. It was beginning to feel as if she'd spent half her life looking for him.

'I have the papers you requested.'

Swiping a cloth over his large hands, he ignored her and began staining the carved piece of wood laid out on a workbench in front of him.

'It's a list of personal assets and properties.'

'You'd think I'd know that if I requested them.'

'You didn't request them?' Not that she'd been there when the call came in, but Carrie on the front desk was normally pretty reliable when it came to—

'Stalking me again?'

'I have *never* stalked you.'

'Some guys might be flattered.'

'I don't think your ego needs any help.'

Had she said that out loud? Maybe he hadn't heard her over the echoing music? The corner of his mouth twitched. Oh, he'd heard. Well, as overjoyed as she was to be a source of amusement to him…

Looking for somewhere to set the file down, her gaze fell on a heavy bed with ornate scrollwork on the posts and a huge headboard carved with curling leaves and branches; incredibly lifelike birds and squirrels were scattered at random intervals. It was practically a work of art. Olivia glanced sideways at him as dense, dark lashes lifted and his intense gaze locked with hers.

The temperature in the room jumped several degrees, a bead of moisture trickling into her cleavage. The woman immediately wanted him to lick the same path it had taken. Even the professional's mouth was dry.

'Did you make that?' She waved the file in the general direction of the bed.

'Showing an interest in what I do the next step in your plan, is it?'

She had to know. 'Are you this judgemental with everyone or have I been singled out for special attention?'

'You want my special attention, sweetheart, all you got to do is ask.'

Shaking her head, Olivia wondered why she was surprised. She should be getting used to it by now, and the accompanying reaction from her body when she realised she was standing within a few feet of evidence he was *good with his hands*.

'You can leave the file.'

He was dismissing her after she'd trekked halfway across the city in temperatures the equivalent of the face of the sun? Olivia didn't think so. Not till they'd cleared up a few things.

'Mr Clayton.'

'Blake.'

'If I'm going to work with you—'

'Work with me. Hmm.' He dropped the brush in the can of wood stain. 'Still haven't figured it out, have you?'

'Figured what out?'

'Didn't you go to some fancy law school to learn all this stuff?' He wiped his hands on the cloth again.

'All *what* stuff?'

'Stuff like who calls the shots.' Tossing the cloth aside, he continued holding her gaze. 'You won't be working *with* me. If I hire you, you'll work *for* me.'

Technically true, but she could argue a technicality. 'I'm employed by—'

'Seriously—' the corner of his mouth tugged again '—consider the T-shirt.'

'*They* pay my salary.'

'And Warren Enterprises pays *them*. Way I figure it— since I've just been handed the keys to the kingdom—that means *I* pay you.'

Not until he signed the papers, he didn't.

'So if I'm stepping up to the plate—' a potent smile began to form on his lips '—you get to be at my beck and call, day and night. I holler, you come a-runnin'.'

Summoning the professional demeanour expected of an employee of one of Manhattan's most respected law firms, Olivia stopped herself from running through the endless possibilities involved with being at his beck and call, day and *night*.

Wait a minute. She was playing messenger girl so he could prove a point? Her eyes narrowed. 'Trust me when I tell you I'm not paid anywhere near enough for that kind of service. I'm good at what I do, Mr Clayton. That's why I'm here. I can work *with* you, represent Warren Enterprises' best interests and ensure a smooth transition for you to head of the company. But I'm not going to bring you coffee, I'm not going to jump when you snap your fingers—' she stepped across the room and set the file down beside him '—and I'm not a messenger.'

The slow hand clap started when she was halfway across the room. 'You practice that on the way over?'

Olivia kept going, the words 'justifiable homicide' jumping into her head. She was almost at the door when a large hand captured her elbow, causing her to jerk in surprise. She swung round. She was a heartbeat away from allowing the training of her former career to kick in before she realised where she was and who he was. Horrified by what she might have done, she took an immediate step back, bumping her spine into the doorframe.

She closed her eyes. 'Please tell me you didn't stain this doorframe before I got here.'

When she opened her eyes again, he was setting a palm on the wood beside her neck. Immediately glancing at her one remaining escape route, she watched another large palm flatten on the wall beside her waist. Like it or not, she wasn't going anywhere. Not without hurting him.

'Nice speech,' he commented.

'I meant every word of it,' she said with a lift of her chin, trying desperately to ignore the erratic thudding of her heart. One man should *not* be that breathtakingly gorgeous up close. She took a deep breath and stifled a moan. He absolutely shouldn't smell that good.

For a second she felt a little bit dizzy. She could really do with some air that wasn't filled with testosterone. Everything around him contracted and went fuzzy again, leaving her unable to focus on anything but him. Her gaze went to the full lip she was so attracted to—the one she wanted to kiss, lick with the tip of her tongue, suck and maybe even nibble a little.

When had she got so sexually frustrated? She tried to remember the last time she'd been on a date—the kind with the remotest possibility of ending in great sex.

Well, *that* was depressing.

'If you're not up to the task, maybe I need to find another lawyer.'

Thank you! It was exactly how she needed him to be. If he added charm—or, worse still, seduction—to an already potent mix, she would be in deep, deep trouble.

Not to mention naked. *Fast.*

'For the record, Mr Clayton, underestimating me is a bad idea.' And she wasn't kidding about that. Thanks to her former profession, she could have him flat on his face on the floor in less than ten seconds and when it came to her present occupation— 'I've been assigned to the Warren accounts since I joined the firm. I know the company inside out and back to front. You won't find anyone more qualified than me.'

He frowned. 'You worked for Charlie?'

'I met him.' She softened a fraction at the mention of the father he'd lost. 'But I didn't work with him.'

'For him,' he corrected.

'*With* him,' Olivia argued. 'That's how we do things at the firm: we work *with* our clients. It's a long-term partnership based on mutual trust and common goals.'

'I'm not looking to get married, sweetheart. I'm looking for someone to do what I tell them to do when I tell them to do it. Is that a problem for you?'

'You tell me to jump, I ask how high?'

'Works for me...'

Over. Her. Dead. Body.

Her breath caught as his head lowered. *What was he doing?* When he stilled, his face inches away from hers, every fibre of her body ached with an almost crippling desire to be kissed. How could she dislike him and want him so badly at the same time? Maybe the heat was getting to her. They said people did things they wouldn't normally do during a heatwave. Olivia just wished she was the kind of girl who hid behind excuses when they did something stupid.

'What's wrong, Liv?' he asked in a low, excruciatingly sensual rumble. 'Not good at taking orders?'

'Depends what they are,' she replied in an equally low voice. And what they were doing at the time.

Don't go there, the professional warned the woman.

When a knowing smile began to form in his eyes, she frowned, swiftly getting back to business with, 'I won't do anything illegal.'

'Unless I'm mistaken, a big part of your job would be to make sure *I* don't.'

'Whatever trouble you get into away from Warren Enterprises isn't my concern.'

'I'll keep that in mind when I'm only allowed to make one phone call.'

The man had no shame. Raised on a diet of discipline and obeying the letter of the law, Olivia had never considered herself the kind of woman who would be attracted to a bad boy but apparently she'd been wrong. Who knew?

'I assume I can't schedule any meetings north of the border.' She analysed his reaction with a tilt of her head.

'Probably best not,' he replied without giving anything away.

She sighed heavily. 'Is this how it's going to be every time we try to have a discussion?'

'That's what we're doing, is it?'

She aimed a narrow-eyed glare at him.

'So what's it to be?' he asked. 'We got a deal?'

'I'm not going to come running when you holler.'

'Where's the fun in that?'

'I think you'll find it would be more fun for one of us than it would for the other.' Inwardly groaning at the fact she was encouraging him, she moved on to the next point. 'I have no problem working outside office hours, but you can't call me in the middle of the night.' Her errant gaze dipped to his tempting lower lip. 'There are boundaries I'm not willing to cross.'

'Like never mix business with pleasure—you have a rule on that, right?'

As it happened, yes, she did. Olivia *liked* rules. It was part of the reason she loved the law so much. A single set of rules for everyone to follow, there for the protection of all. It was an even playing field and she was less likely to mess up as badly as she had before if she worked within the boundary lines.

'Yes,' she replied.

'Why am I not surprised?' He shook his head. 'But you're still not getting it. I'm not questioning your capabilities. If they sent you to deal with this, I'm sure you're up to the task.'

Then what—?

'But here's how it's gonna be, sweetheart. The only advice you get to give me is law-related—you don't question my decisions unless it's something that might get me prosecuted, sued, or both—and there's no First Amendment for free speech in this arrangement. We clear on that?'

Olivia blinked in surprise as the woman inside her purred like a cream-filled cat. Suddenly she understood why Charles Warren had chosen him as his heir. He didn't sound like a man who didn't want the responsibility of the legacy that had been left to him; he sounded like a man taking charge and more than up to the task.

It was exactly how Jo had described him: *sexy as sin*.

Who *was* this man? Tilting her head, she looked at him more closely. Her curious gaze whispered over his face, taking in every detail from the crease lines at the corners of his dark eyes that suggested he laughed more often than she'd had evidence of thus far to the small scar on his chin her fingertips itched to touch while she asked how he'd got it.

'*Liv*—' his deep voice held what sounded like an edge of warning, forcing her gaze back up '—we clear?'

Right. Negotiations. *Focus.*

'No middle of the night phone calls,' she insisted.

She could do the maths. Her dreams of late plus that voice on the other end of a phone line multiplied by the never-ending heatwave they'd been experiencing equalled the road to insanity.

'Not unless it's something I need an answer to right away,' he allowed.

'You holler expecting me to come running, I'll tell you to go to hell.'

'I'll keep that in mind.'

Olivia nodded firmly. 'Then we're clear.'

'Good. I want to go through personal assets first. Can you handle that area?'

She nodded again.

'We'll start looking at the properties on the list you brought me tomorrow.'

Another nod, then, without warning, the tip of his thumb brushed back a strand of hair from her neck, the light graze of work-roughened skin sending a sharp jolt through her body that tightened her abdomen.

'Now that's settled,' he said in a seductively rough rumble as the backs of his fingers trailed lazily over the sensitive skin below her ear, 'I think we should discuss your rule…'

What rule? She had a rule?

Blake watched the movement of his fingers, his head lowering. 'How set in stone would you say that is?'

Oh, this was bad. This was *really* bad.

It felt good.

Breathing ragged, pulse erratic, her heart threatening to beat a hole in her chest, Olivia felt the hand on the wall slide to her waist. The fingers on her neck moved to her nape as his gaze focused intently on her mouth.

'Blake…' Her voice was thick, the unspoken plea caught somewhere between *stop* and *don't stop*.

The tip of his thumb brushed against her jaw as his gaze lifted to search her eyes and a slow smile began to form on the sensual curve of his mouth. 'That's a step in the right direction.'

'What is?'

'My name. It's the first time you've used it.'

It was?

'Say it again,' he demanded, his smile growing. 'Practice makes perfect.'

The sparkle of amusement in his eyes snapped her to her senses. What was she doing? He wasn't caught up in the moment the way she was. He knew *exactly* what he was doing. Worse still, he knew what it was doing to *her*.

Never in all her born days had she been more tempted to play the tease and hand out a little payback. But since she was pretty sure playing up to him would give him exactly what he wanted...

As if the wall would magically move and place some distance between them if she just pushed hard enough, Olivia leaned back and fought through the fog of residual desire and a rapidly descending red mist to form a lightning-fast list of defensive moves she could use without causing any lasting damage. It didn't matter that he was bigger and stronger than she was—she'd been trained for that. Step one: verbal warning.

She opened her mouth and sucked in a sharp breath.

'Hey, Anders, we're going to the deli,' a voice called, making her aware the music had stopped. 'You coming?'

'Did I mention I owe you one for my new call sign?' He stepped back and responded with, 'Right behind you.'

Olivia frowned as she exhaled. He couldn't leave. They weren't done yet.

'We'll pick this up in the morning—nine a.m.—first place on your list.' To her complete astonishment and immeasurable irritation, he flashed a grin that knocked her on her ear. He even had the unmitigated gall to add a wink before telling her, 'I'll bring my own coffee.'

There. Weren't. Words.

Olivia followed him through the door and down the hall. 'Mr Clayton—'

'We're back to Mr Clayton again?'

'This is a professional relationship, nothing more.'

'Don't remember agreeing to that.'

'As I said, there are lines I won't cross.'

'Lack of adventure noted.'

'It's got nothing to do with a lack of adventure.' She

followed him down the first flight of stairs. 'You seem to be under the impression—'

'That you're attracted to me?'

'I am *not*—' Her breath caught when he turned without warning and she found herself looking directly into his eyes again, up close and personal.

How did that keep happening?

Placing large hands on lean hips, he nodded firmly. 'Add lying to me to the list: *don't do it*.'

'I wasn't—'

'Yes, you were.'

Well, yes, she was, but he couldn't know that. What part of dealing with a lawyer hadn't he got? Did he think she couldn't look into his sensationally dark, fathomless eyes and conceal what she wanted? How did he think lawyers negotiated with other lawyers?

She lifted her chin. 'You're not the first difficult client I've worked with, Mr Clayton.'

'Blake. And worked *for*...'

The question slipped out before she could stop it. 'Does this tactic work for you with women?'

'This one isn't?'

'No.'

'You sure about that?'

Oh, he was annoying.

The corners of his mouth twitched with barely suppressed amusement as he dropped his hands to his sides. 'You want something to eat before you head back?'

'No.' She faltered, remembering the manners drummed into her from an early age. 'Thank you.'

'Then I'll see you tomorrow.' He flashed another grin as he turned away. 'Try not to miss me too much.'

Olivia shook her head as he jogged down the second flight of stairs. The man was unbelievable. But if he thought he had the upper hand, he was mistaken. She could maintain her professional decorum under trying circumstances. No way was she screwing up two careers inside a decade. Henceforth, she was enacting a strictly at arm's length policy. No encouraging him through verbal engagement, no rising to the bait—even if she had to bite her damn tongue off—and if he ever got close enough to do the whole addle-her-senses thing he was so good at...

Yeah, she really couldn't let that happen again.

Continuing down the stairs, she allowed herself a brief foray into fantasy where she could hand out a little quid pro quo. In that universe she would have the same effect on him as he had on her. She would play on it, winding him tight, getting him so hot and hard for her, he'd *beg*—

She took a deep breath and blew it out with puffed cheeks. Since that train of thought wasn't helping any, she started looking for loopholes in his stupid rules as she made her way back to the office. Women like her didn't have hot, steamy casual sex with men like him—even if they were tempted.

Really, *really* tempted...

CHAPTER THREE

BLAKE walked around the vast expanse of space that had been one of Charles Warren's last purchases. The view of Central Park's lush green treetops, rolling lawns and duck ponds beneath the sharp contrast of the Manhattan skyline was spectacular, there was no denying that. But could he see himself living there?

Hell, no.

'Pretty amazing, isn't it?'

Olivia followed him around with a file cradled against her breasts and the same transparent enthusiasm as a realtor looking to make a sale. It wouldn't last. After several days in her company one-on-one, Blake knew she started the day in a better mood than she ended it. He liked to think he'd had something to do with that.

'Amazing would be one word.' Turning towards her, he pushed his hands into the pockets of his jeans. 'Little over the top, don't you think?'

Everything about the place had been over the top since they arrived on the red-carpeted steps outside one of New York's most prestigious landmark hotels. A liveried doorman had touched the peak of his cap as they stepped into the revolving doors. The manager had met them in the foyer, shaken Blake's hand and practically fallen over himself to make it clear he could get anything from anywhere at a moment's notice. There had even been maids in traditional uniforms who magically scurried out of sight when the doors to the penthouse were opened. Blake had hated every moment.

Even while he stood inside three floors of some of the largest square footage known to Manhattan apartment-kind, he could feel the walls closing in on him.

'It's...opulent...' she replied after some thought.

'Opulent would be another word.'

Looking at the long sofas placed at right angles to a massive wood-burning stove, he took his hands out of his pockets, sat down, and stretched his arms along the cushions at the back. As he set his feet on the glass coffee table, he saw Olivia frown in disapproval before she controlled her expression.

'You could redecorate.'

'What would you change?' he asked, idly swaying his feet from side to side. When she frowned again, he stopped the movement and stifled a smile. There were times she made it too easy for him.

'It's not mine to change.'

'If it was...'

Her gaze flickered briefly to his, then away. She'd been doing that a lot. Different sides of an elevator, more than an arm's length away when they were walking, subtle side-steps if he moved any closer—he'd noticed them all and each and every one had either amused or bugged him to varying degrees.

'I'm afraid that doesn't fall under the remit of my professional opinion,' she replied as she wandered around the room.

'Humour me.'

'I don't think that's in my job description either.' Smiling sweetly, she turned to face him; she decided several items of expensive furniture provided a safe distance between them.

'Kills you to even think about breaking a rule, doesn't it?'

'Your rules, not mine.'

Seemed to Blake she'd been pretty damn close to breaking a rule when he'd been inches away from kissing her. But since thinking about reminding her had the same effect on his body it always did, he lifted his feet and pushed upright. 'May as well check out the bedrooms.'

'I'll wait here.'

'Where I lead, you follow.'

She lagged behind more noticeably on the second floor than she had when he'd looked at the large kitchen with its black marble counters or through the rounded bay windows overlooking the reflecting pool and plantings in the plaza's courtyard. She remained silent while Blake threw open random doors to increasingly decadent bedrooms and mosaic-tiled bathrooms; each and every room possessed a chandelier whether it needed one or not.

Feet sinking into the deep-piled carpeting in the master bedroom, he walked across to the giant bed, sat on the edge and bounced a couple of times before looking to where Olivia watched warily from the door.

'Take a seat.' He patted the covers. 'If we're lucky we might see a camel before the harem gets back.'

'It's not that bad.'

He held her gaze and waited.

'Okay,' she admitted reluctantly. 'Maybe it's a *little* over the top.'

It was the kind of understatement the place could use in Blake's opinion. Restless again, he walked to the windows. 'Remind me how many properties I own in Manhattan.'

'Fifteen.'

'Current value of this place?'

'Fifty-three million...give or take...'

When he looked over his shoulder—brows raised in disbelief—she cut a smile loose, distracting him from the ridiculous price tag with how it lit her up from inside. She should smile like that more often, he thought, forcing his gaze to look out of the window again. For a moment, when her reflection came into focus on the glass, he watched her looking at him. Her smile faded as she bit her lower lip and checked him out from head to toe. She did that a lot. It was her 'tell' in the game they were playing, his way of knowing she was bluffing when she'd claimed she wasn't attracted to him.

'Sell it,' he said firmly, forcing his gaze from her reflection to the clear blue sky above the city. 'There's a private jet on that list, isn't there?'

'Three of them,' she replied with resignation. 'Let me guess, you want to sell them, too.'

'Explain to me why I need three private jets.'

'Senior executives use them to—'

'Join the Mile High Club?' His gaze sought her reflection again. 'Understandable. The restrooms on commercial airlines can be a tad tight when it comes to wriggle room.'

She sighed. 'You're very cynical when it comes to people with money. Isn't that going to be a problem when you look in the mirror?'

It had taken long enough. Blake bit back a smile, 'Is that an opinion?'

Pressing her lips together, she breathed deep, striving for what remained of the patience he'd been purposefully testing. 'I don't see why we're visiting these properties if you're going to sell everything.'

'And now she's questioning my decisions...'

'Fine,' she replied. 'That's eight properties and three private jets, bringing your running total to approximately one hundred million dollars.'

Resisting the addition of a *congratulations*, she opened her file, made a note, snapped it shut and left the door. Blake turned away from the window and followed her into the hall, his mood improving by the second.

'Hold off on the sale of a jet. Apart from the Mile High possibilities, we might need it when we go to look at the overseas properties.'

She swung around to face him. 'You never said anything about taking trips overseas.'

'Is your passport out of date?'

'That's not the point.' She frowned as he closed the gap between them. 'I can't drop everything and go jetting around the world with you so you can spend five minutes looking at each of the places you're planning on selling.'

'Who says I'm planning on selling them?'

'Aren't you?'

'Depends.'

'On what?' She arched a brow as she looked into his eyes. 'Whether or not they look like something thrown together from a tsar's yard sale?'

The corners of his mouth twitched. 'Meaning you think it's more than a *little* over the top. Could *you* live here?'

'No,' she admitted reluctantly.

'What would you do with it?'

She sighed again. 'Sell it to someone who could.'

'Uh-huh.' He nodded.

When he stepped into her personal space, she lifted the file and hugged it against her breasts like a shield. Glancing away, she held her breath for a moment before sizing him up from the corner of narrowed eyes. 'You want to look at every property, no matter where it is?'

'Maybe.'

'Do you have any idea how many properties you own overseas?'

'Is there a prize if I get it right?'

'It could take *weeks* to visit all those countries.'

'On a tight schedule, are we?'

Cocking her head, she came back with, 'You tell me.'

Closing his thumb and forefinger over the file, Blake tugged and watched her reaction when the instinctive tightening of her hold caused the backs of his fingers to brush against the skin between the lapels of her jacket. She sucked in a sharp breath, her eyes darkening a shade. But when he smiled in response, she let go of the file and lifted her chin in defiance.

The woman had a unique way of looking at him: As if she was hinting heavily she could drop him to his knees with very little effort and he was lucky he was still upright. It was one heck of a turn-on for a man whose personal preference ran to strong-willed women. They were right up there with women whose confidence in their abilities added to their sex appeal and who knew what they wanted in the bedroom and weren't afraid to demand it. She'd find he could be very accommodating with the latter. He might not stick around long enough for anything to get complicated but when he took a lover there was no question in her mind he was one hundred per cent with her.

He took a great deal of pride in that.

Turning his upper body to make room, he opened the file and pretended to read the contents. 'You want to tell me what the real problem is?'

'Meaning?'

The way Blake saw it, it was one of two things. 'Either you hate the idea of taking an all expenses paid trip around the world—' which didn't seem likely '—or you hate the idea of taking that trip *with me.*' Closing the file, he turned and lowered his voice. 'Worried about breaking your mixing business with pleasure rule if you spend more time with me?'

'No.'

'No?' he challenged softly.

While tapping the spine of the file with the palm of his hand, his gaze wandered over her face. The arch of her brows, the length of darkly spiked lashes, the sparkle of warning in her eyes—she really was something.

'There's a reason that rule exists,' she said tightly.

'Office romance gone bad?'

'That would be none of your business.'

'Married, huh?'

There was a small noise that almost sounded like a growl. 'You are the most—'

'I've been told.'

'You really don't care what people think, do you?'

It was said as if it was a completely alien idea to her, something Blake found telling. Appearances mattered, judging by the number of times she straightened the endless selection of suits that had to be *hell* to wear during the heatwave they were experiencing, but it went deeper than fashion. Her personality was adjusted according to the demands of her profession, even if it meant suppressing what she thought and felt—the latter explaining why she'd been able to follow his rules for as long as she had when Blake wouldn't have lasted five minutes.

'Does it matter?' he asked.

'If you care?'

'What people think…?'

She frowned. 'Yes.'

'Why?'

Long lashes flickered as she looked over his shoulder and considered her answer. 'Because the attitude we project tends to influence the attitude we receive in return.'

A hint aimed at him, no doubt.

Blake laid the file against her breasts when she looked into his eyes again. 'Then maybe you should try being nicer to me.'

Her mouth opened then closed, her lips pressed together to stop herself from saying what she thought.

Time for a little prodding. 'Know what I think?'

She took the file. 'I'm sure I'm about to.'

'I think frustration makes you testy.'

The hand holding the file snapped down to her side. 'If I'm testy it might have more to do with the fact you're hardly the easiest person in the world to work with.'

'Work *for*.' When she turned and headed for the stairs, Blake followed at a leisurely pace. 'You're really struggling with that part of the arrangement, aren't you?'

'I'm not used to winging it,' she announced in a voice that echoed down the hallway. 'Did it occur to you if you told me what it is you're thinking of doing with all this money, I could plan ahead?'

'Lack of organisation isn't the reason you're frustrated, sweetheart. You don't want to think about kissing me. Trouble is, you can't *stop* thinking about it. You're angry. Probably blame me for it...'

She spun around to face him at the top of the stairs. '*You* are the most arrogant man I have ever met.'

'You should get out of the office more.'

'This attitude won't help in the boardroom.'

Since he didn't plan on ever stepping into one it was a moot point. Blake smiled a slow smile at how close she was to losing her temper. It was about time. If he'd been her, she'd have strangled him by now.

'Don't do that,' she warned.

His smile grew. 'Do what?'

'You know exactly what you're doing.' She wrinkled her nose. 'And trust me when I tell you, you *really* don't want to play this game with me.'

'Don't want to like me, do you?'

'If I did, you wouldn't be making it easy,' she muttered. Scowling, she turned a little too quickly. Her eyes widened when the toe of her shoe slipped over the edge of the top stair and her heel caught. The file dropped from her hand as she swung her arms out to her sides for balance, grasping for a railing just out of her reach.

Before she fell, Blake snagged an arm around her waist and hauled her round against him.

Grabbing handfuls of his shirt, she uttered a breathless, 'Thank you.'

'You're welcome.' He smiled. When she tried to move he tightened his arm. 'Give it a minute.'

If her heart was thundering as loudly as his it would do them both good. He'd never have forgiven himself if she'd tumbled headlong down two flights of stairs. But as her breathing slowed, his concern, tempered by relief, was replaced with something more potent.

She blinked once, twice; the fingers holding his shirt loosened and her palms flattened as if she couldn't stop herself touching him.

Then her gaze lifted.

With her guard down, he was shown how truly expressive her eyes could be. Curiosity threaded with need, confusion tangled up in desire—and those were just the things he could recognise. Everything she was feeling danced in the light of a blue flame he was drawn to with the same compulsion he felt to draw air into his lungs. Did she have any idea what she was willing him to do when she looked at him like that? The effect it had on his body when she had her hands on him? He searched her eyes for a hint of power in the knowledge, feeling marginally better when he couldn't find it. If she knew, he'd be in trouble.

As her palms slid across his chest and down his arms, he tensed, unable to stop the telltale sign from happening; it was almost as if part of him wanted her to know. Her gaze lowered as she felt it happen, hands sliding down to his elbows, her mesmerized expression suggesting she was watching what she was doing as if it was some kind of out-of-body experience.

Blake studied the soft sheen of hair against her forehead before lowering his chin and looking at her hands where they rested against the rolled up sleeves of his shirt. Such small, fine-boned hands, such a light touch, but he could feel the effect of it scorching into his veins, transforming his blood to the same consistency as lava: thick, heavy and fiery-hot.

Damn, they were going to be good together.

When their gazes lifted, she focused on his mouth.

'Do it,' he demanded in a huskier voice than he'd have preferred.

'Do what?' she asked in a thick voice.

'Kiss me.'

She shook her head.

'You're thinking about it.'

'No, I'm not,' she lied.

Moving his fingertips in slow, soothing circles on her back, Blake silently willed her to forget whatever was holding her back. 'If you spent less time trying to pretend this isn't here we might get along better.'

'I don't want—'

'Yes, you do.' Raising a hand, he used the backs of his fingers to brush her hair off her cheek. 'You've been thinking about the kiss that never happened.' Just like he had. 'Wondering what it would have felt like if it had…'

Why should he be the only one tortured by it?

Turning his hand, he traced his fingertips over her jaw to the sensitive skin below her ear. She leaned her head towards her shoulder in response, dutifully arching her neck to allow him access as her eyelids grew heavy. Her body couldn't hide the truth any more than his could.

'Don't you want to find out, Liv?' He dipped his head and saw the lift of her chin bring her mouth closer to his.

'You'll have to fire me first.'

'I'm not going to fire you,' he answered in the same husky-edged tone as before. 'You'll have to quit.'

'I'm no quitter,' she replied, an incredibly sensuous smile curling her lips.

'Neither am I.'

When she breathed deep and exhaled on a hum of what sounded distinctly like pleasure, he stifled a groan. The slow slide of her lower lip between her teeth, the hooded gaze she had focused on his mouth—she was testing him, wasn't she? If she was, it was a test he was failing.

Sensing the balance of power shifting, he took a short breath. 'Word of warning, sweetheart—I never said anything about making it impossible for you *not* to kiss me.'

There was a flash of light in her eyes.

'I think…' she said in an intimate tone as one of her hands slid back up his arm, '*you…*'

Blake's body tightened with anticipation as she angled her head and moved closer.

'Should…' A fingernail trailed tantalisingly over his skin where the collar of his shirt touched his neck; her palm flattened as she lowered her hand to his chest. 'Keep this apartment…'

What?

Lifting her chin, she brought her mouth closer to his. She looked up at him and informed him, 'The ceilings are just about high enough for your head to fit in here.'

Fixing him with a heavy gaze that said *gotcha*, she leaned back against his arm and smiled tightly. 'You might want to let me go now. I'd hate to have to hurt you.'

Judging by her expression, he doubted she'd hate it that much. But conceding a hand didn't mean the game was over. Releasing her, he stepped to the side and bent down to retrieve the file. 'What next?'

She arched a brow as she tugged her jacket straight.

'On the list.' He waved the file back and forth.

'Another penthouse...'

'Any chance this one doesn't have a guy in a top hat at the door?'

'I doubt it.' She reached for the file.

When she tried to take it from him, Blake held on, waiting for her to look into his eyes before he smiled meaningfully.

'We're not done.'

She lifted her chin, a smile sparkling in her eyes and hovering on her lips.

'I know.'

Relinquishing the file, he turned towards the stairs and held out an arm. Suddenly the next few weeks didn't feel like such a chore to him any more. He should probably thank her for that. As it was, he would have to up his game. The way he saw it, by the time he was done she was either going to kiss him or kill him.

He smiled as she stepped past him. 'Mind the step...'

Olivia rolled her eyes.

CHAPTER FOUR

BREATHING deep, Olivia mentally continued banging her forehead on the edge of the breakfast counter.

Stupid, stupid, stupid...

She should never have told her friends how tough she was finding it dealing with Blake. They'd talked about little else ever since. There was no escape from him now.

'I think you should quit working with him,' Jess said over the rim of her mug. 'If you're on a diet, it doesn't make sense to hang out by the dessert cart.'

Jo cut to the chase. 'Apart from the fact you work with him, what's the problem? Run it past us.'

'It would just be sex.' Olivia shrugged.

Jess stared at her as if she'd lost her mind, 'Not seeing that as a problem unless it's really *bad* sex.'

Nope. She was pretty sure it would fall into the rock-her-world category, judging by her response to his most recent tactics. Since she'd started slipping up and playing him at his own game, he'd pulled out the big guns, breaking down her defences with his irreverent sense of humour and targeting her biggest weakness with his obvious skills in the art of seduction. He was, without doubt, the most annoying man she'd ever met but at the same time there was something almost roguishly charming about—

Jo narrowed her eyes as she saw Olivia smile. Olivia

avoided her gaze and cleared away her breakfast things. 'I've got to go. I have calls to make before I meet Blake at Union Square.'

'There doesn't automatically have to be a consequence for letting go,' her friend said from the bedroom door.

Grabbing her jacket and her briefcase, Olivia pushed her feet into her favourite pair of heels. 'There's no point letting go with a guy like him.'

'They don't all have to be keepers.'

'I'm not looking for a keeper.'

'Doesn't mean you don't recognise keeper qualities when you see them... Great sex is on everyone's wish-list.' She shrugged. 'I say go for it if this guy does it for you. How often does *that* happen?'

They both knew the answer to that.

'It's about time you had some fun...'

Blake most definitely fit the bill in that department. There wasn't anything about him that yelled steady, stable or long-term. Worse came to worst, she'd already vowed she'd do her damnedest to make sure he caved before she did. If there was one thing that bugged her more than arrogance, it was smugness.

'Know what I'd do if I was in your shoes?' Jo asked.

'Shoes are off limits. Don't make me do an inventory.'

Linking their arms at the elbow, her friend walked her to the door of their apartment. 'I'd cut my inner bad girl loose and make it impossible for *him* not to kiss *me*.'

Except the problem wasn't about kissing or not being kissed by him. Maybe—just once in her twenty-eight years—she should have fun with a man who could take her on with a distinct chance of winning: a trait she'd long since recognised in Blake. If anything, with her background, it would be freeing as hell.

'It's okay, you know.'

'What is?' She blinked.

'Letting go a little and having fun. You can't stay shut off for ever, Liv. Not when you have so much to give.'

Despite the fact she wasn't sure she was ready to take that step, Olivia hugged Jo before heading down the hall to the elevator. If she let go and allowed herself to get emotionally involved again there was a danger she might open a door it had taken a long time to close. She had an all-or-nothing personality but, with a great deal of time and effort, she liked to think she'd learnt to control her emotions the way she should have a lot earlier. It was better that way, safer for all concerned. Unfortunately, at times it was also something else...

Lonely.

And now she was starting her day even more in need of fun than before. *That would help.*

'I'm starting to think you sleep in a suit.'

'What makes you think I wear anything in bed?' Walking along the busy sidewalk, she glanced sideways at him while yet another inner bad girl comment slipped off the tip of her errant tongue.

'Understandable in this weather,' his deep, rough-edged voice replied. 'Dial up the air con, wait for that first whisper of cool air on your skin as you kick off the covers.' He nodded. 'I'm a big fan of sleeping naked.'

Great, now she'd spend the rest of the day thinking about him lying naked in bed—waiting for her—watching while she dialled up the air conditioning and came back to join him so they could pick up where they'd left off.

She was beginning to feel like General Custer with advance knowledge of how the battle would turn out.

'A cold shower would help,' she muttered.

Blake took a step closer when she stopped walking,

leaning in to speak in a low, seductive tone that tested what remained of her resolve. 'Turn up the temperature some, we could take one together.'

The woman whose needs had been suppressed for entirely too long dipped a hip towards him, lowered her lashes and fixed her gaze on the strong column of his neck. It would be so very easy to set her lips to the tanned skin there. She could work her way up to his strong jawline, whisper in his ear every little detail of the things she wanted him to do to her beneath the running water of that shower. Looking into his eyes, she caught her lower lip between her teeth.

'You say a lot without words.'

'I have two words for you,' she said in a purposely low voice.

'Let's go?' he asked optimistically.

'We're here.' She smiled.

He glanced at the doorway of the large building beside them, his expression changing. 'You sure?'

'Yes.'

'Right.' A muscle tightened in his jaw but, before she could ask what was wrong, he was halfway up the steps.

Inside the grand foyer, he headed for an area filled with comfortable chairs and large pieces of furniture, his back to her—shoulders tense—while Olivia introduced them to the receptionist and asked for the manager.

'How long did he own this place?' he asked when she stood beside him.

Olivia checked the file. 'Eight years.'

'Ms Brannigan, Mr Clayton, I'm Frank Gains, manager of—' He was shaking Olivia's hand when his gaze shifted. 'Blake?'

'Frank.' Blake held out a hand as he turned.

The older man seemed flustered. 'I didn't know.'

'Didn't you?'

'I didn't make the connection. Your name...'

A confused Olivia looked from one to the other. She had absolutely no idea what was going on. Blake nodded curtly as he dropped his arm to his side. When he walked back towards the entrance without saying anything more, she blinked in surprise.

'He's Charles Warren's son?' the manager asked.

She nodded. 'I take it you've met before.'

'His guys did some of our renovations a few years back. It's not easy to find skilled craftsmen these days, especially for an older building. We didn't want to lose the character of the place...'

Ironic as it was, considering how little of it they'd taken up, Olivia thanked him for his time and followed Blake outside. Standing on the sidewalk, she squinted against the bright sunshine, raising her hand to shield her eyes as she scanned the crowd until she found him across the street in Union Square. He was watching a woman dressed as the Statue of Liberty walk by, plastic torch tucked under her arm while she adjusted the foam crown on her head.

His gaze collided with Olivia's as he waited for her to get close enough to hear him say, 'Sell it.'

Not that it was a surprise, but, 'You didn't know, did you? When you took the job there, you didn't know it was your father's hotel.'

He frowned.

'I asked the manager how he knew you.' When he turned away, she followed him. 'You obviously weren't close.'

'Good guess.'

'But he left you everything.'

As they walked into the farmers' market set up at one end of the park, Blake slowed his pace before stopping to look over some of the produce. 'There's very little left of the Warren gene pool. In the end I figure he had a choice between the family bastard and a cousin who's doing time for illegal possession. If it narrows it down for you, I'm not the one wearing an orange jumpsuit.'

Olivia digested the information while he headed for another canopied stall that had caught his interest. The market in a tree-filled Union Square was an orgy for the senses, with plenty to distract the eye, but her mind refused to let go of the opportunity to get answers to some of the questions she'd had before she met him.

'Here.'

She leaned back when he held a small lump of something creamy-coloured in front of her face, 'What is it?'

'Goats' cheese, with honey.'

'I'll pass.'

'That lack of adventure again.' Shaking his head, he popped the sample in his mouth and chewed. 'Your loss.'

Frowning at the comment, she reached out a hand and snagged another sample from the stand, chewing with a smirk before she blinked in surprise.

'Good?'

'Mmm.' She nodded appreciatively as she swallowed, falling into step beside him as he headed for the next stand. 'Did you know you were his heir?'

'Did it look like I knew when you told me?' He stopped and turned towards her. 'Try this one.'

Olivia accepted the sample without protest, her grimace making the corners of his mouth twitch.

'No?'

'What *was* that?' She frowned at the produce on the stand in disgust.

'Celeriac.'

Taking a mental note of the offence against taste buds,

she followed him to the next stand while trying to scrape the taste off her tongue with her teeth, 'How well did you know him?'

'Does it matter?'

'It's unusual for someone to leave everything they own to a complete stranger.'

'If you say so.' He turned around. 'Here.'

'What is it?' Her eyes narrowed, the celeriac memory causing suspicion.

Blake twirled the sprig of small green leaves between his thumb and forefinger as he held it closer to her mouth. 'You tell me.'

When he brushed one of the leaves over the parting of her lips, she lifted her arm and wrapped her fingers around his to still the movement. A jolt travelled up her arm as soon as skin touched skin, instantly tightening her nipples against the suddenly abrasive lace of her bra. Her gaze locked on his as her breath caught. How did he *do* that?

'I've got it,' she said in a low voice.

'When you put your mind to it, yes, you have.'

She fought the need to smile at the compliment.

Raising their hands, he held the sprig of leaves beneath her nose, the backs of long fingers resting lightly against her lips. 'Breathe in.'

'I know what you're doing,' she mumbled as she dropped her hand.

'What is it?'

Six foot three of increasingly irresistible male, but since Olivia assumed he meant the leaves, she breathed in.

'Mint?'

'Close your eyes.'

'Why?'

When the movement of her lips became a caress against his fingers, his gaze darkened. 'Just do it, Liv.'

Concerned she might give in to the temptation to kiss him if he kept looking at her with an intensity that made it feel as if he were absorbing her into him, Olivia closed her eyes. Theoretically, if she couldn't see him she could pretend he wasn't there. If it wasn't for the touch of his warm fingers against her lips, the scent she found even more addictive with the addition of a hint of mint and the fact she could almost *feel* the air crackling between them.

Somewhere inside her head a white flag was waving.

'Keep them closed.' The rumble of his rough voice resonated through her body, echoing in a hollow place inside her, the existence of which had been denied for a long time.

He really did do it for her.

'Open your mouth.'

While her imagination ran riot with erotic thoughts of him issuing a similar set of demands in a more intimate setting, she took a short breath, opened her mouth and tilted her head back. Placing a small sliver of the leaf on her tongue, the tip of his finger lingered on her lower lip, tracing its shape before sliding along her jaw.

A languid smile formed on Olivia's lips as she chewed.

'Chocolate.' She sighed contentedly. She could taste mint-flavoured chocolate. Apart from the fact it removed the bitter taste of celeriac from her mouth—which was thoughtful of him—combined with his touch, it was bliss.

'That good?'

'Mmm.' Swallowing, she slowly ran the tip of her tongue over her lips, rolled them in on themselves and parted them to draw a deeper breath as she opened her eyes.

'I should taste it,' he said roughly.

'You should,' she agreed.

Reaching out, she wrapped her fingers around his wrist, sliding them down over the back of his hand. He took a half-step closer, head lowering as she lifted her chin. *God*, he was tempting. She *really* wanted to kiss him—just once, so she knew what it was like and didn't have to spend the rest of her life wondering—but with a twist of her thumb and forefinger she had her prize. The opportunity was too good to miss as she held the mint up in front of his face and smiled victoriously.

Realisation sparkled into a glint of amusement when his gaze locked with hers. 'Not what I had in mind.'

'Wasn't it?' She batted her lashes innocently.

'No.'

When his fingertips curled around the nape of her neck, Olivia's heart punched against her breastbone.

Kiss me, the woman in her willed breathlessly.

'You're doing it again,' he said roughly.

'Doing what?'

'You know what.'

She did. That it was having such a strong effect on him was empowering. She wanted him. He wanted her. For the first time it felt that simple to Olivia. All she had to do was take one teeny tiny step over the line and—

Kiss me. The words hovered on the tip of her tongue.

Leaning forward, Blake nudged the tip of his nose off hers, the tantalising jut of his lower lip within millimetres of her mouth as her eyelids grew heavy. Another hand lifted to frame her face, thumb brushing her cheek. The long fingers of the hand on her neck flexed into her hair and made her sink back into his touch. She knew he'd played the seduction card to stop her from asking questions he didn't want to answer. Knew it and should have been irritated by it, but she really didn't want him to stop.

'Blake.' She exhaled his name like a plea.

'Do you know what I hear when you say my name?'

It took considerable effort to shake her head. How was

she supposed to fight this? It felt futile, especially when she couldn't summon the energy to try.

He slid his cheek across hers so he could whisper in her ear. 'I hear: *I want you.*'

'Blake—'

'This guy bothering you?' a voice asked loudly.

Olivia stifled a groan. 'You got to be kidding me.' She turned and glared at the man standing beside them as Blake took a step back. 'Slow day for parking violations?'

'I'm on indecent exposure watch—reckoned if I left it another minute, I'd have to arrest you.' He jerked his head towards Blake. 'Who's your friend?'

'Didn't we agree you guys would stop doing this when I left high school?'

'Should I get my notepad out to take his details?'

She sighed heavily. 'This is Blake. He's a client.'

'Really.'

From anyone else it would have been a timely reminder. 'Blake, my brother, John Brannigan.'

'Last name?' Johnnie asked him without blinking.

'Clayton.'

'Uh-huh.' He nodded. 'And how do you spell that?'

'You run a background check on him, I'll kick your ass,' Olivia warned.

'That's assaulting a police officer.'

'Running a background check on every guy you ever see me with is harassment.' She smiled sweetly. 'Don't make me tell Mom.'

'Go right ahead. She'd appreciate a call more than once a month.'

Low blow.

A call came in on the radio attached to his shoulder, *'Unit nineteen, ten fifty-four…'*

It was an echo from her past—one that still had an effect on her, even after six years. Suddenly it was dark; she could feel rain falling, see coffee cups falling into a trash can and hear a voice calling her name. But at least she didn't get nauseous any more. That was something.

'Gotta go.' Her brother looked Blake straight in the eye. 'Be seeing you.'

Letting the latter slide, Olivia took an automatic step forward. 'What happened?'

'You know the ten codes as well as I do.' He backed away, pointing a finger at her. 'Stay out of trouble.'

Shaking her head, she watched him jog across the square until he disappeared. When she looked at Blake she found a familiar glint of amusement in his eyes.

'You have the police codes memorised?'

'They were funny about that at the academy.' She checked her watch. 'We're early for the next viewing; you want to stop and get coffee?'

His brows lifted. 'You were a cop?'

'Yes.'

There was a brief pause, then, 'Makes sense.'

It did? She glanced sideways at him as they walked to the crossing.

'How long were you a cop?'

'Six months.'

'Not cut out for it?'

'Something like that.' Waiting at the kerb for the signal to change, she glanced up at him again. The smile on his face was different from any of the ones she'd seen before. Her eyes narrowed. 'What?'

'New information. I'm absorbing it and trying to get a mental picture.' He nodded. 'The uniform's working for me.'

Olivia rolled her eyes when his smile turned into something more familiar. The man was incorrigible.

As the traffic stopped, he laid a large palm against the inward curve of her spine, leaning closer as they crossed the street. 'Not the only one who clams up when it's something they don't want to talk about, am I?'

'Meaning I should stop asking questions?'

'Some subjects are easier than others,' he allowed, his gaze focused on their destination. When they were standing in front of the coffee shop, the scent of roasting beans rich in the air, he dropped his arm and turned towards her. 'Why do you need to know?'

'Knowing you better might make my job easier.'

'That the only reason, is it?'

Feeling distinctly as if she were crossing an invisible line, Olivia breathed deep and answered honestly. 'No.'

When he stared at her, she tried to find a way of justifying it that made as much sense to her as it would to him. 'It's part of a cop's job to know why people do the things they do. Everyone has a story—you just have to put the pieces together so you can understand it.'

'You're not a cop any more.'

'True, but lawyers are taught the same thing. If it makes you feel any better, I do it with everyone I meet.' Her gaze lowered to the open collar of his white shirt when she found it difficult to look into his eyes.

If she was being completely honest, she would tell him she didn't want to know everyone's story as badly as she needed to know his. But the fact she'd admitted it to herself was the much needed reminder that had been missing in the square when she came so close to kissing him. Giving in to sexual attraction was one thing, caring about him was another and if she knew more than she already did…

Reaching out, she pushed open the door to the coffee shop. 'Of course you have the right to remain silent.'

'Tell me you still have the handcuffs.'

She chuckled softly. 'You'll never know.'

CHAPTER FIVE

The place was a wreck.

Sidestepping debris, Blake looked up at the broken panes of glass; the beat of several flapping wings echoed around the huge expanse of space as they interrupted the resident wildlife. Most of the second floor had fallen in, as had part of the roof, but he was willing to bet there were some great views of the river from higher ground.

'How sound is the structure?'

'Will need shoring up before we put the second floor back in, but it's not bad.' The man who had met them with the keys stayed with Liv while Blake walked around. 'The details are in the architect plans I brought with me.'

The commercial elevator was shot, but the staircase beside it looked sound enough, barring a few missing steps. Placing a palm on a large wooden crate, Blake bent his knees, twisted his waist and bounced onto the surface, slapping his palms together when he was upright and reaching out a foot to test the first step. When he put weight on it, there was a loud crack.

Liv took a step forward. 'Be careful.'

When he flashed a grin, she rolled her eyes.

Testing each step before he put his full weight on it, he made his way up to what was left of the second floor.

'If you fall and break your neck I'll make sure they put

"terminal stupidity" as the cause of death on the certificate,' she called up to him.

'Feel free to administer mouth-to-mouth,' he called back.

The properties outside Manhattan were looking better already. He'd been right; the view across the river was great from the second floor—area was ripe for development, too. Be nice to have something within a block of the river that wasn't a generic high-rise. Considering how many of them there were, the building had been lucky to survive. When he looked through a gap in the floorboards, he saw Liv peering up at him, her expression a mixture of disapproval and concern. He smiled.

Placing his hands on his hips, he jerked his head in invitation. 'Come on up.'

'I'm good where I am.'

'Where I lead, you follow.'

'Yeah—' there was a short burst of sarcastic laughter '—that's not happening this time.'

'Not good with heights?'

'I have a very long bucket list.'

Making his way across the floor, he stretched tall to see out of the windows on the other side, frowning as he rocked back. View was pretty good from that side too but it was also familiar. He didn't get it. Had it been so damn difficult for his father to talk to him? Considering the envelope he'd been carrying around for longer than he cared to admit, he supposed it had. They'd been one as bad as the other.

The silent admission made him search inside again for a hint of grief or regret. If he was the kind of guy who shared things with others, he might have admitted his biggest fear was that the great vacuum of nothing would expand like a black hole and swallow up the parts of him that still felt alive. Had he felt the same way after his mom died? No. He'd felt relief then. Partly because she was out of pain, partly because it was over and he was free. He'd felt guilty about the latter, but he'd sat on it, tucked it away and pretended it wasn't there. Maybe that was when it had started. By ignoring it instead of dealing with it, the small dark place where he'd buried the things he didn't want to face had quietly grown while he covered up the emptiness with good times, fun, laughter and the kind of freedom of choice he'd never had before.

A hand lifted to his pocket to check the envelope was safe in a reflex born of habit. It was too late to change the past, so what was he doing revisiting it? Why hadn't he told Liv to sell everything and get back to him when it was done? He didn't need to look at it. Now he had. If there were more places he liked the look of he could find himself having to make decisions he hadn't—

'Blake?'

'I'm coming down.'

Fifteen minutes later they were walking in silence to the water taxi and he was holding a cardboard tube in his hand. Slanting a glance at Liv, he found her smiling.

'What?'

'I find it amusing we've looked at millions of dollars' worth of property and this is the first one you've liked.'

'I'm not a millions of dollars' worth of property guy.'

'You are now.'

'I haven't said I'm keeping it.'

'You're thinking about it,' she said brightly. 'That's a step in the right direction.' When he didn't reply, she took a short breath. 'You just need to find your place in this. Give it time, you'll get there.'

'Do I need to remind you about the rule on advice?'

Stopping in front of the taxi landing, she turned towards him. 'What's wrong?'

'What makes you think there's something wrong?'

'You were different when you came back down.'

'Was I?'

'You can talk to me, you know.' She shrugged a shoulder, downplaying the offer with, 'It won't go any further—attorney/client privilege.'

'I've known you two weeks.'

'Is there someone you *can* talk to?' Angling her head, she studied his eyes and blinked in surprise. 'Wow.'

'You don't know me,' he said tightly.

'Does anyone?'

'Don't make this personal, sweetheart. It's not.'

'Fine. You're right. I don't need to know.'

When she turned and walked away, Blake frowned. He hadn't lied to her, hadn't said anything overly harsh, so why did he suddenly feel the need to make amends?

'I'm not going with you.'

She stopped and turned around.

'I live a few blocks from here.'

Jerking his head to the right, he watched her gaze follow the movement and waited for her to put it together. If she'd been quick enough to figure out his reaction to the hotel, he reckoned she was smart enough to work out he hadn't known about the warehouse on his doorstep either. It was getting to the point where it felt as if he should check the ownership on the lease agreement for his apartment.

He'd thought it was a sweet deal at the time.

When awareness entered her eyes, she nodded.

Blake felt some of the tension roll off his shoulders when she didn't push. 'I'll take a look at these plans and let you know my decision.'

'Okay.'

'And, unless I'm mistaken—' he pointed the end of the tube at her '—you've got a party to go to.'

'The benefit.' She nodded again. 'Will you be there?'

He glanced over her shoulder. 'Taxi's coming.'

As it got closer, the yellow and black hull tearing a swathe of white froth on the surface of the water, she remained still, the corners of Blake's mouth tugging in reaction to her inability to leave him.

'*Go*. I'll see you later.'

She clasped the handle of her briefcase in both hands and swung it around her body as she turned away, flashing a bright smile over her shoulder before she sashayed down the dock. Thought he was wrapped around her little finger, didn't she?

Dropping his chin, Blake chuckled as he left. He was going because he owed her; that was all. Knowing him, spending 24/7 with her would bring their relationship to a swift end. And he wasn't ready for that. Not yet.

She owed him for this, *big time*.

'…with the continued support of Warren Enterprises, naturally we hope to see…'

His attention had long since left the continuing conversation between a State Senator, the Mayor and varying executives who surrounded him. They didn't need his full attention for him to follow the gist. Not when he'd decided part of the role of a brand new billionaire was to assume an air of boredom, more interested in the never-ending supply of champagne circulating on round silver platters than anything business-related. Not that it happened too often, but getting drunk suddenly held a lot of appeal to Blake.

Draining his ridiculously fiddly glass, he reached out an arm to set it on a tray as he smiled at the waitress who'd been circling him. 'Don't suppose there's any chance you could get me a good old-fashioned American beer?'

When the bottle arrived, he ignored the accompanying glass, rewarded the waitress with a smile and turned to look at the couples on the dance floor, his gaze seeking the one thing he did find interesting. In a sea of black and white it didn't take much to pick out the shimmering gold highlighted in her hair by surrounding strings of fairy lights, but when the crowd rolled into a different position she disappeared like a ghost. *There.* This time her head turned towards him as long lashes lifted and her gaze locked with his. When the crowd shifted again, he frowned.

Damn that dress.

The rooftop pool deck offered unparalleled views of the Hudson River, Lincoln Centre, Central Park and the city, but even the sight of Manhattan sparkling against the night sky didn't compare to the wondrous sight of the thin-strapped sheath of red silk that left inch upon inch of skin exposed from her shoulders to the dip in her back. Add the way the molten material hugged the curve of her hips, outlined impossibly long legs when she moved and barely skimmed the edges of the small breasts that would fill his palms and—

He ground his teeth together as she waltzed around the crowded dance floor in the arms of a smooth model-type. A couple of years shy of Blake's soon-to-be thirty-three, he'd bet the guy was nowhere near as capable of taking her on. He was batting way out of his league.

Large eyes darkened to pools of midnight-blue by the muted light sought him out again before she focused her attention on her partner as the man led her into another turn. It allowed Blake a momentarily uninterrupted view of the perfection of her back. Desire rolled through him and settled heavily in his groin. He wanted to explore every inch of that skin. He wanted to touch and taste, to bury himself deep and get lost in her, those long legs wrapped around him as she cried out his name, and if that guy looked down the front of her dress *one more time…*

He fought the need to go feral. The guy was holding her too close but Liv didn't seem to mind as much as Blake did, a slither of awareness sliding across his senses when she looked at him from the corner of her eye and smiled. Still thought he was wrapped around her little finger, didn't she? To prove she was wrong, he turned and walked away. She wanted him, she could come find him.

He was leaning on the balcony when she did.

Dangling the neck of the bottle between his fingers, he watched her step up beside him to look over the city.

'Run out of dance partners?'

'Thought I'd get some air…'

As he glanced at her, she tilted her head back, eyes closed and a blissful expression on her face as a light, cooling breeze lifted her hair from her shoulders.

'Mmm,' she moaned. 'This is wonderful.'

Blake counted to ten. He was *not* going to fold first.

Turning ninety degrees, she leaned her elbow on the railing and studied his profile. As her gaze lowered and he felt it every place she looked, both down and back up his body, he ground his teeth together and wondered if she had any idea how thin a line she was treading.

'In case I haven't mentioned it—nice tux.'

Lifting the bottle, he spoke over the rim. 'And I got dressed all on my own.'

'You hate every minute of this, don't you?'

'What gave it away?' He turned his head to look at her, frowning at her expression. 'It's not funny.'

'It's a little bit funny.' She stifled the smile sparkling in her eyes.

'Next time I owe you an apology for something, you're getting flowers like everyone else.'

'I like orchids, rare ones.'

'You'll get daisies and be grateful.'

'I *love* daisies.'

Wouldn't give an inch, would she?

'What is it you hate most?' she asked in a soft voice.

'Where do you want me to start?'

'Pick one.'

'*That*—' he tilted his bottle at the crowd '—isn't a party. At a party—' he leaned towards her and lowered his voice '—people have *fun*.'

'They're having fun.'

'No.' He stood tall again. 'What they're doing is networking and using the auction to demonstrate who has the biggest wallet.'

'Okay, then.' With another slight turn, her shoulder pressed lightly against his upper arm. 'Champagne bottle guy, two o'clock, he looks like he's having fun…'

With a ten minute head start in the crowd-watching department, Blake inclined his head towards her. 'Bad day on the stock market. Drowning his sorrows…'

'Marilyn Monroe lookalike, six o'clock…'

'On the hunt for husband number three, trying to make it look like she knows how to have a good time…'

'Stuck-in-the-eighties guy at eleven o'clock?'

'Celebrating the purchase of a midlife crisis sports car,' Blake said as the man held up a set of keys. 'Using it to score with the woman half his age opposite him who comes from the right breeding stock…'

Laughing, Liv lifted her chin. *'Cynic.'*

'Just telling it how it is, sweetheart.' He winked.

The smile remained in her eyes as she continued looking up at him, lips parting as if she was going to say something then closing as a brief hint of a frown creased her forehead.

'Say it,' he demanded. 'Don't stop to think about it.'

'You really don't want to make that one a rule.'

'Say it.'

'I was just going to say you're doing fine. Everyone has been talking about you.'

Blake bit back the kind of response he would normally have given, taking a deep breath and forcing the truth out of his mouth. 'That doesn't help.'

'Good things,' she reassured him, her gaze slanting up and to the side as she added, 'surprisingly...all things considered...' She smiled mischievously as she looked into his eyes again. 'Some of the women made a lot of highly complimentary comments.'

Lifting his brows, Blake looked over the crowd with more interest. 'Anyone you want to point out?'

'Not particularly.'

The change in her tone made him smile. 'Shame—you could have been my wingman—might have livened things up.'

The second she moved, he turned, stretched his arms out and grasped the railing on either side of her narrow waist. 'They say anything you agreed with?'

'I'm likely to admit that?' She circled a finger in front of his face. 'Head size, remember?'

'How much champagne have you had?'

'Not *that* much.'

'Good.' He leaned closer, angling his face above hers. 'Because I want to discuss your rule again.'

'Now?' Her brows lifted.

'Mmm-hmm—' he nodded firmly '—*now.*'

She peeked over his shoulder. 'Not here.'

'You're saying no one kisses at these things?' Blake took that as confirmation of his appraisal of the 'party'.

'Not if it's someone they work with.'

'Work *for*.'

Setting her palms flat against his chest, she pushed, frowning when he didn't move. 'I can't kiss you here.'

'So when you say "not here", it's not that you're denying you want to kiss me—' which would have been a step in the right direction '—it's that you don't want to kiss me where someone might see you kissing me.'

'I wouldn't have put it that way,' she said a little too defensively for his liking. 'You don't understand.'

'Don't I?' He forced a smile onto his face. 'You want to sneak around for a little midday fun, I'm open to that. You want to act like strangers in public while we get it on behind closed doors, you can forget it.'

'I didn't say that.' She scowled.

'It was implied.' Setting his bottle on a nearby planter, Blake grabbed her hand.

'What are you doing?'

'You're going to dance with me.' He tightened his grip and led them to the dance floor where he turned, hauled her against his chest and wrapped an arm around her waist. 'If you think I'm going to watch you dance with a string of guys under my nose while I pretend there's nothing going on between us, *think again*.'

Incredulity filled her eyes as he began swaying them to the music. 'You think I did that to make you jealous? Oh, you do, don't you? And you're telling me…'

When realisation entered her eyes and she caught her lower lip between her teeth to control a smile, Blake shook his head. 'Oh, no, you don't. You don't get to look happy about it. Not after labelling me a guilty secret.'

'That's not what I said!' She glanced around them. 'Would you *stop* putting words in my mouth?'

The fact she'd lowered her voice so no one could hear didn't help.

'Prove me wrong,' he challenged.

'What?'

'You heard me.'

The look she gave him said he couldn't be serious. 'You want an audience the first time I kiss you? Maybe they should make an announcement so nobody misses it. I know what we could do—we could *auction it*. Someone pays enough money, we could put on quite a show for them. That should make it a party to remember.'

Her eyes sparked with a hint of impending danger. Having waited so long for her to lose her cool, it was a shame he was too pissed at her to appreciate the moment. When she pulled back, he held on, his jaw locked with determination. She wasn't going anywhere.

Without giving him enough time to read her intentions, she relaxed in his arms, angled her head, smiled sweetly and kicked him sharply in the shin.

Lurching forward, he looked up as she told him, 'You can be a real jerk when you want to be.'

His burst of deep laughter caught them both off guard.

After a few moments of gentle swaying—allowing time for the storm to pass—she quietly slipped her hand up his chest and around his neck; her fingertips brushed against the short strands of hair touching his collar.

'You don't get it.'

'Then walk me through it.'

'After the stunt you just pulled?' She raised a brow. 'I don't think so.'

Leaning back, his gaze scanned the crowd. It had been

an overreaction—not that he'd never had one of *those* before—but she deserved better.

'I won't hide,' he heard his voice say. 'Not again.'

The confession made him frown. She was going to be all over that like a rash. Maybe they should find a nice couch for him to lie on while she took notes. But she didn't say anything, her fingertips moving against his neck in a soothing caress until his shoulders relaxed and he looked into her eyes again. 'If I wanted our first kiss to have an audience, I wouldn't have dragged you over here to dance with me, would I?'

The same understanding he'd seen at the taxi landing entered her eyes. 'You wanted us to be seen together, so everyone knew I was here with you.'

It was uncharacteristically possessive of him—and he didn't know where that had come from either—but he sure as hell wasn't telling her. He'd said enough already.

'We arrived together,' she pointed out with a small smile. 'Wouldn't that kind of make it look like a date?'

They'd met in the foyer, but he got her point.

'It might,' he allowed, 'if you hadn't spent the rest of the night avoiding me and dancing with everyone *but* me.'

'You could have asked me to dance.'

'Sweetheart, I don't stand in line.'

'And I wasn't avoiding you. I was…' She clamped her mouth shut.

'Go on.'

Catching her lower lip between her teeth, she grimaced as it slid free. 'Once I'd introduced you to a few people, I stepped back to let you mingle…and find your feet…'

'Woman, don't baby me.'

She arched a brow. 'Wouldn't sticking to you like glue the entire night be babying you? Kinda like holding your hand while you go play with the big boys?'

Okay. She had him on that one.

'You're an idiot,' she said.

A possessive, jealous idiot, apparently—*that was new*. Not a particularly nice feeling, either.

The hand on his neck slid forward when his gaze scanned the crowd again, and her thumb moved against his cheek. Lifting his arm from her waist, he captured her fingers and lowered them to his chest, his voice low.

'Someone will see you.'

Long, darkened lashes flickered as she lowered her gaze to her hand, her fingers flexing as she took a breath, frowned, damped her lips with the tip of her tongue and looked into his eyes again.

Her hand slid back up. 'I don't care.'

'Yes, you do.'

Capturing her hand, he held it over his heart. 'Forget about it. It's my hang-up, not yours.'

She smiled through another grimace. 'Kinda is mine. I've been so hung up on what people might think if they knew I was sleeping with a client that—'

'Jumping the gun a little bit, don't you think?' He smiled. 'I don't know about you, but I don't like to skip any of the steps. I'm all about the foreplay.'

This earned a burst of soft feminine laughter, and he lowered their hands from his chest, took a step back and threaded their fingers. 'Let's go.'

'Where?'

'Consider it working on your lack of adventure…'

CHAPTER SIX

'THIS is a party.'

'*Anders!*' yelled a chorus of voices over the music.

Olivia was mid-smile when a large palm flattened against the small of her back to guide her through the crowded bar. The heated brand of his touch seared into her skin and scrambled her thoughts. She inhaled sharply.

Those hands should come with a warning.

'Aren't we a little overdressed?' she asked to cover up the effect it had on her.

'One of us is.' He tucked the dark ribbon of his bow tie into the pocket of his jacket, loosened the buttons at the collar of his dress shirt and leaned closer. 'Not that I'm complaining, but I'd have to lose a couple of layers to get to where you are.'

Olivia smiled. The dress was worth every impulsive cent she'd spent on her overextended credit card after she'd left him at the taxi landing.

'Nice monkey suit, Anders.'

'You remember Marty,' Blake said when they got to the table. 'He used to work for me.'

'Still does,' Marty corrected.

'Not if you don't start using my name, you don't.'

'I'm using one of 'em.' He winked at Olivia as he gave up his seat and Blake made the introductions.

'Marty's wife, Chrissy, Sam, Duke, Duke's wife, Kate.' He grinned. 'Happy birthday, beautiful.' She blew him a kiss before he looked at the last person at the table. 'And that's Mitch, but you're better not knowing him—what do you want to drink?'

'We got a pitcher of beer,' Marty offered as he appeared with extra chairs. 'Figure we owe you a drink for the Anders. We're getting a lot of mileage out of that.'

Olivia laughed. 'A beer would be great. Thank you.'

'I'll get another pitcher. Everyone, this is Liv.' Blake's lethal hand moved from her back to her shoulder as she sat down, his thumb rubbing across her collarbone to get her attention. 'Don't believe anything they tell you but feel free to cross-examine them till I get back.'

'What makes you think I'll wait till you're gone?' Before his hand left her shoulder, she turned towards Chrissy. 'So how long did you say you've known him?'

'Since high school.' Chrissy smiled as Blake left. 'It's nice to meet you; we've heard a lot about you.'

They had?

'Marty says you're one heck of a pool player.'

That made more sense. Somehow Blake didn't strike her as the kind of man who discussed the women in his life. Not that she was the woman in his life, but—

Moving on, 'Blake went to high school here?'

'Where didn't he go to high school?' Marty asked as he sat down between them and reached past Olivia for a glass and the pitcher. 'He was here for two semesters when we were seventeen.'

'Made quite an impression on the cheerleading squad,' Chrissy added before smiling affectionately at her husband. 'Well, the *majority* of them, anyway…'

'She already had her eye on a bad boy,' Marty explained

with an equally affectionate smile. 'Been keeping me on the straight and narrow ever since.'

Olivia smiled as she took the glass from him. They were cute together. There weren't many married couples within her social or family circles, but it was easy to tell they were still in love. She wondered how much time Blake spent with them, doubting he would look at them and think of their relationship the same way she did—as something she would like one day, with the right guy, at the right time, given the opportunity.

For a second it made her long for something she could never have with Blake. Someone like him, with a grin that knocked her on her ear, a touch that still tingled on her skin even when he wasn't there, who could make her smile every time she thought of seeing him and who would get jealous when she danced with other men...

She could see herself falling for a guy like that.

'Apart from that time in Canada...'

Olivia perked up. 'Canada?'

'What did I miss?' Blake set another pitcher on the table before removing his jacket and dropping it over the back of the chair beside her.

'We were just getting to the good stuff.'

'They're not going to tell you about Canada,' he said as he rolled up the sleeves of his shirt.

'Canada!' The call came from across the table, glasses raised in salute as the toast was repeated and the men took a drink while the women shook their heads.

Blake chuckled as he sat down. 'Nice try, sweetheart.'

She'd. Been. *That*. Close.

'You know all of them from high school?' she asked when she'd relaxed into a couple of laughter-filled hours.

Leaning closer to hear her over the music, Blake shook his head. 'No.'

The fingertips at the end of the long arm that had been casually resting on the back of her chair traced lazily over the skin of her upper arm. He'd been touching her since he sat down. Apart from the fingertips that hadn't been still for more than a few seconds at a time, she had to deal with his leg brushing against hers, the warmth of his breath close to her ear when he spoke in his rough, rumbling voice and a million other little things that tested the final shred of her resistance.

It wasn't that she hadn't known he had sensational eyes but the thought had never entered her head that the light sparkling in them was probably similar to stars in a night sky away from city lights. It wasn't that she hadn't noticed how thick his eyelashes were or been mesmerized by how sensual each of the sixteen blinks per minute every human being took could be. She just hadn't realised they could hypnotize her to the extent where she felt like staring at him long enough to count the beats in case she missed one…two…three, four…

When his gaze locked on hers, a weird shifting sensation happened inside her chest. Almost immediately, it was replaced with something she recognised: *fear*.

Oh, no. She couldn't allow herself to be sucked in—just because he'd introduced her to his friends and spent the evening treating her like a guy treated a girlfriend didn't mean—she *knew* what she'd been fighting and it had nothing to do with—

'Dance with me.'

'What?' Thankful for the invitation to tear her gaze from his, she glanced at the small dance floor on the other end of the room. 'I don't think—'

'You should do more of that.' He pushed back his chair. 'You overthink things.'

Things like the fact she was the only woman in the

room in a floor-length evening dress and he was asking her to dance to music that leaned more towards hip-hop than tango?

'Don't wimp out on me now, sweetheart.'

Olivia shook her head as she stood up. Glancing at his face, the hint of smugness she detected at how easily he'd played her brought a smile to her face as she stepped past him. He was in so much trouble and he didn't even know it.

Head held high, she ignored the number of people staring at what she was wearing as she made her way through the crowd. Thanks to several strategically placed mirrors in a changing room, she knew what Blake was looking at behind her. The knowledge encouraged her to exaggerate the sway created by walking on sinfully high heels. Judging by the fact a woman at a nearby table slapped her man on the head, she must have been working it to the desired level. A fact she had confirmed when she got to the middle of the dance floor and turned in time to see Blake frown before he lifted his gaze.

Hand on hip, she angled her head and beckoned him to her with a crooked finger. He froze for a second, then closed the gap between them, reached out a hand and raised his voice to be heard over the music.

'I don't think we've met.'

Ignoring the implied suggestion of an introductory handshake, Olivia placed them palm to palm, threaded her fingers through his and lifted their arms as she angled her head a little more and stepped into him.

'We talking or dancing?'

As his head lowered, an arm snaked around her waist. 'We've been dancing since we met.'

Smooth. For a moment she was tempted to smile. But she was the one doing the seducing this time, not him.

Recklessly, she decided he was about to see an Olivia Brannigan few people ever laid eyes on. Gaze lowering to his mouth, she ran her hand up his arm and across a broad shoulder until she could dip her fingers beneath the collar of his shirt and curl them around the column of his neck.

If everyone at the table had been given the impression she was his, in a few moments there wouldn't be a single soul in the entire bar who didn't think every gorgeous inch of him was hers. Fighting her attraction to him was exhausting. Giving in to it—even if it was just for a little while—suddenly seemed much easier.

Leaning forward, she dipped down a little, brushed the tips of her breasts against the wall of his chest and slid upwards, rolling her shoulders and smiling when his body tensed. As they began to sway, she moved her face closer to his, her gaze whispering lazily upwards until she was looking into his eyes. Checking to make sure she had his full and undivided attention, she ran her tongue over her lips, then moved her head so she could speak directly into his ear. 'Did you know dancing is the closest thing to having sex in public?'

'Like living dangerously, do we?'

Pressing tighter to his chest, she allowed her lips to brush his ear. 'I still have the handcuffs…'

'Okay—' he reached for the hand on his neck and took a step back '—*now* we're dancing.'

Tightening long fingers around hers, he took another step back, dropping the hand he'd removed from his neck and swinging her out to arm's length before hauling her back to his chest with a sharp tug. Olivia drew a sharp gasp through her lips as his leg stepped between her thighs; the contact was totally unexpected and at the same time thrilling. The hand on her back tightened, steering her around his body as he changed direction. The leg between her thighs moved back a step, he took another sidestep and, before she knew it, she was being moved around the dance floor.

Did he seriously think she was letting him lead?

When his leg insinuated itself between her thighs again, she stepped higher and back, initiating a back and forth stepping motion that slithered the silky smooth material of her skirt between her thighs with each forward thrust of his leg. But just when she thought she was in control again, he stilled. Clasped hands lifted in the air beside them as he bent her backward, his gaze sliding down her throat to her breasts and back up to linger on her parted lips while he drew her upright and moved his face closer to hers. Heaven help her, it *felt* as if they were having sex in public.

But the woman inside her didn't care, particularly when the pressure of his hand on her lower back brought her abdomen into contact with his groin and she made a discovery. He was as turned on by what they were doing as she was; the evidence pressed against her, heat pooling between her thighs in response. Running her tongue over her teeth, she fixed a heavy-lidded gaze on his mouth as she crushed her breasts against his chest and felt a buzz of anticipation hum through her body.

She was so far over the line she couldn't see it any more but, instead of fear, she felt more alive than she had in years. She'd never cut loose with a man the way she wanted to cut loose with him. Every fantasy she'd ever had, every one of the dreams that left her bathed in sweat and tangled up in her sheets since she met him, she could play out with him. It was too good an opportunity to miss. Call it temporary insanity, a vacation from reality, a reward for all the years she'd spent rebuilding her life and buried in work—she didn't care what her conscience labelled it. She needed this, she wanted him and what was even better, she knew *he* wanted *her*.

Adrenalin pulsed through her veins. Where to begin?

Angling her head, she pushed up onto her toes; a hand gripped his shoulder as she used his large body for leverage until her mouth hovered over his and her inner bad girl looked him straight in the eye.

'Hello, lover.'

Realisation entered his eyes a split second before she hooked her arm around his neck and lifted a foot off the ground. Trusting him to support her weight, she lifted her leg forward and up, curling it over his hip before leaning back and lowering her chin. She looked up at him from beneath her lashes, catching her lower lip between her teeth as she silently transmitted her intentions in the way a man like him would understand.

He shook his head a little. *'Don't do it.'*

If it was meant as a warning, he had a lot to learn about reverse psychology. She slowly slid her thigh down his leg. Back onto her toes and she was sliding upward again. She leaned her head back a little, eyelids heavy and lips parting as she breathed deep and exhaled on a note of sensual satisfaction.

If it felt half as good for him as it did for her...

Gripping her waist with unforgiving fingers, Blake lifted her a couple of inches off the ground, practically throwing her off him before he wrapped his arm around her body and spun them around in circles.

She lifted a brow. 'Something wrong?'

For a moment he looked pained.

'Poor baby,' she pouted, effervescent laughter bubbling inside her chest.

Dark eyes glowed, his gaze glancing briefly over her

head. A faster set of turns made the remaining couples around them clear a space while Olivia's heart beat faster and her blood rushed through her veins. She leaned her head back and closed her eyes, throaty laughter breaking free until he brought them to an abrupt stop, dipped her backward and his large body loomed over hers. With his face shadowed, she focused on his breathing, elated to find it as laboured as hers. She couldn't remember the last time she'd felt so exhilarated, so light and giddy and *free*.

Slowly drawing her upright, he pulled her close again, the curves of her body fitting into the dips and planes of his as if they'd danced together a thousand times. When he stepped back, she stepped forward. There was a give and take to their movements that hadn't been there before, a push and pull all too similar to lovemaking. Now, every time he brushed the inside of her thighs with his leg, she savoured the sensation, moving her leg between his as she followed him forward. When she looked into his eyes, the world went fuzzy around the edges again, her entire focus on him and only him. Did he know how much she wanted him?

How much she *burned* for him?

She wanted the glow in his eyes imprinted on her memory, his touch branded on her skin, his taste in her mouth, to breathe in his scent and have his deep, rough voice echo in her ears. She wasn't stupid—she knew an attraction like theirs didn't come along every day. The fact she knew it would flare and fizzle out didn't matter. If anything, it made it feel as if she had to reach out and grab it before it disappeared and was lost to her for ever.

Her gaze tangled with his as the music changed to something slower. He searched her eyes, studied the loose curl of hair lying against her flushed cheek and watched the movement of her tongue as she damped her lips again. A tremor ran through her at the thought of his mouth against hers, demanding the response she was so ready to give him.

As if he knew how close she was to making their first kiss public, he lifted her hand over her head, turning her around and crossing her arm over her breasts before drawing her back against him and setting his other hand on her stomach, his fingers splayed possessively. While he moved their hips in a languorous circle, Olivia leaned her head back against his shoulder, her eyes closed as his head bowed next to hers. Warm breath tickled against the tingling skin at the hollow of her neck, his body heat seeping through the thin layer of his shirt and into her blood.

She smiled. He was trying to slow things down, wasn't he? It was sweet but there was really no need. Not when she'd made her decision.

She arched her back a little and straightened her legs. The smallest sliding movement, but it had the desired effect. Blake swore beside her ear, the hand on her stomach pressing her tighter to him in an attempt to stop her from doing it again. Swaying her hips in the opposite direction to his in response, she chuckled when the expletive in her ear was more colourful.

Turning around, she reached up, curling the fingers of one hand around his neck while the other framed his face. As his gaze consumed her, she knew, deep down inside where *all* women knew, sex with this man was going to be beyond incredible. One look and her body had begun readying itself for him—had been in pretty much the same state ever since. It was the most basic of biological instincts: the need to mate with the strongest of the species. Was it any wonder she'd been fighting a losing battle when she'd been fighting against nature itself? But she was done fighting. She wanted to feel again. Just for a little while. So long as it was nothing more than physical, she'd be fine.

'Kiss me,' she demanded.

'Here?' The glow in his eyes intensified.

She shook her head. 'Everywhere.'

'I had a more private "here" in mind for that.'

'Then take me home with you.'

He searched her eyes. 'Aren't we skipping some steps?'

'We packed them all into one night.'

'If I take you home with me, we'll be packing a hell of a lot more into one night.' He looked over her head, dark brows folded in thought before he reached for the hand on his face. 'We're leaving.'

A blanket of heated, moist air surrounded them as they left the bar five minutes later, the background noise of traffic and a siren echoing over the river from Manhattan a symphony to her city-girl ears as they rounded a corner and Blake stopped dead in his tracks. Tightening his fingers around hers, he took a deep breath, a muscle working in his jaw before he turned towards her.

'Last chance, Liv. If you've had too much to drink or this isn't something you're one hundred per cent certain you want, I'm not going to be held responsible for the regret you'll have written all over your face tomorrow.'

'You're still an idiot.' She smiled softly, touched by the unexpected chivalry that allowed her a chance to back out. 'I'm not drunk, I know exactly what I'm doing and if you don't shut up and kiss me, I may have to kill you.'

'Why don't *you* kiss *me*?'

'Blake, I *promise you*—'

It was as far as she got before his mouth was on hers. No matter how vivid her imagination had been during waking or sleeping hours, or how real some of those fantasies had felt, nothing could have prepared her for the reality of being kissed by him. Not when hunger and need blinded her to everything but sensation. Firm, warm, practised lips moved over hers, his deliciously clean, masculine scent filling her nose and creating a spinning sensation in her head. He tasted so much better than she'd thought he would—a combination of spice and heat with the tantalising promise of hidden depths if she just pushed a little bit deeper. When he coaxed her lower lip with the tip of his tongue, she opened her mouth and dipped inside.

Shivering when he wrapped his arms around her and drew her to him, the sensation of her overly sensitive breasts crushed hard against the wall of his chest forced her to lift a hand to his shoulder to form a vice-like grip. Leaning into him, she demanded more, the hand at his waist sliding beneath his jacket and tugging at the shirt on his back so she could get to skin.

A groan vibrated in his chest before he tore their mouths apart, leaned his forehead against hers and hauled in a breath, his voice deeper and rougher than before. 'I want to tell you we'll take it slow the first time, but I don't think I can.'

'I just asked you to take me home with you before we'd shared our first kiss—what part of that suggested to you I want to go slow?'

'You know you're going to pay for what you did on that dance floor.'

What did he think she'd been aiming for?

She sighed dramatically. 'And yet somehow we're still standing here, talking about it. Anyone who didn't know you might think you'd been bluffing all this time and you're one of those all talk, no—'

Grabbing her hand in a tight grip, he tugged her to the kerb and whistled loudly. *'Taxi!'*

CHAPTER SEVEN

THE woman slept like the dead.

As the first rays of sunlight appeared in the arched windows of his apartment, Blake watched her sleep. He'd never known anyone who slept so soundly, or remained so still. At least *now* she was still. Several times during the night she'd tested the one chivalrous bone he had left by sliding her naked body against his, smooshing her breasts into his side and rubbing her cheek against his chest. Add the small, contented moaning noises she'd made and his body had spent hours in the same state most men woke up in.

Reaching out, he used the tip of his forefinger to lift a strand of hair from her cheek. She looked exactly the way he'd wanted her to look at the start—hair messed up and framing her face, full lips devoid of lipstick, flushed cheeks... *Damn, they'd been good together...*

She was spectacular when she cut loose. It had been more than worth the effort he'd put into breaking through to get to the woman she kept hidden from the world. *She* was more than worth the effort. Whatever guy ended up spending his life with her would be one lucky—

He frowned. Jealous and possessive—apparently he hadn't shaken either one of them off yet.

His gaze slid down her neck to where the sheet was

dangerously close to slipping off her breast, then lower to where an impossibly long leg was visible, bent at the knee. He remembered how those legs had felt wrapped around him and how responsive she'd been to everything he did and said. It did a lot for a man's ego while at the same time leaving him hungry for more. He wasn't done with her. He was nowhere near done.

Realising he didn't know how long he'd been watching her sleep, he quietly rolled away and eased into a sitting position, scrubbing his fingers haphazardly through his hair. He would let her regain her energy, but he couldn't think of a single reason for her to get out of his bed before Monday.

It took another two hours for her to wake up.

Glancing over his shoulder as she came into the living area, he saw her hands smooth her hair back from her face. She had put on the shirt he had been wearing the night before. The movement of her arms lifted the material up her thighs and he appreciated the fact she'd left several buttons undone at the top, allowing a glimpse of the curve of her breasts.

'There's coffee on the counter,' he said before concentrating on what he was doing, one of his feet propped on the workbench in front of him.

'I can't find my dress.'

'It's hanging up in the bathroom.'

'I borrowed your shirt.'

'I noticed.'

A moment later she appeared at his shoulder with a mug cradled in her hands, her lips pouting as she blew on it before hiding behind the rim.

'Sleep well?'

She nodded as she swallowed. 'Mmm-hmm.'

'Was tempted to check for a pulse a couple of times...'

She didn't comment, but he could feel the change in her; it was as obvious as it would have been if she'd exhaled after holding her breath. He was glad. He didn't want her to regret a single second.

'How long have you lived here?'

'A while.'

'It's nice.' She took another sip of coffee. 'Where did you live before this?'

'Here and there.'

'Always in New York?'

'No.' He took a deep, measured breath. 'But you already know that.'

She'd found him, hadn't she?

When she went for a walk around his living space, he lifted his gaze to the windows in front of him and watched what she was doing. She tilted her head to the side and read the spines of his books and DVDs, lightly ran her fingertips over the back of his sofa, lifted a couple of framed photographs and studied them before setting them down. It was the kind of thing people did in other people's apartments, not that it felt any better.

As she made her way back to him, he lowered his chin and concentrated on the knife in his hand. The blade made a soft, scraping sound as he used his thumb to push it away from his body, carefully guiding each stroke, reducing the wood, layer by layer, to get to what lay beneath. Stopping for a moment, he leaned in and blew on the surface.

Liv stood at his shoulder again. 'Do you think you'll stay here now you have so many apartments to choose from?'

'Chatty first thing in the morning, aren't we?'

'I'm curious.'

'You'll get over it.'

'I don't think so.'

When he looked at her and she smiled a small, soft smile, Blake lowered his foot to the floor. 'Look, Liv, this isn't…'

He frowned. He was going to say it was something he wasn't used to. Given the choice, he avoided the morning after the night before. But he couldn't say that without making it sound as if he slept around or giving her the impression what had happened meant more than it did. Not that it hadn't meant something—*it had*—but he couldn't tell her that either, not without—

'I know,' she said, the smile remaining as she lowered her voice to a conspiratorial whisper. 'Wasn't planning on moving my stuff in for another couple of weeks…'

Blake stared at her as amusement danced in her eyes. Shaking his head, he snagged an arm around her waist and tugged her onto his lap. Nudging her hair back with the tip of his nose, he placed a kiss on the side of her neck before telling her, 'Drink your coffee.'

When she laid an arm across his shoulders and lifted the mug to her mouth, he continued working the wood. For a while there was an almost companionable silence, the blade working as Liv sipped her coffee and watched what he was doing. Whether it was because she'd made it easy for him, or the fact she wasn't walking around looking at his stuff, he didn't know, but whatever it was, it felt better. Even if he realised simply sitting with a woman and enjoying her company was something else that was new.

She looked at some of the finished pieces on the workbench, then down at his hands. 'What's this one going to be?'

'Hasn't told me yet.'

'You don't make it whatever you want it to be?'

'Doesn't work like that.'

She studied his profile. 'How does it work?'

'When you get below the surface, it is what it is.' He lifted the piece of wood and studied it from several angles against the light. 'You either work with that or you toss it away and look for something you like better.'

'What if it's hard to get below the surface?'

'Then you need patience.'

When he looked up at her, sunlight from the window glistened in her hair and her eyes. Lifting a hand to the back of her neck, he eased her towards him, pressing his mouth to her warm, pliant lips. It was a gentler kiss than the majority of the ones they'd shared the night before but, like before, it wasn't enough. Tossing the wood and knife aside, he heard them thud and clatter onto the bench as he wound his fingers around her coffee mug and took it from her hand. Setting it down, he slid his arm under her knees, moved the hand on her neck to her back and pushed to his feet, unceremoniously hoisting her higher.

The vibration of a chuckle against his mouth made him lift his head so he could look down at her. As he smiled in reply, her hand slid from his neck to palm his cheek, her thumb grazing the morning shadow he hadn't dealt with yet.

'I can fix that.'

'No—' she smiled back '—I kinda like it.'

'Remember you said that. I plan on kissing a lot of places I missed last night.'

'I don't think you missed anywhere.'

'Let's check, shall we?'

So long as they stayed the way they were and kept things light, there wasn't any reason they couldn't keep doing what they were doing until he'd finished wrapping things up and went back to his life. Light he could do. Fun he could do. Anything more than that, he didn't have in him. He never had. But as he laid her down on the bed and told her he was going to need his shirt back, for a moment he regretted he was not able to give more. Something else that was new.

She was in love.

'Do not say your two favourite words,' Olivia warned him as they walked across a manicured lawn. 'Not till we're leaving.'

As enthralled as she'd been throughout the thirty-five minute helicopter trip from Manhattan—views of the Empire State Building, Wall Street, the Statue of Liberty, Ellis Island and the Brooklyn Bridge eventually being replaced by open fields brimming with wildflowers, corn, and rows upon rows of sunflowers as they got closer to their destination—she hadn't noticed much as they came in to land beyond glimpses of a large gabled roof surrounded by mature trees. But once they'd walked around the corner of a curving privet hedge and the house was revealed to her in all its glory, she fell instantly and irrevocably in love.

If he dismissed it after his usual five minutes she might have to strangle him. Tearing her gaze from dark shingled walls, white shuttered windows and the curving porch beneath twin turrets, she saw Blake's jaw tense.

'Did you call ahead to say we were coming?'

'I do with all the properties we visit. Why?'

He looked down at her from the corner of his eye. 'Three guesses.'

When she looked for a clue, she discovered a line had formed on the steps at the front door. Stifling a smile, she shrugged. 'At least no one is in a top hat.'

He didn't look amused.

Gravel crunched beneath their feet as Olivia prepared to take on the role she normally did and introduce him. But before she'd opened her mouth, the stately silver-haired man at the head of the line inclined his head.

'Master Blake.'

'We can drop the master part, Henry.'

'Of course, sir...'

Blake shook his head, the next person in line bringing a smile to his face. 'Still here, Martha?'

She beamed in reply. 'It's good to see you again.'

Glancing at the others standing with expectant expressions, he took a deep breath and announced, 'Go home folks—take a few days' paid vacation—we can fend for ourselves.' He winked at Martha on his way past. 'Good to see you, too.'

While she blushed and the rest of the staff looked at each other in confusion, Olivia followed him inside, ignoring her surroundings as she stated the obvious. 'You've been here before.'

'Yes.'

'When?'

'I spent a summer here when I was seventeen.'

Before or after the two semesters he'd spent at high school in Brooklyn? It was a source of great frustration to Olivia that the list of questions she'd formed before she met him grew on a daily basis. After sharing a bed at every available opportunity in the last six days, they knew everything there was to know about each other's bodies but anything more than that, not so much.

Setting her weekend bag and laptop at the bottom of the newel post, she turned towards him. 'You can give me the grand tour, then.'

Blake pressed his mouth into a thin line as he dropped his bag beside hers. 'Fine.'

When he walked through an archway into a room filled with deeply upholstered white sofas, she barely glanced at the understated decor: she was more interested in his reaction to being there.

'Living room.' He waved an arm to his side and kept walking. 'Library.'

She had to increase her pace to keep up.

'Den.' He nodded to the right as they walked back across the hall again. 'Billiard room—that's the British version of pool to you and me—dining room...breakfast room...kitchen...'

'Could we go a bit slower?'

He stopped so abruptly she almost ran into him. 'It's just a house, Liv.'

'The word *just* doesn't come close to describing this place.' She looked up at his face, the realisation hitting her that, 'You don't want to be here.'

Correct her if she was wrong, but hadn't it been his idea? There were plenty of other places they could have visited and they'd barely scratched the surface when it came to the Warren Enterprises' subsidiaries.

Pushing his hands into the pockets of his jeans, Blake turned his profile to her, his gaze fixed on a point outside the numerous windows lining a wall of the large kitchen they were standing in.

He shrugged. 'Thought you'd like it.'

'I do,' she said softly, touched by the comment, even if she didn't entirely believe the trip was solely for her benefit. She smiled when he glanced at her from the corner of his eye. 'I love it. But if you're uncomfortable here...'

'When did I strike you as comfortable in any of the places we've visited?'

Barring the one time, good point, but—

'You want to see outside?'

She noted the swift change of subject, but she nodded, struggling to find patience as he opened a door and they stepped onto an expansive stone patio. Down a couple of sets of gently winding steps and around a corner, a large swimming pool twinkled in the bright sunlight, and the promise of a stunning ocean view from the railing beyond drew them forward. As his large hands grasped the metal railing, Olivia blinked at the horizon and added to her question list. How long had he been here? Had his father spent much time with him? What had it been like? Had they been able to talk? Had his mother been here too? Did they visit regularly?

One question barrelled through the others to make it to the top of the list. 'Why are we here?'

When his fingers tightened, she thought he was not going to answer her. Not that it was anything new, but it was really starting to tick her off.

'I don't know,' he replied in a voice so low she almost didn't hear him.

The fact he was frowning told her he wasn't happy he'd said the words out loud. But what got to her was how much it reminded her of the expression he'd worn on the dance floor when he'd told her he wouldn't hide, *not again*.

'You want the helicopter to come back for us?'

'No.' He let go of the railing and took her hand. 'Let's go look at the best part.'

If it was meant to distract her, it worked, at least for a while. Within five minutes of her toes sinking into warm sand she understood the attraction of The Hamptons. In the city it was easy to become bogged down with a million and one things: deadlines to meet, obligations to fulfil, parties to attend and the vagaries of everyday chores causing stress and tension as people tried to squeeze everything into twenty-four hours per day. It was a hectic, fast-paced lifestyle. One Olivia had thought she thrived on.

But while walking along a deserted beach with her hand

held in Blake's she found herself thinking about the things she was missing out on: the simple pleasures in life it was all too easy to take for granted and the important things she'd relegated to some nebulous point in the future. Her time with him was turning into quite a journey of self-discovery. She smiled wryly. The fact he was so reluctant to talk about his life had made her think about her own.

'It's beautiful here.'

'It is,' he agreed.

Once the silence had been interrupted, she felt the need to fill it. *You could take the girl out of the city...*

'It's funny how easy it is to forget Manhattan is an island. I never think about the ocean being so close. It's just there, you know?' She lifted her hand to push back a strand of hair. 'When I was a kid, we used to take a trip to the beach every summer—Jersey, mostly. My brothers played touch football on the sand, Dad refereed and I got to keep score. Killed me I never got to play. Uneven numbers, they said.'

'How many brothers?'

'Four.'

'Sisters?'

'No, took five attempts for my parents to get it right.' Since she'd opened a line of dialogue, she tried something simple. 'You have brothers or sisters?'

If Charles Warren had more than one child, she assumed they'd have been mentioned in the will, but his mother could have married and had children before or after Blake.

'You're allergic to silence, aren't you?'

'It's called making conversation.'

'We were doing fine without it.'

She stopped and waited for him to turn towards her. 'I can't be the first person to try and get to know you.'

'You're not.'

They hadn't fared any better, had they? Not that it was much consolation.

'You know enough,' he said. 'If you didn't, you wouldn't be sleeping with me.'

Blunt but true. 'You're right, I wouldn't.'

'So what's the problem?'

'Oh, I don't know.' She shrugged. 'Not being made to feel like it could be anyone in your bed would be nice.'

He frowned. 'That's how I make you feel?'

'No.' She searched for a way of explaining what she meant without sounding needy. 'But if you make it seem like I'm not even supposed to make idle conversation with you, I *might* feel that way.'

As she broke eye contact, she shook her head a little, questioning what she was doing. She didn't regret the decision she'd made to sleep with him, no matter how uncharacteristically spur-of-the-moment it may have been. But was it so unusual to want to know even the most basic things about him—the details people shared every day without feeling it had cost them something?

She didn't think so.

'You knew what you were getting into…'

Actually, Olivia wasn't entirely certain she had known, not really. Her attraction to him was an unstoppable force of nature, the conclusion as inevitable as the ocean hitting the shore beside their feet. Beyond that, she may possibly have been a tad naive when it came to how casual she could keep things. Sex was intimate, there was no avoiding that.

'So what is it you want?'

Good question.

'You,' she replied without hesitation.

It was the one thing she was clear on. Her body, still aching with sweet reminders of the passion they shared, though satisfied time and time again, was far from replete. But the needs that weren't being satisfied were beginning to demand similar levels of attention. She wanted to know who she was sharing her body with, to understand how his mind worked, why he reacted to certain things the way he did. The very idea of caring as much as she used to about anything or anyone still terrified her but there had to be a middle ground somewhere.

An affair with a man like Blake could be viewed as a kind of stepping stone—a way of testing the water to discover if she could allow herself to feel again without getting too involved. If it meant being brave and going a little further out on a limb than she'd planned, she could do that—but not at the expense of her self-respect. Jumping into bed with a virtual stranger was one thing, continuing to have sex with him without getting to know him better was another—so yes, she still wanted him but—

'Just not like this.'

'Then why are you here?'

'Because I want to be.' She lifted her chin in defiance, in case he told her she shouldn't feel that way.

'This will end,' he said in the rough-edged rumble that still got to her. 'You know that.'

'I do.'

Blake shook his head, frowning harder. 'Make it more than it is, it'll feel worse when it does.'

She shrugged. 'The memory might be sweeter.'

Turning her head, she looked out at the ocean while retreating behind the wall she'd built around the emotions she could feel churning inside. There may have been a time she'd trusted and was led by her heart, but those days were gone. She couldn't allow herself to get sucked into the maelstrom again but there was a balance to be found, she understood that now. It was something she could take from her time with him.

'Liv—'

'I'm done talking now.' She tilted her head back and took a deep breath of salty air, calmness washing over her as the churning began to settle. 'Just getting it off my chest.' Lowering her chin again, she looked down the long stretch of pale sand in front of them. 'How far does the beach go? Do you want to walk to the end?'

'I'm just supposed to forget what you said?'

She arched a brow at him. 'In case you hadn't noticed, that was me letting you off the hook. I can't afford to get emotionally involved with you, so if that's what you're worried about you can set your mind at ease. Not like there's much point, is there? None of this will matter in a few weeks. Once we've finished scratching this itch—'

The next thing she knew, he was pulling her against him, his mouth capturing hers with brutal intensity. There was nothing gentle in the way he kissed her—nothing tender—but Olivia didn't want gentle or tender. She wanted him to need her as much as she needed him, for him to be even a fraction as out of touch with reality as she felt every time he kissed her. When his fingers splayed across the back of her head and his tongue demanded entrance to her mouth, she opened for him. Their tongues tangled as her hands reached for the strong column of his neck.

Wrenching his mouth from hers, he looked down at her and frowned. He was angry. She could see it. Angry because he'd kissed her, because he hadn't ended it or angry with her for saying what she had? She shook her head. She didn't want to argue with him.

Lifting her mouth, she kissed him with the same urgent sense of need she'd felt when he kissed her. When he groaned and lowered his hands to her hips, she smoothed her hands over his shoulders to his chest, her fingertips exploring the hard, sculpted contours beneath his T-shirt.

'Take me to bed,' she mumbled against his lips.

Their relationship may have been sorely lacking in every other form of communication, but in bed they spoke to each other in ways only lovers could. Having felt the effect even the smallest increase in distance between them could have on her, she needed to feel connected to him again, that he was right there with her, feeling what she felt. It was a Band-aid on what could, if she were foolish enough to let it happen, become a massive gaping wound.

They stopped again and again on the walk back to the house—her shoes dropped inside the kitchen door—his T-shirt gone by the foot of the stairs. When the kissing and tearing at clothes became frantic he leaned back, the twitch of his lips becoming a full-blown grin. Emotion seeped through a crack in the wall around her heart and dripped into her chest.

When had she got so crazy for him?

Fusing their mouths together, he pushed through the door to a bedroom and kicked it shut behind him. But at the side of the bed he stilled, his palms framing her face, thumbs beneath her chin as he looked deep into her eyes.

'You're not just anyone, Liv.' The words were husky and low, washing over her like a caress. 'Don't ever think that. Not when you're with me.'

The impact it had on her heart created fracture lines around the crack, the drip of escaping emotion becoming a trickle. Every danger-sensing instinct she possessed screamed *Run!* but she reached for him, hands smoothing over his chest and around his neck, her voice thick as she demanded, 'Show me.'

Once they were back in Manhattan she would have to think long and hard about what she was doing while she was still in control of her emotions. Even if he had been the kind of guy who stayed in one place, anything more than sex could never be possible between two people unwilling to share more than their bodies. But while he filled her world with warmth, sensation and the physical closeness she'd never experienced with anyone else, she clung to him and held on tight in case she never felt it again.

CHAPTER EIGHT

WATCHING Liv withdraw behind the mask she'd been wearing when he met her had made Blake unreasonably angry. At the same moment she'd made it clear he was hardly in a position to throw stones when it came to communication. It wasn't that he couldn't hold a conversation. Politics, sports, the economy, big business versus the little guy, which superhero would win in a fight with another superhero—he could hold a conversation on a vast range of subjects when he set his mind to it.

It wasn't until Liv that he realised how little he said.

While she slept, he headed outside to clear his head—what had happened on the beach replaying on a loop in his mind while he replaced the things he'd said with what he could have said. When it came to anything about his life, there was a subconscious wall he seemed unable to break through, even though he wanted to—for her.

'Not being made to feel like it could be anyone in your bed would be nice.'

He liked to think he'd taken care of that in the one way he knew he could communicate clearly with her—*anyone, his ass*—but when it came to the other stuff? No, he didn't have any brothers or sisters—had that been so difficult to say? And when he'd asked her what she wanted and her answer had been 'you', why couldn't he tell her it was the same for him? He wouldn't have been telling her anything she didn't already know.

After walking a long loop, he ended up back at the railing overlooking the ocean. When he'd said he hadn't known why they were there, it was the closest he'd come to being open, even if it was only partially true. Maybe he'd thought poking the edge of the empty place inside him with a memory-shaped stick might allow something to leak out; maybe he'd thought he would free an emotion he could experience and deal with before he moved on. If that was what he'd thought, he'd been wrong. He still had a big fat nothing.

Leaning his elbows on the railing, he breathed deep and looked out at the ocean, comparing the seventeen-year-old who'd been there before to the man he was now. He hadn't thought he was as messed up as he'd been back then.

Maybe he'd been wrong.

His gaze followed a seagull as it glided on a current of air, wings outstretched, not a care in the world. Used to be a time he felt that carefree. Thing was, he didn't feel so trapped any more either—as if with each property or asset he disposed of he was cutting a string that attached him to the life he'd never even contemplated. By cutting them he was proving *he* was in control, *he* was the one making decisions, he was in charge of his own destiny. But if that was true, he would be standing at the helm, not feeling as if he were adrift on a raft.

The one time he'd felt like himself had been when he'd looked at the warehouse and thought about its potential. He didn't need penthouses or private jets or skyscrapers with high rental incomes. But building something before he sold it on, something he would only be tied to for the duration of the project, wouldn't be so bad. He could take his usual pride in a job well done while providing steady work for the guys who needed it and had families to think about.

Reaching into the back pocket of his jeans for the envelope, he unfolded it and looked down at the numerous stamps and scored out addresses. It was the first time he'd been tempted to open it.

His chin lifted. Why could he hear music?

Waking up alone wasn't a new experience, but it was starting to get a little annoying when she reached out and he wasn't there. Blinking at the empty space, Olivia resolved it wasn't going to get to her, not when she felt so good. Stretching languorously, arms and legs spread wide in the ridiculously large bed and her head pushed deep into decadent pillows, she grinned from ear to ear. There wasn't an inch of her body that hadn't been worshipped. She curled her toes. A few hours with Blake while he demonstrated she absolutely, most definitely was the woman he wanted in his bed had been *heaven*.

Reluctant to wash his scent from her skin, she got up and threw on light cotton shorts and a halter-neck, padding barefoot through the house and deciding to indulge in a little exploration when she couldn't find him. Starting in the library, she wandered along the floor-to-ceiling bookshelves, trailing her fingertips over the rise and fall of the books' spines as she looked around the room. It would be a great place to spend time on a rainy afternoon. She could see herself taking cushions from the chairs and piling them in the window seat, wrapping a blanket around her legs while she tried to work her way through every book. She'd always meant to find time to read more.

In the fantasy world she allowed herself to envisage for a moment, it was how she would spend her time while Blake was in the workshop he'd set up somewhere in the house. Given the choice, Olivia would make it a bench in the same room—possibly over in the corner where a couple of chairs and a lamp were currently standing—so she could watch what he was doing. The way his hands moved, the concentration on his face as little by little he revealed what was hidden beneath the surface of the wood...

She smiled. She loved watching him work.

In the living room, she stopped to look at pictures of generations of famous Warrens on a baby grand piano, frowning at the fact there weren't any of Blake. He should have been there, laughing and smiling with everyone else. When she found a picture of a young Charles Warren, she picked it up and searched for a resemblance. They had the same colouring, she supposed, but knowing they hadn't been close, she refused to see anything more and set the picture down. He didn't deserve to have his son look like him. Not when he didn't have a single picture of Blake as a baby.

In her fantasy world the few pictures she had seen in his apartment would take up space on the piano along with new ones taken on weekends and holidays at the house. Instead of photographs taken sailing or sipping cocktails or—she leaned in to check what she was seeing, shaking her head in amusement—*playing croquet*, there would be pictures of touch-football on the lawn, picnics on the beach, maybe even snowball fights during winter holidays.

When her imagination started adding kids who looked like Blake to the picture she stopped fantasizing. It was the house calling out to be filled with love and laughter. The more she saw, the deeper she fell under its spell.

In need of something to do, she went to the kitchen and searched through the cupboards for ingredients she could throw together to make a meal that wouldn't require culinary skills or allow her to burn the house to the ground.

With the basics laid out, she placed her hands on her hips and turned a circle. The house had to have a sound system. She'd even settle for a—*Ha!* She might have kept the volume down if there had been houses nearby. But the way Olivia saw it—wherever Blake was—he would soon know she was awake. If she fed him and no one died, they could have an early night.

Leaning his shoulder against the door frame, Blake crossed his ankles and folded his arms across his chest, a smile lifting him out of the contemplative mood he'd been in outside. Unaware of his presence, she balanced salad ingredients in her arms, bumped the refrigerator door shut with her hip and made her way to the sink, where she dropped everything and rescued a pepper as it rolled away.

The singing he'd heard from the patio continued, culminating in an enthusiastic if somewhat off-key chorus of, 'La, la, la…la, la, la… La…la…' as Blake chuckled.

When his gaze followed hers to an overflowing pot, he crossed the room and met her at the stove, the hands he placed on her hips making her jump in surprise before he kissed the side of her neck and she smiled in greeting.

Locating the source of the music, he stepped over and turned the volume down, returning as Liv blew on the surface of a loaded spoon and brought it to his mouth.

His reaction made her grimace. 'That bad?'

It really was. He shook his head. 'No.'

When she sighed heavily, he took the spoon out of her hand, turned her around and moved her to the side before lifting her and setting her on the counter. 'Do I want to know what's in the other pot?'

'Pasta.'

'How long have you been boiling it?'

'Ten, fifteen minutes.' She shrugged.

'I'd say it's done then, wouldn't you?'

'I don't spend much time in the kitchen.'

'I guessed.'

Turning off the heat, he set the pans to the back of the stove. 'How have you managed to survive this long without learning to cook?'

'I live in Manhattan, I don't need to cook. We have delis and restaurants and markets where you can buy stuff that's already put together in neat little packages you can heat up in the microwave.'

'If Martha had more notice we were coming you'd have found something similar in the refrigerator.' Checking what she'd left by the sink, he set the things he needed aside and started opening cupboards. 'Last time I was here, she made enough food for an army.'

When he looked at her again Liv had a thoughtful expression on her face. Considering his reaction when she asked questions, he could understand that but he didn't mind talking about Martha. She was one of the few good memories he had from that summer. The kitchen had been different then: a large wooden table in the centre of the room had provided the setting for the three squares a day. A younger, cockier Blake had flirted outrageously with the older woman because he knew it made her blush.

'You want something to drink?' he asked.

'What is there?'

'In this place—name your poison.'

'I'll have what you're having.'

After a trip to the refrigerator, he opened drawers until he found utensils, popping the lids off ice cold bottles of beer and handing her one before he washed his hands at the sink and got to work.

Taking a sip from her bottle, Liv ran the tip of her tongue over her lips. 'Did Martha teach you to cook?'

Lowering his chin, he focused on chopping the pepper into strips, the knife making efficient, even slices. 'No one but Martha cooks in this kitchen when Martha's here.' He took a short breath. 'My mom taught me the basics.'

Giving her an opening hadn't cost him much. It was dealing with the line of questioning she could form from it he wouldn't find easy. Thanks to his upbringing, he had a tendency to think three steps ahead. Don't say anything that might give people a hint where he came from or where he was going. Never mention something that would lead to another question and another until they had enough pieces to put it all together. When he'd said he wouldn't hide, he'd meant it, but the truth was he'd been conditioned to hide. Probably half his problem, now he thought about it.

'Mine tried that,' she replied lightly. 'Still does from time to time. Not that it does her much good.'

He smiled. 'Tomboy, huh?'

'Didn't matter, she tried it with all of us. No division of the sexes in the Brannigan household.'

'Four brothers can't have made your life easy.'

'You have *no idea*.'

No, he didn't. But he was glad about that for many reasons, not least of them being he hadn't had anyone to worry about but himself.

'Were you serious about your brother running a background check on every guy he sees you with?'

'They all do.'

Blake's brows lifted. 'They're all cops?'

'Worried they might find something?'

'No.' He smiled again. 'Are you?'

'You're not on the Mounties' Most Wanted list?'

His smile grew. 'Killing you to know what happened in Canada, isn't it?'

'*Yes.*'

'Can't tell you, sweetheart; I took an oath.'

'Attorney/client confidentiality, remember?'

'Pity you're off the clock then, isn't it?'

'Damn it.' She was silent for a moment, the sparkling memory of an earlier time in their relationship fading in her eyes before she felt the need to add, 'You know I'm not billing you for the hours we're together like this, right?'

'You have to bill me for today and tomorrow. Weekend starts Saturday.'

'Changes my profession a tad, don't you think?'

'You're here because we're looking at another property.' He slanted a glance at her to measure her reaction. 'If you don't bill me, they're more likely to question what you've been doing.'

She thought about that. 'It just doesn't feel right. And anyway—' she shrugged the shoulder nearest to him '—I'm hardly the first person in the world to play hooky, am I?'

'You've never played hooky before,' he said with the certainty of someone who had played it plenty.

'There's a first time for everything.' She smiled, her gaze rolling upward. 'Been kinda fun…'

He was glad to hear it but, 'Bill me for office hours, Liv. Keep it straight with your boss.'

'Not when we're doing…*this*…' she said with a wave of her hand between them.

'We've been doing *this* since the day we met.'

'Not all of it, we haven't.'

'So where do you suggest we draw the line?'

'I don't know,' she said honestly. 'But we'll figure it out.'

'It's not like I can't afford it.'

She could quadruple her rate as far as he was concerned. People with money tended to pay over the odds for the best and, whether he liked it or not, he was now one of those people. Since he'd watched her at work she could consider half of it a bonus for how sexy it was when she talked in legal terms. The way she said 'fiduciary' did it for him every damn time.

'That's not the point.' She sighed.

Setting the knife down, he rinsed his hands again and picked up a cloth to dry them. 'No one knows you're sleeping with me, if that's what you're worried about. It's not like we're having sex in Times Square.'

She frowned. 'Are we heading for an argument? I don't know about you, but I'd prefer it if that didn't happen.'

'There's nothing to argue about. You bill me for office hours, we'll take it from there.'

'No,' she said firmly. 'And I'm not moving on that. Not while we're here.'

Tossing the cloth, he turned towards her. 'So you're gonna do what when we're not here? Check your watch every time I kiss you, or are you going to make a rough estimate of how much time we spend flirting and deduct it from the weekly total?'

'Don't do that,' she warned. 'You're making this more complicated than it needs to be.'

'No, what I'm doing is making it *less* complicated.'

Shaking her head, she set her bottle down and began to wriggle off the counter. 'You're the most stubborn person I've ever met.'

'I'm not holding all the cards on that one.' Stepping sideways, he laid his palms flat on the counter beside her hips and looked deep into her eyes. 'You think I want you doing math in your head when you're with me?'

'That's the whole point of not billing you while we're here,' she said with exasperation. 'I want our time here to be about this…about *us*…'

When she realised what she'd said she frowned, her gaze lowering to his neck. But before he could tell her not to censor herself, her chin lifted, eyes bright with determination as if looking at him as she said the words was some kind of personal challenge. 'Can you give me that?'

Blake was floored by how much he wanted to. In that moment, looking into her eyes, he wanted to give her everything. Anything she wanted was hers; all she had to do was ask. It was the first time having stupid amounts of money held any appeal to him. He couldn't promise her more than he was already giving her from a personal point of view, not when he didn't think he had it in him. But this time in this place he could give her, even if it still didn't feel like enough.

Hands moving from the counter to her hips, he nodded.

The smile she gave him was different from any of the smiles he'd seen before. 'Told you we'd figure it out.'

Reaching up, she palmed his cheek before leaning in and kissing him. Her soft lips explored his as she lifted her legs and wrapped them around his thighs to haul him closer. Hands sliding up from her hips, Blake circled her waist and drew her to him, angling his head to deepen the kiss.

'Thought you were hungry,' he mumbled.

'I am,' she mumbled back. 'But not for food.'

'Think you can stay awake long enough to eat later?'

Liv leaned back and blinked as he slid her off the counter. 'Are you complaining because we don't snuggle? Oh. That's. So. *Sweet*.'

Shaking his head, he allowed her feet to hit the floor before scooping her into his arms and turning around. 'You sleep like a dead person.'

'It's not my fault you tire me out.'

'I happen to *enjoy* tiring you out.'

'I'm obviously not doing as good a job of it with you.' She nodded firmly. 'I'll try harder this time.'

Heaven help him if she did.

She smiled the smile he hadn't pinned down yet. 'Would be nice—just once—to wake up and find you beside me.'

It was something else he could give her.

CHAPTER NINE

'You want more coffee?'

'Please.'

Raising a hand to the back of her neck, Olivia moved her fingers against tense muscles. Sitting at a table for three hours without a break would have made her muscles ache to begin with but working with Blake wasn't helping any. She'd never been so distracted from her work by the presence of another human being. Every movement of his large hands, the rise and fall of his broad chest beneath the dark material of his V-necked T-shirt, the teasing hints of deliciously clean male scent that drifted across to her when he shifted his weight in his chair or—

It was distracting as hell.

Lifting the mug he set in front of her, she cradled it in both hands and leaned back in her chair, blowing on the surface of the hot liquid before she took a sip. When her gaze found his, he was watching her mouth.

'You could just let it sit till it cooled.'

She shrugged. 'Maybe I needed the break.'

'This was your idea.'

True—kind of made a mockery of their time there being about 'us'—but she saw it as a necessary survival tactic. Her hope might have been they'd get to know each other well enough to make it feel as if what they were doing was more than just sex for its own sake—that it could be categorised as a romantic interlude when she looked back on it in her old age. But who could have predicted after a minor breakthrough in the conversation department that the first real change would take place in the bedroom? After endless hours of couldn't-keep-their-hands-off-each-other sex, if she'd known the difference it would make when he made love to her oh-so-slow with soul-shattering tenderness—looking deep into her eyes as she tumbled over the precipice...

Trouble was, she wasn't convinced she'd have done anything different. But the experience had widened the crack around her heart, turning the trickle of escaping emotion into a flow she was fearful she wouldn't be able to stem if it got any worse.

'How many shares does this guy have?' He lifted the paper he'd been reading and turned it towards her so she could see the details.

Reaching out a hand, she called up the information. 'Ten per cent.'

'This one?'

'Six per cent.'

'So Kirby is the largest shareholder on the board...'

'No. *You're* the largest shareholder on the board.' Having decided his lack of interest in money was yet another thing she found sexy, she transferred her attention to how tiny the pen looked in his hand.

'Collectively, they could still outvote me.'

'They're only going to outvote you on something they don't think will make money. That's the way it works when you're a shareholder.'

'Thanks for the heads-up,' he said dryly.

Her gaze lifted. 'I'm just stating a fact.'

'Do I have the word *stupid* written on my forehead?'

'No. But I'm pretty sure I can see the word *touchy*.' She sighed. 'If you hate this so much, wouldn't it be easier to sell your shares with everything else?'

His eyes narrowed. 'You don't approve.'

'Do you need my approval?'

'No.'

'Then why should my opinion matter?' She smiled sweetly. 'If I recall, I'm not supposed to have one.'

Leaning back in the chair, he rolled his neck before tossing his pen on the table. 'I'm done for today.'

'Do you want to tell me what the problem is or shall I take a stab at it?'

'Not a big fan of paperwork.'

'Mmm-hmm—' she nodded '—got that.'

When she continued staring at him, he frowned. 'Might save time if you told me what you're fishing for…'

'Admitting you don't want to take over the day-to-day running of the company might be a good place to start.'

'I don't want to take over the day-to-day running of the company.'

'Because you don't want to or because you don't think you can?'

Blake nodded, pressing his mouth into a thin line. 'I'd stop there if I were you.'

'No, you wouldn't.'

He turned his head and looked out of the windows. 'I don't want the responsibility.'

'Okay.'

He shot her a warning glance from the corner of his eye. 'Don't play me, Liv.'

'Touchy.' She shook her head. 'You're still not easy to work with, you know.' When he lifted a brow, she rolled her eyes. 'Fine. *Work for.*'

A tense silence descended. One she didn't fill for a

minute. Deciding that was ample demonstration of patience—and since talking about work was a safe subject—she set her mug down and rested her elbows on the table. 'Walk me through it. Which part of the responsibility is it that bothers you most?'

He looked into her eyes. 'You won't change my mind.'

'What makes you think I want to?'

'Don't you?'

'Depends how dumb I think your reasoning is…'

'I made it clear from the start how I felt about all this.' He shook his head again. 'Not everyone wants to live the billionaire CEO lifestyle.'

'I think you'll find the majority of people would be willing to try the billionaire part.' She took a short breath. 'Even if you sell everything at knock-down, everything-must-go prices, you're still going to end up with buckets of money. What are you going to do then—let it sit and gain interest? 'Cos it will, you know. Money makes money. It's like bacteria in a Petri dish.'

'Maybe I'm considering giving it away,' he said with a completely straight face.

Olivia's eyes widened in disbelief. 'You're just going to hand it out on street corners? Do you have any idea how long that would take?'

'I could hire you to do it.'

She laughed. 'Sorry to disappoint, but I wasn't planning on making a lifetime commitment to you.'

The comment earned another frown. 'I don't expect you to understand.'

It was getting tough to keep the note of exasperation from her voice. 'Have you considered the difference it could make to your life? You could do what you want when you want.'

'I already do.'

'You could make a difference with this money.'

'Giving it to people who need it wouldn't do that?'

It wasn't that he didn't have the right to do whatever he wanted with his legacy. Of course he did. It was just Olivia didn't get it and since it was wrapped up in her need to understand how his mind worked...

'Thousands of people work for Warren Enterprises.'

He folded his arms. 'I remember the guilt card from the first time you played it.'

'There might be more jobs if you ran the place.'

'Still might. Doesn't mean I have to be there. Didn't you say there are people at the company who know what they're doing?'

Oh, he was *good*. She'd argued with trial attorneys who weren't half as quick-minded as he was.

'There's nothing you want to keep from all this?'

Suspicion narrowed his eyes. 'Like?'

Her gaze slanted briefly to the side. 'Nothing you want to hang on to...'

'I might need a bigger hint.'

'No *properties* that interest you?'

'It's just a house, Liv.'

'Don't listen, baby,' she crooned to the house before aiming a glare at him. 'You can fall for a crappy, rundown warehouse but can't envisage wanting to spend time in this beautiful place? Have you had your eyes tested recently?'

'There's nothing wrong with my eyes.'

Actually, she would have to agree with that. She loved his eyes. She just wished she could read what was going on behind them a bit better.

'The warehouse is different,' he said.

'Different how—apart from the obvious falling apart versus still standing aspect of it all...?'

'I can see the potential in it.' Unfolding his arms, he reached for his mug. 'Maybe he knew that.'

It was said as if he found it difficult to believe even his father knew him that well. Tilting her head, Olivia studied him while she tried to slot the information into place. There was a danger it would take them out of safe topic for conversation territory, but if he thought she was giving up on the house she loved so much...

'You can't see potential in this place?' She tried a tentative, 'Because it has memories?'

'It does.' He nodded.

Not good, she assumed. 'You could make new ones.'

'What makes you think we haven't done that already?'

The need to smile was immediate, the flow of emotion escaping into her chest increasing. But when the intensity of his gaze made it feel as if he could see inside her, she leaned back, frowned and pushed to her feet. Walking around the table, she circled his wrist with her fingers, took the coffee mug, set it down and reached for his hands. 'Come on.'

'Where are we going?'

Releasing one hand, she led him down the hall by the other. 'You'll see.'

In the middle of the library, he lifted his brows in question. 'What am I looking at?'

'It's called a library. The books should be a clue for you.' She stepped to his side, tilting her head as she looked up at him. 'What would you change?'

'No point changing anything if I'm not keeping it.'

'What about the bookshelves?' She looked at the room. 'Would you change them?'

'If they're holding up books, I'd say they're doing their job.'

Leaning closer, she adopted a tone of mild outrage. 'But they painted over all that lovely wood.'

'Not all wood is lovely. They probably painted over it for a reason.'

'When money isn't a problem?'

He shook his head. 'You want to strip the paint off that many shelves, it would be quicker ripping them out and starting again.'

Olivia frowned at the idea, suddenly protective of the room. 'Is that what you'd do?'

'I'd leave them the way they are.' He leaned down and lowered his voice. *'Less work.'*

'So there's *nothing* in here you'd change.'

'Since you've obviously put some thought into it, why don't you tell me what *you'd* change?'

'It's not mine to change,' she replied in an echo of the conversation they'd had at the plaza.

'If it was…'

'W-ell…' she scrunched her nose a little as she fought the impulse for all of two seconds before enthusiasm slipped free '…okay, then.' Releasing his hand, she stepped forward with a spring in her step. 'Nice deep cushions in the window seats—there's too much white in here, so I'd change the drapes. You know—add a little warmth to the colour scheme…'

'That's cosmetic. You're not changing the room.'

'I *like* the room,' she said as she turned towards him and shrugged a shoulder. 'It just feels like there's something missing.'

'Coving,' he said without missing a beat.

'What?'

'Some genius took out the coving.' She tilted her head back and studied the high ceiling. 'Would it be hard to put it back in?'

'No. But finding it might take time. You want to replace like-with-like where you can in a place like this.'

Lowering her chin, she studied his face, trying to figure out if he was talking the way he would if he was consulting instead of making decisions about a place he could call his own. 'So that's what you'd do? You'd hunt around salvage yards or antique stores until you found it?'

Not that she had any idea where people got stuff like that, but she assumed it was one or the other.

'I know a guy. I tell him what I need, he tracks it down.' He shrugged. 'What I can't find, I make. It's because I can reproduce traditional carving people hire me for renovations of old buildings.'

'So you'd do the work yourself.' Olivia smiled.

'Why would I hire someone to do something I can do?'

'And *enjoy* doing.'

'Fine.' Blake shook his head in resignation. 'I'd replace the fronts of the shelves.'

Her smile grew. 'With something carved?'

'Rope, maybe shells, something nautical to reflect the fact the ocean is outside.'

Clasping one large hand in two of hers, she backed away. 'Next room.'

'You've made your point,' he said as he allowed her to lead him across the hall.

'I'm just getting started.'

Stopping inside the doorway, she lifted her brows.

'Billiard room,' he supplied with a hint of amusement in his eyes. 'The big green table gave it away.'

'Do you play billiards?'

'No.'

'You play *pool*.'

'I'd take the billiard table out and replace it with a pool

table.' He shook his head again, the amusement more obvious. 'That's what you want me to say, right?'

'Would leave a lot more space...'

'A whole two feet of it...'

'Wouldn't have to be smack bang in the middle, the way this one is, though. It's a big room.'

'Be a pain in the ass to get out of here.' When he looked at her again and she batted her eyelashes in reply, she was rewarded with a smile. 'And you had time to think about all this when, exactly?'

'That was a pretty long walk you took yesterday.'

'It wasn't *that* long.'

'Yes, it was.'

'Missed me, did you?'

'You want to know what I think could go in here?'

'Go on.'

She pointed to a corner. 'Big-screen TV over there for watching the games. Big leather sofa in front of it. Maybe a bar over here—you could carve something beautiful like the bed you were working on that day...'

'Was that a compliment?' He chuckled when she rolled her eyes. 'If we're putting in a bar, we need a jukebox.'

'Not one of those new ones.' She frowned.

'Rock 'n' roll era—we could put a pinball machine beside it.'

'See?' She beamed. 'Now you're getting it.'

'We're not doing this for every room,' he said firmly.

'Well, duh, we can't have a pool table in every room. Where would our friends sit when they come to visit?' When she realised she'd stepped into fantasy land, she blinked and tugged on his hand. 'Just a couple more rooms.'

It went pretty well in the den, Blake playing along with less reluctance as they decided the furniture could be moved and it was the perfect room to sit around an open fire in winter. It was the announcement of 'one more room, I swear'—the step too far she just *had* to take—that messed it up.

Having only seen it from the hall, she wasn't overly surprised when he lingered in the doorway, allowing her hand to slip from his as she walked further into the room.

'I know,' she said as she sat down at a huge leather-topped desk and swivelled the chair around to face him. 'Kind of oppressive, isn't it?'

Blake's gaze roved over the wood panelled walls as he leaned against the door frame and pushed his hands into his pockets. 'I used to think so.'

The hollow tone sounded a death knell on her plan to let him see the potential for a home in the house she loved so much. Olivia grimaced. 'This is his office.'

'Was.' He looked around again. 'Probably inherited—panelling looks original.'

'It's dark,' she commented cautiously.

'Dark wood to begin with but wood does that over time. Strip the varnish, it would probably look better.'

When his gaze found hers, Olivia's chest deflated. One step forward, three steps back. She didn't know to quit when she was ahead.

'I didn't think. I'm sorry.'

'It's just another room, Liv.'

If it was just another room then the hollow tone of his voice wouldn't make it feel as if everything should be taken out and burned so there was nothing left of Charles Warren. What kind of father didn't try to have a relationship with his son? How could that man have walked around in the guise of a well respected businessman and philanthropist while behind closed doors he didn't have so much as *one photograph*—?

Laying her hands flat on the desk to push the chair back, her gaze fell on one of numerous picture frames on the surface. Frowning, she lifted one as she stood up.

'This is you.' Her gaze slid over the others. 'They're all of you.'

It was his childhood in a patchwork quilt of different sizes and styles of frames. To Olivia, it felt as if she'd discovered El Dorado. He just would have been an adorable baby, wouldn't he? How could anyone have resisted that smile? She bit the corner of her lip when she spotted a later picture.

'Nice hairstyle.' Setting down one frame, she reached for another. 'I take it back.'

'Take what back?'

'What I thought last night.' She pointed the frame in her hand in the general direction of the living room. 'There are a bunch of family photos in the other room.'

'And?'

'There weren't any of you.' she shrugged a shoulder as she set the frame down. 'I thought there should be—blamed him because there weren't—but now I know he had *these*...'

Reaching for a picture taken at the railing by the pool, she frowned at the awkwardness between father and son. There was a visible gap between them, Blake's body language suggesting he was less than happy about having his picture taken. Not unusual for a teenager, but she sensed there was more to it than that.

She shook her head. 'I don't get it. Why aren't there any out there? Did he spend that much time in here?'

Gaze lifting sharply when she realised she'd asked the questions out loud, she searched Blake's face for a sign she'd overstepped. He frowned, his gaze on the backs of the pictures not visible from the doorway as a muscle worked in his jaw.

'He couldn't put them with the others.'

Her brows lifted. 'In case someone *saw them*?'

When he nodded, any feelings of forgiveness she'd had disappeared with the snap of invisible fingers. *'Why?'*

It explained why no one had heard of him. Why he was such a mystery when his name appeared in the will and why it had taken so long to find him. But at the same time it made her ache. She could see his face as he'd said he wouldn't hide, *not again*. To purposely hide a child from the world, denying his existence until he was forced into the open as an adult and pushed into a life he hadn't wanted to live, it was so...*manipulative*... What was worse, she'd been part of it. She'd thought he was insane to turn it down, had been determined he should accept the responsibility of such a 'great' legacy.

Olivia felt nauseous.

'He wasn't allowed.'

'What do you mean, he wasn't allowed?' A hint of barely suppressed anger threaded her voice. She wasn't buying it. There was virtually nothing a man with Charles Warren's wealth and power couldn't do if he *wanted to*.

'He made a deal,' he replied in the same hollow tone.

'What kind of deal?'

'She didn't give him a choice.'

Meaning his *mother*? While frantically attempting to make sense of it all, she tried to work out what it was she could see behind dull, emotionless eyes. Resignation, acceptance—what was it? When it occurred to her what it *might be*, it hit her with the equivalent force of being run over by a speeding truck. It wasn't something she could see; it was something she thought she could sense because she knew how it felt.

Standing in the doorway, so tall, still and in control, one of the strongest-willed men she'd ever met suddenly seemed *vulnerable*. And. It. Killed. Her.

Blake's eyes narrowed almost imperceptibly, his jaw tight as he spoke through clenched teeth. 'Don't do that.'

Oh, yeah, *now* he was angry. But not at his parents, not at the past—he was angry at *her*.

When he pushed off the doorway and disappeared into the hall, something inside her snapped. She wanted to *know him*. Not be made to feel as if she were being locked out of his thoughts and how he felt because she didn't matter. Why make the effort to demonstrate so definitively she wasn't just any woman in his bed if how she felt didn't matter? She'd tried not to get emotionally involved but she couldn't change who she was—not that much. It had been there all along. The churning emotion she'd held so tightly in check constantly bubbled below the surface, waiting for a crack in the shell around her heart to grow wide enough for some of it to escape.

Wavering, she made a vain last-ditch attempt to force it back inside and give the moment of madness an opportunity to pass. But it was too late. She cared about him and in six years' time she didn't want to be haunted by what had happened between them.

'She couldn't walk away with dozens of unanswered questions and 'what ifs'...

Not again.

CHAPTER TEN

'You can't just drop something like that on me and walk away,' Liv's voice said behind him.

Gaze fixed on the door at the end of the hall, Blake sensed the freedom beyond, drawn to it with the same compulsion that made a man kick to get to the surface of deep water so he could haul in air. It was an urge he recognised, the restlessness inside him as ingrained as the screaming instincts he'd ignored when he told her things she didn't need to know.

'Damn it, Blake.' Frustration threaded her voice. 'Would you just stand still for a minute?'

Yeah, he was famous for standing still, wasn't he? Thing was, for a moment, while they'd been talking about changes that could be made to the house, he'd thought—

'Talk to me.'

So she could land another dose of pity on him? He didn't think so. Close to the door, he changed direction, reasoning if he was going anywhere, he needed his stuff.

'Of course, how stupid of me,' her voice said when he was halfway up the stairs. 'This is what you do. It's why you've had so many addresses. You run away.'

Hands clenched into fists at his sides, he froze and fought the wave of anger washing over him. 'You don't know anything about me.'

'Why do you think I'm trying to get to know you?'

Breathing deep, he took another upward step.

'Going to pack, are we?'

It was none of her damn business what he did or where he went. There was a difference between running away and leaving somewhere he just plain didn't want to be.

'That's your life, is it? Every time someone tries to get to know you, you cut and run.' She laughed bitterly. 'So much for not hiding.'

Anything you say can and will be used against you.

Squaring his shoulders, he turned around. 'When did pushing me start to seem like a good idea to you?'

'Being patient wasn't getting me anywhere, was it?' Anger flashed in her eyes. 'You think I like sleeping with a stranger?'

'Seems to me you liked it plenty last night.' He bit back the way any animal would when backed into a corner.

'Seems to me I wasn't *alone* last night.' She lifted her chin in defiance. 'See, that's what I don't get. The stranger I sleep with? He's a pretty amazing guy. That's why I'd like to get to know him better. The man I spend time with during the day—most of the time he's not bad—but he could win Jerk of the Year with very little effort.'

Blake pressed his mouth into a thin line. If she wanted to get it off her chest he could be the big guy and take it, but once she'd spit it all out they'd be done.

She lifted a hand and dropped it to her side. 'What do you think I'm going to do? Try and pin you down to a long-term commitment? Start planning a wedding and naming our kids the second you tell me something about your life? When did I strike you as someone desperately looking for a happily ever after? If I was, I sure as hell wouldn't be looking at you.'

That really shouldn't have bugged him as much as it did. 'Maybe you should tell me what it is you *do* want.'

'I want you. To. Talk. To. Me.'

'So we can work our way through my childhood issues?' He jerked his brows. 'I didn't realise therapist training was part of the course at law school.'

'You think you're the only person who has been messed up by something that happened in the past?' she yelled.

Blake laughed and shook his head. 'You're so far over the line of good judgement now you're flailing.' He looked her straight in the eye. 'You know *squat* about being messed up or what it takes to walk out the other side of it.'

'You think?'

'I know.'

Glancing down the hall, she nodded, eyes glinting with raw emotion when she looked at him again. 'When you've spent six years of your life believing if you'd just done one thing different you might have saved someone's life then you can talk to me about being messed up and what it takes to come out the other side of it. Okay?' She took a breath, shook her head and turned on her heel, her voice cold and controlled. 'I'm done. Talk to me, don't talk to me. Do whatever the hell you want. At least I'll know I tried.'

Blake ground his teeth together, determined he was going to let it go. Just because every time she took a step back he felt the need to take a step forward didn't mean—

'I can't.'

She was on the other side of the banister from him when the words slipped out, surprising him as much as her. Blinking, he shook his head as she stopped and looked at him. What the hell was he doing?

'Yes, you can,' she said in a low voice.

'No.' It took more effort to say it again. 'I *can't.*'

The emphasis made her pause before asking, 'Why not?'

'It's not something I do.'

'You could try.'

'It's not that simple.'

Great, now he couldn't keep his damn mouth *shut*. He tried to figure out why he was still there. Didn't want to leave was the obvious answer. Understanding the underlying cause was a different matter. Since there was only one way he could find out, he sat down on the stairs, setting his feet apart and leaning his elbows on his knees before he looked at her through the carved wooden balustrade.

'I'm not big on sharing.'

'Because it's not easy for you,' she said tentatively.

'Because I'm not any good at it.' He frowned.

Avoiding his gaze, she took a short breath, narrowed her eyes and pointed a finger at him. *'Stay there.'*

Climbing the stairs, she sat down a couple of steps below him, her back to the wall as she waited for him to decide what to tell her.

'I can hold a conversation,' he heard his traitorous voice explain. 'I just can't…'

Form a sentence, apparently.

'It's okay, I get it now.'

Good. Maybe she could explain it to him.

'You didn't get it five minutes ago.'

'That was different.' She shrugged when he looked at her. 'I didn't know why, then.'

And that was all it took to appease her?

'Makes sense…'

It did?

'Easier to tell when someone is holding stuff back if it's something you do yourself. You've always known when I was doing it, even when I thought I had my game face on.' She grimaced. 'I don't find this easy, either.'

'Not like I make it easy for you.'

She rolled her eyes. 'Shocking as it is to believe, it's not actually all about you.'

Okay, he'd deserved that.

She smiled a small smile. 'Has there ever been a time you spit something out without thinking about it first?'

A corner of his mouth tugged wryly. She had to ask?

'I mean personal stuff.'

'No.'

'You're like that with everyone?'

'Yes.'

'What about Marty—you guys seemed pretty tight.'

'We talk the way guys talk.'

'Sports analogies, right?' Her eyes sparkled. 'I can talk in football terms if it helps.'

Blake lifted his brows. 'Know what *would* help?'

'Not patronizing you?'

She'd got it in one. When she studied him again, he waited.

'I can't believe I'm going to say this.' She sighed heavily. 'Tell me what you're thinking.'

'You know the problem with that?'

'Apart from the fact it's lame?'

He let her in on a little secret. 'When women ask that question, whatever a guy was thinking is replaced with what he *thinks* he should be thinking.'

'Is that what you do?' She blinked innocently.

'I tend to ignore the question.'

When the smile softened her eyes, Blake shook his head. Fighting the need to close some of the distance between them for all of ten seconds, he reached for her hand, spreading his legs wider to make enough room to tug her onto the step below him. As she leaned back against his chest, he pressed the tip of his nose to soft summer-scented hair and breathed deep, allowing her body heat to seep into him before he rested his chin on her head and frowned at the tremor he could feel running through her.

Gently rocking their bodies, he waited until he felt her take several long, controlled breaths before the shaking eased and she relaxed into him.

'Right now,' he said in a low voice as he lifted his head, 'I'm thinking I'd really like to know what happened six years ago but I can't ask you to tell me.'

'Why?'

'Bit hypocritical, don't you think?' He looked down at her as she rested her head against his shoulder. 'You share stuff with me, you'll expect it in return.'

'Sharing does tend to involve more than one person.'

'You've got the wrong guy for that.'

'Do you want to try?'

'I can't change the past, Liv. Talking about it isn't going to undo anything.' As he said the words he felt the emptiness inside him grow.

'Shall I tell you what I think?'

She was asking for permission?

'I think we have the perfect scenario for sharing stuff. We're those passing ships in the night. But I don't think it matters if you know someone for five minutes or fifty years, they all become part of your journey if you let them.' The smile sounded in her voice. 'I know that probably sounds dumb to you, but—'

'No, it doesn't. I've met people like that.'

She looked up at him. 'Name one.'

'Matthew Allen. Taught me to carve wood.' He smiled at the memory. 'Grumpy old bastard, but he had tales to tell. He could see things in a lump of wood anyone else would have burnt. Left me his tools when he died…'

A legacy he'd appreciated from a man who had been

more of a father to him in six months than Charlie Warren had been in a lifetime. He'd mourned Matthew's passing. He could access what he'd felt at the time with very little effort.

'And now I know something I didn't know before...'

Nodding, Blake considered what she'd said and thought about the raw emotion he'd seen in her eyes when she'd revealed more than she intended to in the heat of the moment. He liked the idea of being part of her journey—leaving the same indelible imprint on her it felt as if she was leaving on him. What he didn't want was the time they spent together to be seen as a mistake or for it to hurt when she thought about it in the future.

How she felt mattered to him. It may have crept up on him when he'd been distracted by everything else but it had been there for a while.

'If I'm going to try this, you can't look at me the way you did in that room.'

'How did I look at you?'

'Like a kicked puppy.' He frowned. 'I don't need your pity, sweetheart.'

'You thought that was pity?' She looked stunned.

'What was it, then?'

'I can tell you it wasn't pity.' She shook her head. 'The problem with only getting pieces of the puzzle is people have a tendency to fill in the gaps. I went from resenting your father to forgiving him a little to hating him and angry as hell in less than ten minutes.'

Blake was tempted to welcome her to his seventeen-year-old world.

Lowering her chin, she watched as she smoothed her palm over his arm in a light caress. 'I don't understand how someone can hide their child like that. I have a two-year-old niece—Amy—and Johnnie hands out pictures of her to the family like they're fliers. Amy's first smile, Amy's first tooth, the first time Amy held a spoon—poor kid never gets a minute's peace.'

'It's not the same thing.'

'It should have been,' she argued.

Wasn't much he could do about that, was there? But while he didn't agree with the majority of choices his parents had made, he understood some of their motivation. 'Sometimes kids are better kept out of the public eye.'

'That's not what I'm talking about.' She scowled. 'Proud and protective aren't mutually exclusive.'

'Don't get mad, sweetheart. I agree with you.' He smiled, wondering if it had occurred to her the child she was so passionately defending was a fully grown man.

'Why aren't you angry?'

'It was a long time ago.'

'You *should* be angry.'

'You want to go dig him up so you can kick his ass?'

'Don't do that,' she said in an echo of the warning he'd given her. Twisting around, she grabbed a handful of his T-shirt and pushed her fist against his chest. 'That wasn't pity you could see, you idiot. I—'

'I get it.'

It was a lie. He didn't. But the way she was looking at him was tough enough to handle without asking what it meant. His reaction to the unknown emotion he could see in her eyes made the simple act of breathing in and out more difficult. Hadn't she got enough out of him for one day?

As if she'd heard the question, the hand on his arm slipped up to his shoulder and around the back of his neck, adding pressure to lower his mouth to hers. The contact was light, unbelievably sweet, whisper soft and Blake was amazed—considering how much of it they'd done—they could still find a kiss that was new.

When their lips parted and she looked into his eyes, his thoughts returned to what she'd yelled at him. He couldn't imagine her ever being messed up. Not the Liv he knew. Every time she dropped a piece of information into a conversation or during the meandering chatter she felt necessary to fill a silence, he'd been on it, tucking away each detail as if he was saving them for the proverbial rainy day. But what he knew wasn't enough. Not any more. Maybe that was why she'd pushed him.

Blake discovered he was okay with that.

'Can you tell me what happened six years ago?'

She nodded. 'I can talk about it. The compulsory visits to the department shrink can testify to that. He ticked the "not crazy" box—always good to know, right?'

Blake knew what she was doing. He was the master when it came to making light of things that weren't the remotest bit funny.

'You know my brothers are cops.'

'Yes.'

'Did I mention my dad was a cop?'

'No.'

'And his dad before him.' A wistful smile softened the blue of her eyes. 'It's in the blood. My whole life was geared towards becoming a cop. I couldn't wait to sign up.'

'How did your dad feel about that?'

'Mixed feelings, but I like to think he'd have been proud.' Avoiding his gaze, she added a matter-of-fact, 'He had a heart attack two years before I graduated from the academy.'

'He'd have been proud,' Blake said with certainty.

She flashed a small smile of appreciation before continuing. 'After graduation, rookies get partnered with a Training Officer. I got Nick. He taught me a lot. One of the things he kept saying was you can't be a cop if you let your emotions take over. We have to sit on them, push them deep inside so we can do our job. I struggled with that.'

But she'd learnt how to do it, hadn't she? It was a revealing insight into the woman he'd met at the beginning, while at the same time leaving him feeling as if he'd barely scratched the surface.

'I told you about needing to know someone's story to understand why they do the things they do.' She waited for his nod. 'What we're not supposed to do is help people make decisions.' She rolled her eyes. 'I still suck at that.'

'Little bit.' He smiled. 'But there's a difference between having an opinion and telling someone what to do.'

She raised a brow. 'Could we remember that the next time I have an opinion?'

Walked right into that one, hadn't he?

'We can try,' he allowed. Contrary to the impression he might have given her with rules that might possibly have been put there to see how long it would take her to break them, he was interested in her opinion. Didn't mean he had to agree with it or that she would change his mind, but he could make an effort to be less defensive. 'Keep going.'

There was a pause as she took another breath and held it for a long moment. 'On the patch we patrolled, there was an underpass at the edge of a park where homeless people gathered. We would drive by to check in on them. We looked for drug use and underage teens—kept an eye out if anyone was missing or died during the night—that kind of thing.' She shrugged. 'But you get to know people...'

'There's nothing wrong with that.'

'There is if you're struggling with the not getting

involved part of the job.' She sighed heavily. 'Every time we left, Nick had the same look on his face, especially after I got to know Jo. She was my contact. She would tell me when there had been problems, keep an eye on everyone, make sure anyone who couldn't make it to food handouts had something brought back to them. Jo was special—wise beyond her years in many ways.' She smiled. 'Still is...'

'You kept in touch with her?'

'We share an apartment.'

'Takes the phrase "bringing your work home with you" a tad too far, don't you think?'

'Don't judge,' she warned.

If she'd started adopting strays he was with Nick. How much could she realistically have known about the person she'd invited into her home? In a sense he supposed it was exactly what she'd done with him when she decided to share his bed. He frowned at the idea of being adopted like a stray. It was the last thing he wanted from her.

But since it begged the question of what he *did* want...

Her gaze lowered. 'Jo introduced me to Aiden. He was a good kid—messed up—but a good kid.' She blinked several times, as if focusing on something at a distance. 'When he had problems with a guy who was taking his stuff, I talked to him about it and suggested he try clearing the air. I got the usual lecture from Nick on the way to get coffee but he was right. While we were gone Aiden did what I'd suggested and talked to the guy. There was an argument—the guy pulled a knife—and Aiden was stabbed in the stomach. Took us less than ten minutes to get back when the call came in, but he died at the scene.'

When Blake felt another tremor run through her body, he tightened his arms. 'It wasn't your fault.'

'I wasn't holding the knife, but it felt like it was.'

'You made a suggestion. He didn't have to follow it.'

'I was wearing the uniform and he was an eighteen-year-old kid.' She shook her head. 'I should have known better. Or intervened—intervened would have been better...'

Except then she might have been the one who was stabbed in the stomach and died at the scene. Blake would never have met her. He didn't like that scenario.

'Bad things happen.' He frowned at how trite it sounded. 'You cared enough to try and help. I bet that meant a lot to a kid living on the streets.'

'It wasn't enough,' she said in a small voice.

Blake crooked his finger underneath her chin and tilted her face up, leaning down to look deep into her eyes as he repeated, *'It wasn't your fault.'*

'I know.'

'Do you?' He wasn't so sure.

'I want to.' She blinked incredulously. 'That's the first time I've admitted that. How did you know?'

'Guilt looks different on everyone. Same for grief.' He may have been struggling to deal with his inability to feel either one, 'But I know them when I see them.'

'I'm better now, really I am,' she reassured him. 'It just takes time to work through it, you know?'

He brushed the backs of his fingers across her jaw. 'I know, but you can't blame yourself, Liv. We all make choices every day—some big, some small. If we tried to figure out the chain reaction of every single one, we'd go crazy. We won't always get everything right but we can learn from the mistakes and decide what we're willing to live with when we look in the mirror. I don't think anyone can do anything more than that.'

Her brows lifted. 'Wow—that's actually quite—'

'Smart?'

'I was going to say insightful.'

'You could try looking less surprised.' When he smiled and she smiled back at him, he tucked a strand of hair behind her ear before he lowered his arm. 'So is that why you quit?'

'It was the start of it.' She nodded. 'When you're a rookie you know stuff like that is going to happen. Everyone has a bad shift; it's part of the job. But it wasn't one bad shift. They just kept on coming. You think you'll handle it. I didn't. The first time I drew my weapon my hands were shaking.' She looked down and folded her fingers into her palms. 'That's when I knew I was done.'

'And went to Law School...'

'Took me a while to figure it out.' She smiled again. 'But it seemed like a logical move when I thought about it.'

Blake couldn't remember ever respecting anyone as much as he respected Liv at that moment. He knew what it took to pick up, dust down and move on but he'd never known what it took to stand still and regroup the way she had. Possibly because he'd never had anything to fight for—at least nothing that mattered to him as much as the oath she'd taken to 'Protect and Serve'.

Because she was still doing it, wasn't she?

Apart from her concern for the thousands of little guys employed by Warren Enterprises, Blake realised she'd been doing it with him. More than simply serving her position as his lawyer, her opinion was offered—even when he didn't want to hear it—to allow him to see things from a different perspective. If she thought he was wrong, she challenged him, protecting him from the kind of clouded judgement that could get in the way. She was right about that—it had done, more than once in his life, but he wouldn't let it happen with her. He was determined to give her what she wanted. No regrets, only bittersweet memories.

'Thank you—' it was something he should have said before, for more than one reason, but this time '—for telling me.'

'You're welcome.' The blue of her eyes softened with warmth that reached deep inside him, wrapping around the emptiness the way it did when they made love.

Gaze roving over her face, he took in all of the familiar details he still found fascinating. What was it about her that was different from any of the women he'd met before? With Liv, he felt things more intensely: desire, need, hunger. He was frustrated at his inability to give her more than a sexual relationship and that warred with new sensations of jealousy, possessiveness and a newfound protectiveness he felt towards her—even if it meant protecting her from *him*.

Someone with the ability to care as much as she could shouldn't be around someone like him. Not if the emptiness he carried would lead to him leeching emotion from her in an attempt to fill the void. If he thought for a second that might happen he would have to let her go sooner rather than later, whether he was ready to or not.

'You hungry?' she asked, letting him off the hook when it came to his part of the sharing bargain they'd made.

He was okay about that, not because he didn't want to make the effort to talk to her, but because she was right. Even if talking about it helped—which he doubted—it wasn't all about him. Nor should it be.

'Yes.' He smiled with meaning.

'I meant for food.'

He grinned. 'That, too.'

'You're insatiable, you know that, don't you?' She got to her feet and reached for his hands to pull him up.

'Is that a complaint?'

'Did it sound like a complaint?'

Smile becoming a grin as they walked down the hall, he nudged his upper arm off her shoulder and rocked her sideways. 'So it's another *compliment*...'

'It's amazing to me the size of that head doesn't topple you over.'

CHAPTER ELEVEN

'I THINK you should keep this house. It *needs you*.'

'I don't think it's particular about who looks after it so long as someone does. Houses can be funny that way.'

Walking hand in hand along the beach, Olivia took a long breath and smiled. She was happy, closer to Blake since their breakthrough than was sensible, admittedly, but the way she looked at it, a girl had to grab moments of happiness where she could find them, even if part of her was waiting for a pinprick to burst the bubble they were living in.

She tilted her chin and looked up at him. 'Did I point out the advantage of it being in The Hamptons?'

'No, but you're going to.'

'You wouldn't have to be here the whole year round. Most people aren't.' She continued smiling. 'And when you get itchy feet, it's not like you don't still have plenty of places to go. You own places all over the world now.'

'And a choice of private jets to take me there…'

'Precisely.'

'I'd be happy to help you join the Mile High Club.'

'I'm serious.' She laughed.

'So am I.' He winked.

When she rolled her eyes, he stopped and leaned down to kiss her—firm, practised lips drawing a hum of approval from low in her throat. It was a gentle, almost tender kiss—one that had been happening more frequently since he'd started sharing little details of his life with her—but it wasn't always like that with them. There were times it was all about hunger and need, times when it was more about giving than taking, times when it was teasing and times—like this—when it soothed and said everything was going to be all right. Even if she knew it wouldn't.

If she hadn't already known, when he told her about some of the places he'd lived, the people he'd met and she watched his eyes shine with memories she was reminded how different they were. Blake was a rolling stone, free of ties and the burden of any responsibilities beyond taking care of himself, while Olivia was tethered to the people she loved and the place she called home. She was a New Yorker, a Brannigan, a best friend and a lawyer who put long hours into her work—she didn't even know where a relationship with a man like Blake would fit into that. And knowing she'd be willing to find out took a little of the brightness off her day...

'Just think about it,' she mumbled against his mouth.

Leaning back, he used his free hand to brush her hair from her cheek. 'You really love this place.'

'I do.'

He searched her eyes before announcing, 'It's yours.'

A low huff of disbelieving laughter left her lips. 'You can't give me a house.'

'I can do what I want.'

Reaching up, she wrapped her fingers around his hand, lowering it from her face as her smile faded. 'I can't accept a gift that large from you.'

'Yes, you can.'

'No, I can't.' The second huff of laughter was tighter. 'People don't give other people houses.'

'Not like I don't have plenty to spare, is it?'

'Stop it,' she said more firmly, stepping back. 'I'm just saying you should think about it before selling it. Not every decision you make has to be made in a hurry. Some things are worth hanging on to...'

When he frowned at the words, she let go of his hands and turned away, walking ahead of him while berating herself for giving him the impression she wanted more than they had. As obvious as it was she hadn't known the risk she was taking emotionally when she slept with him, when it came to commitment she knew exactly where she stood. What they had would end. It was simply a matter of when.

Why did she have to keep reminding herself of that?

'It's just a house, Liv.'

'You keep saying that.' She turned and walked backwards for a few steps. 'It's not *just* a house and even if it was, I would still feel the same way. I don't want expensive gifts from you. It would feel like—'

A large hand captured her elbow when she turned away, holding her in place as he stepped closer. 'Payment?'

Frustration threaded her voice. 'It's how it might look. *There she goes—the lawyer who slept with a billionaire and got a house in The Hamptons out of it.*'

'I don't care what people think.'

'I do,' she said in a softer voice. 'We're judged by our actions. How can I work with rich and powerful company owners in the future if they suspect my motives? I won't be able to smile at a guy without someone thinking I'm out to get something.'

'They won't think that.'

'They might.'

The hold on her arm loosened, his thumb brushing over her skin. 'I can't give you anything? Flowers, chocolates—

all the usual stuff women are supposed to like—they're all out of bounds, are they?'

A smile hovered around the corners of her mouth. 'I didn't say *that*. What I'm saying is there's a gap the size of the Grand Canyon between a bunch of flowers and a house. You don't have to woo me, Blake. Considering how much time we've spent in bed, I think it's safe to say we skipped the wooing part, wouldn't you?'

'I don't even know what it means.'

Taking a step forward, Olivia laid a palm on his chest. 'I don't need expensive gifts from you—anyone who does isn't worth your time.'

What he didn't know was how great a gift he'd already given her. When she'd told him what happened in the past, he'd done more than tell her what she'd needed to hear. While she'd thought she'd moved on, she realised she hadn't let that day go—carrying the memory of it around with her like a penance. But while talking to him without getting upset, hearing the sincerity in his rough voice and seeing the resolve in his eyes when he told her it wasn't her fault, she'd felt some of the weight being lifted from her shoulders. The department shrink, who had expected her to spend hours reliving the moment Aiden died, people she'd worked with, family and friends—none of them had been able to do that for her. Then along came Blake.

As frightening as it was that he'd seen inside her to something she hadn't admitted to herself, by understanding what had happened he'd given her a gift money could never buy: the first hint of real peace of mind she'd felt in six years.

He shook his head. 'Still doing it, aren't you?'

'Doing what?'

'Preparing me for a new life…'

'Your life *is* different. I think you know that now.' Her gaze searched his eyes, sincerity lacing her voice. 'Sometimes we don't get to choose where we end up. Stuff happens. You'll find something good you can take out of this, I know you will. You've just got to be open to it.'

'What makes you think I haven't done that already?'

Flashing a smile to cover the sudden ache in her chest, she rocked onto her toes and placed a kiss on the corner of his mouth. 'You can be incredibly sweet when you set your mind to it.'

'Don't go telling anyone.'

'Your secret's safe with me.'

Blake circled her with his arms, drawing her close, her body fitting into his in a way that suggested they'd been together for a lot longer than they had. In turn, she wrapped her arms around his lean waist, placed her cheek on his chest and listened to the steady beat of his heart, drawing comfort from the sound.

Sad thing was—if things had been different—she knew he was exactly the kind of man she needed in her life. Despite the things they both still held back, having someone she could lean on during moments when she got tired of being strong, and who could find the words to make her feel like less of an emotional ticking time bomb, sounded pretty darn good to her. She just wished she could find a way of helping him the way he'd helped her.

Blinking as she looked at the sparkling ocean, she took a mental snapshot of the moment and stored it away in her memory for the day he wouldn't be there any more. She didn't want to leave. Not yet. As if somehow she knew when they left The Hamptons it was the beginning of the end.

'We'll forget I tried to give you a house,' his deep, rough

edged voice rumbled above her head. 'Be a bitch to gift-wrap anyway.'

'It would.' She smiled.

When she leaned back to look at him, he lowered his mouth to hers for one of the kisses that lit a flame inside her body. She'd been wrong about the attraction between them flaring and fizzling out. If anything, knowing him better had added a depth and richness to their lovemaking that hadn't been there before. She wanted him *more*, not less. Making love and sharing the moment when they were at their most vulnerable, falling asleep next to him and waking up in his arms—she knew she would miss it when it was gone. He'd be a hard act to follow, too.

'We should probably think about packing.' She sighed with regret, loosening the arms around his waist and backing away. 'The chopper will be here first thing.'

'We still have time.'

'I don't want to leave a mess behind.' She forced a smile to hide any subliminal message he might read into the words. 'You were the one who told the staff we could fend for ourselves, remember?'

Hand held in his again, they headed back up the beach in a silence she didn't feel the need to fill.

'I won't sell it,' he said before they left the sand.

'I'm glad.' Wrapping her arms around his waist again, she clung to his side, his arm draped across her shoulder as she added, 'If you're lucky, next time I'm in The Hamptons, I might look you up.'

'You're gonna call first, right?'

Blake settled back against the pillows, lifting his arm so Liv could curl in beside him before she fell asleep. As her cheek rubbed against his chest, her breasts smooshed against his side, he found himself staring across the room, fingers tracing lazy circles on her back while he thought.

It wasn't the first time he'd found himself focusing on the mental picture she'd helped create of the house he'd told her he would keep. She was right, changes could be made—some of them he would probably enjoy making. Old houses had always been his thing, after all. Not that he'd ever had one he could call his own, but he suspected it would add to the sense of pride he put into his work. But while mentally working his way from room to room, thinking about the changes, Liv was always there. He couldn't imagine it without her.

But even if he had it in him to put down roots, there were no guarantees. Especially when staying put would mean making decisions he hadn't wanted to make—ones he knew would put him in a perpetually foul mood until he worked his way through them. Not wanting to run the company wasn't just the issue of responsibility. Much as it killed him to admit it, part of the problem was—*maybe*—he didn't think he could. If there was one thing Blake hated more than finding something he wasn't any good at, it was being surrounded by people who were better at it than him.

But he could delegate. He'd been known to allocate work to guys who knew what they were doing. Wasn't that kind of the same thing as running a company? But considering doing something he would enjoy—like renovating the warehouse—was one thing, making changes that large to his life was another. *Why was he even thinking about it?*

Liv moved her calf against his leg, her murmur of contentment calming him. He remembered the first morning in his apartment when he'd felt better with her close to him. Then he thought about how it felt worse when the distance between them increased. She was the equivalent of an open fire in the depths of winter. Step too close and flames would consume him, licking his body and igniting his senses until he exploded in a shower of white heat and bright light. Step too far back and he could find himself standing in arctic temperatures that seeped into his bones, numbing him until he wouldn't have the strength to step close to the warmth again.

Was that how it would feel when she wasn't there?

Just the thought of walking away from her made him keenly aware of the cold empty place inside him. He needed to deal with that—plunge into the middle of it and get to the heart of why he couldn't feel anything about the death of the man who had contributed half his DNA. He couldn't stay numb for ever or get angry every time he was faced with something he couldn't communicate clearly. Hadn't talking to Liv the last couple of days proved he could find words if he made the effort?

'We moved around a lot…'

He wanted her to know—to understand why staying in one place and putting down roots was something he knew nothing about.

'It started when I was seven. A guy turned up outside school and argued with my mom. He followed us home, parked outside the house, took pictures.' He felt the blink of Liv's lashes against his chest as he spoke. 'When none of that got him anywhere he hung around at recess, calling me from the other side of the fence, "Hey kid, where's your dad? Ever meet him? I've got a picture—you want to see?"'

Blake could still hear the man's voice and remember what it felt like to see the picture—the sense of curiosity and a childlike awe. 'It was the first time I'd laid eyes on Charlie Warren. I'd hit that age where I was starting to ask the questions kids ask when they notice they don't have two parents. My mom would tell me he was busy or had important stuff to do—how his job made him responsible for lots of other folks. Sometimes she'd just change the subject. Guess it wasn't easy to explain to a kid why you loved someone but couldn't stay with them.'

Pausing to take a breath, he checked to see how he felt about that. When he was a kid it had hurt and made him think his dad didn't care, but now, nothing.

'Within twenty-four hours of seeing the photo we were packed and headed to a new town.' He remembered being angry, not wanting to leave his friends or his school and arguing with his mom until she'd promised him the dog he wanted so badly. They'd never got a dog.

'My mom was always looking over her shoulder after that. Maybe she was right and there were others. After a while, I think it was paranoia. Nobody cared who we were.'

'He was a reporter?' Liv asked in a soft voice.

'Yes.'

'She was protecting you.'

'The only way she knew how. It's why she left Charlie. She couldn't handle the spotlight—didn't want me under it either—finding out she was pregnant made her decision.'

'How many times did you move when you were a kid?'

'I stopped counting. At first, you think it's how everyone lives. By the time you're old enough to know better, you don't know anything else.' He breathed deep, feeling a hint of remembered acceptance. 'When the reporter lost our trail, he headed straight for Charlie to break the news to him he had a kid. Charlie hired a PI to track us down. Gotta give it to him, he had one hell of a stand-up row with my mom when he found us.'

'You'd have done the same thing.'

He would, but he'd never understood how Charlie might have felt until that moment. In the darkness, he could feel the curve of Liv's stomach pressed against his waist and for a moment—before he'd realised what he was doing—he pictured what it would be like to have a full, rounded belly pressed against him and a baby—*their baby*—moving inside her. Stepping into Charlie's shoes and replacing his mom with Liv, he understood how angry his father had been at his mother for keeping his child from him. Liv was right, he'd have yelled, too. He'd have yelled his damn head off.

But the mental image he'd created didn't stop there.

The heated weight in his groin at the thought of what was involved when it came to putting a baby in Liv was hardly a surprise, but what stunned him was how completely okay he was with the idea of her being pregnant with his child, of a new life that would bind them together. He'd never thought about having kids, about a family of his own.

That suddenly he thought—

'Keep going,' she coaxed in the same soft, totally-unaware-of-his-thoughts voice.

'Where was I?' It took a lot to keep his voice even, and Blake didn't know how she couldn't hear his heart racing, his body already kicking into full-on baby-making mode. What the hell was *that* about?

'Charlie found you. He had a fight with your mom.'

Lifting the hand from her back, he swiped it over his face in an attempt to pull himself together. 'When they'd calmed down and talked about it, I think Charlie got it. He'd hit a few reporters in his time and he knew how insecure my mom was. He loved her. Guess he must have, since he never married. So they made a deal. She'd send him pictures and keep him updated—he'd send money and keep the secret till I was old enough to decide what I wanted.'

'He didn't visit?'

'When he could—wasn't always easy for him to keep a low profile. Don't think he found it easy to keep track of us at times, either. My mom could be hit-and-miss with the whole stay in touch part of the deal. Every time he visited she was borderline manic for days after he left. Everyone was looking at us, everyone was talking about us; someone had to have recognised Charlie. It was easier when he didn't visit.' Blake had known that at twelve. He'd resented the man who made life more difficult for him than it already was. 'Not like a handful of days a few times a year was gonna make for much of a father/son bond, anyway. Once I hit my teens, he didn't stand a chance. I wasn't interested in why he wasn't there. Bottom line, he wasn't and I had my mom to deal with on my own.'

'Did she ever get help?'

'Talk to someone who might rat us out? *Hell, no.*' And by the time he'd worked out that his mom might have benefited from talking things through with someone it had been too late. 'If she'd visited a doctor more often they might have found the tumours sooner.'

He'd felt guilty about that. He should have made her go sooner, should have known there was something wrong.

'Is that when you came here?'

'When she collapsed and the hospital emergency room said it was cancer, I made her contact Charlie to pull some strings and get her the treatment she needed.' His pride might have been dented but it had been her only hope. 'After a couple of semesters at high school in New York, they decided I'd spend the summer here. I wasn't given a choice. It didn't go the way I think Charlie hoped it would. By seventeen I had attitude, was getting into trouble, resented the hell out of being here and was stuck with a guy I barely knew. Not like we could toss a football around. He was a lot older than my mom, to begin with.'

Blake ran his palm along her spine before starting to make circles with his fingertips again. 'Looking back, I think it took that summer and the couple of years my mom was sick before she died to straighten me out. If things had been different, there might have been more than one member of the Warren family wearing an orange jumpsuit.'

'I don't think so,' Liv said with a certainty he far from deserved.

She hadn't known him.

'When was the last time you saw him?'

'Her funeral.'

'He didn't try to get in touch again?'

Blake immediately thought of the envelope he'd been carrying around. 'Not till it was too late.'

'He should have tried.'

'I can be pig-headed when I set my mind to it.'

'You?' She pressed a kiss to the skin directly over his heart and rubbed her cheek against his chest. *'Never.'*

He smiled into the darkness.

They stayed silent for a long while after that, a clock chiming the hour somewhere in the distance while Blake tried to make sense of his thoughts. What the hell was he doing thinking about having a child when he had no idea what family meant? Families were something other people had. Granted, it might explain some of the emptiness he carried around, but what if having a family of his own didn't fill it or, worse still, he handed whatever defect it was inside him onto his kids? They didn't deserve that. Neither did their mother. His arms tightened instinctively around Liv. He wouldn't do that to her.

The void within him expanding, he vowed he would let her go before he came close to hurting her. He could do the honourable thing. What he couldn't do was be selfish, give her half a man or one who might some day succumb to the emptiness and leave her living with a shell. A wave of anger crashed over him. It wasn't enough, damn it.

He wasn't enough *for her*.

As if sensing he needed to get lost in her again, she shifted and stretched her body along the length of his, her hands smoothing up his arms and across his shoulders as she whispered, 'Thank you. For telling me…'

It felt like the least he could do. His inability to give her something more when nothing ever felt like enough forced him to fight his most basic instincts and remain passive while she took what she wanted. But as her soft lips moved across his mouth he felt himself drawn to her warmth, the need to move closer to the fire making him roll them over so he could set the pace before he was engulfed by the flames she ignited inside him.

He couldn't get enough of her. Maybe he never would.

Olivia found the letter by accident as she picked up a pair of his jeans. When it dropped to the floor, she bent down to lift it without thinking, unfolding it to see if she could toss it away. Reading several familiar scored out addresses, she froze, turning it over and checking the sender's address above the unbroken seal. How long had he been carrying it around? She checked the date on the postmarks, her brows lifting in surprise.

'How many damn bottles of stuff did you bring with you?' Blake called from the bathroom.

'You think I look this good without any effort?' she called back while frowning at the envelope.

'That's one of those questions there's no right answer to, right?'

Turning towards the bed where their weekend bags were laid out, she debated telling him she'd found it. She loved that he'd shared so much with her but the closer she felt to him, the more there was to lose. The story of his past told in the deep, rough rumble of his voice while he'd held her in the dark had had even more of an effect on her than the fact they'd made love in what had felt like the truest sense of the word.

But why hadn't he opened it? Why carry it around? Why hadn't he told her—?

Lifting her chin, she frowned harder. Just because her heart longed to pour everything she had to give—without restraint—on someone who might need her a fraction as much as she needed him, didn't mean she could throw caution to the wind and go looking for something with Blake that wasn't there. How many times did she need to remember what they had would end before it sank in? Folding the envelope between her thumb and forefinger, she pushed it back into the pocket of his jeans, packing them into his bag as he appeared beside her and dumped an armful of assorted toiletries into hers.

'Is there anything left in Macy's?'

'Remind me never to show you my shoe closet.'

'I'm allowed to give you shoes, am I?'

'I think you'll find that's enabling an addict.' When he shook his head and leaned down to kiss her, she turned her cheek. 'Helicopter's here. We should go.'

It wasn't a lie—she could hear the rhythmical beat of the rotors close by—but the fact she'd taken a step away from him—no matter how small or practical the rejection might have seemed—made Blake frown.

'What's wrong?'

'Apart from the fact I seem to be packing for you?'

'The house will still be here a week from now,' he said in the rough voice she loved so much. 'We'll come back at the weekend.'

Olivia tucked a strand of hair behind her ear before

pulling the zips on the bags. 'I can't next weekend. It's Jo's birthday.'

'We'll be back, Liv.'

'You never know.' She tossed her best imitation of a smile at him as she began filling in the cracks in the wall around her heart. 'Might be another place we like better.'

'Not fooling anyone in this room, sweetheart.' Picking up their bags, he pressed a kiss into her hair. 'I refuse to feel jealous of a house.'

The helicopter was swinging in to land by the time they got to the front door, Blake jogging down the steps with their bags and walking across the gravel with long, confident strides as Olivia reached out a hand to the wooden railing and looked up.

''Bye, house.' She swallowed to loosen the sudden knot in her throat. 'Take care of him for me.'

Knowing he'd never had a place to call home made him a perfect fit for a house calling out to be loved. It might be a part-time relationship, but while he was there she knew he would lavish attention on it in a way that could last more than a lifetime.

Turning, she forced reluctant legs to carry her away. Now they were leaving The Hamptons and fantasy land, it was time for a reality check. Holding her head up, she walked towards the helicopter without looking back.

She'd never considered she would be the one to end it. She wondered why. Was she so desperate to hang on to every last moment until the day he walked away? How much of a masochist did that make her?

Enough was enough. It was time for damage control. She had to give herself a fighting chance of getting over him—something she doubted would be easy, especially if she fell in love with more than his house.

CHAPTER TWELVE

'I ALWAYS figured if someone handed me a few million bucks I'd look happier than you do right now.' Marty dropped onto the stool next to him and ordered a beer.

'Not all it's cracked up to be,' Blake replied.

It earned him a grin, 'Aw, you're just saying that to make me feel better.'

No, he wasn't. He'd been right about making decisions he hadn't planned on making putting him in a perpetually foul mood. The fact Liv was being weird with him wasn't helping any either. Why hadn't she kicked him to the kerb for his attitude of late? It wasn't like her.

'Punishment for being economical with the truth, if you ask me,' Marty said.

Blake tilted his bottle to his mouth. 'You knew my old man had money and I wanted nothing to do with it.'

'Left out the Charles Warren part, didn't we, Anders?'

'Could we knock it off with the Anders some time soon?'

The baseball game playing on a large screen behind the bar took up their attention while some of the lunchtime crowd filtered in, Marty eventually taking a short breath before stepping into touchy territory again.

'So how was your first day at the office?'

'I'm just looking around.'

'Well, while you were—' he made speech marks with his fingers '— "looking around", the rest of the class took a field trip to that warehouse down by the river.'

Blake turned towards him. 'And?'

'Doable.' Marty nodded. 'You'll need to clear those changes you want made with the architect and building control, but yeah—should keep us busy for a while.'

'Good. Bring in as many new guys as you need.'

'Yes, Boss.'

Blake shook his head. 'Don't do that.'

They watched the game for a while, Marty glancing sideways when Blake kept checking the screen of his cellphone. 'Waiting on an important call?'

'No.' He set the phone down and lifted his beer.

'So what's the problem?'

'Apart from the fact I might need a new lawyer?'

If firing her was what it took to make it feel as if they could hold a conversation that didn't involve work, then so be it. Seemed to Blake they'd talked about little else since they got back to Manhattan. But as sexy as he found her, he didn't want to spend time with the lawyer—he wanted to spend it with the woman he'd been with in The Hamptons. Where the hell had *she* gone? He missed her.

'Thought there was something going on with you two.'

Blake frowned as he swallowed.

'Ah,' Marty said.

They sat in silence for as long as Blake could stand it. 'You got something to say, spit it out.'

'It's none of my business.'

'Never stopped you before...'

'Never looked like it mattered before...'

There were loud groans and shouts of complaint in reaction to what was happening on-screen while Blake focused his gaze on the bottle he was turning in circles with his hands. 'It matters.'

There was a long pause, then Marty dived in with, 'Know what I think?'

'I will when you get round to spitting it out.'

'I think you stepped out of the dugout too soon.' He nodded. 'Didn't help any that they sent a curve ball your way with the lady lawyer.'

Blake glanced at him from the corner of his eye. 'Could we do this without the baseball analogies?'

Leaning an elbow on the bar as the game went to commercial, Marty turned towards him. 'Knee-jerk reaction has always been your problem. We've both known that since high school. First day you turned up, you came out swinging and asked questions later. That's what you've done this time. You ask me, you didn't spend enough time prepping for the game. One look at her and you were stepping up to the plate. Understandable—you got eyes—but now you're asking questions and I'm willing to bet some of them you should have asked yourself earlier.'

As the game resumed on the screen, he turned away, leaving Blake to absorb what he'd said. 'Didn't occur to you to say any of this sooner?'

'Ain't nobody getting in your way when you come out swinging.'

'Didn't stop you that first day in high school…'

Marty shrugged again. 'You were taking on half the football team. Someone had to stop you getting killed.'

'I didn't know she was dating the quarterback.'

'Yeah—' he snorted sarcastically into the rim of his beer bottle '—'cos cheerleaders didn't date football players in any of the two hundred other schools you went to. That pretty much *never* happens.'

Breathing deep, Blake looked up at the screen. Marty

was right, he *was* asking questions. Some he'd thought he knew the answers to. Some he'd never asked before. Some it stunned him he even *had* to ask. As to the part about Liv being the reason he'd stepped up to the plate before he was ready? That was probably true, too. He'd wanted her from the moment he laid eyes on her. Still did. Except now he wanted more at a time when he was pretty certain she was backing off. But since he'd never stuck around long enough for a woman to back off before he did, how would he know?

'Had to happen some time,' Marty commented.

'What did?'

'Something to make you think about staying put.'

They sat in silence through two sets of commercials, occasionally lifting their bottles and tilting them to their mouths while Blake tore the corner off the label and rolled it between his fingertips.

'What's it like?' he asked, tossing the paper ball onto the bar and watching it roll away.

'What's what like?'

'Staying put.'

'Depends what you want.' Marty reached across for a handful of mini pretzels. 'And who you want it with.'

That helped.

'You see your life without her in it?'

Blake frowned at the question and got a nod in reply.

'Don't suppose you counted up how long you'd been here before all this happened.' Marty shook his head. 'No. Give it a minute. Use fingers and toes.'

'We'd been busy.'

'We had plenty of work the last two times you came home and it didn't stop you getting itchy feet after six months.' He tossed another pretzel in his mouth and chewed while talking. 'Happens to the best of us—just comes a time when we're ready to put down roots and settle.'

'You got married at *nineteen*.'

'Some of us get lucky earlier than others.' He glanced sideways. 'No one said anything about you getting married, did they?'

Blake clenched his teeth together hard enough to make his jaw ache.

'Mmm.' Marty quirked his brows as he looked up at the screen. 'Might want to figure out how serious you are about her before that reporter comes sniffing around again. He seemed as interested in her as he was in you.'

'*What* reporter?'

'Olivia Brannigan?'

'Yes.' She looked up at the fair-haired man, tucking away the phone she'd been checking for messages as a manila envelope appeared at eye-level.

'I'd like to talk to you about Blake Clayton.'

'And you are?'

'Ed Parnell, freelance reporter.'

Pressing her lips together, Olivia lowered her chin and turned her attention to the remnants of a Waldorf salad. 'I have nothing to say to you, Mr Parnell.'

'You might when you look at the pictures.'

Glancing at the envelope while she wiped her hands with a paper napkin, Olivia reasoned it would be better to know what she was dealing with. It was part of her job as Blake's lawyer, would be remiss of her not to—

Who was she kidding? Of course she was going to look.

Taking the envelope from him, she twisted the tab and slid out the contents, frowning as she flicked through photograph after photograph. Blake kissing her at the heliport on the way to The Hamptons, the two of them laughing at something as they walked along a sidewalk—there were even pictures of her leaving his apartment.

It felt as if something had been stolen from them.

'Your boyfriend is newsworthy. Secret son of famous billionaire inherits entire family fortune?' The young man smiled. 'Rags to riches stories, people love them.'

'I think we're done here.' Lifting the salad container and her empty coffee cup, she pushed to her feet and dropped them into a nearby trashcan. She walked past the fountain and along the dappled path that took her out of the park and into the crowd.

The reporter followed her. 'I'm sure Warren Enterprises shareholders will be fascinated by his plans for the company now he's the majority shareholder. Especially when we take into consideration he's a carpenter. How many carpenters do you think there are running multinational companies, Ms Brannigan?'

'No comment.'

Taking her sunglasses off her head to hide her eyes, she frowned as she headed for the crossing. How dare he suggest Blake wasn't capable of running the company? That man was capable of anything if he set his mind to it. When he wanted something—well, she *knew*, didn't she?

If he ever met a woman he could love, she wouldn't have a single doubt how he felt. Nothing would stand in his way. The woman wouldn't stand a chance. She might put up a fight—he could be annoying as hell—but if he let her, she would see what was standing right in front of her and when she did she would hold on tight and never want to let go.

They would find a way to make it work, *together*.

Olivia had never been as jealous as she was of the imaginary woman who might one day share his life. If he was capable of staying in one place and wanted her as much as she wanted him—

As if thinking about him could conjure him up out of nowhere... She blinked. At first he was just a figure moving towards her in the distance, among a great many others doing the same thing; the fact she'd even noticed was a miracle in itself considering the volume of people on the streets of Manhattan. A second later he was a man. Then a tall man with broad shoulders and unruly chocolate-brown hair who became a stand-out-of-the-crowd, unbearably sexy male with his dark, intense gaze fixed on her and an expression that said nothing and no one was getting in his way.

It was a cruel glimpse of something she hadn't been ready to admit she needed more than her next breath.

As the world contracted, Olivia froze, the wall around her heart crumbling to dust and emotion gushing into her chest. How could she have been so blind? She'd thought it wouldn't be easy to get over him *if* she fell in love with him? There was no *if* about it.

The shaking started in her midriff and radiated outwards over her body, forcing her to clamp her teeth together to stop them from chattering as she experienced the closest thing she'd ever had to a panic attack.

'Will he be optioning shares? I've heard he's been selling off properties. Care to comment on that?'

Blake's gaze shifted sharply to the reporter as he pushed up the sleeves of his dark blue shirt.

'Where has he been all these years? How come nobody has heard of him? Did Charles Warren hide the fact he had a child on purpose—because of the mother, maybe?'

Five strides away. Four, three... His large hands bunched into fists.

'Then we get to you, Ms Brannigan. Nothing like a little

romance to add to the story. When I realised your relationship was more than professional, I did a little research. You used to be with the NYPD. Is it true a homeless teenager died in your arms?'

Blake came to a halt in front of her and glared at the younger man, who took a step back in surprise.

'Mr Clayton, I'm glad you're here,' he said warily as Olivia silently handed over the envelope.

'I'd hold that thought if I were you,' Blake replied ominously as he looked at the photographs.

Summoning every ounce of the control she'd learnt in the last six years, Olivia stepped between them, the professional warning the client, 'Don't say anything.'

She reached up a hand and placed her sunglasses back on her head. She sized up the younger man with a cursory glance. 'Mr Parnell, I think I should warn you, continue stalking my client, I'll slap a restraining order on you so fast you'll be lucky not to be arrested in the next ten minutes for violating it. Print so much as one word that could be considered defamation of character, I will also sue for libel—and when I say "sue" I mean your great-great-grandchildren will still be paying off the debt.'

'You can't—'

'Yes, I can.' She smiled coldly, the chill washing over her body turning her blood to ice in her veins. 'What's more, *I'll enjoy it.*'

He opened and closed his mouth a couple of times.

Olivia raised a brow. 'You realise you'd be taking on one of the largest, most reputable law firms in Manhattan along with one of the richest men in the country?'

His eyes tightened. 'I'm not done.'

'Yes, you are,' Blake said.

The reporter looked at him, baulked at his expression

and beat a hasty retreat. As he did, Olivia took a short breath. 'He won't be the last.'

'I know.'

'Are you ready for that?'

'As ready as I'll ever be.'

Considering the effect it had on his life the last time anyone attempted to make a story out of him, she suspected it was something he would never be comfortable with—she knew *she* wasn't. But she wasn't his mother. She would fight with every weapon in her arsenal and hunt down every slimy, headline-grabbing, muck-racking, gossip-mongering—

'You can't hit them,' she said. 'They'll sue.'

'Be worth every cent.'

'They get more of a story out of it that way.'

He frowned. 'You shouldn't have got pulled into it.'

'It's hard to deny photographic evidence.'

'Will it be a problem for you at work?'

'Nothing I can't handle,' she hoped, but if her entire world crumbled around her ears again she would have no one to blame but herself.

Blake's voice lowered to a rough rumble. 'You didn't tell me he died in your arms.'

Gaze fixed on a random point just past his left ear, Olivia fought to keep her vulnerable emotions out of sight. She couldn't do what she had to do if there was so much as a hint of how she felt visible to him. The fact he'd always been able to see beyond the surface meant she had to draw on acting skills at an award-winning level. But he hadn't asked her to fall in love with him. She would let him go before she had to listen to him tell her they were done.

'You were covered in blood, weren't you?'

'Stomach wounds bleed like a bitch,' she said flatly.

'Don't do that.'

She shrugged. 'It's true.'

'Okay, that's it. I've had enough.' Grasping hold of her hand, he led her back to the park, turning to face her when he'd found a quiet corner. 'What's going on, Liv? And don't tell me it has something to do with that reporter. We both know that's not true. Whatever it is started when we left the house in The Hamptons—so what is it?'

Staring at his shirt while mentally preparing herself, her gaze lifted, button by button, over his open collar, the column of his neck, his tense jawline and the curve of his delicious lower lip until she was looking into the dark eyes she loved so much. She could do this, even if—for a moment—she was angry she had to and rallied against it.

'We both knew this was coming.' She slipped her hand free, curling her fingers into her palm to capture the warmth of their last touch.

'Knew what was coming?'

'The firm has a couple of important litigation cases coming up.' She was lying through her teeth, but she managed to hold his gaze. 'One of my associates familiar with Warren Enterprises subsidiaries will be taking over your case.'

Blake looked as angry as he'd been with the reporter. 'I can choose my own damn lawyer.'

'Naturally, we hope you stay with the firm…'

'Seriously—' he jerked his brows '—that's how you're handling this?'

'You're right; things haven't been the same since we got back to the city.' She could be honest about that. Turned out making the decision to end things and actually going through with it were two entirely different things. She hadn't wanted to let go, had been greedy and hung on for a few more memories while ignoring the reason she felt that way.

'I think it better we call it a day.' She avoided his gaze when it got difficult to keep up the pretence as she tried to figure out how long she'd been in love with him. It might have been lust at first sight, but the moment she'd started smiling when he wasn't there should have warned her of the potential danger. 'There's no point dragging it out till things get ugly.'

'Absolutely, best not drag it out till *that* happens.'

Her gaze slid swiftly back to his. 'What do you want me to say?'

'An explanation would be nice.'

'We both knew what we were getting into.'

'Did we?'

Had the fact she was using *his* reasoning escaped him? Olivia frowned, emotion churning frantically inside her chest. 'You may be tied up in Warren Enterprises business right now but we both know when you're done you'll move on. It's what you do. I knew that before I met you.'

She wasn't telling him anything he didn't already know. She remembered him talking about working with wood, how he did not know whether a piece would be worth keeping until he got below the surface. That wasn't the case for them. When she got beneath the surface she didn't get to choose whether to keep it or toss it away. She was being *forced* to toss it away. Spending each day waiting for the time to come when he would get restless and want to move on would cause her heart to shrivel up a little more with each passing hour, haemorrhaging emotion, bleeding her dry.

'You better be damn certain this is what you want.' His mouth twisted into a cruel impersonation of a smile. 'In case you hadn't noticed, I'm not big on looking back.'

'Don't make me the bad guy in this,' she warned. 'No one's to blame here. We have to be realistic. I know what I'm doing.'

'Beating me to the punch?'

Olivia was hanging on to her control by a thin thread. 'Can you tell me you won't walk at some point?'

'*Liv...*' For a second he looked pained.

'Tell me you won't get restless a month from now, or two months or six.' She wished he could. But she couldn't change him. She didn't want to, not really. If he wasn't the man he was, she wouldn't have fallen for him.

'You think I wouldn't *try* to stay—*for you*?'

'That's just it, Blake. You shouldn't feel you have to do it for me.' She almost choked on the words. 'If this was anything more, you would stay for *you*—and for *us*; if you wanted there to be an "us". The fact I even have to tell you that says it all. You're not ready for this. Maybe you never will be. But I can't wait around for you to decide or watch while you make a half-hearted attempt at staying in one place when your heart isn't in it. What do you expect me to do? Give everything to someone I know one day will walk away? Why would anyone do that? Sometimes we have to be selfish to survive.'

It was more than she'd intended to say but she took consolation from the fact it was as close as she could get to the truth without telling him how she felt. Just to be on the safe side, she stepped back, rolling her lips together to stop anything else from slipping out.

'You done?'

'Yes.' She nodded. 'I'm done.'

When it looked as if he was going to reach for her, she took another step back. If he kissed her she wouldn't stand a chance. She shook her head. 'That won't solve anything.

It's not like we ever had a problem there. But if you care about me—even the tiniest little bit—you'll respect—'

'You think I *don't care*?' The question was thrown at her with enough force to rock her back on her heels. 'You think I *asked* for this? What gave you the impression I need additional complications in my life right now? I didn't ask for *any* of this.'

'You're not angry at me.'

'The *hell* I'm not.'

'Say it, just once.'

'Say *what*?'

'Who you're angry at.' Her voice cracked, the need to reach out, soothe and find the right thing to say to help him the way he'd helped her so intense it almost tore her apart. 'It's not me because who ended this doesn't matter. It was always going to end. So say it—don't stop to think about it—*who* are you angry at?'

'You want me to say my parents, don't you?' His lips slipped over his teeth in a movement closer to a sneer than a smile. 'You think you've got me all figured out. You want to know who I'm angry at, I'll tell you.' Taking a step closer, he allowed her to see the torment in the depths of his eyes. '*Me*. I'm. Angry. At. Myself. Happy now?'

How she felt couldn't have been further from happy but somehow, from somewhere, she found enough strength to continue looking into his eyes. 'Then maybe you should ask yourself why and find a way of fixing it, because even if you could stay in one place for long enough to work on a relationship, I couldn't fix that for you, not alone.'

Taking a step back, he turned his head and looked down the path they'd taken, a muscle clenching in his jaw before he swallowed hard and nodded, his voice hollow. 'I know.'

'But for the record—' she smiled tremulously when he glanced at her '—if you'd let me, I'd have tried.'

'I know.'

Prolonging the inevitable, she watched the blink of his thick lashes as he continued staring into the distance. But the longer she stood there and felt the invisible draw to him, the harder it would be to leave. Stepping closer, she placed a soft, lingering kiss on his cheek, taking a last breath of clean, masculine scent before saying the two most difficult words she'd ever had to say.

'Goodbye, Blake.'

CHAPTER THIRTEEN

'You're not ready for this.'

Thunder rolled ominously through heavy clouds pushing their way over the skyscrapers but Blake walked slowly, even when the heatwave broke; people ran for cover or rushed past him beneath plastic hooded tourist capes and assorted umbrellas.

'If this was anything more, you would stay for you—and for us; if you wanted there to be an "us".'

It was the light bulb moment it had taken for him to see things more clearly. As she'd said it he'd realised he wanted there to be an *'us'*. He wanted it so bad the thought of living without her felt as if he were being pulled apart on some kind of medieval torture rack. He wanted their lives so tangled up nothing could unravel the threads that bound them together. He wanted to hear her laughter and watch her sleep and be amused by the fact she never let a cup of coffee sit still long enough to cool on its own. He wanted to argue with her so they could make up. Have her push him to talk so he could understand things more clearly with a different point of view.

She had little patience, talked too much at times for his liking, hogged the hell out of the covers on their bed—which would have bugged him if they'd met in the winter—but she was smart and bright and funny and tenacious and braver than she realised. And it had taken her to leave for him to know he didn't want to let her go.

But he hadn't stopped her or gone after her because she was right—she couldn't fix him, not alone. Even if she could, he wouldn't let her. It was up to him to make sense of his life so he could offer her more than half a man. He just had to pray she wouldn't find a guy less messed up than him before he worked his way through it and could tell her the things he wanted to say.

The thought and accompanying surge of jealousy lent a sense of urgency to the situation. Stopping dead in his tracks, he ignored the rain falling heavily on his head and bouncing off the concrete around his feet while he gritted his teeth and attacked the emptiness head-on. He dug deep and searched for a place to begin. He refused to believe he couldn't heal himself and build a new life—one he could share with her.

He wasn't aware how long he stood there but it was not that difficult to find a starting point—not when the stakes were so high.

Reaching a hand to his pocket to check the envelope was there, he hailed a cab. Forty minutes later, it had stopped raining and he was walking purposefully along winding paths edged with majestic trees and immaculately tended lawns. It had been fourteen years since he'd been there, but he remembered the way. Beyond modest, moss-green lakes full of ducks and geese, past black squirrels scurrying from pines to lindens; he rounded the corner and pinpointed the weeping beech, its branches skirting the ground above the stones, one more weathered than the other.

Footsteps slowing, he looked around and decided it wasn't too bad a place to end up—peaceful, pretty and private. He was thankful for the latter considering what he was about to do. Reading the names on the stones, he felt the emptiness throb like an old injury he'd convinced himself he never had until he started to stretch the muscle again. He hadn't known Charlie had forgone the family mausoleum. It was nice. Good to know his mom wasn't alone any more. Just a pity they'd waited so long to get together.

'I'm not mad at you.' Their son took a deep breath and ignored the fact he felt like an idiot for talking out loud. 'Not any more. But I was, for a long time. You messed up. But I think you knew that. Least I hope you did. I want to forgive you for sucking as parents, but I can't throw stones in that department until I can prove I'm better at it than you. Maybe one day I'll be able to come back and tell you how I'm doing with that...'

Blake shook his head at how he had questioned his sudden need for a family. It wasn't sudden, but it wasn't just a family he wanted either. It was a family *with Liv*. That was why he couldn't let her go.

'I can't keep being angry or feeling frustrated but I won't blame you for that. I should have dealt with this earlier.' But instead he'd allowed parts of himself to wither away, without nurture, rather than risk getting involved with someone he might damage in the way his parents' actions had damaged him.

Trouble was, while he'd been so focused on the empty place inside him, he'd been ignoring the feelings that had been growing elsewhere.

When another wave of anger hit him that it had taken so long to figure it out he took several deep breaths and fought it off, shaking his head more firmly. He didn't have to make the same mistakes they had. Nor would he continue punishing himself for things that *hadn't* been his fault. He was who he was because of his upbringing but he didn't have to stay that way. He could break the cycle, be the man he chose to be and the kind of father he'd never had to his own kids. The kids he wanted to have some day with Liv, if she'd have him.

'This stops now. I'm sick of running in the wrong direction.' As his voice grew more determined, he felt stronger, the emptiness within him shrinking as if hope held it in a fist and was squeezing tighter with each word. 'There's a time to stand and fight for the things that matter. I've said it before but this time I mean it: I won't hide—not who I am, what I want or how I feel.'

Bet big to win big, that was how he saw it. But he wasn't carrying any IOUs from the past into his new life. Without hesitation, he reached for the envelope, pushed his thumb below the seal, ripped it open and took out the letter.

Leaning her wrists on the metal railing, Olivia tugged out her earplugs and bent forward, gasping for breath. She was *so* unfit. Lifting her head as she continued hauling in air, her gaze took in the Manhattan skyline, Brooklyn's waterfront and the Verrazano Narrows Bridge as the famous orange ferry approached the terminal nearby. She could smell the brine, feel the sea breeze against her damp skin and hear the slap of water against the pilings, but while the familiarity of home would ordinarily have offered a measure of comfort, no matter what she tried, nothing made her feel better. Not when he was gone.

At first it was the little things like the lack of messages on her phone or the sound of his voice when she called to see how his meetings had gone that reminded her of the loss, but since she'd been gradually weaning herself off those things she was able to cope with that. Waking up alone after a restless night of tossing and turning while she tried to find a comfortable sleeping position without his large body to curl into was harder. Seeing his face in several interviews hadn't helped. While she was incredibly proud he was taking on the press on his own terms, every time she found an article about Warren Enterprises' new owner, she absorbed it, reaching out and touching his face as if somehow the ink could transmit the warmth of his skin to her fingertips.

The last time she'd felt anything close to as empty as she did without him, it had taken a new career to get her through. She had put everything into it, filling her mind and the hours until one day merged into the next and she was able to take a breath without hurting. But no matter how hard she looked, she knew she would never find another man to replace Blake. What she was experiencing was self-inflicted grief. But if it hurt as much as this after ten days without him, she'd been right to let him go.

She had to continue believing that.

When another wave of emotion threatened to overwhelm her, she pushed off the railing and walked a circle as she put the earplugs back in and ramped up the volume. Picking up the pace, she pushed her body through the pain barrier, running harder to replace emotional pain with straining muscles, aching lungs and a raw throat. Couple more miles and she would return to the house she'd grown up in to shower and change, filling a few more Blakeless hours with a family barbecue for her niece's birthday, where she could smile and pretend everything was okay.

Even if it felt as if it never would be again.

'I'm pretty sure what you're doing to that chicken is illegal in five states,' Johnnie commented when they gathered around a picnic table in the park.

'And Canada...'

Olivia's gaze jerked sharply upward at the comment

from the second of her brothers as he clinked their beer bottles together. 'What was that?'

'What?' Danny asked.

'The Canada thing—what does it mean?'

'Can't tell you,' he replied with a completely straight face. 'We took an oath.'

She blinked. 'Who did you take an oath *with*?'

'Your boyfriend.' He shrugged.

'My what?'

'Your boyfriend.' Johnnie held his bottle up and spread his fingers. 'Clean record, lays on a pretty decent spread on poker night...'

'Are you talking about Blake?' When she lifted a trembling hand to swipe hair back from her face, she knocked over a plastic beaker, forcing her to scramble to catch it as her mother joined them.

'He sounded lovely on the phone this morning. I'm looking forward to meeting him.'

'You talked to him on the phone?'

Was there a hidden camera somewhere?

'When you went for your run,' her mom replied as if it was an everyday occurrence.

'Pretty straight-up guy,' Danny commented as he reached out a finger towards the icing on the birthday cake and had his hand slapped away. 'Dad would have liked him. He's good with his hands.'

Olivia felt a flush of warmth building on her neck. 'When did you meet Blake?'

'Last week,' Johnnie replied for Danny, looking across at his wife where she was talking to a couple of other mothers and watching Amy play with her friends. 'Wanted to check on the procedure for closing off a road down by a warehouse on the river, we got talking—he mentioned he played poker—so I invited him to the Monday night game.'

'He got dating approval when he lost the pot.' Danny smiled. 'Never mentioned you were dating a rich guy...'

Olivia frowned. 'How much money did you take off him?'

'Let's just say I don't need to worry about making the rent this month...'

Meaning Blake had lost on purpose. How had her brothers not known that? If they were tag-teaming him she was going to kick their—

'He'll tell you about it when he gets here.'

'When he gets here?' On a day when she had virtually no make-up on, still had puffy eyes and—

'Yeah, we figured you were making things difficult for him.' Danny nodded. 'We told him to hang in there.'

'Speak of the devil.' Johnnie smiled.

'Oh, my,' her mother said. 'Isn't he handsome?'

He was also a dead man. Did he think she'd endured ten days of hell so she could go through it all over again? Olivia closed her eyes and took a deep breath before facing him, knowing full well the very sight of him would do what it had done from the get-go. When she turned around her heart crumpled into a tight, painful ball in her chest.

Damn it. It was *so* unfair he looked that good.

She hated him for it.

Blake smiled as Liv headed straight for him with a glint in her eyes that said he was in trouble.

She was beautiful when she was mad.

'What are you doing here?' she bit out, grabbing hold of his sleeve and turning him around without breaking stride.

'I was invited. Didn't the guys mention it?'

'Oh, believe me, they're next on my list.' She cocked an accusatory brow at him. 'And you called my *mother*?'

'What do I know about buying a present for a three-year-old girl?' He held up the bag in his hand. 'I've never bought anything this pink in my life.'

'What are you even doing buying a gift for my niece? We broke up, remember?' She frowned, glancing over her shoulder before she dragged him behind a tree. Letting go of his sleeve, she took a step back. 'Why are you here?'

'Why do you think I'm here?'

'Would I ask if I knew?'

'Have a think about it for a minute.'

When she floundered, he smiled, unable to resist when it had been the longest ten days he'd ever experienced. Lifting his hand, he slid his fingers around the nape of her neck and lowered his head, not caring who might be watching as he fitted his mouth to hers. It felt like a lifetime since he'd kissed her and Blake knew, without a shadow of doubt, he would never, *ever* get enough of her.

He just had to convince her to give them a chance.

When he looked down at her, she still had her eyes closed, her lower lip trembling as she took a long, ragged breath. Her lashes lifted, her gaze meeting his with a flash of vulnerability that completely did him in.

She shook her head, her voice thick. 'I can't do this again.'

'You won't have to.'

Any doubts he'd had disappeared as her eyes filled with tears. While she was crumbling in front of him and his chest cramped, relief washed over him. They weren't so different. She'd been struggling to deal with what was happening between them as much as he had.

'Thought I wouldn't figure out what you were doing?' Before she could say anything, he took her hand and led her to a bench below the tree. 'Sit.'

'I don't want to sit.' She tugged on her hand and sniffed loudly. 'I want you to go away.'

'Do I have to kiss you again?'

'Blake, you can't—'

'Yes, I can.' Tightening his fingers around hers, he pinned her in place with a determined gaze, silently transmitting all of the frustration and longing he'd experienced without her as he fought an internal battle with his need to demonstrate—the old-fashioned way—just how much he wanted her.

Her eyes widened.

'Sit,' he said roughly.

'No.' She frowned.

'Fine, then we'll do this standing up.' Unwilling to release her hand in case she made an attempt at leaving him again, he set the bag at his feet and took a steadying breath. 'Thought I was the one who ran away.'

'I—'

'Got scared.' He lifted his brows. 'You think I don't know how that feels?'

Her swollen lips formed words that never came. A frown, a short breath and then she blinked. 'I didn't think…I mean I thought…'

'No.' He shook his head, the sight of the strong-willed woman who had him wrapped around her little finger struggling to form a sentence creating an overwhelming swell of emotion inside him. 'You didn't. But I didn't help any with that, did I?'

'We knew this wouldn't last,' she protested weakly.

'Did we?' he asked again as he looked deep into her eyes. It might have been true at the start, but things had changed. At least they had for him.

'You don't stay in one place for long.'

'I never stayed in one place for long because I've never

known anything else.' That part she knew, so he tried to explain the cycle the way he understood it with the perspective he'd gained, thanks to her. 'Because I kept moving, I never got attached to anyone. Because I never got attached to anyone, there was nothing to stop me leaving. I didn't think I needed a place to call home. But for a place to be a home I think it needs to be more than just a place. And since I'd never got attached to anyone…'

'There was no one to come home to…'

He smiled. 'Not till now.'

When her brows wavered, he reached out and tucked a strand of hair behind her ear, his fingers lingering on the sensitive skin on her neck before he lowered his arm. Taking another deep breath, he started to lay his cards on the table the way he'd rehearsed over and over again.

'You were right,' he told her. 'I needed to figure out why I was angry and do something to fix it. It wasn't something you could do for me. I wouldn't have let you try. I'm not saying I'm all the way there but I made a start. Thing is, what you said about not being able to do it alone? That's how I feel, Liv. I don't want to do it alone. I feel better when you're there. You're the first person I've ever wanted to run to.'

When her lips parted on a low gasp, he took a half step forward. 'I know I don't make it easy, that's why I need someone in my life who will tell me when I'm being a jerk and kick me into touch when I need it; someone who knows to push to get me to talk things through, even when I don't want to. I need you, Liv. You've no idea how much I need you. You're it for me in ways I can't even begin to explain but I tried to show you when I couldn't find words.'

'I didn't know that's what you were doing,' she said in an impossibly soft voice.

A corner of his mouth tugged wryly. 'Neither did I at the time, but I get it now. It makes sense.'

'It does.' She nodded, but her smile was tentative, as if she still couldn't quite believe what she was hearing.

'I thought about what I wanted.' He threaded his fingers more firmly through hers. 'And I'm here to tell you. I'm ready for this. Now I need to know if you are.'

'I'm terrified,' she confessed.

'Know what scares me?'

She shook her head.

'Losing you.' When her eyes shimmered again he choked, 'Please don't do that, sweetheart.'

'You just gotta give me a minute.'

He held his breath and counted to ten as she blinked and took several deep breaths, reminding him of the time he'd felt her shaking and had held her until it had stopped. While they were the same in many ways, he realised when they'd met they had been at the opposite ends of the scale. Where he'd been struggling to feel things, she'd kept her emotions tightly in check because she felt things so strongly.

'Is that long enough?'

There was a short burst of laughter and then her brows lifted, her voice filled with incredulity as she asked, 'You thought infiltrating my family was the best way to come tell me all this?'

'I couldn't come tell you till I'd fixed as much as I could on my own,' he explained. 'I had to sort out my life so I had one to share with you. I'd planned to come find you when I'd worked through it, but when Johnnie landed at the warehouse and invited me to poker night—lame as it sounds—spending time with your brothers made me feel closer to you till I could see you again. They're like you, you know. You're better-looking, obviously, but they have the same sense of humour and say similar things and they're as proud of how you rebuilt your life after being a cop as I am—not that I had anything to do with it. You know they still worry about you, right?'

'They worry too much.'

'Yeah, I got that. I told them you can take care of yourself.' He didn't tell her the grilling that had accompanied his defence of her when there were still more important things to say. Didn't matter, anyway—he could handle her brothers. 'Talking about you helped. I missed you but I wasn't going to come to you damaged. You deserve better than that.'

'We're all damaged,' she said in a firmer voice as she squeezed his fingers. 'Why do you think this scares me so much? I tried not to care, really I did, but I couldn't stop it happening and when I knew how I felt—knowing you would leave—'

'I'm not going anywhere. I didn't stop to think about how long I'd been in New York this time till Marty opened his trap and pointed it out, but I'd already been here longer than I've ever stayed in one place.' The corner of his mouth tugged wryly. 'I told myself it was because we were busy but the truth is I've been coming back here for years—even if I never found an apartment to stay in. When I left it was more about going where the work was than running away from anything but, now I've thought about it, I think it was a sign I was ready to stay in one place and put down some roots.'

'If you'd told me that I would never have left.'

'If you hadn't left it might have taken me longer to work my way through everything. The thought of losing you proved quite the motivator.' Even thinking about it when she was in front of him created a wave of desperation. He needed everything out in the open, for it to be crystal clear so there was no room for doubt.

Clearing his throat a little less silently than he'd have preferred, he flexed his fingers around hers. 'If we do this, Liv, I need to warn you there'll be no leaving me again. Wherever you go, I'll find you and bring you home so we can work our way through the tough stuff together. I'm talking the whole package here. We'll start slow this time if that's what you need to believe what I'm telling you, but I want to marry you, have kids with you and spend the rest of our lives—'

'Yes.'

Suddenly finding it difficult to breathe, he shook his head. 'You might want to think it through before you give me an answer. I swear I'll be the best husband to you I possibly can but I'm not always gonna get it right. I'm far from perfect. I like to think I'm getting better at the whole talking things through thing but there'll still be times I'll struggle with that. Old habits...'

'You're doing fine.' She smiled.

'We'll still argue.'

'I know.' She shrugged a shoulder. 'But fighting with you kinda turns me on a little bit.'

'It does, does it?'

She nodded. 'Uh-huh.'

'Me, too.' He smiled in reply.

Liv took a small step forward, their bodies inches apart. 'We have a pretty great time making up.'

'Yes, we do.' He looked deep into her eyes. 'But it won't always be the solution to everything. We'll both have to work at this.'

'We will,' she agreed.

'But so long as you're happy, I'm happy, and if there's

anything within my power to give you than you'll damn well *let me* give you—'

'Never thought I'd say this, but could you stop talking for a minute?' She smiled the smile he hadn't wanted to understand until he was searching for something he desperately needed to be there. 'The answer is still yes. I don't need to think about it and I don't need to take it slow. Now we've fixed the communication problem I think we can get through anything together. Neither of us is perfect. Thing is, I don't want perfect. Just as well really, considering I'm in love with you and you can be a giant pain in the—'

'You have no idea how much I missed you,' he said hoarsely, what he could see in her eyes and hear in her voice banishing the last of the emptiness within him and filling it with warmth and light and more love than he had ever thought he could feel for another human being.

'I do if it's half as much as I missed you.' Tears shimmered in her eyes again as she laid a hand on his chest, directly over his thundering heart. 'I was miserable without you.'

Framing her face with his hand, he caught a tear with the tip of his thumb as it spilled from the corner of her eye. 'Me, too. In case you hadn't got it already, I love you, Liv. I've never loved anyone the way I love you. I never will. You're it for me. No more hiding, no more secrets from here on in— What's wrong?'

He frowned as she leaned back and grimaced.

'I found the letter from your father. When we were packing, it fell out of your pocket.'

Wait. 'Was that what happened? There was something about the letter that bothered you?'

'No—' she shook her head '—I wanted to ask you about it, but I couldn't. Every time you shared something with me and I felt closer to you, there was more to lose. I thought

I could distance myself and shut off my emotions, but it was too late. I'm strong, Blake, but…'

'I know you are.'

'Not all the time. I thought letting you go would be easier than watching you leave, but it wasn't.'

'Come here.'

When she stepped in to him and wrapped her arms around his waist, he held her close and frowned at the shudder running through her body. 'You're shaking.'

'Emotional overload,' she said against his chest. 'I might have held it all inside for too long.'

'You don't have to hold anything back from me.'

'Because you looked so happy when I got weepy?'

'Cry, laugh out loud, yell your head off if you need to let something out—I want it all, Liv.'

'Remember you said that the next time I yell at you.' He heard her smile. 'Now tell me about the letter.'

Blake laid his cheek against her hair. 'I carried it too long. Wasn't ready to read it or didn't want to face what was in it when I heard he was gone; doesn't really matter now. I carried a lot of things around for too long. I read it. A lot of it I expected, some of it I didn't. He mentioned the will—you can look at it if you like.'

'No. It's the last letter from a father to his son.'

'Explains a lot about my relationship with him I'd like you to know. I want you to know everything in the same way I want to know everything about you.'

'We have time.' She smiled as she leaned back and her gaze met his. Her feelings glowed in her eyes as she pressed an all too brief kiss to his mouth. 'I love you.'

'I love you, too.' He smiled back and leaned in for a more meaningful kiss; the kind that reminded him how long it had been since they'd shared a bed and made him want to get to one so he could demonstrate more eloquently how he felt when three small words didn't feel like enough.

She sighed when he lifted his head. 'You better come meet the rest of the family before they send out a search party and find us making out.'

'We'll tell them we just got engaged.' He thought about the ring he'd been carrying around in his pocket for more than a week—the past replaced by his hope for the future. It was tempting to give it to her since she'd already said yes and she didn't have a hope in hell of ever taking it back, but he had plans for when he put that ring on her finger. Ones that didn't involve a public place or an audience...

She laughed softly. 'This soon? No, we won't. They'll think I'm pregnant.'

'I'm willing to work on that.' He grinned. 'And since you're using up all the vacation time you've saved over the last few years instead of working on one of those big litigation cases you talked about when you dumped me...'

'Oh, my God—' she rolled her eyes as she leaned back '—is there anything my brothers didn't tell you?'

'Not much after I'd dropped a couple of hands.'

'Don't do that again,' she warned as he reached for the birthday present he'd left at her feet. 'They won't respect you for it.'

'I'll keep that in mind when they come to our place for poker night.' He kept hold of her hand as they walked around the tree.

'You're going to tell me about Canada now, right?'

'When we're married and you can't testify against me.'

'Blake.'

'Yes?'

'Blake.'

He stopped and turned towards her, allowing the meaning to seep into his soul as he heard *'I want you'* wrapped in *'I love you'* and knew with a certainty he hoped all men felt when the time came to settle and put down roots, he'd found his place in the world. Wherever she was would be home for the rest of his life.

'I hear you,' he said roughly. She'd spoken to him from the start, even when she wasn't using words. 'And for the record, I'm your man, Liv. I always will be.'

All it had taken was for her to come find him when he hadn't known he was looking.

* * * * *

PLAYING HIS DANGEROUS GAME

**BY
TINA DUNCAN**

Tina Duncan lives in trendy inner-city Sydney, with her partner Edy. With a background in marketing and event management, she now spends her days running a business with Edy. She's a multi-tasking expert. When she's not busy typing up quotes and processing invoices, she's writing. She loves being physically active, and enjoys tennis (both watching and playing), bushwalking and dancing. Spending quality time with her family and friends also rates high on her priority list. She has a weakness for good food and fine wine, and has a sweet tooth she has to keep under control.

CHAPTER ONE

HER photograph didn't do her justice.

Not by a long shot.

Even though Royce was watching her from half a room away, Shara Atwood was so alive she lit up the room. It wasn't just the sinuous way she was dancing—which he had to admit was incredibly hot—but she seemed to radiate a vibrant kind of energy that made it impossible not to look at her.

And people *were* looking—in their droves.

The young single men at the club were outright staring. The older men, or those accompanied by their wives or girlfriends, were not so obvious. Their eyes slid to Shara whenever they thought they could get away with it without being caught.

Royce fitted neither of those categories.

He was watching Shara because he *had* to.

Because as of an hour ago it was his *job* to watch her.

What irritated him was the fact that he was enjoying it. The prickling sensation under his skin told him that his body was enjoying it even more—a fact that he found doubly irritating.

Shara Atwood was the type of woman Royce despised.

She might be beautiful and sexy, but by all accounts she was also spoilt, selfish and self-centred.

He knew the type and tried to steer clear of them—except when his job made that task impossible.

The reminder of why he was here prompted Royce to straighten away from the wall. He made his way through the crowd towards the dance floor. Everyone moved automatically out of his way. At six-foot-four and being keenly muscled, he had that effect on people. They no doubt thought it was safer to move than to accidentally collide with him.

He stopped on the edge of the dance floor.

Now that he was closer Royce realised that Shara had her eyes closed. She was swaying and twirling in perfect time to the music and ignoring everything and everyone around her—including the eager young man with the light brown hair who was desperately trying to capture her attention.

As he watched, the young man reached out to take hold of her shoulders, but she shook him off without even bothering to look at him, as if he were no more important than a bothersome fly. The young man said something. Royce was too far away to hear what it was, but not too far to read Shara's expression.

A flash of irritation she made no effort to hide crossed her face and then her full lips parted. Whatever she'd said, it must have been cutting. The young man jumped back as if he'd been stung by a wasp. His cheeks flushed a bright fiery red as he turned and stalked off the dance floor.

'Keep on walking, mate,' Royce muttered under his breath. 'And don't look back. She's not worth it.'

The incident was a timely reminder to focus on business rather than on Shara's lusciously full figure and thick fall of sable hair.

He walked across the dance floor and stopped right in front of her.

Then he said her name.

Shara kept right on dancing as if she hadn't heard him.

But she had.

Royce *knew* she had.

To the casual observer her expression hadn't changed, but Royce was an expert at reading body language. He was trained to scrutinise people and assess their reactions. That kind of attention to detail was essential in his line of work.

He'd captured the imperceptible tightening of her mouth and the barely there contraction of her brow. And even though her movements were still fluid and graceful there had been a momentary stiffness—so brief it had almost been invisible—that had run through her curvaceous frame.

It was clear she was irritated by the interruption.

Well, she could be irritated all she liked.

Royce was not like the young pup she'd just sent away with his tail between his legs.

He was a man.

And he didn't like being ignored—particularly when he had a job to do.

'Shara,' he said again.

That was all he said. Nothing else.

But his tone, which fell somewhere between firm and harsh, was one people usually ignored at their peril.

Shara heaved a sigh.

Why couldn't everyone leave her alone?

OK. So she'd made a mistake coming to the club tonight. She knew that. Had known it since the minute she'd walked through the door.

She wasn't in the mood to party. She hadn't been for a long time. The last twelve months had seen to that.

She'd also outgrown the crowd she'd used to run with—a fact she'd realised within minutes of arriving at the club. She could thank the last twelve months for that too.

She had to face it. Coming here tonight was just another poor decision in a long, *long* line of poor decisions. Stuffing up appeared to be a habit she just couldn't break.

'Shara.'

There it was again. That voice. She didn't recognise it. She would have remembered if she'd heard it before.

It was male. Very definitely male. A deep baritone that made her toes curl in the stiletto sandals she was wearing.

Not Tony, thank goodness. How many times did she have to tell the guy she wasn't interested? The way he kept coming on to her was bordering on harassment, and with one man already making a nuisance out of himself she didn't need another.

Perhaps that was why tonight she'd given up on politely rejecting Tony's overtures and given it to him straight.

Tony had been gone for no more than five seconds before this guy with the deep velvety voice had appeared.

If she ignored him maybe he'd take the hint and go away.

'Shara.'

No such luck. There it was again, only harder this time. Like a hammer hitting concrete.

Whoever he was, he wasn't going away in a hurry. That tone spoke of stubbornness and determination—qualities that none of the people in this crowd possessed.

Curious in spite of herself, Shara stopped moving and opened her eyes.

She found herself staring at the middle of a strong, barrel-like chest.

She looked up. And up.

Whoever he was, he was tall.

He was also lip-smackingly gorgeous.

Not that he was handsome in the traditional sense—his face was too hard, too angular. But he was ruggedly good-looking, with a broad forehead, strong, well-defined jaw and a slightly crooked nose that somehow did nothing to detract from his tough handsomeness.

He was perfectly proportioned too. Strongly muscled thighs and a stomach that was flat and hard balanced his broad shoulders and deep chest. And he was so big. Even his hands, which he was holding loosely at his sides, were large.

Would his—?

A hot flush of colour flooded her cheeks. Even though she'd managed to put a brake on her thoughts, she couldn't stop her eyes dropping and felt the breath catch in her throat. He was built in proportion, all right...

A peculiar weakness invaded her knees. What on earth had got into her? Imagine staring at him like that! She'd never done anything like that before. And then an appalling thought occurred to her. God, what if he'd noticed...?

Her eyes snapped to his face.

His total lack of expression meant she couldn't tell one way or another.

Embarrassed by the way she'd stared at his private parts, and annoyed by the weakness invading her knees, she snapped, 'What, damn it?'

Royce stared into the most amazing blue eyes he'd ever seen. They were bluer than the sky on a bright summer's day, brighter than a freshly cut sapphire, and more mysterious than the depths of the ocean.

It would be easy to be captivated by them but Royce was not easily captivated—particularly when her sharp, stinging voice told him the true measure of the woman standing in front of him.

'So you *are* polite enough to look at someone when they're speaking to you, are you?' Royce asked, returning sting for sting with rapier-sharp speed.

Her magnificent eyes narrowed and her chin lifted fractionally into the air. 'Do I know you?'

It was a simple question, but the way she asked it was anything but simple.

Princess talk.

That was the way Royce labelled her tone.

These society babes had a way of talking down to someone when they wanted to. Her tone implied that she couldn't possibly know someone like *him*.

A lesser man might have been embarrassed, or even have walked away. But Royce was made of tougher stuff than that. So he smiled and said, 'No, but we're about to become acquainted.'

Her eyes narrowed some more, then her mouth moved in a disparaging little twist, and somehow, despite being about a foot shorter than he was, she managed to look down the length of her nose at him. 'I don't think so. You're not my type.'

'Don't worry, lady. You're not my type either,' Royce drawled smoothly, not the least put out by her attempted insult. 'I'm here in a purely professional capacity.'

Her expression shifted, lost its regal look. She ran her eyes over him again. She'd done that before, when she'd first opened her eyes. Royce had been disconcerted by his response to that simple look, his blood vessels expanding and heat flowing under his skin.

The same thing was happening again now, and he liked it even less the second time around.

'Well, if you're the bouncer I hate to tell you this but I've done nothing wrong. I'm just minding my own business and dancing. So why don't you go away?' She made a waving movement through the air with her hand. 'Go on. Shoo.'

Royce almost laughed. What she'd said, combined with the action, was just so ridiculous. As if he were a pesky animal she was trying to get rid of.

'I'm not a bouncer. Your father asked me to bring you home.'

Her expression became instantly wary. 'He did?'

Royce nodded. 'Yes. Are you ready to leave?'

Shara shook her head, sending her thick pelt of dark hair swirling around her shoulders.

Royce tried to suppress his irritation. He didn't like doing this kind of job. These days he usually restricted himself to overseeing the business. If he did get involved he chose investigative or security cases, *not* bodyguarding. He allocated those jobs to somebody else.

But this was different. Gerard Atwood, head of Atwood Industries, was one of his best clients—if not *the* best. When Gerard had said protecting his daughter would be a personal favour to him Royce had known he couldn't refuse. Not unless he wanted to lose one of his biggest clients—which he didn't.

'Well, if you need to collect your bag and say your goodbyes make it quick. I want to get out of here.'

Although this was a reputable club that didn't mean Shara was safe. After all, it had taken less than twenty minutes of research for *him* to locate her, so no doubt her ex-husband could do the same.

Even before he'd finished speaking Shara was shaking her head. 'That wasn't what I meant.'

His eyes narrowed. 'Then what did you mean?'

She folded her arms. It drew his attention—*unwilling* attention—to the thrusting swell of her breasts.

She was what his mother would call generously endowed. Somehow Royce knew her breasts would fill his hands perfectly—which was no mean feat, given that his hands were on the large size.

The thought sent a prickle of desire along his nerve-endings.

'I'm not going anywhere with you,' Shara said, looking at him down the length of her nose again.

Her tone stopped the prickle dead in its tracks. 'Yes, you are.'

'No, I am not.'

Royce sighed. 'Why not?'

'I have no idea who you are. I only have your word for it that my father sent you.'

'Good point.' In fact it was a very good point. He hadn't introduced himself. He hadn't explained the situation. He'd been sufficiently distracted by the sinuous sway of her body and then annoyed by the way she'd treated first the young guy and then himself that he'd not only put the niceties aside but also his professionalism.

He should know better than that.

'I'm from the Royce Agency. Have you heard of them?'

She nodded. 'Yes. I have. My father uses them all the time. If I'm to believe their spiel they are the largest and most well-known security firm on the globe.'

'It's not spiel. We are the biggest and the best,' Royce said proudly.

It would be fourteen years next month since he'd started the Royce Agency. He'd only been twenty at the time, operating out of the spare bedroom in his parents' home in northern Sydney. It had taken hard work and long hours to make it what it was today.

Shara shrugged. 'Whatever.'

Royce refused to be insulted. As he'd learned a long time ago, these society babes didn't care about anything or anyone except themselves.

Reaching into his back pocket, he pulled out a brown leather wallet. Flipping it open, he held it out to her.

Her arms remained folded in front of her. 'What's that?'

'My driver's licence. I thought you might want to see some identification.'

She shook her head. 'That's not necessary.'

Royce frowned. 'It's entirely necessary. You can't just walk out of here with a perfect stranger. You can't trust anybody these days. You have to be cautious.'

'Again, you misunderstand me. It's not necessary because I have no intention of leaving with you.'

The silence that followed her words was filled with the sound of music and chatter. Royce ignored it all. So did Shara.

He thrust his wallet closer. 'Take it. Look at it. Because you *will* be leaving with me.'

She sighed and snatched the wallet from his hand.

Shara's head bowed as she examined his licence intently. Royce stared at the luxurious fall of raven-black hair that fell about her shoulders and resisted the urge to reach out and stroke it.

'Royce as in *the* Royce?' she asked, looking up from his wallet and giving him a suspicious look.

'At your service,' Royce acknowledged, holding out his hand.

She eyed his hand as if it was a snake he was extending to her, then with obvious reluctance placed her hand in his.

They both felt what happened next.

Royce just wasn't sure how to explain it.

It reminded him of the zap of static electricity that built up on your shoes on a windy day that zapped your hand the minute you touched something metallic.

Only it wasn't that.

It also reminded him of the pins and needles you got when you accidentally fell asleep on your arm.

Only it wasn't quite like that either.

It was just a…

Well, it was just a sensation—like an energy transfer of some kind.

No doubt there would be a scientific explanation for it if he bothered looking for one.

Shara snatched her hand out of his, her wide eyes fixed on his face. 'So. You…you own the Royce Agency?' she asked, showing the first crack in her composure since they'd met.

'I'm afraid so.'

'Well, Mr Royce, I—'

Royce shook his head. 'It's not Mr Royce. It's just plain Royce.'

Shara looked back down at the driver's licence she still held. 'It says A. Royce right here.' She held up the wallet and pointed with a red-varnished nail to the small print. 'That makes you Mr Royce.'

Royce brushed aside the lock of hair that had fallen across his forehead. 'Technically, I suppose it does. But as far as I'm concerned my father is Mr Royce. Everyone just calls me Royce.'

'Why don't they call you by your first name?'

'Because I don't like my first name,' he explained calmly.

'Why? What is it?'

'That's none of your business.'

'I don't suppose it is.'

Royce felt as if they'd got way off track. 'Well, are you satisfied that I am who I say I am?'

She nodded. 'I am, but I'm still not going with you.'

Royce held on to his temper with difficulty. The fact that she'd rather stay here partying with this shallow crowd instead of honouring her father's request told him a lot about her.

Lack of respect. Selfishness.

He could go on, but what was the point?

It wouldn't get the job done, and the job was the only thing that mattered.

'Please will you reconsider?' he said persuasively. 'Your father was most insistent.'

For a moment she looked undecided, then she waved a hand. 'All right. Lead the way Just Plain Royce. We can't keep my father waiting, now, can we?'

The journey to Atwood Hall was completed in silence.

Royce tried to make polite conversation several times,

but Shara's monosyllabic answers eventually forced him to give up.

When they reached the two-storey sandstone house Shara headed straight for her father's study. She pushed the door open without knocking.

Royce followed her in.

She stopped in the middle of the room then swung around to face him. 'Where is he?'

Royce folded his arms. 'On a plane to New York.'

Her mouth dropped open. 'Then what was all that crap about my father wanting to see me?'

He stared back at her calmly. 'I never said anything about your father wanting to see you. All I said was that he asked me to bring you home. Which he did...' He paused for a heartbeat. 'About thirty minutes before he left for the airport.'

The silence that filled the room prickled at the back of his neck.

Shara's thick lashes dropped down to shield her expression.

Royce didn't feel guilty about the minor deception. Gerard had warned him that Shara was unlikely to co-operate. You had to treat uncooperative 'principals'—which was the industry term for the person you were protecting—in much the same way a lawyer would treat a hostile witness.

With a firm hand and any tactic you could lay your hands on.

If keeping Shara safe meant bending the rules a fraction and allowing her to jump to the wrong conclusion then so be it. He'd do what he had to do—an attitude which had contributed in no small measure to his success.

Finally Shara looked up. 'Why? Why did my father want you to bring me home?'

'He didn't think going to the club was a good idea and I happen to agree with him.'

Her cheeks reddened, although he couldn't tell whether

it was from embarrassment or anger. 'I don't care what you think. What I do, and when I do it, is none of your business.'

'That's where you're wrong. Everything you do from now on is very much my business.'

She frowned. 'What's that supposed to mean?'

'It means that while your father is overseas I will be looking after you.'

Shara blinked, frowned, and blinked again. 'I don't need looking after.'

'No? That's not the way I understand it.'

'Well, I don't care what you understand. I'm a little too old for a babysitter, don't you think?'

'I'm not a babysitter. I'm a bodyguard.'

'Babysitter. Bodyguard.' She waved a hand through the air. Her breasts jiggled. Royce tried not to notice but failed miserably. 'It's all the same to me. Either one is completely unnecessary.'

Although Royce didn't particularly like what he was hearing, he had no objection to Shara speaking her mind. If there was one thing he couldn't stand it was someone saying one thing to his face and then saying—or doing—the exact opposite behind his back.

'Well, your father disagrees,' Royce said calmly.

'I—'

Royce cut her off. 'You're wasting your breath. Gerard warned me that this would be your attitude and he said to tell you that while you're living under his roof you'll follow his rules.'

Her humiliation was complete.

Shara stared at the tips of her red-varnished toenails as if her life depended upon it. Tears pricked at the backs of her eyes but she blinked them away.

She had no intention of bursting into tears. That would only add to her humiliation.

Right now all she wanted to do was curl up into a ball and pretend that the rest of the world didn't exist.

It was a feeling she knew all too well. But she fought against it. If there was one thing the last twelve months had taught her it was not to give in to feelings of helplessness. She had to be strong and stand up for herself.

It didn't matter how many times she got knocked down. She had to pick herself up, brush herself off, and try again.

So she straightened her shoulders, dragged in a breath, and instead of avoiding eye contact lifted her head and deliberately looked Just Plain Royce directly in the eye.

His face was expressionless. She had no idea what he was thinking and frankly she didn't care.

She waved a hand through the air. 'Well, Mr Just Plain Royce, I'm out of here.'

He folded his arms across his impressive chest. 'And where, pray tell, are you planning on going?'

She put her hands on her hips. 'That is none of your business!'

'Correction. As I said, where you go and what you do *is* my business.' His tone was determined. 'My job is to protect you. It will help if I know where you're going at all times.'

Her already straight shoulders straightened some more. 'My father may have hired you, but I have no desire for a bodyguard. You can do what the hell you like, but don't expect any help from me!'

A look that was part resignation, part irritation flashed across his face before his expression hardened. 'Be warned. I intend doing my job, with or without your co-operation. It will be easier on both of us if you work with me, but it's not entirely necessary. If you want to act like a rebellious teenager then go right ahead. I won't stop you.'

Shara would have laughed except it wasn't really funny. She'd been a well-behaved, follow-the-rules, obedient teenager. A real goody-two-shoes, in fact.

Twelve months of marriage to Steve Brady had shown her that being meek and biddable had its drawbacks—big-time!

She'd emerged from the dark tunnel of that period a very different person from the one who'd entered it.

She crossed her arms and raised one eyebrow. 'If you're trying reverse psychology on me then it won't work. I'm a grown adult, able to decide when and where I go without reporting in to somebody else.'

His dark eyes glinted. 'Are you? An adult, that is? If so, then prove it.'

She frowned. 'And how am I supposed to do that?'

'Don't go back to the club.'

Shara raised an eyebrow. 'And what will that prove?'

'It will prove you're adult enough to put your safety ahead of having a good time,' Royce said calmly.

The word 'adult' rankled. She wasn't a child. Her marriage had made her grow up—fast.

She knew what she was doing; she was making a stand.

She was sick and tired of the men in her life—first her father and then her husband—telling her what to do.

She didn't need to add a bossy bodyguard to the list.

If she slunk off to her room with her tail between her legs then wasn't she just handing over her power to Royce?

Well, she'd been there, done that, and she'd suffered because of it.

She could, and she would, make her own decisions.

Mr Just Plain Royce had better start getting used to it.

And why was she calling him that anyway?

Plain was ordinary. Easily overlooked. Royce was neither of those things. In fact just the opposite.

'I don't have to prove anything to you,' she said, clasping her hands together in front of her. 'I'm twenty-three years old. I *am* an adult. And if you think insulting me will force me to co-operate then you're sorely mistaken.'

He held up his hands, a small smile twisting his mouth.

'That accusation is well and truly misdirected, I can assure you. That kind of strategy would never work with you. I know that.'

She raised a brow. 'And how do you know that?'

Royce shrugged. 'Because I've seen you in action. First at the club and then again here.'

She gave him a puzzled frown. 'Meaning?'

'Meaning that using reverse psychology on you would have the reverse effect.' He waved a hand, with a glint in his eyes that made her want to hit him. 'You're determined not to co-operate no matter what. It doesn't matter what I say or do, you're going to do your own thing and to hell with everyone else. If I push all it will do is make you dig your heels in even more.'

Shara gnashed her teeth.

She had a sneaking suspicion that Royce was right—although it would take someone pulling out her fingernails before she'd admit it.

'You haven't got a clue what you're talking about,' she flung at him. At that moment the old grandfather clock in the entrance hall struck the hour. Shara glanced at her watch. 'Well, it looks like you're going to get your way. I'm not going back to the club. Not because you say I shouldn't, but because it's late and I'm tired. Goodnight.'

Without another word she spun on her heel to leave the room, but his next words stopped her. 'Before you go perhaps you'd like to tell me which bedroom is yours.'

Slowly she turned back to face him. Her heart was beating with slow, heavy thumps. 'Why on earth do you want to know that?'

'Because I'll be taking up residence in the room next to yours, of course.'

A hand made its way to the base of her throat, where she could feel the beat of her pulse under her skin. For a moment she'd thought…

Well, she wasn't sure exactly what she'd thought.

But whatever it was it had made her go hot all over.

Her hands slammed down on her hips. 'You most certainly will not!'

Royce gestured to the corner of the room. A large black suitcase she hadn't noticed before was sitting there. 'I most certainly will.'

She shook her head. 'I don't understand.'

'I'll be living here for the duration. I—'

'Living here…? You can't do that!'

'Why not?'

'Well, because you just can't.' Shara blinked rapidly, the blinks timing perfectly with the increased rhythm of her heart.

It was out of the question.

Out of the question for any number of reasons—one of which she didn't want to examine too closely because she suspected it had something to do with the little curl of sensation she experienced low in the pit of her belly every time she looked at him.

'Well, I'm afraid what you want doesn't come into it. As your father is aware, I have a policy of up close and personal at the Royce Agency.'

'What does that mean?' Shara asked suspiciously, her brain leapfrogging into all sorts of thoughts. Just how personal did they get at this agency of his?

'It means I'm guarding *you*, not your house.' He shrugged his broad shoulders. 'I'll be of absolutely no use to you if I'm sitting outside in my car and your ex-husband breaks in through the back door, will I?'

'I guess not.' The suggestion was enough to send a shiver of fear slicing down her spine. It was something that hadn't occurred to her. The very idea of Steve breaking in filled her with dread. She swallowed, clasping her hands tightly together in front of her. 'I just expected—'

'That it would be just like on TV?' he finished resignedly, sounding as though he'd heard it all a million times before. 'Well, it's not. You either show me where you sleep or I'll find out for myself. Either way, I'm staying. And I'm staying where I can keep an eye on you.'

'Have it your own way,' Shara muttered.

If Royce intended to hang around there wasn't much she could do about it. He was too big for her to throw out. And there was no use complaining to the police because he had her father's permission to be here—something that one phone call would establish.

All she could do was call her father in the morning and see if she could change his mind.

If she couldn't she'd just have to put up with the situation as best she could. She'd put up with a hell of a lot worse.

This was no big deal.

All she had to do was ignore Royce.

Just go about her business as if he wasn't there.

Except she had the uneasy feeling Royce wasn't going to be easy to ignore.

'I certainly shall,' Royce said.

He spoke with the kind of confidence Shara envied. That I'm-sure-of-my-place-in-the-world kind of confidence. The kind that made every decision he made rock-solid and unbreakable. He knew exactly where he was going—and how to get there.

By contrast, Shara didn't have a clue where she was going.

Even though she was only twenty-three, she'd taken so many wrong turns in her life it was ridiculous. She felt like a player in a Snakes and Ladders game who always landed on the snake's head and slid back down to the tail.

She felt as if that had just happened again.

Her attempt to stand up for herself and control her own destiny had just been ripped out from underneath her and she'd landed flat on her face—again.

'You'd better follow me,' she said through gritted teeth.

She spun on her heel and stalked from the room.

Royce picked up his suitcase and followed her.

'This is my room,' Shara said, indicating a door with a wave of her hand. 'You can sleep next door. The room is made up. I'll just check that you have some towels.'

'Thank you.'

She inclined her head and went inside. Assured that he had everything he needed, she walked to the door, pausing just inside the doorway. 'Goodnight.'

'Goodnight, Shara.'

The way he said her name made her toes curl in her sandals. She hurried from the room.

An hour later she lay, staring up at the ceiling.

For weeks, if not months, her last thought before going to sleep had been about Steve and the hell he'd put her through—was still putting her through.

But tonight was different.

For the first time in a long time she wasn't thinking about her ex-husband.

Another man had super-imposed himself in her mind's eye.

A large man called Just Plain Royce.

CHAPTER TWO

THE next morning Shara followed the smell of cooking bacon to the kitchen.

Since their housekeeper only came in on weekdays, and didn't help herself to breakfast when she was there, Shara knew exactly who was cooking.

Just Plain Royce.

She was tempted to go back to her room and wait until he'd finished, but that smacked a little too strongly of running away so she squared her shoulders determinedly and walked in.

Royce was standing at the stove, his back to the door. He was wearing well-washed denim jeans and a tight white T-shirt, both of which hugged his muscle-packed body.

Of their own volition her eyes made a sweeping perusal—from his still wet hair, down the strong planes of his back, to his backside and legs.

Her heart kerthumped—then did it again.

He really was a fine figure of a man. Although the fact that she kept on noticing annoyed the hell out of her.

'You've made yourself at home,' she said sarcastically.

He half turned towards her, one thick dark eyebrow raised. 'I hope you don't expect me to live here and not eat?'

She shrugged. 'I'd prefer it if you weren't living here at

all, but we've already had that argument so there's no point having it again, is there?'

'I suppose not.' He paused for a moment and then asked, 'Did you call your father?'

'Yes. You must have known I would.'

'I did. And what did he say?'

Her father had said a lot. About how he was concerned about her. About how he knew what was best for her.

Etc. Etc. Etc.

He had no idea how much she'd changed from the girl who used to live with him. And she couldn't tell him without revealing things she didn't want him to know.

He knew her marriage had been bad, but he had no idea how bad.

'You're still here, aren't you?' she said by way of answer.

'I guess I am,' he said neutrally, turning back to the stove.

Shara eyed the frying pan and the small mountain of chopped items on the cutting board waiting to be cooked. 'When is the army arriving?'

Royce shrugged his broad shoulders. His muscles rippled under his T-shirt, doing strange things to Shara's tummy muscles. 'I'm a big man. I need lots of food. And since I work out regularly it's important to keep up my intake of protein and carbohydrates.' He waved a spatula through the air. 'Do you want some?'

Shara shuddered and made her way to the fridge. 'No. Unlike you, I have a small appetite. Fruit and yoghurt suits me just fine.'

He made a sound that was indecipherable.

Shara turned away from the fridge with a punnet of strawberries in one hand and a tub of yoghurt in the other. 'What does *ugh* mean?'

'Nothing. I just don't approve of women who think they can live on the smell of an oily rag and just pick at their food. The human body needs good nutrition to be at its best.'

Shara dumped her items on the granite benchtop with more force than was necessary. 'You're jumping to conclusions. Do I *look* like the kind of woman who just picks at her food?'

As soon as the words left her mouth Shara regretted them.

Royce turned to face her. His chocolate brown eyes travelled from the crown of her head to the tips of her toes.

He missed nothing in between. Not a single thing.

Shara knew he didn't because she felt that look as if it were a caress.

Her skin stretched tight in every place his eyes touched. Her nerve-endings prickled. Even her nipples tightened in the confines of her bra.

The sensation in her tummy flickered to life again. Only this time it was like the flame on the stove. A solid burn that made her want to press her hand against her stomach.

Finally their gazes reconnected.

Something flared deep in his eyes—something that made her tremble with reaction.

'No, you don't look like a woman on a constant diet.' Was it her imagination or was the timbre of his voice lower than it had been moments before? 'I approve.'

Her heart thumped.

What did that mean?

I approve.

Approved of what?

The fact that she didn't diet?

Or did he approve of her body?

The fact that it might be the latter made a rush of hot blood hurtle through her system.

She wanted to look away, but her eyes just wouldn't obey. They remained locked on Royce as if they were glued there.

Royce didn't look away either.

The air between them began to pulse, as if a soundless drum were beating.

It wasn't until she saw the thick plume of dark smoke rising up behind him that she broke out of her trance-like state. 'Royce! The pan!'

Royce cursed and spun on his heel. With swift efficiency he turned off the gas, swiped a dishcloth from the bench and flapped it in the air to dissipate the smoke.

Bending down, he inspected the contents of the frying pan.

Straightening, he threw her a mind-numbing smile over his shoulder. 'It's a good job I like my bacon crispy,' he said, picking up a spatula and scooping the bacon on to a plate.

Shara eyed the results. 'That's not crispy. That's dead.'

Royce shrugged. 'Each to their own. I happen to like it that way.'

'Are you sure you're not just saying that because you've burnt it? It takes a man to admit when he's wrong.'

His eyes glinted. 'No, I'm not fibbing. This really is the way I like it.'

Shara grimaced. 'I suppose you like your fried eggs with a runny yolk too?'

He flashed her a grin that made her go weak at the knees. 'You bet. Is there any other way to have them?'

Shara smiled back. Then, realising what she was doing, she forced her mouth into a straight line.

This man was not her friend. He wasn't exactly her enemy either. But he *was* standing between her and something she wanted—which was the right to make her own decisions. That right was something most people took for granted. It wasn't until it was taken away from you that you realised how much you valued it.

'I like mine cooked through,' she muttered, and turned away.

Grabbing a chopping board, she began cutting strawberries with all the attention a surgeon would give to the most complicated and delicate operation.

They worked silently for a while. Much as she tried, Shara couldn't stop her eyes from straying back to him.

For such a big man Royce moved with silent gracefulness, each movement precise and self-assured. Somehow she knew he'd make love the same way.

She flushed, dropping her lashes. She didn't know where the thought had come from but she wished it would go back there.

His competency as a lover was of no interest to her.

Why should it be?

She was over men.

Shara took a seat at the breakfast table and began eating. Royce joined her a few minutes later with a plate piled high with food.

'So, tell me about this ex of yours,' he suggested softly, when he'd demolished half of the plate with considerable gusto.

The mention of her ex-husband almost made her choke on a strawberry. 'He's not my favourite topic of conversation.'

'Perhaps not.' He took a bite of mushroom. 'But the more I know about him the easier it will be for me to do my job.'

Shara angled her chin into the air. 'I don't care. I don't want to talk about him. Besides, I've already told you that I don't want a bodyguard, so why would I want to make your job easier for you?'

She had no intention of answering personal questions.

Painful questions.

And she had no intention of helping him. She didn't want him around, poking his nose in her business. It would be safer—for all of them—if he quit and left her alone.

His expression remained unchanged but his eyes had hardened. 'Maybe because it's the polite thing to do? Maybe because it would give two strangers sharing breakfast something to talk about?'

Shara stared at him over the top of her spoon. 'Actually, I think it's impolite to ask someone you've just met personal and intrusive questions. If you feel we must talk then I can think of at least a dozen more interesting topics than my ex-husband. What about the weather? Or the exorbitant price of petrol—which in my opinion has gotten way out of control?'

Royce snapped off the blackened end of a rasher of bacon, popped it in his mouth and chewed. When he'd swallowed, he said, 'I'd much rather talk about Steve Brady.'

Shara put her spoon down on the table less than gently. 'And I wouldn't. Now, unless you want to talk about something else, I'm leaving.'

Royce sighed. 'Stubborn.'

'Yes.'

And she wasn't about to apologise for it.

She had to protect herself.

No matter what it took.

Royce sighed again—even more heavily. 'Will you at least tell me about how Brady is harassing you?'

Shara sat back against her seat. 'Didn't my father tell you?'

'He mentioned a few phone calls and the fact that the guy has been seen hanging around outside the house.'

Shara stared back steadily, keeping her expression neutral. 'Well, there's nothing more to tell. Dad has summed it up nicely. Which is why hiring you is a complete and utter over-reaction.'

She'd tried telling her father that but he hadn't listened. Maybe he sensed that things were worse than what she'd told him.

'I've known Gerard for a number of years,' Royce said. 'He's not the type to over-react.'

Her chin angled into the air. 'Well, in this case he has.'

Royce stared back at her. 'I'll be the judge of that.'

Royce received ample evidence of Steve Brady's harassment several hours later. He walked into the lounge room, where Shara was sitting flipping through a magazine, just as the phone rang.

He noticed the way she jumped like a scalded cat, and watched as the colour drained out of her face.

'Leave it,' Royce ordered as Shara reached a hand towards the phone.

'Leave it?' Shara asked. 'Why?'

'You think it's him, don't you?' Royce asked. 'Your ex?'

A frown creased the smooth skin of her forehead as she nodded her head slowly.

'Let it ring,' he dismissed.

'Why?'

Royce sank down on the lounger opposite and stretched his legs out in front of him. 'Because I said so.'

Her chin jutted. 'That's not good enough. I'm not a puppy dog. You can't order me to sit, beg or roll over any time you feel like it. If you want me to do something I suggest you remember two things.'

He lifted a brow, trying to ignore how damned sexy she looked. 'And what would those be?'

Her chin lifted even higher. She uncrossed her legs and then recrossed them the other way. The action pulled the fabric of her Capri pants tight around her hips. Royce tried not to stare.

'There's this movie I saw once. It's about a guy whose life is going nowhere until he signs up for a self-help programme based on one simple covenant, which is to say yes to anything and everything. It begins to transform his life.'

'Well, that sounds very interesting, but what has that got to do with you co-operating with me?'

Her eyes—they really were the most magnificent colour—seared into his. 'I've spent a year of my life with a man who has told me what to do and what not to do every minute of every day. When I walked out I made a vow not to let that happen again. So if you want me to do something I suggest you try *asking* me instead of *telling* me.'

'Fine. Please don't answer the phone.' He raised the other brow this time. 'There. Is that better?'

'Yes. Much better,' she said. 'The second thing you need to remember is that I'm not going to do anything unless I know *why*. If you don't want me to answer the phone the least you can do is give me a reason.'

Royce stared at her. He couldn't argue with her approach. He was a logical, facts-and-figures kind of guy. If he were in her situation he'd react the same way.

What he *did* object to was the hoity-toity princess tone of voice she was using. As if she was a queen instructing one of her minions.

Normally her attitude would be water off a duck's back. He'd accepted a long time ago that the rich liked to think they were better than everyone else.

He'd never understood the mindset that the measure of a man lay in how much money he had in his bank account or how large his investment portfolio was.

He hadn't understood it when students at the exclusive boarding school he'd attended had made it clear that a scholarship didn't mean that he belonged. All it meant was that some rich person had bequeathed upon him a privilege he wasn't otherwise entitled to.

He understood the attitude even less now that he was a grown man. A *successful* man. For some reason he'd assumed that his achievements would earn him an automatic entrée into the exclusive club of the wealthy.

Not so.

It also seemed to matter where—or was it how?—you made your money. Inherited wealth made you part of the group; earning it yourself didn't.

In Royce's mind the exact opposite was true. Succeeding off your own bat held a hell of a lot more weight in his view than leeching off someone else's success. Just as the measure of a man should be in how he acted and what he stood for rather than some meaningless dollar value.

Royce was no longer interested in being accepted by a group of people who saw the world so differently from the way he did.

So why was he letting Shara's princess tone annoy him?

Royce wasn't sure. So he simply nodded and said, 'OK. I don't want you to answer the phone because if it *is* your ex then answering will give him what he wants. If you refuse to pick up you cut him off at the knees, so to speak.'

'Won't that make him mad?' she asked.

Royce smiled. 'More than likely. But who cares? It sounds to me like he's had his own way for too long. Now it's our turn. We're going to take control of the situation.'

He could tell from her expression that Shara was undecided about his approach, but by then it was too late. They both fell silent as the answering machine picked up the call.

There was nothing for one long minute, and then the phone was slammed down.

Shara winced.

Royce smiled.

The phone rang again almost instantly.

'Ignore it,' Royce said again.

This time Shara shook her head. 'I think I'd better answer it. It might not be him.'

'Then why didn't they leave a message?'

'I don't know. But there's one way to find out, and that's by answering the phone.'

'No. Not yet.'

'This is my home, not yours. I'll do what I like. You can't tell me what to do.'

Royce shook his head. 'This is your father's house, and he's put me in charge.'

Again it was too late for Shara to do anything. The answering machine picked up for a second time. The silence lasted for a couple of minutes this time, before the caller slammed the phone down again.

Royce watched Shara, who was studiously staring at her clenched hands.

Her hair really was magnificent. As dark as a raven's wing and as glossy as the finest satin. His fingers itched to touch it—so much so that he curled his fingers into his palms.

The curve of her cheek was exposed. The skin was milky-white, absolutely flawless and ridiculously vulnerable.

How a cheekbone could be vulnerable Royce wasn't exactly sure, but that was how it struck him.

The phone rang a third time.

Royce studied Shara carefully.

She was staring at the phone as if it was going to jump up and bite her.

Her body language was easy to read. It was painting a very different picture from what she'd told him that morning.

'You lied to me earlier,' he said, in a conversational tone that hid the anger tightening his gut.

He valued honesty above everything else. Not only did he see too much dishonesty in his line of work, but after what Fiona had done to him any form of deception was abhorrent to him.

Her head snapped around. 'I beg your pardon?'

Royce crossed one ankle over the other, rested his hands on his thighs. 'You said your father was over-reacting to the situation, but it's clear to me that you're terrified of your ex-husband.'

She looked startled, then wary. She issued a laugh that fell well short of being humorous, although he was pretty sure that was what she was trying to convey because she'd unclenched her fists and made a concerted effort to look relaxed.

'Nonsense,' she dismissed.

'It's too late to deny it. I believe what I see above what I'm told. My eyes don't lie, whereas people do. I saw your reaction just now.'

She tossed her head. 'What you saw is my frustration at being told not to answer the phone in my own home.'

Royce shook his head. 'Sorry, but I don't believe you.'

She looked about to say something, but at that moment the answering machine picked up.

Shara looked away from him, back to the phone.

Royce grew rigid in his chair as a male voice started speaking. Although *speaking* was a polite word for the filth that came spewing down the phone line.

Foul language and even fouler content.

About how he had no intention of letting Shara go. About the fact that he'd rather kill her first.

Royce tried to look past the surface stuff to the deeper meaning and intent beneath the words.

What he was listening to convinced him that Steve Brady was a sociopathic bully.

Bullying was all about power and control.

Bullies also typically targeted people who tended not to retaliate, who in fact responded in such a way as to feed their negative behaviour.

Which surprised him.

Shara was not that kind of person.

Their short acquaintance demonstrated that she gave as good as she got. He couldn't imagine her allowing herself to be bullied.

But then everything wasn't always as it seemed.

As he should know.

He'd fallen for a woman who'd pretended to be something she wasn't.

He knew first-hand that looks could be deceiving.

In Shara's case he'd seen her fear a moment ago.

It had been genuine. He would bet his career on it.

The question was: why was she pretending she wasn't?

There had to be a reason.

There was *always* a reason.

That was something he'd learned well before starting the Royce Agency. People always had a motive for doing something.

Royce rose to his feet.

Shara's head shot in his direction so fast he was surprised she didn't pull a muscle. 'What are you doing?'

'I'm going to talk to him.'

Her face showed alarm. 'Don't do that!'

Royce ignored her and picked up the phone. 'Brady…?'

The tirade was cut off mid-stream and replaced with screaming silence. Royce let the quietness drag on. He was used to situations like these, and immune to the resulting tension.

He doubted it was the same for Brady. No doubt the silence was playing havoc with the other man's nerves.

As he'd expected, Brady broke the silence first. 'Who is this?'

'My name is Royce. I'm a friend of Shara's.' He spoke calmly and confidently, although his voice hardened as he added, 'And I'm warning you to leave her alone or you won't like the consequences.'

His response was more silence. Uncertain silence. Obviously Brady was trying to come to grips with the sudden turnaround in events.

'My God! It didn't take the little slut long to move on, did it?' His voice was vicious. 'You're not the first, you know. Why don't you ask her just how many men she slept with while she was married to me?'

Royce frowned. If he ignored the content of Brady's words for a moment and concentrated on the way he spoke he would be able to learn a lot.

One, although his tone was vicious Brady had spoken more calmly than Royce would have given him credit for, given his previous tirade. And, two, Brady didn't wait for an answer but hung up the phone—softly.

Both of those things suggested he was very much in control.

Surely that hinted at the fact that Brady was telling the truth?

He'd seen enough musical beds in the homes of the rich and famous during his time running the Royce Agency to know that that kind of behaviour went on all the time.

It was an attitude that sickened him. Although he was no monk, and had had his share of women over the years—some might even say more than his fair share—Royce always remained faithful to the woman he was with.

For however long it lasted—which admittedly wasn't very long.

Why would he want to tie himself to one woman when there was a world of women out there to enjoy?

Back in his parents' day getting married and having children was the done thing. These days things were much more flexible. Some couples got married. Others chose to live together. And others remained single, either through choice or circumstance.

Royce planned on being one of the latter.

But while he *was* in a relationship he treated his woman with respect.

Royce glanced at Shara.

Beautiful, sexy Shara.

Maybe she *had* been sleeping around. Maybe that was why her marriage had turned sour.

It was possible.

But it didn't really matter.

He was a bodyguard, not the morality police.

Nothing excused Brady's behaviour. Abuse of any kind—whether it was verbal, emotional or physical—was inexcusable.

And what he'd just heard—both on the answering machine and during his conversation with Brady—convinced him that Shara had been abused in some way.

A wave of fury rode up his spine.

He was going to take a great deal of pleasure in bringing the other man to his knees.

'What the hell did you do that for?' Shara demanded as Royce dropped the phone back into its cradle.

Royce swung in her direction. 'I beg your pardon?'

Shara jumped to her feet and then wished she hadn't. She was so angry she was shaking, her heart beating nineteen to the dozen. 'You had no right to do that. No right at all.'

She began to pace, her sandals making a slap-slap sound on the tiles, then fading to nothing as she crossed the Aubusson rug.

Thoughts swirled through her head, one after the other, so fast they made her dizzy.

One thought stood out amongst all the others: all her hard work had just been undone in one fell swoop.

Anger ripped through her. Grinding to a halt in the middle of the Aubusson rug, she slammed her hands down on her hips and glared at Royce. 'Who gave you permission to butt your nose in like that? This is precisely the situation I wanted to avoid. You've ruined everything, damn it!'

Royce gave her a puzzled look. 'Perhaps you'd like to explain what it is you think I've ruined, exactly? Because I haven't got a clue what you're talking about.'

'Everything!' Shara raked a hand through her hair, unsurprised to find it was shaking. 'This is precisely the reason I didn't want a bodyguard in the first place. I don't need some stranger interfering in my business. This is *my* situation and I'll deal with it *my* way.'

Royce didn't look the least bit impressed by her outburst.

He was still standing by the phone. Still looking cool, calm and completely unruffled.

The fact that he was so in control while she was falling apart at the seams infuriated Shara no end.

'First, when he hired me to protect you, your father gave me permission to handle the situation *my* way. That's the only way I do business. He knows that. I have to have full control.' He folded his arms across his impressive chest. 'And, second, if what I've seen in the last twenty-four hours is any example of the way you've been dealing with the situation then it's entirely ineffective.'

Pressure built inside her head until Shara thought she was going to explode. She could hardly stand still, but at the same time found that her muscles were locked so rigidly tight she was incapable of moving.

Here we go again.

Another man telling her what to do.

Another man trying to smack her down.

Well, he could try. But he wouldn't succeed.

She glared across the distance separating them. 'How dare you? You conceited oaf! You've known me for all of two seconds and yet you're an expert on me and my way of dealing with situations? As far as I'm concerned your so-called expertise has just made the situation one hundred times worse. I don't care who you are. I don't care if you're one of my father's paid minions. From now on keep out of my way—or there will be hell to pay!'

Satisfied that she'd told him exactly what she thought of him, Shara spun on her heel and stormed out of the lounge room.

She stomped up the stairs to her bedroom and snatched up her handbag and car keys. She had no idea where she was going, but she had to get out of here.

How dare'd Royce put her down that way?

Frankly, she thought she'd done one hell of a job.

She was proud of the way she'd gathered enough courage to leave Steve. She was equally proud of the way she was ignoring his harassment.

It wasn't easy.

Turning the other cheek was damned difficult at times, but she was trying to let his behaviour bounce off her.

So Mr Just Plain Royce could put *that* in his pipe and smoke it!

Exiting the house via the back staircase, Shara breathed a sigh of relief when she reached the garage undetected. She slid the key in the car's ignition and was halfway down the driveway when she gave a victorious pump of her fist in the air.

She was no more than half a kilometre from the house when she stopped smiling. A glance in her rear vision mirror turned her smile into a frown.

There was a black sedan four or five cars back.

The same kind of black sedan that Steve drove.

Every time she made a turn the black sedan made a turn.

Every time she changed lanes so too did the other car.

Which, of course, could mean only one thing: Steve was following her.

Her teeth came together with an audible snap, and a shiver of fear snaked serpent-like down her spine.

'Oh, no,' she said.

Another quick glance in the mirror showed that the black sedan had closed the distance between them. It was now only three cars back, and getting closer all the time.

Her hands clenched on the steering wheel until her knuckles turned white.

'You stupid fool,' she muttered out loud.

When was she going to learn that making decisions in the heat of the moment always backfired on her? When was she going to learn that when she was emotionally upset she almost always made the wrong decision?

She'd accused Royce of making the situation worse not twenty minutes ago, and then what had she done?

Stayed in the house where she was safe?

Oh, no—not her.

She'd had to try and prove a point by sneaking out.

Had she thought of the possible consequences?

No.

Had she waited until she'd calmed down before deciding what her next step should be?

No again.

She hadn't just landed on the snake's head by accident this time; she'd jumped on it all by herself.

'Damn it. When will I ever learn?'

Royce peered through the front windscreen.

He'd been quite content to follow Shara at a distance. Close enough to intervene at the first sign of trouble, but far enough back to let Shara think she'd made a clean getaway.

It could prove interesting.

Where would she go? Who would she meet? What would she do?

The more he knew about her patterns of movement, her routine, the better prepared he'd be to deal with whatever the future held.

Information was power.

That wasn't supposition; it was fact.

But that attitude belonged to five minutes ago.

He'd abandoned the hang-back strategy thirty seconds ago.

For one simple reason.

Shara was being followed.

There was no doubt about it.

Every time Shara made a turn the black sedan several cars behind her also made a turn.

Every time she changed lanes the black sedan changed lanes.

Logic suggested this wasn't a random incident. Logic suggested that Brady had been watching the house and when Shara had left he'd followed her.

Cursing under his breath, Royce pressed the accelerator flat to the floor. The large 4WD leapt forward like a giant predator, gobbling up the grey ribbon of road beneath its tyres.

Thoughts whirred through his head at lightning speed.

Possibilities. Probabilities.

He assessed them all and came up with a strategy to counter each one.

Mixed in amongst all the analysing was a good dose of blinding fury. Not co-operating was one thing, but an outright attempt to evade him was quite another—and completely unacceptable.

The stunt Shara had just pulled reaffirmed his opinion of her.

Her actions were thoughtless and selfish, and he wouldn't put up with such spoilt, self-absorbed behaviour—a fact that he'd make quite clear when he caught up with her.

CHAPTER THREE

SHARA glanced in the rear vision mirror again. The black sedan was right behind her. It was close enough that she could see Steve's angry face framed by the front windscreen.

'What am I going to do?' she whispered.

Thoughts swirled through her head, but no obvious solution presented itself.

She glanced in the mirror again and did a double take.

Surely that was—?

But it couldn't be.

Could it…?

A big dark 4WD she hadn't noticed before was racing down the road behind them.

She'd seen it before. Just last night.

Royce!

Royce was coming to rescue her.

Relief washed through her in waves.

She didn't care how he'd found her. All she cared about was the fact that he had.

'Thank you, God!' she whispered. 'Thank you.'

What she needed now was a strategy. No more going off half-cocked and landing in even deeper trouble. She needed to think…and then she needed to act sensibly.

She could brake. That was one option. Royce would catch up to her even faster. But what would Steve do?

At the moment he appeared content to sit on her tail rather than actually *do* anything. It was an intimidation tactic that was typical of Steve.

But if she slowed would he ram her with his car?

She doubted it.

This was a busy road. There was enough traffic to deter him from doing anything rash that could be witnessed and used against him. Unlike her, Steve thought before he acted.

Her other option was to pull over to the side of the road. That would force Steve either to stop or keep on going. If her car doors were locked and Royce was hot on their tail she couldn't get into too much trouble, surely?

Deciding the latter was the better option, Shara glanced in her side mirror and waited for a break in the traffic. Then, without indicating, she swung hard on the wheel and with a screech of tyres pulled over on the side of the road.

The blast of car horns that hit her eardrums suggested Steve had followed suit, but she waited until she'd brought her car to a halt before having a proper look.

Steve was right behind her.

He was getting out of his car.

Shara started to shake. Her hands grew sweaty. Her heart thumped.

The sight of her ex-husband was enough to make her feel sick and anxious. It was a feeling she remembered all too well. It dominated her consciousness, blotting everything else out.

With a squeal of tyres another vehicle screeched to a halt beside her. A quick glance showed her it was the big 4WD.

Royce.

He ignored the fact that he was blocking one lane of traffic and jumped from his vehicle.

Her relief was so strong that Shara fumbled for the door latch and did the same.

Royce looked so big and solid. So reassuringly safe.

Without thinking, she flung herself at him. 'Boy, am I glad to see you!'

Strong arms closed around her.

Shara was aware of heat and the smell of warm male skin. She was also aware of the strength and power barely contained in the muscled lines of his body.

Cocooned against Royce's chest, Shara felt safe and secure.

She also felt something else.

A ripple of desire.

It was the first time she'd admitted, even to herself, that that was what the curling sensation in her belly she experienced every time she looked at him was all about.

Now she had no choice but to acknowledge it.

It packed quite a punch.

Enough to make her push away from him.

She was just over-reacting to their close proximity and to the adrenalin pumping through her system.

That was all.

It was nothing personal.

If she told herself that often enough she might even believe it.

Royce clasped her wrists and pulled her hands down from around his neck before she could completely disengage herself.

'Stay there,' he said, dragging her behind him so that he stood between her and Steve.

Nothing more was said.

Not a single word.

The air was filled with menace. Filled so completely that it raised the hairs on her arms and the back of her neck.

She could feel Royce's body braced for action, but it wasn't needed. She heard the scuffle of footsteps, the slamming of a car door, and then the screech of tyres as the black sedan raced off, leaving behind a trail of exhaust smoke and the smell of burning rubber.

As soon as Steve had disappeared Royce turned, a heavy frown on his face. Gripping the tops of her arms, he gave her a brief hard shake before putting his face next to hers. 'You little fool. Sneaking off like that was stupid and reckless. What on earth were you thinking?'

Shara blinked, her heart leaping into the back of her throat.

Royce was angry.

Very angry.

Steve had looked at her the same way many times.

Now, as then, she shrank in on herself—both physically and mentally. Her shoulders hunched, her muscles contracted, her breath shortened.

The grey, smoke-filled fog of fear closed around her like a shroud. Suffocating. Deadening. Numbing.

'I...I'm s...sorry,' she stammered. Inside she cringed at how apologetic she sounded. She hadn't heard that particular tone of voice come out of her mouth since she'd been with Steve. 'I wasn't thinking.'

Shame washed through her.

She didn't want to revert to the woman she'd been when she'd been with Steve.

The reasons for staying in an abusive relationship were many and varied, and had nothing to do with the victim's character or strength of will.

It had taken Shara a long time to come to terms with why *she'd* stayed with Steve.

One reason was that she hadn't wanted to admit that marrying Steve had been a mistake. Her father had been against the marriage. He'd told her she was rushing into things. She hadn't wanted to admit that he'd been right.

But the driving force—the thing that had compelled her to stay—was fear.

Crippling, disabling fear.

Steve's threats had quite literally paralysed her into inaction for a long time.

She'd been terrified he'd become more violent if she tried to leave.

Terrified that he'd come after her.

And those fears had proved to be justified, because that was exactly what he'd done.

She dragged in a breath, and then another. Slowly her heartbeat began to return to normal. Her fear began to recede. The smoky fog was washed away.

And her power of thought began to return.

She didn't want to be that frightened woman any more.

She *wouldn't* be that woman any more.

She'd come a long way since then. The last thing she wanted to do was backtrack.

OK, so her marriage to Steve had conditioned her to respond negatively to certain things.

But she could rise above it.

She could *un*-learn it.

Somehow.

Starting now.

Royce stared at Shara. Saw the fear in her eyes and realised *he* was responsible. Heard the stammer in her voice and knew that he was answerable for that too.

Immediately his heart stilled.

He was a fool.

A stupid, thoughtless fool.

He'd scared the poor girl half out of her wits. As if she hadn't already been scared enough.

Taking a deep breath, he relaxed his hold on the tops of her arms and adopted a calm expression. His hands soothed gently up and down. 'It's OK, Shara. I'm sorry I yelled at you.'

She didn't look at him. She was staring downwards.

'I wasn't thinking,' Royce continued. 'I didn't mean to frighten you.'

She was shaking, her breathing coming in short gasps.

'That's it.' Royce deliberately kept his voice low and even. 'Take some deep breaths. In and out.'

Gradually she stopped shaking.

'That's it. You're almost there,' Royce encouraged.

Finally, Shara lifted her head. 'Let me go!'

Royce immediately did as she asked. In fact he went one better. He took a couple of paces backwards. His behaviour had obviously made her feel threatened. Giving her some space would help put her at her ease.

It was important Shara felt safe with him—not just because it would be easier for him to do his job, but because he was not a man who got his kicks out of frightening women. He'd leave that kind of behaviour to the likes of Brady.

'That's it,' he said, relieved to see that her breathing was becoming calmer and deeper. 'You're going to be all right.'

Shara dragged in another calming breath and glared at him. 'All right? I doubt very much if I'm going to be *all right* if you're going to go on creating situations like this one.'

He pointed a finger at his chest. 'You think *I* created this situation?' he asked incredulously.

'I certainly do.'

'And just how do you figure this is my fault?'

She tossed her hair over her shoulder. 'You deliberately provoked Steve on the phone earlier.'

'And how did I do that?'

'You told him you were a friend of mine, and—'

Royce nodded. 'I did. What's wrong with that?'

'Apart from the fact that it's a complete and utter lie, you mean?'

He nodded. 'Apart from that.'

'What you don't know is that Steve is insanely jealous—to

the point of being completely paranoid.' His paranoia had become so bad that she'd had to walk on eggshells all the time. 'All I had to do was talk to a man and Steve thought we were having an affair. And if a guy so much as looked at me Steve was ready to beat him to a pulp.'

'And how am I supposed to know that when you refused point-blank to discuss it with me?' he flung at her, but without his earlier aggression.

Shara tossed her head. 'I didn't want to discuss it any more than I wanted you interfering. But it's too late for that. You've already stuck your oar in and muddied the water.' She dragged in a breath. 'Telling him that we're friends has probably given him completely the wrong idea.'

Again, Royce nodded. 'If it's any consolation, you're right. He accused us of sleeping together.'

Shara gasped, lifting her hands to her cheeks. 'Oh, no! That's terrible. Just terrible.'

'Why is it terrible?'

'Are you mad?' she gasped. 'Haven't you listened to a word I've said?'

He shook his head. 'No, I'm not mad. I'm perfectly sane. And, yes, I've listened to everything you've told me.'

'Then surely it's obvious why I'm so upset?' Her mouth twisted. 'Steve won't like the idea of me being with someone else, that's why! Even if it isn't true.'

Royce had an odd look on his face. 'OK. Let's leave that for a moment. You were about to add something else a minute ago when I interrupted you. What was it?'

Shara frowned. 'You threatened him. How on earth do you think *that* will help the situation?'

'If he has any sense he'll listen to my advice and forget about you, and the situation will be over.'

She barked out a harsh laugh. 'And if he doesn't—and I'm betting he won't—you'll have just made him angry.'

'So?'

So.

One word. Two letters. Simple.

Only it wasn't simple.

Royce had used the word in the context of *So what?* a term normally given in answer to an unimportant or irrelevant statement, indicating indifference on the part of the speaker.

Well, that was all well and good for Royce.

But he hadn't lived in her world.

If he had he'd know that there was nothing indifferent about making Steve angry. If anything, the exact opposite was true—which was precisely why she was so concerned.

Shara wrapped her arms around herself, chilled to the bone.

'It doesn't pay to make him angry,' she whispered.

His expression shifted. It was a subtle thing. It was as if all the muscles in his face had hardened. 'What happens when you make him angry?'

Shara shook her head, tremors making their way up and down her spine. 'He retaliates.'

'He hit you?'

Shara hugged herself even more tightly. 'Once.' She paused for a heartbeat. 'But there are other ways of making someone suffer.'

Although she didn't think it was possible, his face hardened even more.

'I know there are,' he said grimly. 'I'm sorry you had to go through that.'

Shara wasn't sure whether it was the unexpected sympathy or the memories that got to her, but suddenly tears were stinging the backs of her eyes and clogging her throat.

Royce muttered a curse under his breath, pulled her against his chest and wrapped his arms around her.

And suddenly a few tears became a flood.

A flood she couldn't seem to stop.

Her arms slid around his waist as she buried her nose against his chest and cried for all she was worth.

Royce spoke softly to her. She didn't hear a single word. Not one. But the sound of his voice and the rumble in his chest when he spoke was soothing.

Finally she pulled back with a loud sniff. She stared at his shirt and the large patch of damp fabric in the middle. 'Sorry about that. I've made your shirt all wet.'

'Don't worry about it. It will dry.' He looked around. Cars were whizzing by them. 'Let's get out of here.'

She nodded.

But neither of them moved.

They stood staring at each other.

The atmosphere changed. Deepened.

His head began to descend towards hers. Of its own volition her mouth lifted.

And then, suddenly, they were more than a foot apart.

Shara wasn't sure who moved first. Royce or her. Either way, it didn't matter.

Didn't matter because what had almost happened shouldn't have happened.

Royce cleared his throat. 'We need to talk—but not on the side of a road.'

She sniffed again. 'There's nothing to talk about.'

Not about the near-miss kiss. Not about her crying jag. Or anything else for that matter. Her position hadn't changed. Just because Royce had rescued her from a potentially sticky situation it didn't mean she'd changed her mind. She still didn't want him interfering.

Royce frowned. 'Yes, there is. We need to talk about our strategy for handling your case going forward.'

Your case.

Those two words were a harsh reminder that his concern wasn't personal. He was just doing his job.

She knew that.

Of course she did.

So why was there a distinct pang in the centre of her chest?

Shara moved away from the heat and the smell of him. She wiped a hand across her eyes, removing the last traces of tears. 'I repeat: there's nothing to talk about. You're just making the situation worse. Don't you understand that?'

'That's why you didn't want a bodyguard?'

She nodded. 'I want you to butt out. I can't make it any clearer than that.'

Royce folded his arms across his chest and stared her directly in the eye. 'Oh, you're being crystal-clear. Have no doubt about that. But that is precisely the reason we need to talk.'

Shara frowned. 'I don't understand.'

Royce sighed and reached out, fleetingly touched her cheek with his fingertips. It was the lightest of touches, and lasted for barely a second, and yet it had a rippling effect right through her system.

'I know you don't.' His tone was odd. 'And therein lies the problem.'

'Stop talking in riddles,' she ordered.

'OK. You don't like my approach to handling your ex?'

Shara shook her head. 'No, I don't. It's too confrontational. You're just going to escalate the situation. And I won't have that. I *won't*.'

'You may just have to, because—'

Shara stamped her foot. 'Because nothing. I don't care whether my father hired you. I don't care what his instructions are. This is *my* life, and I'm done with everyone interfering.'

Royce stared at her long and hard. His chocolate-brown eyes were veiled but at the same time penetrating. Finally he said quietly, 'No, you'd rather continue to play the victim.'

He might as well have hit her. Her head went back. Her heart leapt into the back of her throat. A shudder so deep and penetrating that it rocked the lining of her soul ripped through her.

She staggered back from him. 'You take that back. You take that back right this minute,' she gasped, barely able to get the words out through numb lips. 'I'm not playing at anything. I *am* the victim.'

Royce inclined his head. 'You *were* a victim. It's your choice whether you continue to be one or not.'

Her hands clenched and unclenched. 'If I were a man I'd hit you into the middle of next week for saying that. I made a choice not to be a victim the day I left Steve.'

'Then why aren't you fighting back?'

He asked the question softly. Somehow that had far more impact than if he'd shouted.

'I *am* fighting back,' she said, but her voice was little more than a whisper.

His eyes didn't waver from hers. 'How? Tell me that.'

The words were blunt and to the point. They attacked without mercy.

Shara blinked, an unsettled feeling attacked the base of her spine. 'I left him.'

Royce waved a dismissive hand. 'I'm not denying that, but what have you done since then?'

'I—' She snapped her mouth closed. 'Well, I—'

What *had* she done?

Her mind sifted through the catalogue of her actions since Steve's harassment had begun and she didn't like what she was seeing. Ignoring his behaviour, turning the other cheek, avoiding going anywhere she was likely to run into him. Not exactly fighting actions, were they?

'Everything you say and everything you do regarding your ex-husband is submissive. It's as if you've chosen a course of passive resistance where he's concerned.' His eyes bored into hers, serious and determined. 'You don't want to be confrontational because it will make him angry and if you make him angry, then he'll retaliate. You're feeding his power over you. Can't you see that? You're letting him keep control. If you don't break that pattern of behaviour nothing will ever change. He'll always have a hold over you.'

Shara stared at him and kept on staring.

The breath was locked in her lungs so tightly they felt as if they were going to burst. Her heart was beating so fast and so hard she was sure her ribs would crack at any moment.

He was right.

She didn't want to admit it, but he was.

It was as if Royce had stripped away an invisible veil that had prevented her from seeing her own actions clearly.

'God, I'm such a fool,' she said, burying her face in her hands.

Royce grasped her wrists and pulled her hands away from her face. 'No, you're scared. I understand that. Fear does strange things to people. No doubt you've become conditioned to react the way you have.'

She released a bitter laugh. 'You're right. I thought I was being tough and strong by ignoring Steve's harassment. But I can see now that all I've been doing is what I learned to do during my marriage.'

'Which is?'

'Keep the peace. Don't provoke. Play it safe. The only difference between now and then is that I've been doing it long-distance.'

'Don't beat yourself up over it. It's perfectly understandable.'

She snorted. 'You think?'

He nodded. 'I *know*.'

'I think you're being overly generous, but thank you for saying it.'

'Don't thank me. I never say anything I don't mean. What you need to do now is focus on the future.'

Shara hadn't allowed herself to think too much about the future because Steve's harassment had chained her to the past. Now, for the first time, she had a glimpse of a future in which she was free and in control of her own life.

As if reading her mind, Royce said, 'Keep in mind that the dynamic has changed. *I'm* involved now. That adds an entirely new dimension to the situation. The bottom line is that you don't have to be scared any more. I won't let anything happen to you. I'll keep you safe.'

Shara stared up at him, an emotion she couldn't quite define sweeping through her. 'I want to believe you. I really do. But you don't know what he's like.'

Royce shrugged. 'I don't need to. I've dealt with some pretty tough characters in my life.'

'Still—'

'Still nothing. I'm an expert. Brady isn't. He doesn't stand a chance against me. I *will* protect you. That's a promise.'

Shara wanted to believe him. Wanted to believe him so badly that she could taste it.

But that meant placing her trust in a complete stranger.

Her trust *and* her safety.

But what choice did she have?

'Trust me,' Royce urged, as if he sensed all the doubts swirling around in her head.

She nodded her head jerkily.

'Truce?' Royce asked, holding out his hand.

'Truce,' Shara said, taking his hand.

A tingle of something that felt very much like electricity shot up her arm. As it did so a disturbing thought jumped to the forefront of her brain.

Royce might protect her from Steve, but who was going to protect her from Royce and the magnetism that had burst to life between them?

Royce wanted Shara to return to the house with him, but she refused.

'If you're worried about your car, don't be,' he said. 'I can have someone come and pick it up.'

Shara shook her head. 'Why put someone else to the trouble when I'm already here?'

Why indeed?

Royce had to admit that her attitude grated on him—but for all the right reasons.

Fiona had had little or no respect for her father's household staff. She'd dropped clothes willy-nilly on the floor and had left towels in the bathroom in much the same way.

The fact that Shara hadn't jumped at his suggestion hinted that she was different.

It was only a little thing, admittedly, but Royce had learned that a person's values were reflected in *everything* they did—both the big and the small.

Shara's response just didn't gel with his initial impression of her.

But then his impression of her was changing all the time, wasn't it?

When the household security system—a system *he* had personally installed—had alerted him to the fact that Shara was sneaking out of the house, he'd been furious.

Stupid and *thoughtless* were two of the more polite words that had sprung into his mind. So too were *irresponsible* and *reckless*.

The stunt she'd pulled had reinforced his opinion that she was spoilt and self-absorbed, but their conversation just now forced him to acknowledge that that wasn't entirely true.

Shara had refused a bodyguard out of a misdirected sense of self-preservation. Scraping back the surface had revealed a woman who was strong and courageous.

Because it took courage to admit when you were wrong.

And it took courage *and* strength to face your fears.

And that was exactly what Shara was doing.

She might have gone about it the wrong way, but she *was* trying.

He couldn't help but admire her for that.

'Coffee, I think,' Royce said when they entered the house. 'Unless you'd prefer something stronger?'

Shara shook her head, sending her hair swirling around her shoulders. 'I don't need anything stronger. I'm not going to fall apart on you again.' She smiled a twisted kind of smile. 'One meltdown a day is my limit.'

He laughed, pleased that she wasn't taking herself too seriously. 'You didn't have a meltdown. You just—'

'Had a meltdown,' she said dryly.

Whatever it was she'd had, she'd regrouped marvellously.

He shrugged. 'Everyone has a release valve that goes off occasionally. That's what keeps us sane.'

'I can't see *you* bawling your eyes out.'

Royce grimaced. 'I must admit I prefer hitting the gym.'

'Maybe I'll think about doing the same thing next time.' She picked up the kettle. 'How do you take your coffee?'

Royce told her, and watched as she bustled around the kitchen.

She moved with an easy grace that obviously came naturally. It was a pleasure watching her move about.

'So, if you don't hit the gym, what do you do to relax when the pressure is on?' he asked.

'Listen to music,' she replied promptly.

'What kind?'

She shrugged. 'Nothing too heavy. I like pop and light classical music. If I close my eyes I can lose myself in a song. It's a great way to escape—if only for a little while.'

Royce remembered the way Shara had been swaying and twirling to the music the previous evening. He cocked an eyebrow. 'Is that what you were doing in the club last night? Trying to escape?'

She grimaced. '*Trying* being the operative word. Except I kept getting interrupted. First by Tony and then by you.'

'Tony is the guy you gave short shrift to?'

She plonked a mug down in front of him with more force

than necessary. The coffee rolled around the edge of the cup but somehow managed not to spill.

'That's a rather cutting remark,' she said, taking a seat opposite him.

'I'm just calling it as I saw it,' he returned unapologetically.

He'd been on the receiving end of that kind of dismissal once before and he knew how it felt. Fiona had laughed in his face for thinking she'd ever been serious about him. That laugh had cut him to the quick.

'Well, for your information, Tony has been making a nuisance of himself. He won't take no for an answer. Last night I had to tell him straight to leave me alone.'

'I see,' he said, digesting this new piece of information and realising that it put a different slant on the scene he'd witnessed.

'Or are you one of those guys who thinks that no means yes?' Shara asked, breaking in on his thoughts. 'Because if you are then we're not going to get on at all.'

Royce held up his hands. 'Not me. No means no in any language. I have a strong sense of right and wrong. It's one of the things that led me to starting my business.'

'Good.' She tapped her fingertips on the tabletop. 'If Tony had two brain cells to rub together he would have backed off earlier. The ink is barely dry on my divorce papers. My ex is still harassing me. The last thing I want is to get involved with someone else. Is that so hard to understand?'

Royce shook his head. 'Not at all. In fact it's perfectly understandable.'

Royce remembered how he'd felt when he'd discovered Fiona had betrayed him. He'd been sure he'd never get involved with a woman again.

He had, of course.

Sex was a powerful motivator. He had no intention of living the rest of his life like a monk.

There was, however, one major difference.

Since Fiona he had always maintained a cool distance emotionally in all of his relationships.

If he'd been using his head back then he would have known that something wasn't quite right about their relationship. In fact, he'd have known there was something downright fishy about the whole situation.

If he'd had his wits about him he'd have seen through the web of lies and deceit and seen Fiona for exactly what she was—someone who was using him for her own ends.

At the time he'd thought her interest in him—and the case—was sweet. Instead all she'd been doing was pumping him for information—both literally and figuratively.

'You say that as if you're speaking from personal experience,' Shara commented, breaking in on his thoughts.

'I am. I doubt that any man—or woman, for that matter—reaches the grand old age of thirty-four without having been burned once or twice.'

She raised one neatly plucked eyebrow. 'Once or twice?'

Royce stared back. 'Once. I always learn from my mistakes.'

CHAPTER FOUR

SHARA was staring at him, a mixture of sympathy and sadness in her eyes.

Royce ignored the former, but the latter made his heart constrict.

Such a young and beautiful woman shouldn't have so much sadness in her eyes.

Royce wanted to take her hand in his and say something—anything—to banish that unhappy look.

To make her smile.

Or laugh.

It wasn't an appropriate reaction—just as almost kissing her by the side of the road earlier hadn't been appropriate.

He stared deeper into her eyes and saw a question burning there. It was clear she wanted to ask him more about what had happened, but he had no intention of trading war stories.

He hadn't even told Travis and Jackson, his two closest friends, what had happened with Fiona. The last thing he wanted was anyone feeling sorry for him. The important thing was that even though he'd been hurt at the time the experience had provided an invaluable life lesson.

Getting involved warped your viewpoint.

Emotions fuzzed your objectivity and made you vulnerable.

He'd acted like a stupid fool with Fiona, but—as he'd just

told Shara—he'd learnt his lesson and had no intention of repeating the same mistake twice.

Something in his expression must have warned Shara not to pursue the subject, because after taking a sip of her herbal tea she said, 'You mentioned that having a strong sense of right and wrong led you into starting your business?'

Royce grasped the change of subject with both hands. 'Kind of. To be honest, I had a whole other career mapped out. I was going to be the world's next Bill Gates. The security business picked me rather than the other way around.'

She raised an eyebrow. 'And how did it manage to do that?'

Royce rubbed the side of his jaw with his fingers. 'I've always had a thing about supporting the underdog. I guess it came from being bullied as a child.'

'*You* were bullied? I find that hard to believe,' she said, making no attempt to hide her incredulity.

'Why?'

Shara blinked, then waved a hand towards him. 'You just don't look the type.'

'Because I'm big?'

She nodded.

'Big doesn't necessarily mean aggressive, you know.'

'I suppose not.'

'Strange as it may seem, my size was one of the reasons I was picked on in the first place. I was taller than everyone in my class. A couple of the other kids assumed that because I was big I was also tough. They decided to see just how tough I was.'

'You mean...?'

He nodded. 'They decided to fight me whether I wanted to fight or not. I hated it.'

'I can imagine,' she said.

'After I'd been beaten up a few times my dad decided we'd better do something about it.' His smile was rueful. 'He enrolled me in a local karate class. I never looked back.'

'So instead of getting beat up you did the beating instead? Why do men always have to be so macho? Surely there was a better way of dealing with the bullies than meeting violence with violence?'

Royce shook his head. 'You have it wrong. Martial arts training gave me confidence. I wasn't scared any more. And because I knew what I was doing I could dissuade most of the bullies without hurting them. Strange as it may seem to you, I actually abhor violence.'

'You sure picked a strange profession, then.'

He grinned. 'Not really. My business is mostly about prevention. I can't stop other people from behaving aggressively, but I can protect others from being hurt. Which is exactly what happened at school.'

Shara frowned. 'I'm not following you.'

Royce picked up his cup to prevent himself from reaching across and smoothing the small furrows on her brow with his fingertips. 'If I saw another kid being picked on I stepped in before the situation went too far. I made it clear to the bullies that they'd have to deal with me if they did anything.'

'And did they heed the warning?'

'Some did. Some didn't,' Royce replied, taking a sip of coffee.

Shara raised an eyebrow. 'And the ones who didn't?'

'Let's just say that they didn't need a third warning,' he said simply, his gaze steady on hers.

Shara drew away from him, looking horrified. 'What did you do to them?'

He frowned at her reaction and leaned across the table. 'I think you've got the wrong end of the stick. If you're imagining bloody noses and broken bones then you couldn't be more wrong. I don't operate that way. The only thing that got injured was their pride.'

'I see.'

'I hope you do. Because the last thing I want is for you to think that I'm some kind of thug.'

Not only was his professional reputation important to him, so was his personal one. A man should protect his character as solidly as he protected himself.

Shara shook her head, sending her hair swirling around her shoulders. 'How could I think that after what you did this morning?'

Royce frowned. 'You've lost me. What did I do this morning?'

'When you got angry you reminded me so much of Steve that you frightened me. As soon as you realised what was happening you immediately backed down.'

Royce still didn't get the point. 'I did. So?'

She smiled an odd kind of smile. 'Steve would never have done that. He seemed to enjoy scaring me.'

The admission made him grit his teeth as a wave of fury rode up his spine. It nauseated him to think about what Shara had had to endure.

Royce took a deep breath, surprised by the depth and intensity of his reaction. He'd dealt with numerous sleaze-buckets over the years—had witnessed more sordid and downright awful situations than he cared to think about. But he accepted them as part of the job.

It was a fact of life that those things existed.

There was no point getting emotional about it. Doing so was just a waste of time and energy and achieved nothing.

Instead, he dealt with ugly situations the same way he dealt with everything.

With discipline and self control. And with calm, cool logic.

So why the hell was he sitting here wanting to smash something at the thought of what Shara had had to endure?

Royce wasn't sure, but his reaction set alarm bells ringing.

'Unfortunately I'm not surprised. These guys get their rocks off pushing other people around.' He curled his lip. 'But you don't have to worry about that. Be assured that Brady won't touch you while I'm around.'

Shara stared at him with big wide eyes, 'I think I'm beginning to believe you.'

Shara could hardly believe those words had come out of her mouth, but they had.

Royce's confidence was reassuring. So too was the strong sense of justice he'd just been talking about.

But talk was cheap. Actions always spoke louder than words—and the way Royce had come to her rescue this morning, paired with the way he'd backed down when he realised he was frightening her, were ample evidence that he meant what he said.

She could, she was beginning to realise, trust Royce—at least to some extent.

She pushed her empty mug away. 'It's still a big leap from dealing with a couple of schoolyard bullies to operating your own business.'

He flashed her another of those bone-melting smiles that made her heart turn over. 'I know. In fact it's a bigger leap than you can even imagine.'

'Go on.'

'My career transformation started when I was hauled up to the headmaster's office one day and accused of hacking into the computer network to change the grades of some of the students.'

'But you didn't,' she said without hesitation.

Royce raised an eyebrow in her direction. 'You sound very sure.'

'A man with a strong sense of justice wouldn't cheat like that.'

'Well, your instincts are right. I had nothing to do with it.'

'So what made them accuse you?' Shara asked, resting her chin on her cupped hands.

It was only human nature to be curious about someone you were going to be sharing a house with for the foreseeable future, Shara assured herself. It wasn't as if she was interested in him or anything like that.

'They had no proof, if that's what you're asking. Their excuse was flimsy, to say the least.' She gave him an enquiring look. 'They thought I was the only student capable of hacking into the system.'

'Obviously you weren't, since it was someone else.'

He nodded. 'Exactly. I can understand why they thought it was me, though. I have a knack for computing. Since it was one of my subjects they knew that. Still, I was furious at being unjustly accused with so little evidence.'

'I can imagine.'

It was the kind of injustice that Shara could understand. When Steve had first turned on her shortly after their wedding she'd been bewildered. But quickly on the heels of her confusion had come the question: What have I done to deserve this?

'So guess what I did?' Royce asked.

The question dragged Shara back to the present. 'I wouldn't have a clue.'

'I offered to find out who the hacker was,' he said, with the same panache as someone pulling a rabbit out of a hat.

Shara sat back in her chair. It was an idea that hadn't even occurred to her. 'That's a unique solution—but how on earth could you do that?'

'Actually, it was quite easy. The hacker was an amateur compared to me, so tracing him wasn't difficult.' Royce pushed his chair back from the table and crossed an ankle over a knee. 'But it gave me the idea that maybe it would be challenging, not to mention more interesting, doing that kind of thing for a living instead of straight computer work. So I decided to find out. I approached a well-known security company to see if they'd give me a part-time job.'

It was a logical step, although Shara very much doubted it would have occurred to *her*. 'And did they?'

'No, they laughed in my face. They thought it was hysterical that a schoolkid thought he had something to offer them. But that was a mistake.' Another of those heart-melting smiles flashed across his face. 'What they didn't realise was that, one, I don't like being laughed at, and, two, defeat is not a word in my vocabulary.'

Shara was beginning to realise that—which meant that he was a good man to have on her side. 'So what did you do?'

He leaned conspiratorially closer and beckoned her to do the same with a crooked finger. He waited until she'd pushed her cup aside and leant across the table before saying softly, 'I hacked into their computer system.'

Shara almost choked on her own tongue. 'You didn't!'

Royce nodded. 'I most certainly did. I left a message in the inbox of every employee of the company telling them that if they didn't hire me they'd regret it.'

Shara stared at Royce open-mouthed, then threw her head back and laughed. Not a delicate little giggle but a full-on belly laugh. She couldn't remember the last time she'd laughed like that.

Finally she sobered. 'I shouldn't be laughing. That really was very naughty of you.'

'I know. But do you blame me?'

Shara thought about that. 'I suppose not. Although with your sense of right and wrong I'm surprised you didn't think you were crossing the line.'

'Considering there was no malicious intent involved and that I signed my name to the e-mail, I figured I wasn't doing any harm other than proving that I was determined.'

'Oh, I think you managed to prove that,' she said dryly.

'The company obviously thought so too.'

Shara frowned. 'Don't tell me they threatened you with the police?'

Royce shook his head. 'No. In fact just the opposite. They were on the phone the next day with all kinds of offers.'

Again it was an answer she hadn't been expecting. 'Are you sure you're not making this up?'

'Scouts' honour,' Royce said, giving her the three-fingered salute that usually accompanied the saying. 'It takes quite some skill to bypass the security of a security company, you know.'

'I hadn't thought of it that way, but I suppose it does.' Not only was he determined, he was clever right along with it. 'Did you accept?'

'Of course. I worked with them through the rest of high school, learning the ropes and the various aspects of the business. Then, while I was at university, I started my own business.'

'And now you're the largest and most well-known security firm on the globe?'

'The biggest and the best,' Royce said proudly.

Shara frowned. 'I was less than gracious the last time we discussed this. I apologise. Obviously your success is well deserved.'

'Thanks, but your apology isn't necessary.' He pushed his mug away. 'Now, enough about me. Let's discuss our strategy moving forward.'

'Do we have to?' Shara demanded. 'I'm sick to the back teeth of talking about Steve. I don't even want to *think* about him.'

'I'm sure you don't. But we need to go over a couple of things. After that we won't mention Brady again unless we absolutely have to. Deal?'

'All right,' she agreed reluctantly.

Royce stared at her for a long moment. There was something about the lack of expression on his face that made the hairs on the back of her neck stand on end.

'I want you to take out an Apprehended Violence Order against Brady,' he said quietly.

Shara frowned. 'I've heard of them, but I'm not sure how they work.'

'An AVO is used to protect a person against both acts of violence and the threat of violence. It covers everything from physical assault to non-physical abuse, such as harassment or intimidation. The order itself doesn't give a person a criminal record, but the clincher for us is that a breach of the order *is* a criminal offence.' He leaned forward. 'If Brady crosses the line once the AVO is in place we can have him arrested.'

Shara shook her head even before he'd finished speaking, her hands clenched tightly together in her lap. 'I don't think that's a good idea.'

Royce frowned. 'Why?'

'Because it's too confrontational, that's why.'

Royce stared at her—hard. 'I thought we'd already had this conversation. Don't tell me you're back-pedalling already?'

Shara bit down on her lower lip. 'I'm not back pedalling. I'm just…'

He raised a brow. 'Just what?'

'Exercising caution.'

Royce sighed and leaned across the table. 'Well, I hate to tell you this, Shara, but caution just isn't going to cut it.'

She read the determination written on his face. It was unsettling. 'You're serious about this?'

He nodded. 'I am. Very serious.'

Shara gripped the edge of the table. 'What you're suggesting is suicide.'

'No, it's not. Brady can't touch you without going through me first.'

Shara eyed the rock hard muscles of his shoulders and arms.

Of all of the things Royce had said to her—the promises and assurances—what he'd just said was the most reassuring. If Steve came up against Royce it would be like pitting a domestic cat against a lion or a tiger.

Royce was a professional.

He'd proved that more than once.

Maybe it was time she started listening to his advice.

She nodded before her courage deserted her. 'OK. I'll do it.'

'Good. I'll get Jackson on to it right away.'

'Jackson?'

'Jackson Black. He's a friend of mine and a very good lawyer,' Royce explained. He paused for a moment, then asked, 'Can I take it that you'll co-operate from now on? There'll be no more incidents like the one this morning?'

Shara nodded.

'Good. We have a much better chance of success with us both working together.'

Shara grimaced, not so sure she wanted to work together with Royce.

After that near-miss kiss earlier, working together could prove altogether too dangerous.

'What is it?' Royce demanded when he saw her grimace.

'Nothing. I'm just being stupid.'

'I'll be the judge of that.'

She shrugged. 'When I left Steve I promised myself that I'd stand on my own two feet.'

'You are.'

She shrugged again, drawing his attention to her breasts. 'It doesn't feel like it. Not when I'm relying on you to protect me.'

'Give yourself a break, Shara,' Royce said, speaking in no uncertain terms. 'No one is completely self-sufficient. If you have a leak you call a plumber. If you have car trouble you take it to a garage. If you're sick you go to a doctor. There's nothing different about this situation. You're being threatened and I'm an expert at protection. End of story.'

'I suppose so.' She paused. Looked away then back again. 'How long do you think this is going to take, anyway?'

She rested her elbows on the edge of the table. The action squeezed her breasts together, deepening her cleavage in the low neckline of the white T-shirt she was wearing. Royce found it difficult not to stare. In fact he found it impossible not to.

She had a fantasy-filled bra. He was a man who liked curvy women. Maybe it was because he was such a big man himself. Skinny women did nothing for him. Somehow he knew Shara's breasts would fill his hands perfectly, and his fingers itched to pull off her T-shirt and bra and discover the truth for themselves.

As he watched her nipples tightened to beads under the thin fabric. She'd noticed him staring and her body was reacting.

Suddenly the air around them was filled with electric tension.

His eyes shot to her face. She was staring at him, twin stripes of colour flagging her cheeks.

The realisation that she was being turned on by his look sent a surge of hormones racing through his body. His erection was hard and fierce and instantaneous beneath the zippered seam of his trousers.

Shifting on his seat, he willed his body under control.

He didn't want to be attracted to Shara. Not only was she the principal, but she was cut from the same mould as Fiona.

Both came from rich families and both had been raised by doting fathers who had spoiled them rotten at every turn. The result, of course, was that they were selfish and self-centred. They took more than they gave.

Royce preferred women who'd forged their own path in life the same way he had. They could be models or lawyers.

It didn't matter. All that mattered was that they appreciated what they had because they'd earned it, and that they respected others because that was how it was meant to be.

'This?' he asked, focussing his attention on the conversation at hand.

'Yes, *this*.' She waved a hand through the air. 'You being here? Getting Steve off my back?'

'That depends.'

'On what?'

With a shrug of his massive shoulders, Royce drew his long legs out from under the table and lifted one leg to cross an ankle over a knee. 'On lots of things. Each case is different, I'm afraid. I can't tell you when it's going to end.'

'Surely you must have some idea?' she asked, sounding desperate.

'I'm afraid not. But we're about to change the rules. That might be enough to make Brady back off.' He stared at her, a cold feeling invading his insides at what he was about to say. 'Or it might not. It might make the situation worse—just as you feared.'

She paled.

Royce didn't want to frighten her. She'd already been frightened enough. But he had to lay his cards on the table. It was only fair that she knew what to expect.

'I hope not,' she gasped.

'I hope not too. But being forewarned is being forearmed. If he does anything once we've taken an AVO out against him then we'll have him,' Royce said with satisfaction.

He'd love nothing better than to see the other man in jail.

There was nothing new about that. He believed in justice. He liked to see the bad guys get their comeuppance. It was one of the reasons he'd started the Royce Agency in the first place.

So his reaction was perfectly normal.

Except it wasn't.

There was something different about this situation.
Something different about his reaction.
It was subtle, but it was there.
And, whatever it was, he had the terrible feeling that it had something to do with the woman sitting in front of him.

'How I wish I had your confidence,' Shara said with a sigh, her fingertips making circular patterns on the top of the table. 'I'm tired of being scared.'

'Well, if you feel that way maybe you should do something about it,' Royce suggested.

'Like what?' she asked, curious in spite of herself.

She would do anything not to be scared any more.

To feel safe.

Free.

'Why don't I give you some karate lessons?'

It was the last thing she'd expected him to say. She barked out a laugh and waved a dismissive hand through the air. 'I don't think so.'

'Why not?'

She stopped laughing. 'You're serious?'

He nodded. 'Of course I am. I happen to believe everyone—particularly women—should know the basics of self-defence. The world isn't a safe place. Things happen. People end up in the wrong place at the wrong time. They should know how to protect themselves. Knowing you possess those skills will give you confidence. There have even been studies showing that by projecting that confidence you're less likely to be attacked in the first place.'

Shara stared at him doubtfully. 'I'm not very athletic.'

'You don't have to be. I'm not talking about turning you into a black belt who can take on ten men at one time.'

'I should hope not,' she said, with another laugh.

At the same time a quiver of sensation swept through her. It was all too easy to imagine Royce taking on ten men—

and winning. She could imagine his muscles rippling as he moved. Could imagine the gleam of danger darkening his chocolate-brown eyes to black.

'All I'm talking about is teaching you a couple of moves that will get you out of trouble. You'd be surprised how effective a few simple blocks and punches can be.'

Blocks and punches?

He had to be out of his tree.

Shara shook her head. 'Thank you for the offer, but I don't think I'd be any good at it.'

He stared at her for such a long time that Shara began to feel uncomfortable. 'What?' she demanded.

'Attitude is nine-tenths of battle. If you want confidence then you need to start acting confidently. Don't admit defeat before you've even given it a try.'

Shara stared at him. 'What is it about you? Are you a bodyguard or a psychologist?'

He shrugged. 'I little bit of both, I suppose. An amazing amount of what I do involves getting inside other people's heads. I guess some of it rubs off.'

She cocked her head to one side. 'I also have the sneaking suspicion that you don't believe in wrapping things up in cotton wool.'

Royce shook his head. 'No, I don't. I don't see any point in beating around the bush. I call it as I see it. So, how about it? Are you up for the challenge?'

Shara shrugged. 'I can't very well say no now, can I?'

His eyes gleamed. 'You could, but you wouldn't be talking the talk or walking the walk.'

'I know. I know. If I want confidence then the first thing I have to do is act confident.' She thumped her hands palms down on the table. 'OK. I'll give this karate gig a try. What do I have to do?'

His eyes skimmed over her. 'The first thing you have to

do is change. Put on something that's loose-fitting and comfortable. And lose the sandals.'

Shara shrugged. He was the expert. He obviously knew what he was talking about.

She climbed the stairs to her room and did as he suggested, finding a pair of loose-fitting white trousers she usually wore over her swimsuit to the beach. She left her white T-shirt on. It was stretchy and comfortable so it should fit the bill.

They reconvened in the lounge room.

As she entered Shara's mouth ran dry.

Royce had also changed. He was wearing a pair of black loose-fitting cotton pants and a singlet that bared the steely strength of his broad, bronzed shoulders to her hungry gaze.

She came to a skidding halt just inside the doorway, her heart beating like a runaway train and her mouth so dry she had to lick her lips to moisten them.

If she'd had reservations about this karate lesson before, one look at Royce quadrupled them.

She hadn't given the physical aspect of Royce's suggestion any thought.

Now she did.

She was going to have to touch him.

He was going to have to touch her.

Already she was more aware of him than she wanted to be.

To use one of his own phrases, karate now sounded much too 'up close and personal' for her liking.

Royce saw her at that moment. His eyes ran over her, a gleam in their depths suggesting he approved of what he was seeing.

'Good, you're here,' he said, waving her further into the room.

Shara smoothed her moist palms down over her curvy hips. 'I'm really not sure about this.'

He raised one thick, dark eyebrow. 'You're not chickening out on me, are you?'

It was a challenge and they both knew it.

Courage.

That was what she needed.

And loads of it.

What had he said before she'd agreed to this insane suggestion?

Yes—that was it.

Talk the talk and walk the walk.

So that was what she did.

She dragged in a breath, walked into the room, and said, 'No, I'm not chickening out.'

Royce studied Shara as she walked into the room. She'd followed his instructions and changed into a pair of white loose-fitting pants which were partially see-through.

Not completely—just enough to make the outline of her shape visible.

And what a shape it was.

Lush. Curvy. *Womanly.*

Hormones raced crazily through his system, hardening muscles and other parts of his anatomy.

Suddenly he regretted offering to give Shara karate lessons.

He'd trained many people over the years—women included. He'd also had numerous sparring partners. He knew what was involved.

Being close.

Touching.

Normally those things didn't bother him.

Today they did.

Which was ridiculous.

He was a professional, not an amateur.

He knew the importance of separating his personal feelings from the job at hand.

There was no doubt in his mind that he could get through this session with the same cool aplomb he would have if he was teaching a man.

He'd pushed some of the furniture back and put the coffee table in a corner of the room, leaving the entire Aubusson rug free for them to work on.

Before he could change his mind Royce went and planted his feet in the middle of the rug, right in front of Shara.

'OK, let's start with some simple blocking techniques.'

Shara was so close he could smell the scent of her fragrance. She'd pulled her hair back into a high ponytail on the back of her head. Although he preferred her with her hair down, the ponytail highlighted her spectacular bone structure and made her eyes appear bluer than blue.

'The first block I'm going to show you is a lower block. It's used for blocking both strikes and kicks.'

Shara nodded. 'OK. Where do we start?'

'Watch me. I'll show you how it's done first.' He braced his feet shoulder-width apart, then put his right arm by his side and tucked his left arm up under his shoulder. 'This is the starting position. Then, leading with your elbow and forearm, move the left arm across your chest, blocking your middle area. At the same time swing the right arm in a circular motion, protecting the lower area.'

Royce demonstrated the movement several times.

Shara stared at him with studied concentration, eyes slightly narrowed, a furrow forming between her brows.

'Now you try,' Royce suggested.

Shuffling her feet into position, Shara moved her arms into the starting position. 'Is this right?'

'Yes—now have a go at the block.'

Shara tried, but her arms tangled. 'I'm sorry. I did it wrong.'

She sounded almost anxious. 'Don't worry about it. Hardly anybody gets it right the first time. Here, let me help you,' Royce said, moving even closer.

Then he did what he'd been dreading and anticipating all at the same time.

He touched her.

CHAPTER FIVE

SHARA dragged in a breath. When she'd mucked up the move she'd tensed, half expecting Royce to yell at her.

Only he hadn't.

Instead he'd dismissed her error with barely the blink of an eye.

Which wasn't what she was used to.

Steve had shouted at her all the time.

If the spaghetti sauce she'd made wasn't thick enough he'd bellowed at her as if it was the end of the world. If it was too thick he'd bawled her out just as loudly. If the bed wasn't made tightly enough to make a coin bounce he'd criticised her, and if his shirts weren't ironed to absolute perfection there had been hell to pay.

The constant stream of abuse and the barrage of insults had resulted in her living in an almost constant state of anxiety.

It would take some time getting used to this new state of affairs—but she was looking forward to it.

Royce stepped towards her. He was so close she could feel the heat radiating off his body and smell the scent of his soap or deodorant.

Her nerve-endings twitched as if they'd just been plugged into an electrical socket. Her skin was taut and tight, as if it were being stretched over her bones.

And then he touched her.

Shara tried not to jump. She really did. But she wasn't sure she was entirely successful because Royce gave her a sharp glance.

'Get into the starting position again,' he instructed.

Was his voice deeper than it had been a minute ago? Huskier?

Shara snuck a peek at him through the shield of her lashes. He was staring at her cleavage in a way that instantly made her nipples tighten.

Starting position?

The only positions that sprang into her head had nothing to do with karate but came straight from the pages of the *Kama Sutra*!

Forcing her attention back to the task at hand, Shara adopted the starting position.

Royce placed one hand on her left upper arm and the other on her left wrist. 'OK, relax.'

Relax?

Who was he kidding?

She had as much chance of releasing her tensed muscles while he was touching her as she did of flying to the moon.

'Let me guide you through the movement.'

His hands moved on her arms, leading her step by step.

He would be a good lover, Shara decided, trying to ignore the touch of his hands on her skin. He would lead her to a mind-bending climax with the panache and precision of a conductor conducting an orchestra.

Theoretically speaking, of course.

Because she wasn't the least bit interested on a personal level.

Definitely not.

Although it *did* make her wonder about the woman Royce had been in love with. The one who had hurt him.

What had *she* been like?

And what had gone wrong between them?

'OK. Repeat the movement with that arm only.'

Shara blinked. She felt like an idiot. She'd been too busy imagining what kind of lover Royce would be and hadn't concentrated on what he'd shown her.

Shara tried the movement again—and got it wrong.

'I'm sorry,' she said.

'Stop apologising. It isn't necessary,' Royce said.

He sounded totally normal. That deepening of his voice had either been her imagination or just a momentary something-or-other.

He was fine now.

All business.

She might as well be a department store dummy for all the effect she had on him.

Whereas *her* system felt as if it was going to go into complete meltdown.

'Lead with your elbow across your body,' Royce instructed.

Shara tried again—and got it wrong. The words *I'm sorry* were sitting on the tip of her tongue, but she swallowed them back.

'Again,' Royce instructed.

She did it again.

'Better.' He paused for a beat. 'Again.'

She repeated the move half a dozen times until Royce was satisfied.

'Good.' He nodded his approval. 'Now let's do the right arm.'

His hands were on her again. Confident and sure. By the time she'd mastered the right arm movement to Royce's satisfaction she was hot and more than a little bothered—and it had nothing to do with the lesson and everything to do with Royce.

'Now let's put it together.'

They worked for an hour on two closed-fisted blocks, the jab and the elbow strike.

By the time they finished Shara was exhausted—and strangely satisfied.

How could a few simple moves make her feel strong and powerful?

Shara wasn't sure. Maybe it was the endorphins that had been released into her bloodstream as a result of exercising, or maybe it was simply a psychological reaction to doing something positive and proactive in case she needed to defend herself.

Either way, that was exactly what had happened.

'So, what did you think of your first lesson?' Royce asked.

Although she'd enjoyed it immensely, Shara was reluctant to say so.

Because the truth was that it wasn't just the karate she'd enjoyed but the touching too.

And therein lay the problem.

She was playing with fire.

And fire tended to burn.

She'd been burnt before…and she didn't want to be burnt again.

Shara was taking such a long time answering that Royce tensed—although why that should be the case he had no idea.

Her answer shouldn't matter to him one way or another.

Although that wasn't quite true.

If anything, he should be hoping that she'd hated their session and had no desire to repeat it.

That would be the safe outcome.

Safe…?

Oh, yes.

Definitely safe.

Because the opposite was…

Well, it was fraught with danger.

Shara was the principal. He was the bodyguard. He should maintain a professional distance.

But, despite what common sense demanded and professional etiquette dictated, Royce still hoped that Shara would say, *Yes, I liked it and I want to do it again.*

Because *he* wanted to do it again.

Not just the karate, but the touching too.

Which was just not on.

He knew better than to get involved with a client—particularly a rich woman like Shara. They always had their own agenda, and what they wanted was usually at the centre of it.

All he had to do was think about how Fiona had seduced him to suit her own ends to know that.

Although comparing Shara to Fiona wasn't entirely fair, Royce admitted reluctantly.

Shara's situation was pretty straightforward and her agenda was clear: make her ex stop stalking her.

Shara was also quite a different kettle of fish from Fiona— as he was beginning to discover.

Today had been pretty intense. He'd put Shara on the spot more than once. In every instance not only had her reaction been genuine but she'd risen to the occasion beautifully.

Still, alarm bells were ringing, and if there was one thing he'd learned it was to listen to his instincts.

He opened his mouth to retract his offer to give her more lessons, but before he could get a single word out Shara spoke.

'It was great.' She sounded strangely breathless, and there was a look in her eyes that made his hormones go ballistic. 'Maybe we can do it again some time?' she suggested casually.

Royce couldn't explain what happened when he heard her answer. He should have been disappointed. Should have said he'd changed his mind.

But he did neither of those things.

He really did believe that it was important for Shara to learn self-defence.

It was a legitimate reason for continuing with the lessons.

He wasn't justifying it.

And it certainly had nothing to do with Shara personally.

He raised an eyebrow and said, equally casually, 'How about tomorrow?'

The next day was Sunday. As well as practising what he'd taught her the day before, they worked on two more blocks, and a punch as well as a kick.

They were almost at the end of the lesson when Shara folded her arms and shook her head. 'I can't do that. I might hurt you.'

Royce laughed.

She loved it when he laughed. It was a deep, rumbling sound that created an answering vibration deep inside her.

'You won't hurt me,' he denied. 'I'm bigger and stronger than you are.'

Oh, yes, he was bigger and stronger—and absolutely gorgeous with it. A fact that had been in her face throughout this session. There was something incredibly sexy about the hard contours of his body that made her not only want to look, but to touch too.

'That may be so, but I'd still prefer to keep practising that kick in the air,' she said.

Royce let the cushion he was holding drop to his side. 'Kicking in the air is OK to get an idea of the movement, but it's impossible to develop a powerful or useful kick that way. You can only learn how to generate power and speed by kicking something solid.'

Still she hesitated.

'Come on, Shara. It's important. Women have stronger legs than arms. I want you to know how to kick properly.'

She sighed. 'You're going to make me do this, aren't you?'

He nodded. 'Yes, I'm going to make you do this. And there's not a snowball's chance in hell that you're going to hurt me, so forget about it.'

Shara stared into his face. Concern and stubbornness were a potent mixture, she decided.

For the first time she registered just how much Royce was going out of his way to give her these lessons.

Her hands dropped to her sides. 'Do you know I haven't thanked you for doing this?'

'You don't have to thank me.'

'Yes, I do. You're investing time and effort helping me when you could be doing other things.' She paused for a heartbeat, emotion clogging the back of her throat. 'It's a long time since anyone has done that for me.'

Royce frowned. 'I find that very hard to believe.'

'I don't know why you should. Dad is a workaholic who can barely give me the time of day. Steve is a taker not a giver. The only thing he's ever given me is grief, and I hardly think that counts.'

Royce's frown had deepened. 'I'm sure you have friends that—'

Shara waved a hand. 'Steve made it very difficult for me to make new friends, and my old crowd—the ones that I was at the club with the other night... Well, let's just say I've outgrown them. Anyway, I just want you to know that I appreciate what you're doing for me.'

Royce stared at her long and hard. 'You're welcome. You can show your gratitude by kicking me.'

Shara laughed. 'That's sneaky.'

'I know. That's something you should remember about me. I'll use any tactic to get my own way. So—into position.'

Shara waited until Royce was holding the cushion braced in front of him and then she kicked.

Royce lowered the cushion. 'What a wussy kick! Surely you can do better than that?'

Shara stared at him, noting the teasing glimmer in his eyes and the half-smile tilting his lips.

She leaned her weight on her back foot and then flashed him a smile. 'You want harder? I'll give you harder.'

Pushing off her back foot, she snapped her leg forward and kicked the cushion as hard as she could.

Royce absorbed the impact, his muscles bunching as he braced his body. 'That was excellent! Whoops!' he said as she stumbled against him.

She'd kicked so hard the momentum had carried her forward—straight into Royce.

She landed against his chest.

His arms closed around her.

She looked up.

Their eyes met.

Romance novels were full of what they called 'moments frozen in time'.

Shara had never quite understood what they meant.

Now she did.

The world faded. Shrank until nothing existed but the two of them.

There was no past.

There was no future.

There was just this one moment in time.

And then it was gone.

Just like that.

As if the present had been snuffed out and the world had restarted with them standing several feet apart.

This time there was no question about who had moved first.

Royce had.

He'd turned away, breaking eye contact and shattering the spell that had bound them together for that brief instant.

What Shara found so disconcerting was the fact that she *hadn't* moved.

She'd just stood there.

Waiting to be kissed.

Because certainly that was what had been about to happen.

Why had she just stood there, waiting for him to kiss her as if that was what she wanted?

Because it wasn't.

Was it...?

Her breath hitched and her heart thumped when she realised that she wasn't quite so sure of her answer to that question as she should be.

By mutual consent their karate sessions and the break they shared together afterwards became a daily event.

Shara looked forward to it almost as much as she dreaded it.

'I'm enjoying the karate more than I ever imagined I would,' Shara told Royce several days later. 'I didn't think I would, you know.'

'Why not?'

Shara shrugged. 'I guess because I've never exercised much. But I like the way it makes me feel.'

The karate workouts had given her a new-found appreciation for working her body. Everything from the feel of her muscles expanding and contracting to the sense of co-ordination she felt as the different parts of her body moved in sync.

There was also a sense of achievement associated with mastering a new movement or refining her technique. It was a feeling she hadn't felt since high school, when she'd done well at exams.

'I know what you mean. After a session I always feel more—well, *balanced* for want of a better word.'

Shara nodded her agreement. 'And you were right. I *do* feel more confident. Not quite ready to take on ten men at one time, but I think I could get out of trouble should the need arise. Given what I went through with Steve, that's a pretty big deal.'

'I'm sure it is. You should be really proud of the progress you've made,' Royce said, flopping down on the sofa. 'You're doing amazingly well for a beginner.'

'Thanks. You've made it easy. You're a good teacher.'

And he was.

He was patient and supportive. When she was struggling to master a new move he worked with her, using encouragement and praise instead of criticism and disapproval to achieve the desired results.

'I try.'

That was something else she'd noted about Royce. He was modest. Although he was successful, and had the kind of ultra-confidence that oozed out of every pore, he didn't have a big head.

'You do more than try. You succeed.' Shara hesitated a moment, and then said, 'I wanted to be a teacher, you know.'

'No, I didn't know. What stopped you?'

'My father. He thought it was a waste of time.'

Royce was clearly surprised. 'Why? I would have thought he'd be pleased you'd chosen such a worthwhile career.'

She laughed, but there was no humour in it. 'The only career a woman should have, according to my father, is to be a wife and mother.'

Royce was so clearly gobsmacked that it took him several minutes to answer. 'You have to be kidding. That is...'

'What? Archaic? Primitive? Antiquated? All of the above?'

'Definitely all of the above.' He shook his head. 'I don't know what to say.'

'I know the feeling. That's exactly how I felt when my father started talking about it. He explained how important it was for me to make the right choice. He wanted me to marry someone from a wealthy and reputable family. Someone who would help him expand his business empire. In other words he wanted to marry me off as some kind of a business transaction. He even had a list of potential candidates. He didn't care what I wanted. As far as he was concerned he knew best. He *always* thought he knew what was best for me.'

'So that's why you married Brady,' Royce said thoughtfully, phrasing the remark as a comment rather than a question.

Shara barked out a laugh. 'I'm afraid not. Steve doesn't come from a wealthy or well-known family.'

'So he was an act of rebellion?' Royce asked.

She shook her head. 'Nothing so dramatic, I'm afraid. If I'd wanted to rebel I'd have gone to university like I wanted to. My mother left me a trust fund. I'm sure the trustees would have released the funds for an education, even if it was against my father's wishes.'

'So you married for love instead of duty?'

Shara frowned as she thought about that. 'If you'd asked me that at the time I'd have said yes, but now I'm not so sure. If you want to know the truth I don't think I ever loved Steve.' She was saddened by the admission. It was another of the many mistakes she'd made. 'I think I latched on to him because I was desperately looking for a way to escape my father. What I didn't realise was that I was jumping straight from the frying pan into the fire.'

'I can't argue with that. Brady is obviously some piece of work.'

Shara scratched the side of her head. 'Do you know I never realised how similar Dad and Steve are until just now? Obviously Steve is a far more extreme case than my father, but they both like using threats to get their own way. Do you remember that first night, when you brought me home from the club? You said that my father had asked you to tell me that while I'm living under his roof I'm to follow his rules. He said that so often when I was growing up that I got sick of hearing it.'

'I'm sure he meant well,' Royce said tactfully.

Shara shrugged. 'Maybe he did. I'm not sure. All I know is that he made me miserable in the process.'

Shara stared at Royce. He was so different from the other men in her life.

He wasn't a bully. He didn't browbeat her to get his own way. Nor did he take pleasure in putting her down.

But, much as she liked and respected him for those and other qualities he possessed, there was still one thing she couldn't get past.

He liked things done *his* way.

Royce had told her so himself—more than once.

On the night he'd brought her home from the club he'd told her that he had to have full control, and during one of their karate lessons he'd admitted that he'd use any tactic to get his own way.

Well, she'd had enough control to last her a lifetime. She wanted the freedom to make her own decisions.

Which was precisely why she had to ignore her attraction to Royce.

There was only one role she wanted him to play in her life—and that was her bodyguard.

On Friday they were so absorbed in their lesson—and in each other, although Royce didn't want to think about that—that they worked for almost two hours.

'OK. I think that's enough for the day,' Royce said, finally calling a halt. 'You've done well.'

Her arms dropped to her sides. 'I could do with a glass of water. Do you want one?'

Royce nodded and followed her to the kitchen. As usual, he enjoyed watching her move about.

The phone rang. Royce reached out a hand and picked up the receiver. 'Hello.'

When there was no response he said hello again. His answer was silence.

Out of the corner of his eye he could see Shara watching him.

These phone calls happened every one or two days. If he answered there was always silence. But there was no mistaking the waves of animosity coming down the line.

If Shara answered the response was mixed. Sometimes there was silence. Sometimes there was the traditional, if uncreative, heavy breathing. At other times she was hit by a barrage of abuse that made her slam the phone down.

Royce had discreetly had the phone records checked. All the phone calls came from payphones. Shara didn't recognise the voice, but the tinny sound suggested whoever was calling was using a voice-changer.

'If that's you, Brady, then listen up. Shara doesn't want to see you. She doesn't even want to talk to you. So leave her alone.'

This time he didn't wait for a response. He slammed the phone down with the secret hope that it would give the other man a headache.

'He's never going to give up,' Shara said, plonking a glass of water down in front of him.

Every time one of these calls arrived the shadows reappeared in her eyes—something that made Royce more and more angry.

Royce grasped her hand. 'Of course he is. Don't let these calls get you down. That's exactly what Brady wants. Don't give him the satisfaction.'

She squared her shoulders. 'You're right. I'm done with letting him have power over me.'

Royce grinned. 'That's my girl.'

Shara nodded and took a sip of her drink. Royce watched her lips close around the glass. Watched her head tilt back. Watched the movement of her throat as she swallowed.

Dragging his eyes away, Royce took a long slug of water.

'I have a question for you,' Shara said.

'Shoot.'

'How do my appointments fit into your super-duper protect Shara strategy?'

Royce put his glass of water down. 'What sort of appointments are we talking about?'

'I do charity work.'

She might as well have said that she did magic tricks. Or rode to the moon on a bicycle.

Neither was more astonishing than what she'd actually said.

Although why he should be so surprised he wasn't sure. Plenty of women did charity work. He just hadn't figured Shara would be one of them.

It was dawning on him—slowly—that the image of her he had fixed in his head was wrong. Cracks the size of elephants were appearing in his mental vision.

Why he hadn't seen it sooner Royce had no idea. The truth had been staring at him almost from the beginning.

The courage Shara had demonstrated in leaving Brady and trying to deal with his harassment on her own touched him deeply. It wasn't often that you met someone—man or woman—who had to face the kind of things that Shara had had to face.

He'd also thought she was spoilt.

Huh!

What a laugh that was.

Perhaps financially she'd been spoilt, but she'd been starved of her father's attention which was far worse. And in a clear demonstration of her inner strength neither of those things had had a detrimental effect on her character.

Royce realised he was guilty of pigeonholing Shara without any evidence to back up his opinion. He'd made a superficial, not to mention sweeping comparison of Fiona and

Shara's backgrounds and immediately shoved them into the same category.

But he'd been wrong—on all fronts.

To date Shara had proved herself to be stubborn and determined, honest and open.

Royce stared at her and realised Shara was still talking. He tuned back in to the conversation just in time to hear her say, 'On Monday I have a meeting with some people regarding the planning for a charity ball which is their main fundraising event of the year. It's not the kind of thing I'd like to cancel.' She paused for a heartbeat. 'This particular cause is close to my heart.'

Royce gave her an enquiring look.

'My mother died of ovarian cancer,' she said huskily.

'I'm sorry. How old were you?'

'Twelve.'

His heart contracted. 'There's never a good time to have a parent die, but I imagine twelve is one of the more difficult ages.'

Shara nodded. 'Especially for a girl. Mum and I were close. Her death left a huge gap in my life. My father didn't know what to do with me.'

Given what he knew of Gerard Atwood, Royce could imagine that a grieving near-teenager would have been a challenge for him.

'Well, there's no need to cancel. I'll simply come with you.'

Shara was frowning.

'What is it?' Royce asked.

She shrugged. 'How will I explain you being with me?'

'You can explain it however you like. Although I suspect telling the truth will only make you—and them—uncomfortable. Why don't you just say I'm a friend who's going to lend a hand?' He paused for a moment. 'It's not too far from the truth, you know. I do a bit of volunteering myself.'

'You do?'

He nodded. 'The Royce Agency runs a free anti-bullying programme for schools called Kid Power.'

'Because you were bullied as a kid?'

He nodded. 'It's a cause close to my heart—just as the ovarian cancer charity is close to yours.'

'Well, in that case I'd love to have you come along.'

'Are you sure you wouldn't rather wait outside?' Shara asked on Monday, stopping on the pavement outside the building that was their intended destination.

'I can't do that,' Royce said. 'Up close and personal, remember?'

After their recent karate lessons Shara was beginning to think they were already *too* up close and way, *way* too personal.

'Royce, it's an office building. I'll be surrounded by people. What could happen to me here?'

'Plenty.' Royce folded his arms. 'Brady could have followed us here.'

'But he didn't, did he? I noticed the way you kept on checking the rearview mirror on the way here.'

The fact that he was so vigilant was reassuring. He really was a consummate professional. But above and beyond that she also knew he was a caring person who would do whatever he had to do to protect her.

'I don't think he did,' Royce said. 'But protecting someone is about not taking chances. And don't forget I thought I saw him watching the house a couple of days ago.'

Shara hadn't forgotten. Even though Royce wasn't one hundred percent sure it had been Steve—the guy had been wearing a baseball cap, sunglasses and an oversized jersey—it had still been depressing news.

Royce waved to the building behind them. 'There are multiple entrances and exits in this place. I can't cover all of them.

Brady could simply walk in and confront you. I'm not taking that chance.'

He was right. It was better to be safe than sorry. 'OK. Let's go.'

They rode up in the lift in silence. Shara announced their arrival at Reception, and they were shown into a meeting room where the other attendees had already gathered.

Noreen, the committee chairperson, came up to them. Before Shara had the chance to make introductions Noreen jerked her head towards Royce and asked, 'Who is the mountain?'

Straightening her spine, Shara raised herself to her full height. Once she might have let a comment like that go. Now she wouldn't.

Steve had loved putting her down. He'd seemed to get some kind of perverted pleasure out of doing it.

Back then she'd been too frightened to defend herself. Now she wasn't. At least not with someone like Noreen.

'Don't be rude, Noreen,' she said.

'No offence intended,' Noreen said, glancing at Royce.

'None taken,' Royce said.

The fact that he sounded amused rather than annoyed didn't alter the fact that Shara was pleased she'd said something.

It made her realise how far she'd come.

The Shara she was today wouldn't put up with half the abuse Steve had given her.

If a man didn't like the spaghetti sauce she'd made she'd tell him to like it or lump it.

If the bed wasn't made tightly enough to bounce a coin she'd tell a man to make it himself.

The realisation was...

Well, it was liberating.

It was as if a physical weight had been lifted off her.

She actually felt lighter—as if she were floating several feet above the floor.

She introduced Royce to the other attendees before taking a seat.

Royce sat down beside her.

Their thighs brushed under the table. Shara jerked her leg away. 'OK. Let's get started, shall we?'

Noreen opened the meeting with a progress report on what had been achieved since the last time they'd got together. Shara tried to concentrate, but found Royce's presence a distraction.

'OK. Let's move on,' Noreen said. 'I'd like to focus now on the prizes for the auction. Do we have any volunteers who are willing to contact the people who donated prizes last year and see if we can persuade them to provide something again this year?'

'I'm happy to do that,' Shara said.

'Excellent.' Noreen pushed a sheaf of papers across the table. 'Here are the names and phone numbers, plus a list of what they donated. Given the state of the economy, I suspect we're not going to get them all back on board—which means we need to spread our net wider. Any suggestions?'

'I'm happy to donate a free security assessment of someone's home and make recommendations on what they need to do to resolve any deficiencies,' Royce said. 'I'm also happy to contact a few of my business associates to see if they'll donate something.'

'Excellent, excellent,' Noreen said. 'Anyone else?'

'You didn't have to do that,' Shara whispered to Royce as several other people pitched in with suggestions.

He shrugged. 'I'm happy to do it. As I said yesterday, I'm more than willing to support a good cause.'

'Still, it was nice of you to do it.'

And she didn't want him to be nice, because that just made him even more attractive.

CHAPTER SIX

ROYCE leaned back in his chair and watched as Shara addressed the meeting.

She was formally dressed, in a classic white suit and a black silk blouse, with subtly applied make-up, a French braid, and simple gold jewellery.

She looked elegant and businesslike—and so beautiful that she took his breath away.

Still, he much preferred her the way she was just after one of their karate lessons. A little dishevelled, with strands of hair escaping her ponytail, her eyes sparkling like a gazillion sapphires.

With difficulty he forced his attention back to what she was saying. She was currently outlining the programme for the actual event itself.

She was talking about serving times and collection times and break times. When the music would start and when it would finish. At what time the auction would begin and what time it would end.

It was clear she'd put a lot of time and effort into the event. It was also clear she'd done this before. She knew exactly what she was doing—expertly fielding questions as they arose, clarifying the finer details when required.

Royce found himself as captivated by this side of Shara as he was by the woman he'd already come to know.

* * *

When the meeting had been concluded they made their way to the lift.

'I hope you didn't mind me getting involved in the meeting?' Royce asked, pressing the 'down' button.

'Why would I mind?'

He shrugged. 'A bodyguard should be seen and not heard. Even then he should only be seen when he needs to be. It's my job to blend into the background.'

Shara laughed out loud. She couldn't help herself. 'I don't think it's possible for *you* to blend into the background.'

'Too much of a mountain?'

Too much of everything!

Good-looks. Sex appeal. Charisma.

For a second Shara was afraid she'd made the comment out loud. The answer had flashed into her head so quickly her brain hadn't had the chance to edit it.

But Royce was looking at her so normally she couldn't have.

'I'm sorry about the comment Noreen made,' Shara offered, the incident still rankling.

Royce shrugged. 'It's water off a duck's back. I've been called worse things in my time, and no doubt I'll be called a good many more.'

'Still, she shouldn't have said it.'

'Forget it. I have.'

'OK.'

At that moment the lift arrived with a soft *ping*. The doors slid open. Royce held an arm across the opening to prevent the doors from closing and then waved her inside.

Shara walked past him.

Her arm brushed against his.

A shot of electricity flashed up her arm.

Her eyes flew to his.

What she saw in his eyes made her heart stop.

* * *

Royce followed Shara into the lift.

The air was locked tight in his lungs. His heart was doing the exact opposite, loosening up the floodgates and sending his blood rushing from one end of his body to the other with supersonic speed.

Instinct had always served him well. Several times it had even saved his life.

This time it abandoned him. Dumped him smack-bang in the middle of a place he shouldn't be.

Because, without thinking, Royce bent his head and claimed her mouth with his. He kissed her as if he'd been waiting years to kiss her instead of days.

As his mouth plundered hers Royce admitted what he hadn't wanted to admit until now: he'd wanted her from the first moment he'd seen her, swaying so sensually on the dance floor.

And the crazy thing was that Shara was kissing him back the same way. With not a second's hesitation and enough hunger to set his pulse flying.

Royce fed a hand into her hair. He held her head steady as his mouth continued to move over hers.

Her hands clutched at his chest, grabbing a fistful of his shirt.

Even that small amount of contact was enough to make his senses go haywire. Desire was zinging off the inside of his skin and sending a shudder through his tall frame.

It was an amazing feeling.

The rush grabbed him.

Held on.

Wouldn't let him go.

Wherever the rush was going, he was on board for the ride.

Shara went up in flames the minute Royce's mouth claimed hers.

There was no other way to describe it.

She could feel the heat.

Feel it scorching through her, stripping her of everything but the truth.

She wanted Royce.

There. She'd admitted it.

The stomach-curling sensation and the electrical charge that literally zapped through her body every time they touched was good old-fashioned sexual desire.

Lust.

It pounded through her.

Minced her resistance into a pile of mush.

Flattened her common senses into non-existence.

Thought vanished.

All that was left was sensation.

A wild uproar of sensation that lifted her to her toes and made her cling to him as if she never wanted to let him go.

It didn't matter that what they were doing was wrong.

The part of her consciousness that recognised that fact had gone into hiding.

The *ping* of the lift sounded again. Awareness of where she was, who she was with and what she was doing came flooding back.

She sprang backwards, almost falling over her own feet in the process.

The world rushed back at her so fast that she felt dizzy. For those few extraordinary moments it was as if all of her focus had converged on Royce.

His mouth.

His arms.

The feel of his body against her.

Now she slowly turned her head.

Two men were standing in the opening of the lift, grinning at them.

Mortified, she dropped her chin towards her chest.

She was aware of Royce turning, and then he said with a hint of humour, 'What floor?'

Shara cringed inside.

What was wrong with her? Wasn't her life complicated enough without getting involved with someone else?

Royce glanced at Shara as the doors slid shut behind the two guys, who had got off on the fourth floor.

She was standing as still as a statue, her body visibly tense. Her hands were clenched at her sides so hard that the knuckles had turned white.

So far she hadn't said a single word to him.

Royce wasn't even sure that she'd looked at him.

As if she sensed his eyes on her, she turned on him, her eyes spitting blue chips of ice. 'What on earth did you do that for?'

It was a good question.

A *very* good question.

Because the honest-to-God truth was that he *hadn't* been thinking.

When her arm had brushed against his all rational thought had flown straight out of the window. Instinct had made him reach for her.

Instinct...and desire.

Oh, yes. He couldn't forget that.

The desire had risen up inside him, grabbed him in its tenacious grip and simply refused to let him go.

'Well? Answer me!' Shara ordered, reverting to the imperious, hoity-toity tone of voice she hadn't used for some time. 'Do you always try to kiss your clients?'

She had a knack for going straight for the jugular.

'No, I don't,' Royce replied calmly, watching her with dark narrowed eyes. 'In fact, I make it a rule not to mix business with pleasure.'

'Really?' She tossed her head and flung her hand in the air. 'Then what was that...that *fiasco* all about?'

She'd done it again.

Put him right on the spot with another pointed question.

A question that he had no answer to.

His gut shrank to the size of a pea.

A *fiasco*...?

She thought their kiss was a *fiasco*?

Hardly.

He could think of any number of descriptions to describe the conflagration that had taken hold of them, but a fiasco would not be one of them.

'You enjoyed it as much as I did,' he accused.

Royce wasn't sure exactly where those words had come from. He certainly hadn't intended saying them.

What he *should* be saying was that their kiss had been a mistake and one that wouldn't be repeated.

But Royce always told it the way it was. Even if the truth was unpalatable, it still needed to be said.

Shara blinked her big blue eyes at him, her expression suddenly guarded. 'No, I didn't.'

'Yes, you did.'

She blinked again. Her mouth trembled. 'You're imagining things.'

Royce shook his head.

This was the first time he could remember Shara trying to dissemble—and she wasn't doing a very good job of it.

Desire was surging up inside him again. The rush of it made his head spin.

Instinct took over a second time.

He did two things simultaneously.

He took a step towards her and he slapped a hand against the emergency stop button.

The lift came to a jerking, juddering halt.

Shara took a stumbling step backwards. 'What...what do you think you're doing?'

Those blunt questions just kept right on coming—as if they were bullets fired from a gun.

What *was* he doing?

Royce wasn't sure, but he knew he was going to keep right on doing it.

'Proving a point,' he murmured, and he backed her into the corner of the lift.

'What...what point?'

'That you enjoyed our kiss as much as I did.'

'I— You—' She snapped her mouth closed.

'Admit it, and I won't kiss you again,' he whispered.

Her gaze collided with his. A strangled and indecipherable sound emerged from the back of her throat.

She couldn't do it.

She couldn't look him in the eye and lie.

It just wasn't in her nature.

Triumph raced through his system, arousing everything in its path.

Shara didn't know what to think—or feel.

The glitter in Royce's chocolate-brown eyes was a clear message.

He wanted her.

The thought sent excitement racing up and down her spine. So too did the sheer male smell of him.

His eyes were on her mouth.

Every nerve-ending tingled in anticipation. Each muscle was straining—not away from him, but *towards* him.

Somehow their bodies must have recognised the deepening sexual tension in the confined space. Without either of them seeming to move the gap between them was demolished. Her soft curves were plastered against the hardness of his.

Their mouths came together with a sizzle, lips moving

hungrily as they matched kiss for aching kiss. Royce hauled her to the tips of her toes as his lips prised hers open. His tongue darted into the warm depths of her mouth.

Shara felt her legs buckle beneath her. If it weren't for the arms supporting her she would have fallen.

Shara pressed herself against him. The action squashed her aching breasts against the hardness of his chest. Winding her arms around his neck, she buried her fingers in the thick crispness of his hair, moaning as she felt his tongue delve into her mouth again.

Suddenly Royce lifted his head.

Shara wanted to drag his mouth back to hers, but she heard what Royce had obviously heard because his head was cocked to one side.

'Are you OK in there?' a male voice called.

Were they OK?

Shara couldn't answer for Royce, but for her part she was very far from being OK.

Her breathing was rushed and shallow, her breasts heavy, and there was a moist dampness at the juncture of her thighs that signalled just how far-reaching an effect he'd had on her.

Royce, who had been staring upwards, dropped his gaze to hers.

His face was expressionless.

He dropped his arms to his sides and stepped away from her.

Then he called out. 'We're fine. I accidentally pressed the emergency stop button.'

'OK. We'll have you out shortly.'

'Well, it can't be too soon for me,' Shara muttered. 'I can't wait to get out of here.'

She needed fresh air.

And distance.

Lots and lots of distance between her and Royce.

She also needed a brain transplant.

Or maybe a libido transplant.

She wasn't quite sure which.

All she knew was that as soon as his mouth had claimed hers her resolve not to respond had disappeared in a puff of smoke.

The lift jerked and then began moving. More slowly than it usually did. At a snail's pace.

Shara moved to stand in front of the doors.

Royce grabbed her arm and spun her to face him.

'Let me go.' Her voice sliced at him, and she yanked away her arm, which tingled where he'd touched.

Royce did as she asked. 'Before we leave this lift I want one thing clear,' he said, in a deep, firm voice.

Shara didn't respond. Knowing Royce, he'd say what was on his mind whether she prompted him or not.

'This ends right here.'

'This...?'

'This attraction between us. There will be no more kissing.'

Whatever she'd expected him to say, it wasn't that. She didn't know whether to be relieved or disappointed by his response. Her ambivalence annoyed her.

Even that was an understatement.

She was angry.

At herself—and Royce.

She tossed her head, jutted her chin, and slammed her hands down on her hips. 'You bet it won't. I don't know what you were thinking and I don't care. After what Steve has put me through the last thing I need is the hired help coming on to me. Got it?'

Royce froze.

He was angry.

More angry than he had a right to be.

Not just at Shara for her comment about him being the hired help—although he was disappointed by the remark.

He was angry at himself.

For creating this situation.

And he *had* created it.

He was the one who had grabbed Shara.

He was the one who had kissed her.

He was normally very much in control.

But he was beginning to sense—with the sensitivity of a jackhammer against concrete!—that his reactions to Shara were far from usual.

Kissing her had been the start of the lunacy.

Kissing her for a second time and pressing the emergency stop button had taken the madness a step further.

'Thank you for the timely reminder. I'm here to protect you. Nothing else. Let's keep it that way.'

Royce kept to his word.

Shara should have been pleased, but she wasn't.

Instead, she felt strangely disappointed. She also felt uncomfortable. She vacillated between wanting to apologise to him and then berating herself for feeling sorry for him.

It went on like that for two days.

By the end of the second day Shara had had enough.

She flung the magazine she'd been trying to read without any success down on to the sofa beside her and stomped into the kitchen, where Royce worked on his laptop and mobile phone every day.

'OK. Do you want me to apologise?' she demanded, stopping just inside the kitchen door and jamming her hands down on her hips.

Royce looked up slowly from his laptop and leaned back in his chair.

He really was the most handsome man. Every time she looked at him he took her breath away.

'Apologise for what?'

'For calling you the hired help,' she said.

Royce shrugged. 'That's entirely up to you.'

'But you don't care one way or another?'

'No. I don't.'

Shara stared at him. 'Well, whether you care or not, I'm sorry. I should never have made the comment. It was wrong. I lashed out without thinking.'

Having said what she'd come to say, she turned to leave. She was at the door when he said her name quietly behind her.

Slowly she turned to face him. 'What?'

'Thank you for the apology.'

She inclined her head. 'You're welcome. As I said, I should never have made the remark in the first place. As my old nanny used to say, "We all have to put our undies on the same way."'

Royce stared at her, then flung his head back and burst out laughing. When he finally calmed down he asked, 'Your old nanny said that?'

Shara could hardly speak. Royce looked twice as handsome as he usually did when he laughed like that. 'She did. She was a blunt and down-to-earth woman. It was her way of teaching me that everyone is equal.'

Royce nodded. 'So that's where you get it from.'

Shara frowned. 'Get what from?'

'Your frankness. If you haven't noticed, you're pretty direct yourself.'

Shara shrugged. 'Mrs P was with me for six years. I wouldn't be surprised if some of her attitude rubbed off on me.'

When Royce didn't say anything else Shara turned to leave again. This time she didn't even reach the door before Royce stopped her.

'Before you go, there's something we need to discuss.'

Again she turned slowly, and again her heart went berserk.

'What is it?' she asked, sounding so breathless she was barely able to recognise her own voice.

'We have a court date for the AVO.'

The air hissed from her lungs. For a minute—just one—she'd thought Royce was going to discuss their kiss with her. She didn't know whether to be relieved or disappointed that he hadn't.

'When?' she asked.

'Two weeks today.'

Shara absorbed the information. She'd expected the news to make her feel anxious, but it didn't. She was a little nervous, which was perfectly understandable, but that was about it. 'OK.'

'I think that will send a clear message to Brady. Hopefully he'll back off.'

That could well be the beginning of the end.

She greeted the thought with mixed feelings.

Obviously she was ecstatic at the thought of bringing Steve's campaign of terror to an end. But it also meant that Royce would walk out of her life.

That was a *good* thing, she assured herself.

So why then was there a distinct pang in the middle of her chest?

'Let's hope so.' She hesitated in the doorway. Waved a hand at the files and laptop. 'Do you have time for another karate lesson? Or are you too busy?'

Royce stared at her.

Shara laughed and waved another hand through the air. 'Forget it. It's a bad idea. I shouldn't have said anything. I need a break, that's all. I'll read a book or something.'

'How are the donations going for the ball?'

'I've called all the companies who donated something last year. I've left messages for some of them, but almost everyone I've spoken to is going to donate again.'

Royce whistled through his teeth. 'That must have taken some doing.'

She smiled. 'I had to twist an arm or two, but most of them were happy to help out.' She waved another hand. 'I'll get out of your hair now.'

Royce didn't respond. He just kept on staring at her with chocolate-brown eyes.

She didn't need to explain why a karate session was a bad idea. After the kiss they'd shared in the lift they both knew that they'd be inviting disaster.

She turned to leave for a third time. Had actually taken two steps into the hallway when he said her name again.

'What?' she asked over her shoulder.

'I could do with a break too,' he said slowly. 'Go and get changed. We'll meet in the lounge room in five minutes.'

'What are you *doing*?' Royce muttered to himself under his breath as he walked into the lounge room at the allotted time.

This was foolhardy at best, and at worst complete insanity.

Shara was waiting for him, dressed as she usually was in the almost see-through white cotton pants and a figure-hugging T-shirt that outlined the generous swell of her breasts and enough cleavage to make his body harden.

'OK. Where do we start?' she asked.

Royce took a seat on the sofa. 'I'd like you to demonstrate what you've learned so far.'

There was only one way he was going to survive this session, and that was by adopting a hands-free approach.

'Come on,' he said. 'Let's see what you remember.'

Shara got into the first starting position and one by one went through the various blocks, punches and kicks he'd taught her.

Royce tried to concentrate on her technique.

But more and more he found his focus drifting to other things.

Like how serious she looked as she concentrated on doing each movement to the best of her ability. The frown creasing her forehead and the little moue she made with her lips.

And of course the other huge distraction was her body.

Her muscles flexed and released. Her belly contracted. So, too, did her buttocks.

And then there were her breasts. They jiggled ever so slightly with every movement. And every jiggle made his body harden more and more, until he was ready to jump to his feet and—

No!

Don't even think about it.

If he did he was likely to become undone.

But, try as he might, he couldn't control where he looked or how he felt.

Shara was almost at the end of her demonstration when the phone rang. Her arms immediately dropped to her sides, her expression growing tense.

Royce clenched his teeth. His patience was growing thin at Brady's daily dose of terror.

Reaching out, he pulled the plug from the wall socket.

'Continue,' he said, waving a hand.

'You can't do that.'

'Of course I can. If it's important they'll call you on your mobile.'

What he meant, of course, was that if it was anyone other than Brady they would call her on her mobile.

Shara picked up where she'd left off. When she'd finished, she asked, 'What next?'

If he had any sense he'd end the session then and there. Instead, he rose to his feet. His heart was pounding. 'You're ready to do some very basic sparring. I want you to attack me. Hit, kick, punch. Whatever you like. I'll block you and make an attacking movement of my own. Then we'll try it in reverse.'

'OK.' Shara aimed a punch at his belly. Royce blocked, dipped, and then aimed an answering punch gently to the side of her head.

This time she kicked and then punched him. Royce blocked both moves, spun around, and aimed a kick at her knee.

After about ten minutes Royce said, 'OK, your turn. This time I'm going to attack you. I want you to concentrate on defending yourself.'

Shara raised her hands in defensive mode.

As quick as a flash Royce made a soft chop to the side of her neck. 'Hey, that was too easy.'

'I wasn't ready,' Shara protested.

Royce moved more slowly this time, aiming a fist at her solar plexus. Shara blocked him with a throw of her left arm, then moved into a punch.

Royce blocked her effortlessly. 'Well, well, well. You're full of surprises, aren't you?'

She grinned. 'You bet.'

Royce backed off a pace to see what Shara would do.

They danced around on their toes, hands raised in fighting position. Shara aimed a punch towards Royce's chest. He blocked it with a swing of his left arm.

Royce moved to the left, feinted, quickly put his left foot behind her right ankle and pushed. Surprise and momentum sent Shara tumbling to the floor.

Royce followed her down, pinning her to the rug with his weight.

The feel of her beneath him sent a shimmering wave of heat through his entire body. The cushioning fullness of her breasts and the welcoming dip of her hips sent his blood pressure skyrocketing.

Royce took both of her hands in his and pinned them to

the carpet on either side of her head. He'd never thought of karate as foreplay, but that was exactly what it felt like.

Excitement had been building from the moment Shara had suggested the session.

In the last ten minutes it had gone right off the charts.

Breaking point had come and gone in the blink of an eye.

Royce didn't think twice. He didn't think at all. He simply bent his head and crushed her mouth with his.

Shara kissed him straight back.

Excitement rushed through him. So potent it made his blood fizz and stretched every inch of his skin.

In an action as ancient as time Royce pressed his erection against her. Shara moaned and tugged her hands free. Her arms wrapped around his neck, her fingers weaving into his hair.

Royce trailed his mouth over the delicate arch of her cheekbone to her earlobe, where he sucked on the sensitive flesh.

Shara's body moved restlessly beneath his.

From her ear, his mouth moved lower, trailing a path of liquid fire down her throat. He paused at its base, his tongue flicking against her frantically beating pulse, before moving lower still.

He buried his face between her breasts and inhaled her scent. It circulated in his bloodstream like heady wine.

'Yes,' Shara muttered, her hands clutching at his shoulders, her nails digging into his flesh.

Royce ran his hands over her bone-melting curves, undecided on which part to linger, trying to enjoy each delectable inch of her all at once.

He raised his head and stared down at her.

Her eyelids lifted slowly, as if they were heavy. The fire he saw in her eyes echoed deep inside of him.

'You're wearing too many clothes,' he said, in a voice he hardly recognised as his own.

Shara nodded, as if she were incapable of speech.

With the aid of her wriggling, Royce pulled her T-shirt up over her head. He stared down at what he'd revealed: ripe breasts spilling out of the cups of her bra.

His loins kicked, and then kicked again even harder.

His blood pulsed so strongly he could feel it beating against the underside of his skin.

'Do you know how long I've wanted to see you like this?' he asked, the question dragged from deep inside him.

Shara shook her head.

'For ever,' he whispered.

It was the most incongruous answer. It didn't make sense. And yet on a primitive level, where DNA met energy and created life, it was true. True in a way that he couldn't even begin to understand.

Sliding a hand beneath her back, he unfastened her bra and slowly stripped it away.

His breath caught in the back of his throat

Slowly he raised his hands. For several moments they hovered in the air, and then he cupped a breast in each hand. As he'd thought more than once, she fitted him perfectly. As if she'd been made just for him. The pads of his thumbs rubbed across her nipples, which immediately sprang erect.

Shara moaned and arched her back, pressing against him.

He played with her breasts for a few more moments before dropping his head and drawing one hard bead into his mouth, rolling it with his tongue.

Shara thrashed her head from side to side, a keening cry that sounded half-pleasure, half-protest coming from the back of her throat.

And then she moved.

Her clutching hands left his shoulders and ran down over the hard planes of his back, exploring as she went. She tugged on the hem of his T-shirt. Lifting his head, Royce helped strip it away.

His hands immediately went to the waistband of her white

trousers. He didn't linger over their removal. He was too aroused to take things slowly.

His pants quickly followed.

When one of her hands insinuated itself between their tightly pressed bodies Royce knew exactly what was coming. Still, nothing could prepare him for the first delicate touch of her fingers on his erection.

When her hand closed around him, Royce froze. So much pulsating energy rushed to where she touched that he shuddered. When her hand moved he shuddered again.

'Enough,' he growled, barely able to get the word out as he clasped her wrist and pulled her hand away from him.

He was so aroused he was shaking.

A line from an old tune popped into his head.

There's a fine line between pleasure and pain.

He was on the border of that line right now.

He'd never visited this particular place before.

Never felt the way he felt right now.

CHAPTER SEVEN

WHEN a hand settled hotly between her legs, Shara felt a rush of heat that shook her to the very foundations of her being. Clutching at Royce's powerful back with claw-like fingers, she gasped as his fingers delicately probed the centre of her heat, his lingering caress driving her wild with anticipation. When his hand danced a rhythmic tattoo on the nub of her desire Shara felt as if she was about to shatter into a million pieces.

As if realising how close she was to coming, Royce used his free hand to caress her slowly, as though trying to soothe the flames his other hand had ignited.

It didn't help.

She was beyond help.

She couldn't take much more. She was at the very brink of a throbbing abyss. Royce kept her on the very edge, as if he enjoyed torturing her.

His fingers left her and were replaced by the probing hardness of his erection. Shara circled his waist with her legs, hooking her ankles together to hold him captive against her. She rotated her hips, urging him to enter her and end the suspense, the torture.

As she moved against him Royce moaned, but still he didn't give her what she so desperately wanted.

Lifting her head, Shara nipped at his bottom lip with her teeth.

'Now. Please now,' she begged brokenly.

As if her plea was exactly what he'd been waiting for, Royce thrust inside her.

They moaned in unison.

For several long moments neither of them moved. Shara could have stayed that way for ever, enjoying the silken hardness of him filling and stretching her.

And then there was no more thought as Royce started to move within her, a slow rhythm at first, then faster. Shara moved with him, matching thrust for nerve-quivering thrust, tightening her legs around his waist and pulling him deeper and deeper.

The tension built, spiralled, and threw her sky-high.

In the next instant the world exploded into a mass of sheer sensation. A pulsating throb started deep in her womb and extended outwards until every bit of her was consumed by it. Her internal muscles clenched around him, her fingers clawing at his back.

Royce gave one final thrust, finding his own release with a muttered cry.

Shara's limbs felt heavy and molten. Royce shuddered against her.

The wild beat of his heart matched the hammer of hers.

What they had just shared had been the most incredible experience of her life.

But as her heartbeat slowly returned to normal Shara plummeted back to earth with a bang.

Her mind was filled with visions of what had just happened.

Of hands and mouths, touching and tasting.

Everywhere.

She wished the memories would disappear, but they were indelibly imprinted on her memory banks.

Even in the good times with Steve sex had never been so intense or exciting. The passion that had sheared through her with Royce had turned her inside out.

The fact that it had been so intense disturbed her.

A frisson of...

Of what...?

Anxiety? Panic?

She wasn't sure what.

A frisson of *something* rippled through her like a gust of cold wind.

'I can't do this,' she said, pushing against Royce's shoulders. 'I'm sorry. I just can't do this.'

Royce heeded her urging and rolled on to his back.

Shara scrambled to her feet and snatched up her clothes. Hugging them to her chest, she glanced at Royce to see if he was watching her.

He wasn't.

His eyes were closed.

Quickly she pulled on her clothes to cover her nakedness.

When she was done she remained standing where she was, not sure what to do. She wanted to run out of the room and go somewhere. Anywhere. As long as it was away from Royce.

But that smacked of running away. Given her resolve to stand up for herself, she didn't particularly want to take the cowardly way out.

Her eyes roamed his naked figure. She wished the action left her immune but was very much aware that it didn't.

When she got to his face she was disconcerted to find that his eyes were open and he was watching her. Embarrassed heat flooded her cheeks and made the tips of her ears burn.

He moved to get up.

Shara turned her back on him.

She heard the rustle of clothing. She imagined him putting on his trousers and shirt. Imagined the ripple of muscle and the scent of warm male skin as he did so.

The images were so vivid that Shara scrunched up her eyes, but it didn't help.

'You can turn around now,' Royce said dryly.

If anything the heat in her cheeks burned even more hotly. Slowly—reluctantly—she turned to face him.

'Let's get straight to the point, shall we?' Royce spoke as calmly as if he were discussing the weather or the price of a loaf of bread. 'What just happened shouldn't have happened. Right?'

Relief poured through her. So too did an entirely unexpected pang of disappointment.

Hands clasped tightly together in front of her, Shara nodded. 'No. I mean yes. It shouldn't have happened. I just don't want to get involved again. I...I don't think I can handle it.'

It wasn't just about sex.

It was about the exchange of power.

With men it was always a one way street—with the woman on the losing end.

Well, she'd been there, done that. She wasn't going there again.

Straightening her spine and squaring her shoulders, Shara stared him straight in the eye.

Royce nodded.

Her heart plummeted to her toes and stayed there.

There was a sinking sensation in the pit of her stomach.

Both were quite patently ridiculous reactions.

She wasn't disappointed by his agreement. She wasn't.

This was what she wanted.

Wasn't it?

'I understand,' Royce said with another nod.

He sounded calm and in control, but inside he was a seething mass of emotions.

He didn't understand it.

He should be applauding.

Shara was saying everything he wanted to hear.

She wasn't clinging.

She wasn't trying to turn the situation to her advantage.

So why was he so displeased with her response?

Royce wasn't sure, and that made him even more displeased.

He was an analytical kind of guy.

Logical.

He knew that one plus one equalled two—not twenty.

So why did nothing about this situation make sense?

He knew that getting involved with Shara was wrong—and not just because he couldn't afford a distraction on the job.

It was more than that.

Alarm bells had started ringing almost from the beginning.

There was something about Shara that had got under his skin from day one.

Her hoity-toity tone had got his back up when normally such an attitude would have bounced straight off him.

His reaction to what she'd endured at the hands of Brady had been...

Well, it had been *emotional*, damn it!

Not professional. Not detached. Not anything it should have been.

It was as if his sympathy for her had sucked him over a line he hadn't crossed since the day he'd learned the truth about Fiona—and that was more than enough to make him wary.

'Good,' Shara said.

Her voice sounded flat.

Royce searched her face.

Did she feel the same way he did? That what they'd shared had blown his mind and just about everything else?

No, he had to forget about that or he was a goner. He had to concentrate on the reasons they shouldn't get involved.

'You've just gone through a marriage break up. You're being stalked by your ex-husband. The last thing you need is another man in your life,' he said, repeating her words back at her. 'That makes perfect sense. I completely understand.'

Shara was nodding. 'That's right. I don't.'

'And I'm here to do a job,' Royce said. 'I can't do that properly if I get involved. I need to stay objective.'

'Of course you do,' she said. 'This makes no sense for either of us.'

She was being helpful.

And co-operative.

But he wanted neither of those things.

It didn't matter how many 't's he crossed or how many 'i's he dotted, he wanted her. It went against every rational thought he possessed but that didn't change anything.

Thankfully, before he did anything stupid, like kiss her again, his mobile phone started ringing. Extracting the phone from his pocket, he glanced at the screen and frowned.

He looked up. 'I'm sorry but I'm going to have to take this. It's the Los Angeles office.'

Shara inclined her head, her face expressionless. 'No problem. We've said all we needed to say.'

As Royce watched her walk out of the room he couldn't help feeling she was wrong about that.

What was he going to do?

Royce rubbed his jaw.

Damn. What was the matter with him? The answer was simple. He had to bring in one of his people to finish this job while he concentrated on the high-profile case he'd just received.

Gerard Atwood would understand, he was sure. There were a number of points in his favour.

One, the AVO was in place and would no doubt be upheld by the courts in a fortnight's time.

And, two, he only hired the best people. Shara would be more than safe with any of his operatives.

He just had to figure out who he could use.

That new girl Kelly Walker had impressed him with her work so far. He'd even been thinking of giving her a promotion.

He frowned.

But, no, Kelly was working the Reynolds case.

Bob Brisket, then. If his memory served him correctly Bob was the only operative available at the moment. But even as the idea formed Royce dismissed it. Bob wasn't the right person. He was a good investigator, but too abrasive for bodyguard duty.

Well, there had to be a solution.

He snapped his fingers in the air and smiled. He had it. His friend Travis Knight could help him. Travis had worked with him before. He knew the ropes. In fact, Travis was one of the best—despite the fact that he preferred trading on the stockmarket for a living.

Picking up his mobile, Royce rapidly punched in the number.

'Travis, old buddy. Long time no speak,' Royce said when Travis finally picked up the phone.

'Royce, where have you been? I was beginning to think you'd fallen off the face of the earth.'

'Not quite.' Royce laughed. 'I've been busy, as usual. What about you? Still playing around with that computer of yours?'

'I'll have you know I work very hard on that computer of mine,' Travis replied, mock-indignantly.

'Sure,' Royce joked. 'For all of three hours a day.'

'Sometimes I push myself and make it four,' Travis joked in return. 'How's business with you?'

'Fine. Fine. Couldn't be better,' Royce murmured quietly. 'But I'm in a bit of a bind at the moment. I need to ask you a favour.'

'Done,' Travis replied promptly. 'You name it.'

'Do you mean that?'

'Of course I do. Do you really think I'm likely to say no? You, Jackson and I may not be the Three Musketeers, but we come damn close. One for all and all for one. You know that.'

Royce did know. Which was precisely why he didn't want to take advantage of Travis.

'Thanks. I'm involved in a case at the moment and the Los Angeles office has just booked me in to protect a visiting celebrity without bothering to check my schedule,' Royce said with frustration. 'Not that I want to miss out on this one. It's high-profile and comes with a fantastic fee. That's why I need you to take on the assignment.'

As soon as the words were out of his mouth Royce stopped, hardly able to believe what he'd just said.

Had he really just asked Travis to take over the Taylor Zane case?

Royce replayed his words back in his head.

Yes, that was exactly what he'd said.

It was the exact opposite of what he'd intended to ask, which was for Travis to look after Shara while *he* took care of Taylor Zane.

How had that happened?

Royce wasn't really sure, and really didn't care.

Because the minute he'd said them the words had felt right.

Although it sounded ridiculous even to his own ears, he didn't trust anyone else to protect Shara.

He shook his head. He must be going crazy.

Travis obviously thought so too, because he said, very doubtfully, 'Royce, I haven't done anything like that for a while. Surely you have someone else on your team who could take over?'

'Not for this particular client. I need someone I can really trust. And that's you,' Royce answered emphatically. 'I'd do it myself, except I'm needed here.'

And he *was* needed here. The almost daily phone calls from Brady were proof of that. So too was that brief glimpse he'd had of what he was sure was the other man in disguise.

Gut instinct was telling him to stay on Shara's case. And if there was one thing he'd learned it was to listen to his instincts.

Staying on the case had nothing to do with the incredible sex they'd shared.

He was just doing his job.

Shara stayed in her room for the rest of the day.

She tried to pretend she wasn't hiding, but the way she tensed every time she heard a noise somewhere in the house forced her to admit that that was exactly what she was doing.

Rightly or wrongly, she didn't want to face Royce.

They'd had sex in the middle of her father's expensive Aubusson rug, for goodness' sake.

Mind-blowing, nerve-twisting, gut-wrenching sex.

Sex that had been so explosive it had torn her entire thought processes to shreds.

How could she have done something so stupid?

It was another poor decision in the long line of poor decisions she just seemed to keep on making.

Another snake's head she'd jumped on all by herself.

Finally hunger drove her from her bedroom in search of food.

Slipping a peach-coloured bathrobe over the top of her nightdress, she carefully opened her door, trying to make as little noise as possible.

The last thing she wanted to do was wake Royce.

She wasn't ready to face him yet.

She was too scared.

Scared...?

The word made Shara stop dead in her tracks halfway down the stairs.

She wasn't scared.

Was she...?

The breath caught in her throat and her heart did a strange *kerthump* in her chest. The question cut through the web of chaotic thoughts that had besieged her since she'd taken refuge in her room.

Yes, she was scared.

But she wasn't scared of Royce.

She was scared of herself.

Afraid of how she'd react.

Because there was one fact she couldn't escape.

Regardless of why she shouldn't get involved with Royce, she already was—whether she wanted to be or not.

Royce was lying on his back with his arms folded beneath his head, staring at the ceiling, when he heard the creak of a floorboard. Almost simultaneously his laptop began beeping, indicating movement in the house.

Either they had an intruder, or Shara was up and about.

Given that none of the downstairs motion detectors had gone off, Royce could only presume it was Shara.

Which left him with a decision to make.

Stay where he was...or get up and follow her.

Royce knew exactly what he should do.

Stay in bed.

It wasn't as if Shara could go anywhere without him knowing about it. The household security system would alert him if she tried to leave the house—although where she would go in the middle of the night he didn't have a clue.

So he should stay in bed where it was safe.

Safe...?

The word made Royce jack-knife into a sitting position, his body growing rigid, muscles locking.

Safety played a large part in his life. The security business could be rough, and it could be tough. He'd been in dangerous situations, life-threatening situations, more than once and no doubt would be again.

But did he really see Shara as dangerous?

Beautiful? Yes.

Sexy? Yes.

But *dangerous*...?

The breath locked tight in his lungs, and his heart did a massive leap in his chest as the answer seared into his brain.

Yes, Shara was dangerous.

She was getting under his skin.

Making him think things he didn't want to think.

Making him *do* things he didn't want to do.

Like making love to her in the middle of her father's Aubusson rug.

Like making him turn over Taylor Zane's case to Travis so that he could stay and protect her.

Like making him follow her in the middle of the night when he should really stay in bed.

Because, whether it made sense or not, that was exactly what he was going to do.

He couldn't explain it. He didn't even begin to try.

He simply dragged in a breath, swung his legs over the edge of the bed and rose to his feet.

Then, pulling on a pair of worn denims, he went after her.

A sound in the doorway made Shara jump ten feet in the air. Her heart pounded, her hand going to the base of her throat.

She looked towards the source of the sound—and froze.

Royce was lounging in the doorway, watching her.

Her heart stopped and then kick-started again. Her mouth was parchment-dry. A slow burn started deep in her belly.

He looked absolutely mouthwateringly gorgeous. Like a sexy advertisement for denim jeans.

Because that was all he was wearing.

His jeans had obviously been slung on in a hurry. They

sat low on his hips, the zip only half done up and the button hanging open.

His chest was broad and deep, the skin smooth and golden-brown. Her eyes drifted lower to the rippling display of muscle on his belly before dropping lower still, to the tantalisingly undone button and the zipper just beneath.

A deep shuddering breath escaped her constricted throat as her eyes travelled back upwards.

His hair was tousled and the shadow of a beard was beginning to darken his strong, square jaw.

Her eyes met his.

Desire sizzled along her nerve-endings.

He was looking at her as if...

As if...

As if he wanted to strip her naked and take her where she was standing!

The knife she was holding clattered to the benchtop. 'Don't sneak up on me like that,' she said, dragging her eyes away from him.

'I didn't sneak. I walked.' He levered himself away from the doorjamb and walked further into the room.

Shara couldn't look away, her eyes captured by the ripple of his muscles as he walked.

'You obviously didn't hear me.'

Shara wasn't surprised. She'd been deep in thought. Not about the sandwich she was making. Not about whether to have mustard or pickle.

No, she'd been thinking about that taboo subject.

Royce.

And then suddenly he was here, as if her thinking about him had somehow conjured him up.

Swallowing, she picked up the knife and gestured to the sandwich. 'Are you hungry?'

'Yes.'

Her eyes shot to his face. There was something in the way

he'd said that one word and something in the glitter of his eyes that suggested they weren't just talking about food.

Her already frantically beating heart took off at a gallop. She licked her lips. 'I meant do you want a sandwich?'

'No.'

His monosyllabic answer sent hormones hurtling through her system, setting off one vibration after another against her nerve-endings.

'Then what *do* you want?'

The words burst out of her mouth at the exact same time the thought popped into her head. She hadn't meant to say them out loud. She would have stopped them if she could, but it was too late.

It was still a good question.

Because she couldn't shake the feeling that their conversation was operating on two levels.

Royce stared at her without speaking. His eyes were still glittering, and the angles and planes of his face seemed to be standing out more sharply.

Shara swallowed. And swallowed again.

She dropped the knife for a second time and wrapped her arms around herself. 'I mean why are you here?'

There was any number of answers Royce could give to that question.

He was hungry. Or he couldn't sleep. Or he'd come downstairs for a book.

But Shara hoped it was none of those things.

Rightly or wrongly, she hoped that he'd heard her come downstairs and had followed her.

It was a damned good question.

In fact both of them were.

It wasn't the first time Shara had put him on the spot.

She seemed to be making quite a habit out of it.

And each time the questions made the truth jump up and smack him in the face.

Because, if only to himself, he had to answer them honestly.

Question: What do you want?
Answer: You.
Question: Why are you here?
Answer: You.

That was why he'd got out of bed and followed her.

That was why he was standing here like a dumb jerk, with his insides so twisted in knots he could hardly think straight.

Royce wasn't sure when he'd decided he was going to make love to her again.

Had it been a split-second decision made when he'd heard the creaking floorboard? Or had he made it when he'd walked into the room and seen Shara standing there looking so beautiful?

Or was it the fact that *she* was asking the difficult questions while he was hiding from the truth?

And he *was* hiding from the truth.

Because the truth was that he wanted her.

'This is why I'm here,' he said, and reached across the distance separating them and hauled her into his arms.

Shara leapt into the kiss with a hunger that left her shaking inside.

How could she want Royce so much?

So much that she *ached* for him?

She didn't know and didn't care.

By the time Royce lifted his head they were both breathing heavily.

They stared at each other, dark eyes locked with blue. They didn't talk. They barely seemed to be breathing. As if the slightest movement might break the spell that bound them together.

Neither did they touch each other—unless you counted the hard points of her breasts whispering feather-like against his sleekly muscled chest through the thin fabric of her nightgown and robe.

The look in his eyes was incredible. So hot that it created a fire inside of her.

Royce ran a finger down her cheek to the corner of her mouth, which was tingling from his kisses. 'That's why I followed you. I want to make love to you again.'

Her breath hitched. 'What about not mixing business with pleasure?'

Royce shrugged. 'I'm the boss. If anyone can bend the rules it's me. You have to decide whether this is what you want or not.'

Shara dragged in a deep breath. And then another.

Her eyes landed on his mouth and a quiver of longing ran through her.

The cowardly part of her wished that Royce had just kept right on kissing her. It would have been easier if he'd swept her away into a maelstrom of passion.

But his words wouldn't let her do that.

They confronted her.

Forced her to make a choice.

It should be an easy one.

Step back. Say no. Put an end to all this nonsense.

But somehow she just couldn't do it.

Couldn't do it because she didn't *want* to do it.

What she wanted was Royce.

The realisation made the air lock tight in her lungs.

It was no use pretending any more.

No use trying to ignore what was impossible to ignore.

She wanted the guy.

She wanted the guy more than she'd ever wanted Steve.

More than she'd ever dreamed was possible.

Her heart turned over as she lifted her eyes to his. 'I want you.'

A flash of triumph crossed his face. Shara didn't care. All it proved was that he wanted her as much as she wanted him.

'Are you sure?' he asked.

Shara nodded. 'I'm sure.'

And, strangely, given her record for making poor decisions, she *was* sure.

Even before she'd finished speaking Royce had swept her up against him, his mouth crashing down on hers.

With their mouths still fused Royce pushed her robe off her shoulders. It dropped unnoticed to the floor.

His hands immediately went to her nightdress, which he tugged up to her waist, then over the obstacle of her breasts. Their mouths disconnected only long enough for him to reef it over her head and toss it over his shoulder.

Shara writhed against him as his hands cupped her breasts.

Her fingers went to the zipper of his jeans. As she pulled it the rest of the way down her fingers brushed against his straining erection. His body shook and shuddered.

His hands made long sweeping movements over her body. Skimming some parts and lingering in others. When his fingers probed the moistness between her silken thighs she cried out loud, her nails clawing at his shoulders.

He was watching her with such a molten look in his eyes that her knees buckled. She would have fallen if he hadn't acted quickly. He caught her with one strong arm. The other made a sweeping motion across the kitchen bench.

Once he'd cleared a space he lifted her on to the edge of the bench and moved between her spread thighs.

'Please,' she begged. 'I want you.'

She hooked her legs around his hips and urged him towards her, needing him to hurry.

And then he was inside her, filling her with silken heat,

and she shuddered, clenching her muscles against the hard fullness of him.

'Look at me,' Royce commanded softly.

Shara opened heavy lids and locked her gaze with his. She couldn't look away as he started to move inside her, setting up a primitive rhythm she was powerless to deny.

And still they looked at each other. As inner tension built to an exquisite crescendo their eyes clung to each other as surely as their bodies did.

There was no more thought, just feeling. Their lovemaking was hard and fast, the sheer force of their passion cocooning them in a world of pure sensation. So intensely did Shara feel each stroke inside her body that it was exquisite torture. Torture she wanted to end, and at the same time wanted to continue for ever.

When the final pleasure crashed upon them in waves she cried out. From the sound of his own cry Royce found his own climax seconds later.

Shara collapsed against him. Royce closed his arms around her and buried his face in the curve of her neck. They stayed that way, panting, for several long moments.

Finally Royce lifted his head, a rueful smile lifting the corners of his mouth. 'First the lounge room and now the kitchen. Do you think we're ever going to make it to a bed?'

Shara burst out laughing, a blush heating her cheeks. Then she stroked her hands down over the hard planes of his back. 'I sure hope so. Why don't we go and find one now?'

CHAPTER EIGHT

SHARA woke slowly, stretching her arms and legs. When she felt a warm, hard body behind her, she froze.

Memories of the night before flooded through her like a series of still photographs.

Royce standing in the kitchen doorway, wearing nothing but a pair of low-slung denim jeans.

Royce staring deep into her eyes and saying, 'This is why I'm here,' just before pulling her into his arms and kissing her.

She rolled on to her side and found Royce leaning up on one elbow, staring down at her. His hair was mussed, a sexy stubble darkening his jaw.

'Good morning,' he said, a small smile lifting the corners of his mouth.

'Good morning,' she said, trying to smile back but not quite managing it.

He obviously sensed that she wasn't entirely comfortable with the situation, because he reached out and stroked a hand down her hair. 'Any regrets?'

She thought about that for a moment. 'Regret is the wrong word.'

'Then what is the right word?'

She searched her mind, trying to put a label on what she was feeling. 'I'm not sure. Concerned. Uncertain. Anxious.'

They were both talking quietly. Shara wasn't sure why. It wasn't as if anyone could overhear them. But somehow their hushed tones seemed appropriate.

Royce was no longer smiling, his chocolate brown eyes serious. 'Because of Brady?'

'Partly.' Suddenly lying facing Royce no longer seemed right. She shuffled up on to the pillow, clutching the sheet to her breast, and stared straight ahead.

Royce pushed himself into a sitting position and swivelled to face her. 'Tell me what you're thinking.'

Shara pleated the sheet with her fingers, a knot in her stomach and a lump in her throat. 'I don't know how to explain it. All I know is that whatever else relationships are all about they are also about the balance of power. Women usually end up on the losing end of that equation.'

'Not always.'

She shrugged, staring at her fingers as they worked the cotton fabric into a concertina and then smoothed it back out again. 'Perhaps. But in my experience they are.' She turned and gave Royce a fierce look. 'I'm *never* going to hand power over to a man again. I'm *never* going to lose sight of myself again.'

Royce didn't rush to answer her. Finally he said softly, 'I'm not Brady. I'm not even remotely like Brady.'

'No, you're not. But you're a strong man. I'm not talking about physically. I'm talking about mentally. You're determined and stubborn and you like getting your own way.'

'I—'

She held up a hand. 'Don't deny it. You told me so yourself. You said that you'd handle this situation *your* way. That's the only way you do business. You have to have full control.'

He inclined his head. 'And I won't apologise for it. When it comes to the job—particularly when someone's safety's involved—it won't work any other way. I'm an expert. I'm trained in these situations. You're not. But that's the job. Outside of it—'

'Outside of it, what? You're different?'

'Yes, I *am* different. My parents brought me up to respect women. Their relationship is very much a partnership. In their marriage the balance of power you mentioned is well and truly equal. My mother wouldn't have it any other way.' He smiled. 'You'd like my mother. She is one of the most generous, warm-hearted people I know. But she's also one of the strongest.'

Shara wasn't quite sure what to say to that. 'I only have your word for that.'

'Yes, you do. Just as you only have my word for it that I will respect you while we're together and treat you as an equal.'

That was all he said.

He didn't try to persuade her.

Didn't try to sway her opinion in any way.

He just stared at her unwaveringly.

Shara stared into his chocolate-brown eyes.

She thought back over the last week or so.

She'd learned a lot about him in that relatively short period of time. But now, looking back, one thing struck her more deeply than anything else.

She'd recognised some time ago that Royce was different from the other men in her life, but it had only just dawned on her *how* different he was.

Royce was the first man—the *only* man—who had sought to empower her rather than dominate her.

It was as simple and yet as profound as that.

The knowledge rippled through her like a wave.

Royce had invested time and effort to teach her karate. To give her the skills and the confidence to fight back in a situation that until now had made her feel cowed and powerless.

He'd also encouraged her, supported her and listened to her.

'I believe you,' she said slowly.

'Good.' Royce drew her into his arms and brushed her mouth with his in a kiss so tender it made her want to weep. 'Let's just take one day at a time.'

'Yes,' she breathed, feeding her hands into the hair on either side of his head. 'Just one day at a time.'

'How did you break your nose?'

Royce rubbed the bump and laughed. 'Don't tell me you're still harking back to the movie version of what I do? I can assure you that I'm no James Bond.'

He was wrong about that.

He was very much like James Bond.

He was just as good-looking and he had the same kind of head-turning charisma. He was charming and capable and efficient, not to mention suave and sophisticated.

Had she mentioned good-looking?

Yes, she was sure she had.

He also possessed an I'm-sure-of-my-place-in-the-world and I-can-get-out-of-any-situation kind of confidence.

'So, how *did* you break your nose?' she asked again, determined not to let him put her off.

He laughed. 'I hate to disappoint you, Shara, but I broke my nose falling out of a tree when I was eight years old.'

'Oh.' She couldn't hide her disappointment.

He laughed again.

'You must have some interesting stories, though.' Shara refused to be thwarted. She found what he did for a living fascinating. 'What's the most bizarre case you've ever worked on?'

Royce rubbed the side of his jaw thoughtfully. Then his eyes lit up. 'That would have to be Zeus.'

If she remembered her history correctly, then Zeus was the king of all the other gods and the ruler of Mount Olympus. She was imagining a nasty crime boss similar to the Godfather when she prompted, 'Zeus?'

He nodded. 'Yes—Zeus the Chihuahua.'

Shara sputtered. 'A Chihuahua? You're pulling my leg!'

Royce shook his head, then made the sign of the cross. 'Cross my heart and hope to die. His owner, Mrs Pemberton, lives in New York. She was going on a Caribbean cruise with someone who was allergic to dogs. She hired me to doggy-guard Zeus while she was away.'

Shara searched his face. 'You're having me on?'

Royce shook his head. 'No—and get this: Zeus came complete with a dog collar made from a small fortune in diamonds. I never could figure out whether it was the dog she was worried about or the stones.'

'You're making this up. You have to be.'

'I'm afraid not. The lady has more money than sense. And damn but that dog is ugly.'

Shara laughed, as she was sure he'd intended.

She laughed a lot around Royce—and it felt good.

'So, tell me, what does the A stand for?' Shara asked.

Royce shook his head even as he gave a rueful laugh. 'Don't you ever give up?' he asked, referring to the fact that every day for the last week she'd asked the very same question.

'Nope,' she said, her blue eyes sparkling with mischief.

Daringly, she slid her hand under the sheet until her fingers closed around him, immediately feeling him swell beneath her touch.

He moaned and closed his eyes, his back arching ever so slightly.

'Are you sure you don't want to tell me?' she drawled, moving her hand slowly up and down.

'You witch,' he accused, swiftly rolling over and capturing her hand between their bodies. 'You shouldn't have done that!'

Shara let a small smile play about her mouth. 'I shouldn't?' she asked innocently.

Shaking his head, Royce laughed. 'No, you shouldn't. You won't get an answer now. I have other things on my mind.'

With a small tug under the sheets she prompted, '*Mind?* I thought it was another part of your anatomy that was paying attention.'

Shara loved the freedom she felt to touch Royce and tease him the way he did her. Loved the way his body responded so quickly every time she touched him, too.

With his chocolate-coloured eyes sinfully locked on her breasts, Royce gave a wicked grin. 'Oh, there's more than one part of my anatomy that's engaged at the moment. There are my eyes, which are absolutely captivated by your beautiful breasts.'

His hands lifted and palmed the weighty globes. Her skin leapt to his touch, her breasts peaking into tight nubs.

'And then of course there's my hands,' he muttered raggedly, dark eyes fixed on the way his hands were playing with her rock-hard nipples. 'They're very busy at the moment.'

The quicksilver flash of desire slid over every nerve-ending as she pressed her aching breasts into his hands.

'And you're wrong.' His voice was getting huskier by the minute. 'My mind is very much occupied. At the moment, it's busy thinking about what you look like when I enter you. The way your eyes widen at first and then close for a minute. And when they open again they're not a sparkling blue any more. They're a deep, dark purple.'

An inarticulate sound escaped her strangled throat. The combination of stroking hands and the tantalising picture his words evoked were turning her on so much she was shaking with it.

As if realising she had a desperate need to be kissed, Royce feathered the lightest of kisses across her mouth.

'No,' Shara protested as he moved away, lifting her arms up around his neck, trying to tug his head back down to hers. She wanted him to kiss her properly, to take her mouth in that hungry and possessive way he had.

She *needed* him to kiss her that way.

But he was stronger than she was, and he obviously had something else in mind, because his head dipped and he trailed a string of feather-light kisses down her throat and into the valley between her breasts.

Shara quivered under his delicate touch. But she needed more.

'Royce, please…'

Royce felt his body clench spasmodically as he heard Shara's moaned plea.

He looked into her face, seeing the wanting stamped there. Her cheeks were flushed, her eyes dilating. If he could capture on film or on canvass what she looked like when he made love to her he would. It wouldn't be a picture for public consumption. It would be for his eyes alone. He didn't want anyone else to know what she looked like when he pleasured her.

'Please what?' he asked, placing another delicate kiss on the slope of one breast.

An inarticulate sound escaped her throat.

'This?' he asked softly, as he lowered his head and flicked at one rose-pink nipple with the tip of his tongue.

'Yes,' she gasped, grabbing his head and pulling him back down to her.

His body clenched again—even harder.

The same line from that old tune popped into his head again.

There's a fine line between pleasure and pain.

Well, Royce was pretty damned sure he'd just crossed it.

With a groan he took one nipple fully into his mouth. As he did so, he trailed his fingers gently over the swell of her tummy.

She quivered.

Her response gave him a heady rush of pleasure. Never had giving a woman pleasure meant so much to him. Nor had he received so much in return.

She did things to him no other woman had managed to do.

He dipped a finger into her belly button as he explored the smooth, soft skin of her stomach. Slowly he trailed his fingers down until they slipped between her thighs. He just let his hand rest there. Temptingly. Tauntingly. Enough to make her arch her pelvis up towards his waiting hand.

'You're so hot,' he whispered against her breast. Delicately, he probed her moistness with his fingers, moaning out loud when he felt how wet and ready she was for him. His body jerked as he was struck by a wave of such powerful desire he couldn't breathe.

As if remembering the prize she still held captured in her hand, Shara started to move against him. Rapidly losing what little control he had left, Royce rolled her under him.

Her legs spread invitingly.

Royce lifted his head to watch her reaction as he entered her. At first her eyes widened slightly as she felt his fullness within her. Then her lids fluttered closed with a look of sheer bliss crossing her face. And then they opened again and he was drowning in deep, dusky, midnight purple.

That look alone fired a spark through him. He began to move. Deep, powerful thrusts. Her face tightened as he increased the tempo.

And then she was there.

She threw her head back, her hair a dark splash of colour against the pillow. Her mouth opened, her teeth biting delicately at her lower lip before she cried out.

And then his mind went blank as he too slipped over the edge into a spiral of sensation that racked his whole body.

'I still want to know what the A stands for,' Shara said a moment later in a wearily satisfied voice.

Royce laughed. 'Too bad. Now, you witch, unless you want me to have my wicked way with you again, I would suggest you get that gorgeous body out of bed.'

Shara looked as though she was seriously considering staying.

'Oh, no, you don't,' Royce said, wagging a finger in the air. 'We've barely been out of this bed all week.'

Shara pouted. 'Don't tell me you're getting tired of me already?'

He dropped a hard kiss on her pouting mouth. 'Not by a long shot.'

As he got out of bed Royce was struck by the notion that it would be a long, *long* time before he tired of her.

'Tell me something?' Shara asked.

They'd collapsed on the sofa following a karate session during which one thing had led to another and the Aubusson rug had got a workout of a different kind.

Royce opened one eye. 'What?'

Shara lay sprawled across his chest, her chin resting on her bent arm. 'I want to know about the woman who hurt you.'

His other eye snapped open. His body tensed in an automatic reaction he was too late to prevent.

He could tell from the slight widening of her eyes that Shara had noticed his response.

Royce deliberately made his muscles go slack. 'Why?'

Her index finger stroked over his skin. 'You know all the skeletons in my cupboard.'

Royce tapped the tip of her nose. 'Not all of them. I know you love Abba and have a secret weakness for blueberry pancakes.'

Shara groaned. 'I wish I'd never told you that. I'm going to get fat if you keep making them for me every morning.'

'Quit complaining. Our karate sessions more than work off that little indulgence.' He ran a hand down her back and over her bottom. 'Besides, I love your curves. You're what a real woman should look like—not those stick figures on the covers of magazines.'

'And was the woman you were involved with a stick figure? Or rounded like me?' she asked, proving that she wasn't about to let the subject go.

He shrugged. 'The relationship was meaningless. It's hardly worth talking about.'

'Well, I think it is.'

Royce recognised the look on Shara's face. She could be as stubborn as he was.

He sighed and closed his eyes. 'It's simple, really. It was in the early days of my career. I'd been hired by a wealthy businessman to find out which of his household staff was stealing antiques from his home. Fiona was the daughter of the house. She showed an interest in me from day one.'

Shara stole a quick kiss. 'And why wouldn't she? You're handsome and sexy and smart. Not to mention that you make terrific blueberry pancakes.'

'That earns you another kiss,' he said, putting words into action.

A long, drugging minute later he lifted his head. 'Anyway, to cut a long story short, it turned out that Fiona *was* the thief. She had a cocaine addiction she'd somehow managed to hide from everyone. She was stealing from her father to support her habit. She almost got away with it too—until I finally twigged to what was going on.'

'And how did you do that?'

He shrugged. 'I walked in one day and found her using. I added one and one together and came up with the right answer. She admitted what she'd been doing and begged me not to tell her father.'

Shara's eyes were locked unwaveringly on his face. 'And what did you say?'

'That I had no choice.'

Not only had he had a legal not to mention a moral obligation to do his duty to his client, but supporting Fiona's lies would have made him no better than she was—and that was something he just wouldn't do.

Shara was nodding her head, as if she agreed he'd made the right decision.

Royce stared at her.

Of *course* she would agree.

Her values were much the same as his.

She was as open and honest as he was.

'So what happened?' Shara asked, breaking in on his thoughts.

'That's when things turned ugly. She told me that she'd just been using me to keep tabs on my progress.'

He remembered that last scene vividly. It was imprinted on his brain.

'I'm sorry.'

He looked at her. 'Don't be. It was a long time ago. Besides, it taught me an invaluable lesson.'

She raised a brow. 'And what's that?'

'That it's better to think with your head than your heart.'

'Oh.'

Shara couldn't think of anything to say.

'You sound surprised,' Royce said, brushing a strand of hair off her face.

'I guess I am. I just…'

'You just what?'

She shrugged. 'I don't know. It just sounds kind of…cold to me.'

'Does what we share feel cold to you? Because it sure as hell doesn't to me.'

As if to prove the point, he ran his fingertips down her back to her buttocks, where they lingered for a mind-bending moment. The trail of sensation he left in his wake was anything but cold. In fact just the opposite. It felt so blisteringly hot she felt it deep inside her.

She shook her head. 'No, it doesn't feel cold.'

'Doesn't it make sense to think logically about what you're doing rather than just diving in head-first? It does to me. And I bet it does to the hundreds of divorcees who didn't take the time to realise they were totally incompatible before tying the knot.'

Shara frowned. She couldn't speak for those divorcees. She could only speak for herself.

As if reading her mind, Royce asked, 'If you hadn't been so desperate to escape your father would you have married Brady? I'm betting you wouldn't.'

Shara wanted to argue with him—she wasn't quite sure why—but she couldn't.

Looking back, there had been signs that Steve was a control freak. Once or twice there had even been hints in his behaviour that he had bullying tendencies.

Hindsight was a fine thing. She hadn't realised how she'd ignored those warning signs by simply sweeping them aside. Why?

Because at the time her father had been her most immediate problem. She'd latched on to Steve as if she was a drowning woman and he was a life-preserver. If she'd let him go...

Well, she hadn't wanted to face what would have happened—which was precisely why she'd overlooked those telltale signs that all had not been as it should and proceeded anyway.

She'd been forced to acknowledge more than once that when she was emotionally upset she almost always made the wrong decision—including the time she'd tried to slip away from Royce.

She nodded. 'You're right. It's far better to think with your head than your heart.'

The day of the court hearing arrived far too quickly. It was a dose of reality they could both have done without, but Royce was proud of the way Shara walked in, with her head held high, back ramrod-straight and chin angled challengingly. She was there to do battle and it showed.

He was prouder still as he watched her performance in the courtroom. It was exemplary. When the judge asked her a question she followed Jackson's instructions to the letter.

Keep it simple, Jackson had told her. Try and answer each question directly, without over-answering. Be calm and precise. And under no circumstances let Steve provoke you.

Afterwards Royce hugged her against his chest. 'We are going to celebrate!'

Shara looked up at him, her blue eyes wide in her face. 'We don't have to do that.'

Royce slid his hands into the small of her back. 'I know we don't, but I want to. I was so proud of the way you handled yourself in there that I was fit to burst.'

She smiled. 'Burst, huh?'

He nodded. 'It could have been ugly.'

She laughed, some of the tension in her face easing. 'I couldn't have done it without you.'

'Sure you could.'

She shook her head. 'No—seriously. Knowing you were there made all the difference. I knew I was safe with you to protect me.'

A sudden movement behind Shara caught his attention.

Brady!

A wave of anger rocked Royce on his heels—so intense that he heard a roaring sound in his ears.

A man who treated women the way Brady had treated Shara was not a man at all. He was the scum of the earth.

Royce stepped around Shara, blocking her view.

It was one thing to face Brady in the formality of the courtroom, where he was unlikely to say or do anything offensive or hurtful. It was quite another to meet him in a normal everyday setting like the corridor they were standing in, with no lawyers, judges or guards to prevent him from being his usual ugly self.

Royce hugged her to him. 'I think you're underestimating yourself.' Swinging her in the opposite direction, he grabbed her hand. 'Come on. I have just the place in mind.'

The restaurant Royce took her to overlooked Balmoral Beach. 'This place has the best seafood.'

They took their time discussing the menu. Shara finally decided on roasted Kingfish, with a beetroot, baby spinach and feta salad, while Royce chose the crisp fried whole snapper with bok choy and Asian sauce.

Since they were celebrating Royce suggested champagne. When the waiter had poured the sparkling liquid and departed Royce raised his flute. 'What shall we toast to?'

It was on the tip of her tongue to say *To us*, but that hardly sounded appropriate. It suggested something permanent—and neither of them wanted that.

Did they?

Shara was no longer so sure. Somewhere along the line she'd got in deeper than she'd intended.

Royce was a very special man. He'd helped her become the woman she was always meant to be, and he treated her as no man had ever treated her before.

As if she were a princess.

She raised her glass and stared deep into his chocolate-brown eyes. 'How about to life?'

'I like that.' Royce clinked his glass against the side of hers. 'To life.'

'To life,' Shara echoed.

'What else?'

'What do you mean what else?'

'Well, I'm feeling on a high. I think we should toast something else. In fact I think we should toast anything and everything under the sun just for the sheer heck of it.'

Shara smiled back. In this mood Royce was impossible to resist. Quickly on the back of that thought came another. Royce in *any* mood was impossible to resist.

'Well?' he prompted.

Shara drew back in her chair, hands in the air. 'Hey, don't look at me. I came up with the first toast. Now it's your turn.'

'OK. Fair enough.' He rubbed the side of his jaw thoughtfully, then raised his glass. 'To infinite possibilities!'

'Infinite, huh? There speaks an eternal optimist.' They clinked glasses again. 'To infinite possibilities.'

'OK. Your turn.'

Shara put her glass down on the table. 'I think we'd better slow down, otherwise I'm going to get drunk.'

Royce picked up her glass of chilled water, handed it to her, then picked up his own. 'Here—this should keep you sober. What's our next toast?'

Shara thought about that. *To us* was still sitting on the tip of her tongue, but it was no more appropriate now than it had been five minutes ago.

She held up her glass of water. 'To new beginnings.'

She'd expected Royce to smile. Instead he lowered his glass to the table and frowned. 'Don't think about Brady. He has no place in this celebration.'

'I wasn't thinking about Steve, I was thinking about—'

She broke off, her eyes dipping to the white linen tablecloth.

'Thinking about what?' Royce asked.

You.

For a minute she thought she'd said the word out loud. Because when she'd spoken about new beginnings she'd been thinking about him. And the new beginning she'd envisaged was of the two of them—together.

Which was quite patently ridiculous.

There were taking one day at a time. Keeping things casual.

Only the way she was feeling was anything *but* casual.

'I was thinking about the future and those infinite possibilities you were talking about,' she said, trying to force her lips into a smile. Only they weren't co-operating. 'Once this situation is over, the world is my oyster.'

The thought should have made her deliriously happy—but it didn't.

Because once the situation with Steve was over Royce would walk out of her life.

There would be no more karate sessions.

No more talks.

No more seeing him smile or hearing him laugh.

Shara swallowed—hard.

Then did it again.

Royce flashed her a megawatt-bright smile. 'Well, that's OK, then.' He raised his glass in the air. 'To new beginnings.'

They went backwards and forwards for another ten minutes, each toast becoming sillier and more outrageous.

Finally Shara flung her hands in the air and called it quits. 'You can't make a toast to blueberry pancakes!'

'Why not?'

'Because you just can't.'

Throughout lunch Royce's eyes never left hers—not even for one second, as if what she was saying was earth-shatteringly important and deserved his full attention.

He picked up her hand every so often and twined his fingers with hers. Sometimes he kissed the inside of her wrist, and the look in his eyes made her wish they were somewhere more private where she could draw his mouth down to hers.

After lunch Royce suggested a walk along the beach.

Shara looked down at her suit. 'I'm a bit too dressed up for a paddle.'

'Says who?' He grinned. 'The world is your oyster, remember?'

His grin was infectious. So much so that Shara found herself smiling back. 'So it is.'

She kicked off her court shoes, scooped them up with two fingers, and jumped on to the sand. 'Race you to the water!'

Royce beat her hands-down, but Shara didn't care, waiting patiently while he pulled off his shoes and socks and rolled up his trouser legs.

They walked the length of the beach with the water lapping at their ankles, their fingers intertwined.

They were near the end of the beach when his hand tightened uncomfortably around hers.

'Royce?' she prompted, but he wasn't looking at her. He was looking into the distance with a frown on his face. 'What is it?'

He turned back to her, the frown turning into a smile. 'Nothing. I just thought I saw...' He shook his head. 'It doesn't matter.'

Afterwards they went home and made slow, languorous love.

And as her heartbeat returned to normal Shara realised that she hadn't been this happy in a long, *long* time.

Smash!

Shara bolted upright and automatically reached out a not quite steady hand to turn on the bedside lamp and look around.

When her eyes landed on broken glass, she stared at it.

Where had it come from?

And then it dawned on her—the window had been broken!

'Stay still,' Royce ordered.

He was two steps ahead of her. He was already out of bed, pulling on the low-slung jeans that always made her mouth water, and assessing the situation with narrowed eyes.

'Where are you going?' she asked as Royce headed towards the door.

'Outside. Stay there,' Royce ordered again in a hard voice. 'I'll be back in a minute.'

'I'm not going anywhere,' she said.

She watched his muscular back and tight denim-clad butt as he stormed out of the door. She could hear his heavy tread as he took the stairs two at a time before he raced through the lower level and continued outside.

Shara kneeled on the bed to take a closer look. Someone had thrown a brick through the window.

Shara shivered as she surveyed the scene. The brick had missed the bed by a matter of inches. A little bit closer and it would have hit Royce.

She paled, her insides trembling.

Swinging her legs over the edge of the bed, she used her toes to find her slippers. She rose shakily to her feet and then on wobbly legs walked to the brick and picked it up.

She weighed it in her hands, then turned it over—only to drop it again as if it had bitten her when she saw what was written on the other side.

You're dead.

She staggered back towards the bed and dropped down on to it, the crudely carved message holding her full attention.

Shara stared at the message. Her initial shock was wearing off. In its place was a deep, burning anger that burrowed inside her until it was bone-deep.

Shara welcomed the feeling. A month ago this incident would have made her feel sick and anxious. And it would have made her feel like a victim.

Now anger and frustration dominated her.
She had no doubt Steve had thrown the brick.
Who else would do such a vicious thing?
The big question was: who was the message for?
For her? For Royce? Or for both of them?
And what did it matter?
What mattered was that the situation couldn't be allowed to continue.

CHAPTER NINE

ROYCE stopped in the doorway, his face grim as he looked at Shara. His hands were bunched into fists at his sides, the knuckles showing white. Anger swelled inside him, but he forced it back.

Now was not the time to let the emotions raging inside him free rein. Right now he had to make sure Shara was OK.

Striding across the room, he sat down beside her.

'Did you see anybody outside?' she asked.

Royce stiffened. 'No. Whoever it was they're long gone.'

'It was Steve,' she said flatly.

Royce nodded, doing his best to keep his voice even as anger ratcheted up his spine. 'I suspect so.'

Shara nodded her head towards the brick. 'There's a message.'

Leaving her where she was sitting, Royce picked up the brick using a corner of the bedspread. He'd have it dusted for fingerprints but he suspected there wouldn't be any.

He turned the brick over and read the crudely carved message. Biting out an expletive, he stared at the engraved letters with an icy calm that was far worse than any level of anger could be.

It seeped through his skin and into his bones, freezing his insides to sub-zero.

This was his fault.

Fairly and squarely.

There was no one else to blame.

How many times had he told himself that emotions fuzzed your objectivity and dulled your ability to handle a situation the way it should be handled?

Yesterday he'd been so wrapped up in Shara that he hadn't even realised that Brady had followed them from the courthouse.

It had been luck, not training and experience, that had led him to that brief glimpse of the other man when they were on the way back to the car.

He'd consoled himself with the fact that nothing had happened.

But it had happened *now*.

There was no doubt in his mind that Brady had watched Shara and himself together. No doubt in his mind that it was doing so that had provoked this reaction.

Their lunch at the restaurant and their walk along the beach afterwards flashed across his mind.

No wonder he hadn't seen Brady. He hadn't been able to stop looking at Shara. The sadness he'd noticed in her eyes when he'd first met her was gone. She looked...

Well, she looked happy. And relaxed. And so beautiful that she took his breath away.

Hell, he'd been acting like a man, damn it!

A man—*not* a bodyguard.

A man moreover who had lost his emotional detachment.

A man who—

No!

He put a brake on his thoughts.

Dragged in a breath.

Reproaching himself would achieve nothing.

What he had to do now was focus. Or should he say *re*focus?

OK. So he'd got in deeper than he should have for a little while. Lost his perspective. That was no big deal.

All he had to do was take a step back. Or ten. Or however many it took to re-establish his normal objectivity.

If that meant returning to a strictly professional relationship then so be it.

Shara was the principal.

He was the bodyguard.

Full-stop.

End of story.

He glanced at Shara. 'I suggest you sleep next door in the guestroom.'

She waved a hand. 'I have to clean up this mess.'

'No. That's the last thing I want you to do. The police will want to have a look at it.'

'The police...?'

'Yes, I'm calling it in.'

'Do you think they can prove it was Steve?'

Royce shrugged. 'I don't know. I doubt he's left fingerprints. It's the early hours of the morning—the best time to make an attack because most people are asleep. If we're lucky someone saw him, or he ran a red light somewhere. But, frankly, it's a long shot.'

'Oh.'

She sounded disappointed. Royce was aware that the responsibility for that sat squarely on his shoulders too.

'Get some sleep,' he said, and walked out of the room.

Shara didn't sleep. Instead she lay staring up at the ceiling in the spare bedroom.

She heard movement in her bedroom. And voices. She wasn't sure whether it was the police or operatives from the Royce Agency.

It didn't really matter.

She'd bet money on the fact that they'd be unable to prove that Steve had anything to do with throwing the brick.

Steve wasn't stupid; he'd have covered his tracks.

Finally the house fell silent. She waited for Royce to come to bed but he didn't.

She almost went in search of him, but she didn't want to disturb him if he was busy.

Around four a.m. she fell into a fitful slumber that was filled with bad dreams. The nightmare played out like a series of snapshots.

Royce with a brick hitting his temple.

Royce with bright red blood streaming down the side of his face.

Royce lying prostrate on the floor.

Not moving.

Lifeless.

Shara could feel anxiety filling her from the toes up. As if someone had taken a jug of fear and angst and was pouring it down her throat.

Until she was completely filled to overbrimming.

Until she was choking on it.

A scream tore from her throat.

She came awake with a start, jack-knifing into a sitting position. One hand was at her chest, where her heart was jumping around like crazy, the other went protectively to the base of her throat, where she could feel her pulse racing to a similar beat.

Royce burst into the room with a force that almost took the door off its hinges. He turned on the main light and the sudden brightness made Shara blink like a startled rabbit.

He scanned the room with hard eyes. He was wearing the low-slung jeans and nothing else. His body was tensed so that each muscle stood out prominently. 'What is it? Is it Brady?'

Shara shook her head.

His eyes narrowed. 'Then what is it?'

She took a deep breath. It juddered in the back of her throat. 'I had a bad dream.'

He visibly relaxed. 'Is that all?'

She nodded, waiting for him to stride across the room and gather in his arms.

But he didn't. He stayed exactly where he was.

Shara stared at him, puzzled and more than a little bit hurt.

'Well, I'm not surprised. You received quite a shock tonight.'

'So did you,' Shara said, not able to shake the images that were seared onto her retina.

'I'm used to it. You're not.' He paused for a moment. 'Well, if that's all, I'll leave you to it.'

Shara frowned. 'Aren't you going to join me?'

He shook his head. 'I have things to do.'

'I see,' she said.

But the truth was that she didn't see. She didn't see at all. She'd heard the words. Of course she had. She'd even processed them. But they didn't make sense.

It sounded...

Well, it sounded as if Royce was making an excuse not to be with her. That 'I have things to do' had sounded like the equivalent of *I have to wash my hair* or *I have a headache*.

Maybe she was just being oversensitive—and maybe she wasn't.

Either way, she couldn't shake the feeling that something was wrong.

Royce wanted nothing more than to stride across the room and gather Shara in his arms.

When he'd heard her scream he'd frozen.

That had never happened to him before.

Normally his reaction to emergency situations was automatic. Without question.

He didn't think. He just acted. Whatever he had to do, he did it.

But this time he'd hesitated—if only for a moment.

With fear.

Not for himself, but for Shara.

Which just went to prove that he was too close. Way, *way* too close. On *every* level.

So instead of rushing across the room to hold her he forced himself to stay exactly where he was.

'Are you sure you're OK?' he asked.

She nodded. Her eyes dominated her pale face. She looked anything but OK, but he couldn't afford to comfort her.

'OK. I'll see you in the morning.'

She nodded again.

There was hurt and confusion in her eyes.

Royce hardened his heart against it.

Still, closing the door was one of the hardest things he'd ever had to do.

As soon as Royce left the room Shara rolled over and buried her head in the pillow.

Tears were pricking at the backs of her eyes but she refused to let them fall.

She didn't want to think about Royce and why he was acting so strangely. Frankly, it hurt too much—as if someone was stabbing her in the chest with a sharp knife.

Instead her mind went over the night's events, then drifted back over the past few months.

It was as if she was seeing things clearly for the first time. As if a veil had been lifted from in front of her eyes.

She'd thought she was taking her life back.

Thought she was standing up for herself.

But really she'd only been paying lip service to that goal.

There had always been someone else standing in front of her, fighting her battles for her.

She'd escaped a domineering father by turning to a man she hadn't even realised was far worse.

She'd put up with abuse that no woman should have to put up with.

And when the breaking point had come what had she done?

She'd gone running back to Daddy.

Her insides shrank in on themselves.

Since then she'd followed a path of passive resistance—until Royce had made her realise what she was doing.

Even then she hadn't really stepped up to the plate. She'd been hiding behind the law, behind Royce, behind anything she could lay her hands on.

But she was over that. Now, finally, she felt cold and determined and ready to fight. *Really* fight. She'd had enough. It was time to end this.

And one thing was clear.

If she wanted to deal with this problem once and for all then *she* needed to deal with it.

Alone.

Without assistance.

The answer wasn't going to be found in a courtroom.

Or hiding behind Royce's back.

It was going to be found inside *her*.

She had to find the guts to do what she hadn't done in the first place and stand up to Steve.

The realisation made her feel oddly calm—and oddly in control.

Her courage had been growing along with her confidence. She was ready to do this.

There had to be some way out of this mess.

But what?

Think, girl, think.

And then it came to her.

It didn't come at her like a bolt out of the blue. It was more as if another veil had been removed from her eyes.

In reality she'd known the answer for a long time. Royce had told her all she needed to know. She just hadn't been ready to listen at the time.

What she needed now was a plan that could turn the theory into reality.

Reaching out, she picked up the phone and dialled a number she remembered by heart.

Dawn was only just breaking, but he answered on the eighth ring. 'Hello?'

'Hello, Steve,' Shara replied calmly.

There was a stinging silence.

'Shara? Is that you?'

'Yes, it's me,' she said, speaking quickly, determined to show no hesitation—and no fear.

'What do you want?' he asked.

Her hand tightened around the phone. 'I just called to tell you I received your message.'

'What message?' he asked innocently.

She barked out a laugh. 'Oh, come on, Steve. Let's not pretend, shall we?'

Another silence followed. This time she sensed his surprise.

And she could understand why.

She hadn't talked to him the way she just had for a long time—if ever. She'd been too frightened of the consequences.

'I don't know what you're talking about,' Steve denied.

'Of course you do. Only little boys throw bricks through windows and then run away. Be man enough to admit what you did.'

'Don't play with me, Shara,' Steve warned. 'No doubt you and the he-man have the phone tapped and plan on trying to trap me into admitting something I didn't do. Well, it won't work. I'm too smart for you.'

For a second—just one—she wondered whether he was right.

But no.

She couldn't afford to think that way. Attitude was nine-tenths of battle. She had to walk the walk and talk the talk.

She was no longer a victim, and it was time she started acting like it.

Her hand tightened around the handpiece. 'Who's playing?'

'You are. If you think you can outsmart me you're wrong.' He paused for a moment. Even through the telephone line she could practically hear the cogs of his mind turning over. 'I'll say this much, though. This is between you and me. You had no right bringing anyone else into it. Lose lover boy.'

The implication was clear. As clear as if he'd added the words *or I'll do it for you*.

The suggestion was so ludicrous that Shara couldn't help but laugh. 'Don't even think about it. Royce would take you apart piece by piece.'

'That's what you think.'

'No. That's what I *know*. He'd make mincemeat out of you in two seconds flat. But that's beside the point.'

'Then what *is* the point? Why are you calling me?'

She dragged in a breath. 'I'm fed up with this situation. Why don't we get together and talk about it? I'm sure we can sort it out like two rational human beings.'

There was a long silence. 'What about the Restraining Order?'

'What about it? You didn't let that bother you when you delivered your message last night.' She paused for a moment, and then said. 'You're not scared, are you?'

It was a deliberate ploy. She knew Steve wouldn't be able to resist such a provocative taunt.

'Of course not,' he denied quickly. 'But if you're thinking about getting someone to photograph me with you so that you can say I broke the Restraining Order then it won't work. I'll make it clear that you invited me. And just in case you're thinking about lying then remember that the telephone records will prove that *you* called *me*—not the other way around.'

'I'm not planning on having someone take a photograph of you.'

No, she was planning something far more effective than that.

'OK. When and where?'

Shara thought rapidly, sifting through her options. She needed just the right place for the half-formed plan in her mind to work—somewhere public and open and, even more importantly, somewhere guaranteed to have a lot of people.

She wanted them visible.

'Bonito's,' she said, naming a popular café she and Steve had been to numerous times before. 'Ten o'clock for coffee and a chat.'

With that she hung up the phone. He'd be there. She knew he would. He wouldn't be able to help himself.

The sense that something was wrong between Royce and herself intensified the following morning.

As was usual, Royce was in the middle of cooking breakfast when she walked into the kitchen.

He always woke before her. He was one of those people who got up as soon as their eyes opened. Shara was the exact opposite. She liked to take her time, snoozing for a few minutes before she was ready to greet the day.

'Good morning,' she said, walking into the room.

She walked towards Royce like a homing beacon. Her intention was to wrap her arms around his waist from behind and then wait for him to turn and give her a good-morning kiss.

Royce threw her a brief smile over his shoulder, said an equally short good morning, and then turned back to the stove.

Shara stopped dead in her tracks. She stared at his back for a long moment, a sense of unease rippling down her spine.

After standing there for another minute, with not another word or look, let alone a good-morning kiss, she diverted to the fridge.

'You didn't come to bed last night,' she said, trying to keep her voice light and even.

'I slept in another room,' he said, addressing the contents of the frying pan. 'I didn't want to disturb you.'

'You wouldn't have disturbed me.'

In fact just the opposite. She'd wanted nothing more than to have him in bed with her, the hard, warm length of his body beside her, his arms wrapped around her.

'You needed the sleep.'

The hairs on the back of her neck prickled as her sense of unease deepened. She stopped part-way to the kitchen bench, a tub of yoghurt in one hand, a punnet of blueberries and a banana in the other.

'Don't tell me what I need or don't need,' she said, addressing his back.

Particularly when he had it wrong.

What she'd needed was *him*.

She almost blurted the words out loud, but she swallowed them back. Given how stand-offish and unapproachable he sounded, it was hardly the appropriate thing to say.

'You *didn't* need to get some sleep after all the fracas?' he asked, tossing the question over his shoulder.

Their eyes met. His were blank. Empty. Totally without the warmth she was used to seeing in them.

A shiver ran down her spine and her stomach shrank to the size of a pea.

'Is something wrong?' she asked, her heart beating anxiously in her chest.

She was still staring at his back intently, which meant that she saw the infinitesimal tightening of his muscles. 'No, nothing is wrong.'

But everything was wrong.

It *felt* wrong.

Royce looked and sounded different.

And she couldn't figure out why.

She wasn't imagining things.

And it hurt.

It hurt more than she cared to admit.

Royce was pretending to work—pretending because he couldn't forget the look of hurt confusion in Shara's eyes when he'd deliberately tried to blank her out—when his computer started to beep.

His head snapped up, a frown on his face.

Pulling the keyboard towards him, he tapped a few keys to take him to the household security system. The beeping indicated that the outside perimeter of the house had been breached.

One look at the monitor confirmed someone near the garage at the back of the house.

Was someone—Brady?—coming in?

Or was someone—Shara?—going out?

There was only one way to find out.

He was on his feet and racing towards the back of the house in two seconds flat.

He reached the rear door, only to find it locked. Cursing under his breath, he ran for the front door, noticed an open window and made a quick diversion. He squeezed through the opening, which he only just fitted through, and rounded the house in time to see Shara's car disappear out of the gate at the end of the driveway.

This was the first time she'd tried to give him the slip since that very first day. For a moment all he could do was stand there. He couldn't believe this was happening—not after everything that had happened between them.

'Damn it!' he hurled. 'What is the woman doing now?'

Running at full tilt, he headed for his 4WD. Shara had a head start. There was no time to lose.

He was in and had the motor running in a time that would have shamed an Olympic runner. He took off with a screech of tyres, leaving in his wake a trail of smoke and the smell of burning rubber.

As he drove his brain went to work on this latest development.

Why had Shara tried to give him the slip now?

Royce wasn't sure, but his gut instinct warned him that whatever it was it wasn't good.

Although he was already going well above the speed limit he flattened the accelerator to the floor. The 4WD surged like a hungry monster.

He raced through the streets.

His head turned left and right, searching for a glimpse of Shara's small red sedan.

He had to find her—and fast.

Shara clenched the steering wheel with sweaty hands.

She was a jumble of emotions. So much so that she could hardly string two thoughts together.

Although she was nervous about confronting Steve, her forthcoming meeting with him paled into insignificance beside what had happened this morning.

She'd been so determined not to hand over her power to a man again, and yet that was exactly what she'd done.

She hadn't seen it happening.

It had crept up on her.

And this time it was even worse.

Because this time she'd handed over the most precious thing she possessed.

Her heart.

Royce slammed on the brakes, sending the 4WD into a skidding fishtail.

Car horns blared around him. Abuse was yelled out of windows, along with a few obscene gestures. Royce ignored it all as he brought the car under control and executed a turn.

He'd just caught a glimpse of a red sedan on one of the cross streets. Although there were plenty of red sedans in Sydney, there wasn't a lot of traffic about—and it was the first car he'd seen that looked remotely like Shara's.

It was a target. The best hope he had at the moment.

Hurtling around the corner, Royce gave chase.

Shara pulled her car into a parking slot directly opposite Bonito's. She took a deep breath and looked over at the café.

Steve was already there, waiting for her.

Shara hadn't expected that. Although perhaps she should have. If Steve thought he was being set up it would be logical he'd want to reconnoitre the place. Being here before her would mean he had plenty of witnesses to say that she'd approached him, not the other way around.

Grabbing her bag, she got out of the car, locked it, and hurried across the road.

Steve was drinking what looked like a cappuccino. He didn't bother asking whether she wanted something as she sat down opposite him. He knew this wasn't a social occasion.

She wouldn't be able to swallow anything anyway. She wanted to get this over with so that she could think about Royce and what she was going to say to him when she got back to the house.

Because she had to say something.

She had to *do* something.

She couldn't just sit back and let Royce break her heart.

A lump formed in her throat. She swallowed it down and forced thoughts of Royce away.

Now was not the time.

She'd deal with Royce *after* she'd dealt with Steve.

She leaned back in her chair, as far from Steve as possible. 'So here we are.'

Steve nodded, watching her warily.

Her eyes ran over his face. In the past she'd found him so frightening. Now she didn't. Not in the same way.

Now she saw him for what he was. Not an all-powerful monster. Just a man. A bully, with a mean streak a mile wide.

Her heart started to thud uncomfortably in her chest and she took a deep breath.

It was time.

Royce frowned through the windscreen as the red sedan pulled into a parking space and the sole occupant alighted from the car.

It was Shara.

There was no doubt about it.

Although he was still too far away to make out her features, he recognised the outfit she was wearing and the magnificent fall of her hair.

She hurried across the street and took a seat at a table on the footpath outside a busy café.

His eyes narrowed on the man opposite her.

Ice slid down his spine.

His teeth clamped down tight.

It was Brady.

Royce stared—and kept on staring.

One thing was apparent.

Their meeting was no accident. It had clearly been arranged. There was no doubt about that.

Shara had deliberately and intentionally gone behind his back to meet her ex.

Betrayal bit hard and deep. So hard and deep that it left him gasping for breath.

He would not have believed Shara capable of such subterfuge.

He really wouldn't.

When he'd realised he was guilty of pigeonholing her he'd looked back on her behaviour with new eyes—and it had been quite an eye-opener.

Her reactions had appeared as if they were completely without artifice.

When he'd accused her of being a victim she hadn't hesitated to tell him that if she was a man she'd hit him into the middle of next week. And when she'd realised he was right she hadn't tried to hide her reaction. Instead she'd buried her face in her hands and called herself a fool.

The list just kept going on and on.

Her lack of embarrassment about having a meltdown and her frankness in admitting that she was tired of being scared and that she wanted more confidence.

Even the first morning she'd woken in his arms she'd been open about her feelings, telling him that she felt uncertain and anxious.

He'd been convinced that where Shara was concerned what you saw was what you got.

And yet here they were, Royce thought bitterly.

He thumped the steering wheel—hard.

Then again—even harder.

Then with considerable effort he pushed his feelings aside.

Right now he had a job to do. The fact that Shara had obviously agreed to meet Brady didn't alter the fact that having done so put her in danger.

His heart began racing. Adrenalin pumped through his

veins. Danger lurked in the air. He could smell it. He could taste it. He could touch it with his hands.

What did he do now?

He could, of course, come to a screeching halt at the kerb outside the café, jump out of the car, and snatch Shara to safety.

But he had to consider Brady's reaction.

If Brady saw him coming it could push him over the edge. Who knew what he might do?

Throwing the brick through the window had been a violent gesture. A café had knives. A bottle smashed on the edge of a table could become a lethal weapon in less than a second.

No, a stealthier approach was called for.

It would be safer.

Royce assessed the area through narrowed eyes.

There was a side street running along one side of the café. If he drove around the block neither Brady nor Shara would see him. He could sneak up on them.

The other big advantage of that plan was that Brady had his back to that particular corner. If he was careful—and he usually was—he could steal up behind Brady without the other man even realising he was there.

Swinging hard on the steering wheel, Royce made a sharp right turn and raced around the block. There were no spaces available, so he drove up a driveway and parked on the pavement in one neat manoeuvre.

He jumped out of the car even before the engine had stopped. Then, keeping close to the wall, he edged towards the corner. Once there, Royce leaned forward—just far enough to take a quick look around the end of the painted brick wall.

Brady's back was maybe ten to twelve feet from him.

Royce braced his feet against the pavement and was about to throw himself around the corner when he heard Shara speak.

'You are a pathetic loser,' she said, her voice strong and clear and cutting.

His heart lurched with shock. He froze to the spot, unable to move.

What was she *saying*? What was she *doing*?

Provoking Steve was asking for trouble.

'What did you say?' Brady's voice was low and dangerous.

'You heard me.' Shara sounded strong and self-assured. 'You are lower than a snake's belly. Just a weak little bully who gets his rocks off by pushing other people around. Well, I came here today to tell you that you don't scare me any more. You are just—'

Shara broke off at the same time as a scraping sound hit his eardrums.

Everything happened in slow motion then.

At the same time it happened so fast that it was a blur.

Royce flung himself around the corner just in time to see Brady push himself up off his chair. It fell to the ground with a loud crash that made heads turn in their direction.

Shara jumped to her feet. She didn't back away. She just stood there.

Royce was running as fast as he could, but it felt as if he was moving through an invisible glue which was dragging at him, slowing him down.

He saw Brady draw his clenched fist back in preparation for throwing a punch.

Royce was too far away to stop it happening.

'Block!' he screamed. 'Block, damn it.'

But his instruction wasn't needed. Shara was already moving into action, her body jack-knifing straight, her left arm shooting upwards to block the punch that was already halfway to her face.

She blocked.

And then she punched.

Brady staggered backwards before crashing to the ground.

Several patrons jumped to their feet. A waiter arrived, demanding to know what was going on.

Royce ignored all of it.

He grabbed the tops of Shara's arms. 'Are you all right?'

She nodded, shaking her hand in the air. 'I think so. Although my wrist hurts.'

Royce swung on Brady, who was rising to his feet. 'Down,' he commanded, as if he was ordering a dog to sit. 'Or, as God is my witness, I will punch you so hard you won't ever get up again.'

Brady subsided back to the ground.

Royce glared at the waiter. 'Call the police.' Then he gave a general stare around the café. 'Don't any of you leave. You're witnesses to what happened here.'

The police arrived. Asked questions. Took statements.

Royce wanted to wrap his arms around Shara and hold her close, but the knowledge that he'd crossed a line he'd promised himself he'd never cross stopped him. Instead he contented himself with standing at her side the entire time.

Finally it was over. Brady was taken away in handcuffs.

Royce led Shara to his 4WD. After seeing her inside, he rounded the bonnet and got in beside her.

What had just happened—what had almost happened—flashed across his mind.

He saw again the fist directed towards Shara's face. It if had connected it could have broken her nose or her eye socket or worse.

Worse still was seeing his reaction with the benefit of hindsight.

He'd frozen—again.

Which just went to prove that taking a step back and re-establishing their professional relationship had been the right thing to do.

So why, then, was there an ache in his chest that threatened to consume him?

CHAPTER TEN

SHARA glanced at Royce for the hundredth time since they'd got into his 4WD.

He hadn't spoken a word since they'd driven away. His profile looked as if it had been cut from the hardest and most unyielding granite. His hands were gripping the steering wheel so tightly that his knuckles had turned white. The atmosphere was so thick you could cut it with a knife.

They were halfway home before Shara got up the nerve to break the silence. 'Well? Aren't you going to say something?'

His hands clenched and unclenched around the steering wheel. 'Not while I'm driving.'

His words were clipped and abrupt.

'I know you're angry, but—'

He spared her the briefest of glances. 'I'm not angry. I'm beyond anger. But I would rather postpone our conversation until we get back to the house.'

Shara fell silent, a deep frown creasing her brow. She glanced at Royce again from beneath the shield of her lashes.

Royce wasn't lying. He wasn't angry. He was…

Cold. Emotionless. Distant.

Even though he was sitting right beside her, he might as well be sitting a million miles away.

Her insides turned to ice. She wrapped her arms around herself.

As soon as they were inside the house Royce turned to her. His arms were folded in front of his chest, his face grim. 'I thought I'd seen an end to this nonsense, but I should have known better. What on earth possessed you to sneak out of the house like that? How dare you go behind my back and meet Brady?'

Royce hadn't spoken to her this way for a long time. Not since those first few days when they'd clashed over her need for a bodyguard.

Stalling for time, she asked, 'How did you know I'd gone anyway?'

'I connected my laptop to the in-house security system the day I arrived and I've been monitoring it ever since. But that is beside the point. Why on earth did you agree to meet Brady? And why on earth didn't you tell me he'd contacted you?'

She remained silent.

Royce was speaking to her like a bodyguard.

Not like her lover.

This conversation underlined the radical shift their relationship had undergone since last night.

Why he'd changed, she didn't know.

The important thing was that he had.

'Shara?'

She dragged in a breath, trying to ignore the pain in her chest which she knew was the feel of her heart breaking into a million pieces.

She angled her chin into the air. 'I arranged the meeting.'

She heard the air rush from his lungs.

'Are you *mad*?' Royce roared.

'Don't yell at me!' Shara ordered.

She was proud of her reaction. Not that long ago if anyone—particularly a man—had shouted at her she would immediately have shrunk in on herself.

Now she had the guts to counterpunch—just as she'd had the guts to punch Steve in the face.

Royce dragged in a breath, then said calmly, 'I repeat. Are you mad?'

'No. I'm not mad. I just decided it was time to end this once and for all.'

As she spoke Shara realised that the decision to end this once and for all didn't just apply to Steve.

It also applied to Royce.

It had to.

She'd asked Royce if anything was wrong and he'd said no.

Once she would have sat back and let him get away with his behaviour. She'd have let him go on hurting her.

Now her self-preservation instincts were much stronger.

She was much stronger.

Even though it was going to be the most difficult thing she'd ever had to do she had to cut Royce out of her life before he hurt her any more than he already had.

And she knew just how to do it.

'By getting yourself killed?' Royce demanded, breaking in on her thoughts.

'You're exaggerating.' She waved a hand in his direction. 'You trained me yourself. The odds were on my side. At the worst he might have knocked me out or given me a black eye. But that's a small price to pay for my freedom, don't you think?'

Royce stared at her, his eyes so wide they were deep, dark pools. 'Let me get this straight. Are you saying you *planned* this? Are you saying you intended for him to hit you?'

She nodded.

Royce's big body jerked as if he were a marionette and an invisible hand had just yanked on his strings. 'What on earth would make you do something so stupid?'

'It wasn't stupid,' she said defensively. 'It makes perfect sense.'

'And just how do you figure that?'

'You said it yourself.'

He frowned. 'Said what?'

'You said, and I quote, "If Brady crosses the line once the AVO is in place we can have him arrested."'

'I didn't mean for you to set yourself up,' he said sharply.

'I know you didn't. So don't go beating yourself up over it. I made the decision because I'm tired of this entire situation. I wanted—no, I *needed* it to be over so that I could get on with my life.'

Royce stared at Shara.

Why did he have the feeling that she was talking about more than just the situation with Brady?

Why did he have the feeling that she was talking about *him*?

'What are you saying?' he asked.

He waited for her to smile. Make some kind of light remark about the world being her oyster or something similar.

But she didn't.

In fact there was something about her expression that wound his stomach into a tight ball.

Something was wrong.

He knew it. He could *feel* it.

His gut instincts were finely tuned and usually accurate.

The eyes that met his were ice-blue, with not a skerrick of warmth in them. 'I'm saying that it's over. Finished.'

His stomach muscles tightened some more. 'What is?'

She waved a hand through the air. 'Everything. Including us. I've come to my senses, you see.'

Her voice was cold. Her eyes even colder.

Royce frowned. 'What do you mean you've come to your senses? About what?'

'About what's been going on here.'

His eyes narrowed at her tone. 'And what exactly *has* been going on here?'

'You've taken advantage of me.'

Royce reared back as if she'd slapped him. 'I've *what*?' he bit out incredulously.

'You took advantage of me,' she replied in that same calm tone. 'Your job was to protect me, not seduce me. Is this how you get your kicks? Seducing frightened women into sleeping with you?'

'No. It is not.' He walked further into the room. His movements were stiff, uncoordinated. 'I do *not* make a habit of sleeping with clients. The way you're talking anyone would think I forced you to sleep with me, and we both know that's not true. You were more than a willing participant.'

She nodded. 'You're right. I was. If you want to know the truth I confused gratitude with desire.'

Royce stiffened. The length of his spine contracted, vertebra by vertebra. 'Explain,' he snapped out.

She shrugged. 'You made me feel safe for the first time in a long time.'

He heard the words. Of course he did. He wasn't deaf. But for several long seconds they made no sense to him.

And then they did.

They ripped through his psyche like a bulldozer ripping up concrete.

His hands clenched into fists at his sides. 'Are you saying that you slept with me out of *gratitude*?'

She nodded. 'That's exactly what I'm saying.'

Memories flashed into his head.

The day he'd rescued her from Brady Shara had flung herself at him and said, 'Boy, am I glad to see you!'

Just the other day after the court hearing Shara had said, 'I knew I was safe with you to protect me.'

Hell, she was right.

Why hadn't he seen it before?

His chest felt tight, as if a heavy weight was crushing it.

He opened his mouth to say something—he wasn't sure what—but just as quickly shut it again.

What was the point?

Their relationship was over. He'd already decided that. Her betrayal in going behind his back had merely nailed that decision solid.

It no longer mattered why she'd slept with him—except it did.

It mattered one hell of a lot.

Royce clenched his hands into fists. Dragged in a breath.

All he wanted to do was grab her and demand some answers. But that would be a mistake—because he would be allowing his emotions to make decisions for him.

If ever there was a time to apply cool, calm logic to a situation it was now.

'Fine,' Royce clipped out, making a slashing movement with his hands. 'I won't bother you again.'

She seemed to pale, but surely that was his imagination.

'You most certainly won't,' she said, using her best hoity-toity tone. 'You won't get the chance.'

Royce raised a brow.

'Steve is in jail, therefore your services are no longer required.'

Royce frowned. No matter how unpalatable and distasteful he found the conversation, and her accusations, there was no way he was going to leave her unprotected. 'That may only be temporary. He could be out on bail within twenty-four hours.'

She shrugged, looking completely unconcerned. 'That doesn't matter. Don't you see? Standing up to him the way I did today set me free. I'll never be scared of him again. And he knows it.'

Royce searched her face. Her inner strength shone as brightly as her outward beauty. 'You mean that, don't you?'

She nodded. 'I do. That's why I had to meet him alone. I had as much to prove to myself as I had to prove to Steve. If it's any consolation, you've helped me reach this point.'

It was no consolation at all. Although it proved that Shara had had a damned good reason for going behind his back—an acceptable reason, even—he still felt as if a big, dark thundercloud was hanging above his head.

'I'll fight to keep him in jail,' Shara continued. 'I don't want any other woman to have to go through what I've gone through. But Steve no longer has the power to hurt me.'

Royce stared at her.

He couldn't argue with her rationale.

Like most bullies, Brady had targeted Shara because she was unlikely to retaliate. After her performance today he would know that was no longer the case.

Shara was right.

There was no reason for him to stay.

Which should have been cause for celebration.

Why, then, did it feel as if she'd just shot him through the centre of his chest? As if the life force of his blood was gushing from his body and draining away?

His spine lengthened until he was standing as tall as it was possible for him to stand. Every muscle in his body was as stiff as a board.

He wanted to rant and rave. He wanted to demand that she take back every word. He wanted to tell her that he was staying and that was that. End of story.

But none of that made any sense.

So he simply said, 'Fine,' for the second time in as many minutes.

For a split second he thought he saw a shadow of pain flit across the surface of her eyes, but he decided he was mistaken.

Without saying another word he spun on his heel and stalked out of the room.

He didn't say goodbye.

He couldn't.

Royce didn't remember walking into the lounge room and zipping his laptop into its case. He didn't remember walking up the stairs and packing his belongings. He didn't remember getting in his car and driving away.

He was operating on automatic pilot.

He didn't want to think. Or feel.

It wasn't until a car horn blasted behind him that he came back to reality.

He stared at the traffic light and registered that it was green. From the continuing blare behind him it obviously had been for some time.

He pressed his foot down on the accelerator. The car surged forward.

He drove for about a hundred metres before he slammed on his brakes. The action earned him another horn blast, this time accompanied by a couple of expletives.

Royce rested his head on the steering wheel. His heart was racing, his breathing short and shallow.

It felt as if he'd sprinted that last one hundred metres.

His lungs felt fit to burst.

He felt fit to burst.

He thumped a clenched fist on the steering wheel and then did it again.

This was all wrong. Wrong on so many fronts he could hardly count them.

He'd thought this was what he'd wanted, but it wasn't.

Driving away from Shara had made him realise that this was not what he wanted at all.

He'd spent so much time thinking and analysing and rationalising and trying to be his usual cool, logical and reasonable self that he hadn't even realised he'd been fooling himself.

Slamming the car into gear, Royce spun it around. Then, pressing his foot to the floor, he hurtled back in the opposite direction.

Shara sank down in the middle of the Aubusson rug, trailing her fingers over the fine weave.

Tears were close, but she refused to let them fall.

This was where she'd fallen in love with Royce.

Right here in this very room.

She could see him now, in the black loose-fitting cotton pants and singlet he'd always worn during their karate lessons. She could see his smile and the lock of hair that fell across his forehead.

She could hear him saying, 'Again!' in that determined voice of his as he pushed her to do her best.

He'd given her so much—probably without even realising he was doing it.

And how had she repaid him?

By letting him walk away without telling him the truth.

Worse, by telling him a bunch of lies that reduced what they'd shared to a travesty.

Her fingers stilled on the carpet. Her body grew rigid. Her eyes widened.

She pressed a hand to her chest, her mind whirling with thoughts.

'My God, I've done it again,' she whispered out loud. 'How could I be such a fool?'

Once again she hadn't taken the time to think things through.

She'd been hurt.

So hurt that she'd lashed out without thinking.

She should know by now that making decisions in the heat of the moment always backfired on her. When she was emotionally upset she almost always made the wrong decision.

Why hadn't she remembered that?

She thought back to the conversation they'd had on the roadside. It felt like eons ago.

Royce had accused her of playing the victim, of choosing a course of passive resistance where Steve was concerned.

And wasn't she doing the same thing now, with Royce?

Royce had taught her to fight back—so why wasn't she fighting now? Fighting for the man she loved instead of showing him the door?

She should have stamped her foot, or used one of his own manoeuvres against him and forced him to tell her what was wrong. She should have used every piece of ammunition she possessed to fight for her man.

She'd found the courage to confront Steve. Now she needed the courage to tell Royce exactly how she felt about him.

Shara scrambled to her feet.

Then she raced for the stairs, snatched up her car keys and headed for the garage.

Royce swung hard on the steering wheel and with a screech of tyres fishtailed into the Atwood Hall driveway.

His eyes widened, the breath locking tight in his lungs as Shara's small red sedan loomed in front of him.

She was travelling at a rate of knots—practically hurtling down the driveway.

Reacting automatically, he slammed on the brakes and swung hard on the steering wheel, trying to avoid a collision.

He briefly registered the look of panic on Shara's face before she did the same thing.

The only problem was she'd swung her car in the same direction as his.

Royce cursed and pressed even harder on the brake, even though it was impossible to depress it any further.

Thankfully their quick thinking worked.

When the two cars came together it was with the kiss of

bumper bars. Royce didn't need to look to know that there would barely be a dent.

He sat where he was for a count of ten, waiting for his heart to slow.

Then he pushed the door open and got out.

'Are you mad?' he roared. 'Are you trying to get yourself killed for the second time today?'

Shara slammed her hands down on her hips. 'Don't yell at me.'

Her eyes were a fiery blue but Royce didn't mind. Anything was better than the way she'd looked at him earlier. As if he wasn't there. As if she was looking straight through him.

'I'll yell at you whenever you deserve it. Where on earth were you going at a thousand miles an hour?'

She lifted her hands off her hips and jammed them down again. 'Excuse me? *You* were driving like a maniac. You almost hit me.'

'But I didn't.'

'What are you doing here anyway?'

Royce folded his arms in front of his chest and stared her straight in the eye. 'I came back to call you a liar.'

She blinked. 'What did you say?'

'I said you're a liar,' Royce replied calmly.

'And just how do you figure that?'

Royce dragged in a breath.

Images from the last few weeks flashed across his brain.

Shara laughing.

Shara teasing him.

Shara staring up at him with eyes like stars as his body thrust into hers.

He took a step towards her and then another. 'You did *not* sleep with me out of gratitude.'

She didn't answer him. She just stared at him with deep, fathomless eyes.

He took another step towards her, clasped the tops of her

arms. 'Simple gratitude would not make you look at me as if you want to eat me alive. Simple gratitude would not make you cry out my name or dig your nails into my back when I made love to you. I may make you feel safe, but I also make you feel a hell of a lot more than that.'

To prove it Royce swept her into his arms, right there in the driveway.

He kissed her as if there were no yesterday and no tomorrow. As if this moment in time was all that existed.

When they were both breathing heavily, Royce lifted his head and put her away from him.

Shara's lashes flickered open. She stared at him with desire-drenched eyes. This was the soft, wonderful woman he was used to seeing.

'Now look me in the eye and tell me why you lied,' he said softly.

Shara blinked and blinked again. The daze of desire slowly faded from her face. Something flickered in her eyes, and then the air whooshed from his lungs as she punched him forcefully in the chest.

His wide eyes fixed on her face.

Had he thought she was soft and wonderful?

Huh!

Try strong and angry!

'What did you do that for?' he demanded.

'Because you deserved it.' She shook her hand in the air. 'That hurt.'

'Serves you right.' He took her hand in his and gently massaged it. 'You're going to make me regret teaching you karate if you're going to start picking fights with everyone.'

Shara angled her chin into the air. 'Steve deserved it, and so do you.'

'What makes you say that?'

'You know why, damn it! You rejected me.'

He *had* rejected her. And by doing so he had hurt her. He'd caught a brief glimpse of her pain but he hadn't wanted to acknowledge it.

Because acknowledging it meant confronting what was inside him.

Leaving her had made him confront it anyway.

'I know I did. I'm sorry.'

She didn't look the least bit appeased. 'Why? Did I do something wrong?'

He smudged his thumb across her lower lip. 'You didn't do anything. It was me.'

'I don't understand.'

He sighed. 'I know you don't.'

'Well, you're not leaving here until you explain it to me,' she said, thrusting her hands on to her hips. 'So start talking!'

Royce stared at her for a moment, and then he flung his head back and laughed.

Shara really was a changed woman.

His chest swelled with pride...and something else.

'I realised that when I was around you I was acting like a man—*not* a bodyguard. Doing so could have put you in danger.' She opened her mouth to speak, but before she could Royce continued. Shara had proved that she was the bravest woman he'd ever met. He had to prove that he was her equal by doing the same thing. 'At least that's what I told myself.'

Her eyes narrowed in on him. 'So if you weren't worried about putting me in danger, what made you back off the way you did?'

'Can't you guess?'

Shara stared at him for a long moment, then shook her head.

Royce dragged in a breath. He'd faced some dangerous situations in his time. Even life-threatening ones. He'd dealt with each and every one of them with courage and daring.

And yet telling Shara how he felt was almost enough to

bring him to his knees. 'I was losing my emotional detachment. You more than anyone know how vulnerable that can make you feel.'

He heard her sharp inhalation of breath. Saw her eyes widen. 'You mean you—?'

Royce ran a finger down her cheek. 'Yes. I mean I love you.'

'You do?' She frowned. 'But if you love me why did you push me away?'

'Because I was scared.'

'You? Scared?' She sounded incredulous—as if it were impossible that he could feel that way.

'Yes, me.'

'But you're not scared any more?'

'No, I'm not. Driving away from you was the hardest thing I've ever had to do. I just couldn't do it. I had to come back.'

She stared him straight in the eye. 'Do you know where I was going when we almost collided?'

Royce shook his head, his heart doing a stutter-step when he realised how close he'd come to hitting her. 'No. I just hope it wasn't another hare-brained scheme of yours.'

'It wasn't hare-brained,' she protested.

'You're not safe to be let out on your own,' Royce continued, as if she hadn't spoken. 'You need me around to keep you out of trouble.'

'I agree.'

'I mean it. You—' He slammed his mouth closed. 'What did you say?'

'I said I agree.'

'You do?'

She nodded. 'I do. In fact I think I might need a permanent bodyguard.'

His heart thumped. He glanced at their cars, which were still sitting nose to nose, then turned back to Shara. 'Where *were* you going?'

She stared at him. Her magnificent blue eyes were filled with an emotion that made his heart beat even harder. 'I was coming to find you.'

'You were?'

She nodded. 'I was. Do you want to know why?'

His heart stopped thumping and made a massive leap into the back of his throat. 'Yes.'

'Because I decided I'd made a mistake. I sent you away because you'd hurt me, but watching you leave was even more painful. You taught me to stand up and fight, so I was coming to find you—to fight for my man.'

His heart swelled until it was fit to burst. 'Do you mean it?'

Her eyes met his. 'Yes, I mean it.'

Royce stopped breathing. So many thoughts and feelings rushed through him that he didn't know which way was up.

Not sure what to say, not sure what to feel, he pulled her into his arms and crushed her mouth with his.

By the time he lifted his head they were both breathing heavily. 'Are you sure?'

She nodded.

'Say it,' he demanded.

She didn't question what he meant. She obviously knew he wanted to hear her say the words.

'I love you,' she murmured softly.

And it was there in her face.

It had been there for him to see, only he'd been too blind to see it.

The glow in her face. Her eyes gazing at him like stars.

Royce closed his eyes and savoured the words, felt them filling his bloodstream. He opened his eyes and stared down at her.

'You *have* to tell me now,' she said breathlessly.

He frowned down at her, taking in the mischievous gleam in her eyes. 'Tell you what?'

'What the A stands for.'

He laughed. 'Do I have to?'

Shara nodded. 'If you love me, you have to tell me.'

'That's blackmail.'

'Quit stalling.'

'Aristotle,' Royce muttered.

Shara wrinkled her nose at him. 'Awful.'

He nodded. 'Awful. Promise you won't ask me to give any of our children such an awful name.'

Her expression changed. 'Children? You want to have children with me?'

'I certainly do,' he said firmly. 'Although I want you to myself for a while first. Let's wait until we've been married for a couple of years before starting a family.'

'Married…?'

That was it. That was all she said.

He cupped the side of her face. 'Maybe I shouldn't have mentioned it yet. It's probably too soon. I know you had a bad time with Brady, so I can understand if you're a little hesitant about getting married again. But I want to put my ring on your finger. I want the world to know you're mine. So think about it.'

'I don't have to think about it.'

Her expression was so serious that his heart dropped to the pit of his stomach and then kept right on going. 'But—'

She laid a finger across his lips. 'No buts.'

'But—'

'Let me finish.'

Royce snapped his mouth closed. She could finish—but he wasn't taking no for an answer. Defeat was not a word in his vocabulary.

Shara smiled. 'You're not very good at following instructions.'

'What are you talking about?'

Her eyes twinkled. 'If you want my co-operation what do you need to do?'

His face cleared. Then he dropped on one bended knee. 'Shara Atwood, would you do me the honour of becoming my wife?'

Her eyes misted. 'Why?'

'Because I love you with all of my heart.'

Shara flung herself at him. 'Of course I'll marry you. Just try and stop me.'

His lungs seized, then started working again. He let out a whoop that could probably be heard throughout the entire neighbourhood and then swooped, taking her mouth with his.

* * * * *

MILLS & BOON®
Christmas Collection!

Unwind with a festive romance this Christmas with our breathtakingly passionate heroes. Order all books today and receive a free gift!

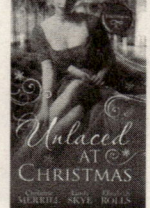

FREE GIFT!

Order yours at
**www.millsandboon.co.uk
/christmas2015**

MILLS & BOON®

Buy A Regency Collection today and receive FOUR BOOKS FREE!

4 BOOKS FREE!

Transport yourself to the seductive world of Regency with this magnificent twelve-book collection. Indulge in scandal and gossip with these 2-in-1 romances from top Historical authors

Order your complete collection today at
www.millsandboon.co.uk/regencycollection

MILLS & BOON®
The Italians Collection!

2 BOOKS FREE!

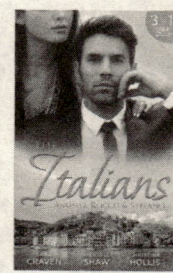

Irresistibly Hot Italians

You'll soon be dreaming of Italy with this scorching six-book collection. Each book is filled with three seductive stories full of sexy Italian men! Plus, if you order the collection today, you'll receive two books free!

This offer is just too good to miss!

Order your complete collection today at
www.millsandboon.co.uk/italians

0815_ST17

MILLS & BOON®

Why shop at millsandboon.co.uk?

Each year, thousands of romance readers find their perfect read at millsandboon.co.uk. That's because we're passionate about bringing you the very best romantic fiction. Here are some of the advantages of shopping at www.millsandboon.co.uk:

* **Get new books first**—you'll be able to buy your favourite books one month before they hit the shops

* **Get exclusive discounts**—you'll also be able to buy our specially created monthly collections, with up to 50% off the RRP

* **Find your favourite authors**—latest news, interviews and new releases for all your favourite authors and series on our website, plus ideas for what to try next

* **Join in**—once you've bought your favourite books, don't forget to register with us to rate, review and join in the discussions

Visit **www.millsandboon.co.uk** for all this and more today!

MILLS & BOON®
By Request

RELIVE THE ROMANCE WITH THE BEST OF THE BEST

A sneak peek at next month's titles...

In stores from 16th October 2015:

- **Ruthless Milllionaire, Indecent Proposal**
  – Emma Darcy, Christina Hollis & Lindsay Armstrong

- **All He Wants for Christmas...** – Kelly Hunter,
  Natalie Anderson & Tori Carrington

In stores from 6th November 2015:

- **In the Tycoon's Bed** – Maureen Child,
  Katherine Garbera & Barbara Dunlop

- **The McKennas: Finn, Riley & Brody** – Shirley Jump

Available at WHSmith, Tesco, Asda, Eason, Amazon and Apple

Just can't wait?
Buy our books online a month before they hit the shops!
visit www.millsandboon.co.uk

These books are also available in eBook format!